Olivia

Twisted

Vivi Barnes

Olivia
Twisted

This book is a work of fiction. Names, characters, places, and incidents are the product of the author's imagination or are used fictitiously. Any resemblance to actual events, locales, or persons, living or dead, is coincidental.

Copyright © 2013 by Vivi Barnes. All rights reserved, including the right to reproduce, distribute, or transmit in any form or by any means. For information regarding subsidiary rights, please contact the Publisher.

Entangled Publishing, LLC
2614 South Timberline Road
Suite 109
Fort Collins, CO 80525
Visit our website at www.entangledpublishing.com.

Edited by Stacy Abrams
Cover design by Kelley York

Print ISBN   978-1-62266-028-5
Ebook ISBN   978-1-62266-029-2

Manufactured in the United States of America

First Edition November 2013

The author acknowledges the copyrighted or trademarked status and trademark owners of the following wordmarks mentioned in this work of fiction: *Oliver Twist*, *The Wizard of Oz*, Alice in Wonderland, AstroTurf, Internet Explorer, Polo, Coke, Domino's Pizza, Stepford Wives, *Twilight Zone*, Chevy Camaro, Tylenol, Google, Styrofoam, J.C. Penney, Walmart, Playtex, *What Not to Wear*, Ducati, Windows, *WarGames*, Facebook, Hummer, *Dr. Who*, LinkedIn, AOL, "Whiskey Dream Kathleen," Twitter, eBay, iTunes, Tupperware, *Wall Street Journal*, Band-Aid, Photoshop, Xbox, Mercedes, Starbucks, *Annie*, *Sense and Sensibility*, YouTube, Post-it, iMac, Matchbox, OpenGL, Cheshire Cat, Unix, Linux, United Way, University of Richmond, Princeton University, Betty Boop, Los Angeles Dodgers, Human Rights Campaign, National Center for Transgender Equality, Amazon, Spill Canvas, JavaScript, Fanta, iMovie, *The Adventures of Huckleberry Finn*.

To Mom for inspiring me to follow my dreams.

And to Aunt Elaine for introducing me to Oliver Twist *in the first place.*

0 1 0 1 0 0 0 1 0 1 0 1 1 0 1 0 1 0 0 0 0 0 0 1
1 0 1 1 1 1 0 1 1 1 0 0 0 0 0 0 0 0 0 1 1 1
1 0 1 0 0 1 0 0 1 1 0 0 1 0 1 0 1 1 1 1 0 1 0
0 1 0 0 0 0 1 1 1 0 1 0 0 0 1 1 0 1 0 0 1 0 0
0 1 1 1 0 0 0 0 1 0 1 0 1 1 1 1
1 0 0 1 1 0 1 1 1 1 0 1 1 1 1 0 1 0 1
0 0 0 1 0 0 1 1 1 0 0 1 0 0 0 1 0 1
0 1 0 0 1 1 0 0 0 1 0 0 1 0 1 0 0 0 1
1 0 0 1 1 1 0 0 1 1 1 0 0 0 0 0 0 1
1 0 0 1 1 1 1 0 0 1 0 0 1 1 0 0
1 0 0 0 0 1 1 1 0 0 0 1 0 1 1 0 0 1 0
1 0 0 1 1 1 1 1 0 0 0 1 0 0 1 1
0 0 1 1 1 1 0 0 0 0 0 1 0 0 0
1 0 1 0 0 1 1 1 0 0 1 0 1 1 0
0 0 0 1 1 1 1 0 0 0 0 1 0 1 0 1 0 0

CHAPTER ONE

"Thus, a strain of gentle music, or the rippling of water in a silent place, or the odour of a flower, or the mention of a familiar word, will sometimes call up sudden dim remembrances of scenes that never were..."

—Charles Dickens, *Oliver Twist*

LIV

I should be used to this by now—the emptiness that fills me when I become homeless for the stretch of a car ride. I've done this more times than I can count, but the truth is that it sucks. Every. Time.

Occasionally, my case manager, Julia, glances at me in the rearview mirror. She knows better than to attempt conversation in a useless effort to comfort me.

Or maybe not.

"Bernadette looked so sad about saying good-bye to you, Olivia," Julia offers in a whine that's supposed to come off as sympathetic. "It's nice that they loved you so..." She falters when I turn my withering glare on her reflection.

Nice? Yeah, Bernadette and Marc loved me so much that they wouldn't take me with them when they moved to Hawaii. I seriously thought the last home would be *the* last. I swallow hard—*I refuse to cry*—and turn my gaze back to the blur of trees as we breeze by on the highway. Julia makes another half-assed attempt at conversation, but I tune her out.

The drive to my new home from Bernadette's is only about twenty minutes once you cross the James River. Julia's GPS announces various rights and lefts, sending us through a maze of streets dotted with small, scrawny trees. The pastel-colored houses are pretty much clones of one another. Über middle class.

Julia parks in front of one of the clones—a white house with a bright-green lawn and orange and pink flowers lining the front picture window.

I've stayed in uglier places.

She pops the trunk to get my suitcase. I step out and lean against the car, not realizing that I'm audibly sighing until Julia throws me a *poor baby* look. Ignoring her, I sling my backpack over my shoulder, one step ahead as I walk up the stone path. She scrambles to follow me with the suitcase.

Julia presses the doorbell. One thing I've noticed in my years of being shuffled around? A home's doorbell seems to be a reflection of its personality—buzzing for the no-nonsense, cathedral chimes for the snobs, light singsongy bells for the artsy-fartsy. As she releases the button and the cock-a-doodle-dooing ends, my first impression of this home is that the owner might be insane.

Finally, the door opens and an unsmiling woman greets us with nothing more than a raised eyebrow. Her hair is about the same color brown as mine, except short and kind of frayed-looking.

"You must be Mrs. Carter." Julia thrusts her pudgy hand toward the lady. "I'm Julia Winters from the Richmond Department of Social Services."

Mrs. Carter looks at the hand for a moment, maybe trying to decide whether it's safe to shake, then slowly offers hers.

"This is Olivia, the young lady you've been expecting." Julia's open-palm gesture at me announces, *Ta-da!* Mrs. Carter just presses her lips together. I'm guessing she's in her forties or fifties, although she might look younger if she'd attempt a smile.

Julia's eyes bounce back and forth from her to me like she's watching an invisible tennis match. It's not like she hasn't seen this before: the disinterest, the annoyed "why are you bothering us" mood from the new foster parent. But she always looks so hopeful and happy. Clueless.

Julia clears her throat. "May we come in?"

Mrs. Carter opens the door wider and we step inside. A sickeningly sweet odor almost knocks me over. For some reason, I think of *The Wizard of Oz*, when Dorothy is drugged by inhaling the scent of poppies. My eyes burn from the shock of blue floral country decor. And yes, there are the roosters the doorbell promised. They fill every space—clocks, paintings, pillows. As Mrs. Carter leads us to the breakfast room table, my eyes are drawn to a ceramic rooster cookie jar sitting on the kitchen counter. It's paired with rooster salt and pepper shakers that frame the floral centerpiece on the table.

This isn't a home; it's a museum for old ladies.

Mrs. Carter is watching me now, offering no more than the occasional "okay" and "uh-huh" in response to Julia's blabber. I attempt a smile and fail.

"And she's been top in her class each year." Julia turns her honey-sweet smile on me. I disregard pretty much everything she says. She's paid to care. "Why, she won a contest just this year in computers, or something."

"Computer programming." I flick a tiny crumb from the table.

"Yes, that's right, computer programming." Julia reaches for my hand. I jerk it away, but she doesn't seem to notice. "The last school she went to was one of Virginia's best private institutions. For a sixteen-year-old, she's really mature. We're so proud of our Olivia. You'll love having her here."

Our Olivia?

Mrs. Carter doesn't say anything. She just looks at me. I look back at her without blinking—two can play the staring game. Finally, her attention redirects to Julia.

"I'm sure she'll be fine," Mrs. Carter says in a thin voice. "My husband felt it'd be a good idea to be foster parents. He's thoughtful that way."

It's almost like she spit out the word "thoughtful." *Trouble at home?* I feel like asking. After a few more minutes of small talk, Julia finally decides it's time to make a break for it. We stand up and she wraps her thick arms around my shoulders.

"Everything will be fine, just fine," she whispers. I stand there, my posture as stiff as I can make it. It always amazes me how she can utter the same words every time she drops me off at a foster home. It's like I'm just here to get my hair done or something. I wonder if she'd think everything was "fine" if our situations were reversed.

Julia and Mrs. Carter walk to the front door, Julia her usual chitter-chatter self. I sink back down in the chair and continue my visual tour. Yep, roosters pretty much everywhere.

Seriously, what the hell? I toy with a leaf from the plastic fern on the table and wonder if their backyard is made up of AstroTurf.

Mrs. Carter walks back into the room. "Do you want something to drink?" she asks in a passable effort to be polite.

I smile. At least, I press my teeth together, which I hope looks like a smile. "No, thank you."

She sits across from me and studies her small hands. Her nails are almost nonexistent. Maybe she's a biter like me.

"So am I your first foster?" I ask.

She nods.

"Do you have any kids?"

"No. I'm not able to have kids," she says quietly, still not looking at me.

"Oh."

We sit for a few more minutes, not talking. I pick at my cuticles, so much so that I'm surprised they haven't starting bleeding. I feel like screaming—or maybe throwing the little rooster shaker—just to break the silence.

I try to stay polite. "May I see my room?"

She looks almost startled. "Of course. This way."

Mrs. Carter leads me across the living room and into a small hallway with four doors. I look with interest at the pictures that line the wall, mostly of her and a blond guy I assume is her husband. She actually looks happy in the pictures, younger.

"This is your bathroom. We have our own. That's our room at the end of the hall." She closes the first door and moves to the next. I'm thinking this tour will take all of thirty seconds.

"This will be your room while you're here," she says, opening the door to a very plain, rooster-free-thank-God white room. A light-green spread covers the twin bed and a small desk stands next to a tall dresser. Flowered curtains over the window are the only homage to her obvious obsession with country living. She's watching me now, so I put my bag next to the bed and manage to mutter, "Thanks."

"Dinner will be ready in about an hour. You can have some time to yourself until then." She pulls the door shut behind her as she leaves.

The room is nice enough, I guess. A quick peek out the window reveals a spectacular view of the neighbor's white fence just a couple feet away.

My own suburban jail.

My eyes are drawn to the Bible on the nightstand. I stare at it for a moment. Bibles were always on nightstands in shelters we stayed at when I was little. Like our souls were desperate to be saved. I grab it and bury it among the extra sheets and blankets in the bottom drawer.

I unpack my clothes and set up my books on top of the dresser. The blue laundry bag that took up most of my suitcase swells with clothes I didn't wash before leaving Bernadette's. I toss the bag into the corner, then pull the laptop Bernadette gave me out of my backpack.

There are no free Wi-Fi networks available, so I select the one with the strongest signal and type "password" in the password field, then try the same with neighboring signals. Nothing. I sigh and lie back on the bed. I'll have to get the router password from the Carters later.

I don't realize I fell asleep until I hear a light tap, startling me awake. "Time for dinner." Mrs. Carter's soft voice barely penetrates the closed door. I get up to join her in the kitchen.

"Did you wash your hands?" she asks, removing a

casserole dish from the oven.

"Yes," I lie. *What am I, four?* I take the plates off the countertop to set the table but Mrs. Carter grabs them from me.

"I'll get these," she says. "You can set the napkins."

Yes, wouldn't want the foster kid to break the precious plates. Napkins are much safer. I shiver, remembering the time I did break one. It was years ago, but the stinging slap from Mary Elizabeth's cruel hand when I broke one of her everyday plates is still fresh in my memory. I don't think I'd even be standing here today if it had been one of her good plates.

The door on the side of the kitchen opens and a man in a dark pin-striped suit walks in. "Well, hello there," he says, not looking surprised to see me standing in his kitchen. "You must be Olivia. I'm Derrick."

I recognize his face from the pictures. He's tall and seems to be about the same age as his wife, with thick, wavy blond hair and a dimple that forms in his cheek when he smiles. I guess he's nice-looking in a businessman sort of way.

He reaches over to hug his wife around her waist and kiss her cheek. She doesn't kiss him back.

We sit down for dinner and I have the food halfway to my mouth before realizing they're both staring at me with their hands outstretched. Oh. I put the fork down. Holding hands is way outside my comfort zone, but I grit my teeth and extend my palms. The Carters barely touch me—mostly fingers on fingers—but it's enough to give me the heebie-jeebies. As soon as Mrs. Carter says amen, I yank my hands away, wiping them on my jeans. I think I'll fold my hands in front of me from now on.

I start on the roast chicken. It tastes pretty good. Nothing like my last home, where Bernadette could barely boil water. We ate out most of the time, which suited me just fine.

"Well, Miss Olivia, why don't you tell us about yourself?" Mr. Carter says. He shifts his glance to his wife, whose eyes are focused on her plate. "Denise, remember what the agency rep said? She was top of her class. Great with computers. I love it!" He winks at me. "I'm a computer nerd myself, you know."

I'm surprised by his warmth, a stark contrast to his wife's personality. How could they have possibly ended up together?

"I like designing apps, mostly," I say, declining a second helping of mashed potatoes. "My last school had a pretty good programming class, so I learned a lot."

"Well, we have a computer in the living room, so feel free to use it any time you need," Mr. Carter says, halfway into a bite of peas.

"Oh, that's okay. Bernadette—the woman I lived with before—bought me a laptop and let me keep it. As long as there's wireless I'm good to go."

Mrs. Carter's head pops up. "I'm sorry, but I only permit one computer in this house. I'll need to put your laptop away."

"Excuse me?" I'm sure I misunderstood.

"I'm going to need your laptop," she says firmly. "I'll give it back when you graduate or if you leave before then. You'll have it for college."

Oh, hell no. "I need to keep my laptop. Most of the work they give us in school is online."

Mrs. Carter takes a deep breath, slowly closing and opening her eyes as if talking to a belligerent child. "Olivia, the Internet has too much questionable content. The one in the living room is suitably set up for *appropriate* use." Her eyes flicker for just an instant at Derrick.

"But…"

"No buts. Well? Are you going to say something or not?" she asks in a borderline whiny voice without taking her eyes off Derrick. He grimaces and looks pleadingly at me.

I groan inwardly. What the hell is *wrong* with this woman? My natural instinct is to keep fighting her on this, but one wrong word and I'll be back in Julia's car. "All right, fine. I'll give it to you." Great. By the time I graduate it will be completely archaic. I'll have to think of a way to get it back later.

After dinner, I help clear the table and wash dishes, trying to pretend I can't hear the Carters arguing quietly between themselves. Finally, claiming a headache, Mrs. Carter heads to her room with some pills and a small cup of what would look like water if I hadn't seen her pour something from a square glass bottle. Mr. Carter grabs a dry towel with a rooster print and stands next to me, taking the dishes after I rinse them.

"Listen," he says, "I know Denise can be pretty rigid at times, but she means well. She's going to love having you here in no time at all. I already do. And please feel comfortable coming to me if you have any concerns, at home or at school. Okay?"

I smile and nod. No way in hell will I be bringing any problems to him. The one thing I've learned about being in foster homes—keep your mouth shut. If you have problems, deal with them on your own. Otherwise, you'll find yourself transferred, punished, or ignored.

He tries to put his arm around my shoulders, but I shudder and almost throw the wet plate at him to dry. He raises an eyebrow but doesn't say anything. I bite my lip, feeling bad but what do I say—I don't like to be touched? I've had enough touching in my lifetime, thank you very much. I dip into the soapy water for the last dish and hope that he got the hint.

Mr. Carter invites me to watch TV with him in the living room, but I politely decline and head to my room instead. Putting on the "I'm happy to be here" act is tiring, and I just want to be alone.

As I've done since I was ten, I pull out the childish, crumpled handwritten list from my bag and lie on the bed to review my checklist for The Perfect Family. Since I've never been permanently placed, I use it for the foster homes.

Kind and caring parents.

Well, Mr. Carter seems okay, I guess. I think ice could actually freeze to Mrs. Carter's ass.

No drinking. No drugs.

Whatever it was she poured into that glass wasn't water. And I also doubt this is a onetime thing for her, from my experience with alcoholic foster parents.

No punishment.

Too soon to know, but I'll be out of here fast if they so much as raise a hand against me. I've had enough of that in my life.

My own room.

Totally, check! No sharing space with bratty kids who put ants in my bed as a sick joke.

Love.

I stare at the word, wondering at what point in my life this one started mattering less. I no longer believe in love, no longer believe in the strength of a family that can get a person through the hard times.

I finger my mother's locket—the only treasure I have from her and the only thing I own that means something to me. Yes, my mother loved me all the way up until the day they scraped her dead body, riddled with drugs, off the street. My last foster parents told me they loved me right up until the day they moved to Hawaii. They said it was too difficult to go through the adoption process, so I got left behind.

That's what love is.

I scratch through the word with a pencil. No happy endings for me. I won't be conned again. I might accept friendship or guidance.

Never love.

. . .

Z

It doesn't matter how many times I've hacked these accounts, the excitement when I break them burns through me as if my blood is on fire. The toughest give the biggest rush—the ones with so-called "uncrackable" codes or behind strong firewalls. This one wasn't complicated, for sure—Micah had already cracked the administrative password on the security system— but the kick-ass feeling lingers as I log on to the account.

I lean back, lightly drumming my fingertips on the keyboard. In fact, this one was easy enough that it's obvious to me that Jen screwed it up on purpose.

"Z?"

The door to the office opens and Nancy walks in, closing the door behind her. "What's up?" I ask without looking up.

She sits down in the chair across from me. "I made you a plate. It's in the fridge."

"Thanks."

She sighs, drawing my eyes to her. With her hands clasped in front of her and red hair pulled back into a tight bun, she's in full "mom" mode. Which means I'm probably not going to like this conversation.

"We missed you again," she says. "What are you working on that you'd miss dinner two nights in a row?"

I wave a hand at the monitor. "Jen slipped up again."

She peers at the screen, frowning. "I was afraid of that. Bill mentioned something today when I spoke with him."

I grow cold at that. If Bill's aware of it, I'm not catching her mistakes in time. I shove the keyboard away and lean back. "Yeah. Well, I thought I'd be able to fix it before he noticed."

"He noticed. I told him you were on top of it."

"Thanks."

"He's on his way here, though. He might want to talk with you."

I stare at her. If he's coming here because of this, I'm in deep shit.

Nancy smiles, though it's strained. "Relax, you'll be fine. But you need to talk to Jen. Tell her Bill's not going to let her go just because she tries to screw things up."

"I have. She doesn't listen."

Nancy considers that, her lips pursed. She picks up a stone paperweight and twirls it in her hand. "Maybe you should think about…"

"No," I say firmly.

"I'm not suggesting you get back together, so calm down. Just…be nicer. She's competent. She probably wants attention."

"She can get that from someone else."

Nancy sighs, putting the paperweight down and looking at me directly. "I'm not trying to tell you how to do your job. But you need to consider these girls' feelings. That's all I'm saying."

"Did you have this same conversation with Jen about what she said, what she did to Maggie?" Nancy doesn't respond. "I didn't think so. Before you try to make me feel guilty, why don't you go chat with her about acting like a jealous—"

"That's enough. I know you're angry, but Maggie made her own choices. She would've left regardless of the things Jen said to her. You can't break up with these girls and expect them to get over it the next day. It doesn't work like that." Nancy stands to leave, turning back to me once to say, "Think about it, at least. As long as Jen's angry, she risks everything. You're the only one who can fix this." She leaves, closing the door behind her.

I turn back to the screen, typing out B-I-T-C-H and translating it into binary. Maybe it's childish, but I'm tempted to print it and stick it on Jen's door. Not that she'll get it.

It doesn't make me feel less guilty, though. I know the main reason Maggie left, and it was because of me. Jen might've made it worse by rubbing our relationship in Maggie's face, but I did nothing to stop it. That single fact will always haunt me.

My phone buzzes and I check it. A text from Sam with two words that make my stomach clench: *Bill's here.*

It takes all of one minute for him to find me. I stand as he enters the office, my fingers twitching nervously. He walks to the desk, the *thump* of his cane the only sound in the room. Bill Sykes used to be decent-looking, sophisticated even, but finding himself on the wrong side of a gun with a former partner and getting steel placed in his leg changed him.

Nancy insists he's really kind "once you get to know him," which is stupid because I've known him for years now and "kind" isn't even in the same universe as a word to describe him. She says he started up this home because he hated the idea of kids on the street. I say he started it because he saw an easy and cheap way to make a shitload of money. Still, I've made a similar shitload, so I keep my mouth shut.

Bill sits across from me, smoothing out the seam of his pants and laying the cane across his legs. Only then do his icy blue eyes find mine, cutting into me even as he nods at me to sit. This is not going to be a pleasant visit.

"Z," he acknowledges in the quiet voice that belies the snap of his eyes.

"Bill." I try to keep my voice steady.

He's twirling his cane in his lap, almost idly if I didn't know better. "I thought you were going to talk to her."

I cringe at the implication in his voice. "I did. But she doesn't—"

"She's sloppy. If I hadn't stepped in, they would've been able to trace the source to this house. You of all people should know what's at stake here."

"I'll talk to her again."

"You need to do more than talk." His voice rises only slightly but he may as well be shouting. "Do whatever it takes to get her to shape up or I'll flush her. Do you understand?"

I swallow hard. "Yes."

A long pause, then, "This is two now, Z." Each word is enunciated carefully, a dagger pricking at my skin. "The next one better shine."

"I understand."

He pulls a file from his jacket and hands it to me. "Your new target. This one has proven to be difficult." He leans forward, his long fingers steepled together. "We've tried different access codes, insiders, everything, but nothing has gotten through. He's got firewalls that make me think it's Fort Knox he's sitting on. This might be better suited to your expertise."

My expertise. Social engineering. In spite of the situation, my skin starts to itch with the anticipation of a challenge — it's been a long time since I had one that was uncrackable. I open the file and review the picture of an old man. Shouldn't be too hard. Older people tend to be more sentimental in their passwords. Just a little research and I'm sure I'll be able to find a way in. "No problem," I tell Bill.

He nods and leaves me without another word. I sink back into the chair and toss the file onto my desk, grateful that he had a job for me to deflect some of his anger about Jen. For the moment, at least, I'm off the hook.

Jen. She's a smart one, so I know it's not a matter of incompetence. Better for Bill to think it's something easily solved with a kiss rather than the fact that someone I brought on can't handle the job. Better for me, for sure.

As for the next one…the thought of bringing on someone else just to fail makes me cringe. It's not like we even need new recruits. Bill is testing me, expecting me to make up for my lack of judgment, which means I don't really have a choice. But whoever it is better be good, or I'm toast.

CHAPTER TWO

"Who can tell how scenes of peace and quietude sink into the minds of pain-worn dwellers in close and noisy places, and carry their own freshness, deep into their jaded hearts!"

—Charles Dickens, *Oliver Twist*

LIV

The crowing of a rooster interrupts my sleep. I rub my eyes and blink in confusion, wondering how I ended up at a farm.

I hit the snooze button on top of the deceptively plain white alarm clock. Of course. Trust the Carters to find the one damn clock in the world that has a rooster crowing as its alarm. I flip the sound switch from "rooster" to "bell."

I thumb through the few clothes I have in the closet and take out a navy top and jeans, the most normal outfit I can find. The worst first impression I could make would be to show I'm different.

The top button on the shirt is missing. My next attempt is a plain white tee that I've never worn, but it's a little too snug. I grit my teeth and kick at the overstuffed laundry bag, wishing I'd had the chance to clean the clothes I usually wear, but Bernadette's washing machine was on the fritz. I tug hard at the shirt to make it stand away from my chest, sighing as it returns to its clinging state.

Damn it. I take back what I said earlier. The worst first impression I could make would be to look like I'm wearing the wrong size. Bernadette told me I have one of those bodies girls would kill for, which was her kind way of saying I have big boobs. She was going to take me shopping before Hawaii, but she ran out of time. I swallow hard, hating that I miss her and Marc now. Of all the houses I've lived in, theirs was the only one that started to feel like a real home. I yank the hem of my shirt down and push the thought of them away.

When I get to the dining room, Mr. Carter is already there, dressed in a business suit, bowl of cereal in front of him.

"Good morning, Olivia," he says with a smile. "Want some cereal?"

"Okay." I slide into the seat next to him and pour some of the corn flakes and milk into the second bowl.

"So, ready for your first day of school? Should be fun, right?"

I try to smile, but my idea of fun does not include switching schools a couple months before the end of the year. And as a bonus, I'm super shy, which makes it even harder to find friends.

I swallow a bite of cereal. "Mr. Carter, just so you know, I'd rather not tell anyone I'm a foster kid. Some people act like they feel sorry for me when they find out."

"I understand." He reaches over to me, but I jerk away. He raises an eyebrow. "Well, I want you to know that you can talk to me anytime, okay? Anytime at all."

No thanks. "Where is Mrs. Carter?"

He runs his tongue along his teeth and glances toward the hallway, where their bedroom door is closed. "Ah, she's not feeling well today. Usually, she leaves for the office early, so I'm afraid you won't have much help from her in the mornings. But I'll be here to drive you to school every day before I go to work."

"Oh. That's okay, I'll take the bus."

Honestly, I hate the bus, but it's better than having to rely on him for rides. What I need is a car.

His hand lifts as if to touch my shoulder, but then he seems to think better of it when I lean away slightly. He takes a ten-dollar bill out of his wallet and hands it to me. "For lunch. Looking forward to hearing about your first day tonight at dinner."

Ten bucks? I start to tell him that lunch doesn't cost anywhere near that much, but he's already walking out the kitchen door to the garage. I slide the bill into my pocket and grab my backpack. In a way, it's good to have something to do today instead of being stuck at home with icy and probably hungover Mrs. Carter, but the idea of going to a new school makes me a little sick to my stomach. In the years I've been moving around, it's never gotten easier.

At ten past, I'm standing at the bus stop with a couple other kids from the neighborhood. Rarely have I experienced a bus ride without at least one girl giving me the bitch-slap look for one reason or another. In this case, it's a gum-smacking girl with a bright-pink streak highlighting her long brown hair. The spiky-haired guy standing next to her is holding a cigarette, sporting an eyebrow piercing, and grinning at me in a way that makes me cross my arms over my stupid, overdeveloped chest.

Her narrowed eyes move from me to him and back again. "What are you looking at?" she asks, then whispers something to the smoker. He shrugs, his eyes still trained on me. I glance in the opposite direction, hoping like hell the bus will get here soon. *I need a car. I need a car.* I resolve to look for a job as soon as the last bell rings today.

A few other kids join us and immediately start laughing and chatting with the smoker and his friend as the bus appears. It squeals to a stop and the doors fold open. The other kids climb up the steps, glancing at me but not acknowledging me otherwise.

"Hey, new girl. Sorry about Candy. She can be such a bitch," the smoker says, grounding his cigarette into the sidewalk. He gestures grandly to the door and I step up.

It's not shocking that Candy and her crew park themselves in the last rows. I walk down the aisle and find a seat precisely in the center. The bus jerks forward and my new neighborhood crawls by. From a higher vantage point, I can see that my first impression of the neighborhood was accurate. The houses *are* clones—all shaped like big boxes, with the same windows, same doors, same twiglike trees spaced evenly apart. It's like living in a kid's cardboard play set, complete with Matchbox cars parked on quiet streets.

The smoker plops into the space next to me. "This seat taken?"

"Aren't you supposed to be sitting back there?" I look to the rear of the bus. Candy's infuriated face tells me she believes he's in the wrong seat, too.

"Hey, she does talk!" He claps his hands as if in delight, reminding me of a seal. A punk seal. "I was beginning to think you were mute."

Is this guy for real?

"I'm Tyson. What's your name?" He slings his worn backpack forward and hitches his knee up on the seat in front of us. The reek of smoke hovers around him like an invisible fog. I'll be pissed if I smell like cigarettes later.

"Olivia."

"Olivia? That's a name for old people," he says, laughing. I grimace and turn to the window. "Hey, kidding. Pretty cool name, Olivia. Do you go by Livy or what?"

"No." My friends usually end up calling me Liv, but I'm guessing he won't be on that short—make that now nonexistent—list.

"Tyson!" Candy calls from the back. "Get back here."

He puts an arm around the seat. I twist my shoulders away, but he doesn't get the hint.

"So…you're seventeen?"

"Sixteen."

"Cool. Sophomore? Or a baby junior?"

Baby? I don't bother to answer. I hate the way he's looking at me, like I'm something to eat. With my luck, I'll end up in class with this jerk.

Of course, I'm right.

Having stopped by the office to pick up my schedule, I find myself standing in front of my first class—Computer Science— waiting for the teacher, Ms. Walsh, to acknowledge me and doing my best to avoid Tyson's smug look.

Ms. Walsh finally turns to me and takes my schedule. "Okay, let's see…Olive Westfield. Welcome, Olive."

"It's Olivia," I say quietly, ignoring the snickers from the class. "That's a typo."

The name on my schedule says Olive Westfield. Seriously.

Olive. The secretary refused to change the name in the system, claiming she has to follow the process for researching my records. She didn't look in a hurry to do it.

She also didn't notice that I watched her type her user name and password into the computer's admin site.

"Oh, okay. Olivia." Ms. Walsh smiles and hands it back to me. "That's a nice old-fashioned name. Is it a family name?"

I try to smile as if I know why my mother gave it to me. She probably picked it off someone's bottle of prescription meds. But I don't say anything. Teachers usually don't know about my situation. If they do, they sometimes act like I'm some sad abuse case in need of saving or a freak no one should trust. I don't care. Well, at least not on days when my clothes fit me. I keep my arms crossed over my chest, uncomfortably aware of all the eyes staring at me.

"Well, Olivia, this is kind of a strange day to start, but hopefully you can just jump right in. We're practicing for a competition that many of our students are participating in this weekend. You can take that seat over there." She points to an open spot in the middle. Of course, it's next to Tyson. *Crap, I knew it.* I slide through the middle row into the empty seat.

Tyson smiles and leans over to me, the stink of stale cigarettes heavy on his breath. "I get the hottest girl next to me. Cool."

"And I get the biggest jerk," I snap back. Maybe it's a little harsh, but I can't help it. The way he looks at me is just…gross.

I hear a snort and see the guy directly behind Tyson smirking. His eyes move toward me for an instant before sliding back to his monitor.

"Seriously, that's awesome," the girl on the other side of me says. "Hi! I'm Sam." She has an easy, open smile and friendly eyes. Her cropped blond hair frames her smooth, perfect features—a model's face.

"Olivia."

"Tyson's an asshole," she says in a loud whisper for the obvious benefit of Tyson, who glares at her.

I like Sam already.

Ms. Walsh is now talking with another student who walked in, and everyone else is talking among themselves. I glance around. Tyson is chatting with the person on the other side of him, and Sam is texting. No one is paying attention to me. I open the school's admin site and type the secretary's log-in and password in the box, smiling when I get the welcome screen. My student records are easy to find, and I quickly adjust the spelling of my name—Olive to Olivia. So much for their stupid process. I take a pen from my backpack and write an "ia" over the "e" on my paper schedule.

Now at least I don't have to go through the entire day being called Olive.

I can feel Sam's eyes on me, so I quickly log out of the admin screen without looking at her.

"Okay, class." Ms. Walsh claps her hands together. "Practice day! We'll be splitting into pairs again. For those of you who are not competing this weekend, please let those who are have the first go. Then you can take your turn as part of Group Two." She hands a girl in front a stack of papers. "Alyssa will hand out the assignment to the Group One participants for the first task. Remember, it's not only about speed but accuracy, so focus. Those who are competing, this is very similar to what they'll be giving you this weekend." Ms. Walsh directs her gaze to me. "Olivia, you can pair up with Sam here." She smiles.

I breathe out, relieved, ignoring Tyson's exaggerated sigh of disappointment. I glance at Sam as she takes her paper. "Are you competing?"

"Hell no," she says, snorting as if I suggested something offensive.

I stand up to move behind her at Ms. Walsh's instruction to the class. We're supposed to learn from each other. I glance at Sam's paper—it's an easy one. I could do it in my sleep.

After Ms. Walsh says "Go," I watch as Sam draws a trapezoid using OpenGL code. I had assumed she wasn't very good, but it's just the opposite. She's really fast, fingers tapping the keys perfectly, with no errors. She's concentrating hard, but it seems pretty easy for her. I'm fascinated at her speed, and kind of shocked, considering her reaction to my question about whether or not she's competing. She raises her hand before anyone else is finished.

Ms. Walsh checks Sam's trapezoid then claps her hands together. "We have a winner! Congratulations, Sam." She hands her a small package of hard candy. When Ms. Walsh turns away, Sam flings the candy toward me, her eyebrows raised as if to say, *I wasted my time for this?*

The rest of the class finishes their trapezoid assignment, then we switch. Another student hands out the Group Two assignment, and I almost laugh out loud when I see it. Not that I would tell Sam, but I've done this one before.

Ms. Walsh tells us to start, and immediately I start entering an algorithm to determine possible outcomes of a tic-tac-toe game. A waste of time, since everyone knows the game can be played a million times without a winner, a fact I learned the hard way a long time ago, thanks to my horrible older foster brother, Frank. He told me I had to play him until I won. It didn't take long before I realized there wouldn't be a winner.

He wouldn't stop playing, though, and would threaten me if I tried to quit. It was my foster sister Dani who rescued me from going into another hour playing with that jerk. He just laughed and said he'd have a different game for me the next day.

The next game he tried to play…

Sam taps me on the shoulder, making me jump. Shoot, I've stopped typing. I shake off the memory I've tried so hard to block and refocus my attention on the assignment. Just another minute…

"Done!" a boy in the row behind me calls out. It's the same one who snorted when I called Tyson a jerk, only now his look is smug. He's the cliché of a smart guy, from his geeky square, black-rimmed glasses to the buttoned-up Ralph Lauren Polo. His eyes are on Sam, who's tsking with hands on her hips. She's smiling, though, so I'm guessing they're friends.

"Yes, of course. Congratulations, Z," Ms. Walsh says. *Z?* She hands him a bag of candy, which he immediately opens. He pops a piece into his mouth and raises an eyebrow at me. I turn to the front, my face burning, and quickly type the rest of the data to complete the assignment. Everyone else is still working.

Sam sits back in her chair as we wait for the others to finish. "You did great," she says in a quiet voice. "Programming is easy for you, huh?"

"I guess. It was my favorite class at my last school. I thought I was pretty good, but now I'm not so sure."

Sam glances back at Z and smiles. "Oh, yeah, he's fast. Don't feel bad, though. He beats everyone."

"Is he competing this weekend?" I ask hopefully. Something tells me this guy thinks highly of himself and could be taken down a notch or two. Maybe it's the name—Z. Who names their kid Z?

I start to ask how I can sign up when she snorts. "Z? No way. Talk about a waste of time."

So much for that idea.

. . .

Z

Sam is chatting up the new girl. I watch her smile and nod toward me as she whispers. I can't hear her, but I know that look. I try narrowing my eyes and shaking my head to get her to lay off, but she ignores me. Ever since Sam started working with me, she seems to think it's fun to try to set me up with any girl who breathes. She's probably bored, since we haven't worked on bringing someone to Monroe Street in a while. Still, I can't think of anything that irritates me more, and she knows it.

The new girl turns her head slightly to catch me in her peripheral vision. I stare at her openly, even rudely, taking in the slender neck, long dark-brown hair tied with a simple band, smooth cheeks turning pink under my scrutiny. I chuckle as she swivels around in her seat to face the front. Pretty, for sure. But same as every other girl, so easily intimidated.

With the exception of Sam, who shakes her head at me. *Asshole*, she mouths. I pop another piece of candy in my mouth and grin at her, rewarded when she turns around in a huff. It's not long before a message pops up on my computer.

What is your problem?

I type, **What problem?**

Stop being rude.

Stop being... I stare at the chat box for a moment, wondering what I should put. So many words go through my mind. So I opt for the one that sums them all up: yourself. I almost laugh at the ridiculous conversation. Sometimes it's refreshing to just act like a kid.

She ends the chat as the bell rings. Walsh calls out, "Remember everyone, the competition is on Saturday at nine o'clock. Come support your school, even if you're not participating."

Tyson is the first to his feet as he faces the new girl. "You did good, Brainy," he says, reaching out to rub her shoulders. Of course he'll hit on her. Dumbass Tyson hits on anything that moves. I can't hear her response but notice that she ducks away from him to follow Sam out the door. I grab my backpack and follow, close enough to hear their conversation but not join them.

"So where are you headed?" Sam asks.

"English Lit," the girl responds.

"Ah, well, History for me. Let me see." Sam grabs a piece of paper from her and peruses it. "Cool, we have the same lunch period. Do you bring from home or do your parents give you cash?"

She hesitates, then says, "Well, um, Derrick gave me money."

Sam glances over her shoulder at me for just a second, and in her eyes I can almost see the wheels turning. Is she kidding? I scowl but she's already turned back to the girl, saying, "Great! I have to go through the line, too. How about joining me so you don't get stuck with someone like Tyson? Although, thank God, he's not in our lunch period. So what do you say?"

I move past them, not waiting to hear the girl's response.

I don't need to. It's her first day, she has no friends—of course she'll want to eat with Sam. And Sam will try to dredge up information on her, coming back with nothing. Same old, same old. Overeager Sam has failed to find anyone that actually fits the criteria, but it doesn't stop her. Even though we're partners and supposed to be looking out for each other, trying to tell her what to do doesn't work, so sometimes I have no choice but to sit back and watch her fail.

Sam catches up to me at my locker, now alone. "Hey, what do you think? About Olivia," she says.

I grab my English Lit folder, feigning interest in the pages inside. "Who?"

She slides between my locker and me so I'm forced to face her. "The new girl. You know."

"Not impressed."

"What do you mean? She's obviously good. If she hadn't stopped typing for a second, she would've kicked your ass." Sam smirks. "She's probably even better than you."

"I seriously doubt that."

"You just need to get over your ego, that's all."

I wrap my arm around her waist, enjoying the wide-eyed shock in her eyes, and flip her around so she's out of my way. Then I turn back to the locker.

Sam leans against the open metal door. "Come on. She obviously doesn't play by the rules. Did you see her hack into the admin site?"

That sparks my interest. "Why'd she do that?"

Sam shrugs. "I don't know. She wasn't in long, and I didn't get a good look. I didn't see how she got in, either." Her expression turns thoughtful. "You know, I think she's got some weird family situation going on. Maybe I can peek into that locket of hers to see who she's hiding."

"What gives you that idea?" Although I should know—Sam is nosy as hell.

"She called the person she lives with by his first name. It's a long shot, I know, but I'm going to do some research next period. Want to come?"

"No, you can handle it." Sam's fourth period is Student Assistant, which she loves because she can get information not accessible by kids. Not usually accessible by student assistants, either, but then no one has to know that Sam has an A-plus in snooping.

"You never want to have any fun," she says, pouting. I ignore her. Sam likes playing the drama queen just to get under my skin. I wouldn't tell her, but now I'm curious. If this chick is playing around in the school's admin site, there might be more to her than the sweet, shy, boring girl she appears.

Bill's words haunt me. *The next one better shine.*

We'll see.

CHAPTER THREE

Oliver: If you're good, good things will happen to you.
The Artful Dodger: [sarcastic] Where'd you learn that, the workhouse?

— a film adaptation of *Oliver Twist*

LIV

"So you're a foster, huh?" Sam asks during lunch.

I almost choke on my pizza. "Um, yeah, how'd you know?"

She laughs. "I know everything. Really. Doesn't take me too long to find out what's going on at this school. So, how do you like your foster parents?"

I think for a moment. Do I like them? Do I even care? "Denise isn't really the social type. Derrick is okay, I guess." Annoying, but okay.

"Tell me about some of your homes."

I take a sip of my Coke to stall, not sure that I like Sam after all. "Not much to tell. They've mostly been in smaller towns than this. The last home was pretty good, but they moved to Hawaii."

She raises her eyebrows as if to say, *And?*

"Um, before that, they had lots of kids. I wasn't really part of the family. It's been like that mostly, some better than others." I am not getting into details with her.

She nods. "Yeah, that sucks. I don't have parents either."

That surprises me. "You're a foster? Or adopted?"

"Neither." She laughs at my confusion. "I live in a group home. You know, abandoned kids, orphaned kids, kids in trouble. It's not bad. Nancy lets us pretty much do what we want."

"Oh. Sounds…nice."

"It's great. You should come check it out if things get unbearable around your place. Trust me, it's not like other homes, and you don't have to worry about a bunch of stupid rules. We have a lot of freedom."

Yeah, I know of homes like that. I stayed in one years ago, and mostly what I remember is that there were bullies, and I seemed to be a magnet for them. Bullies scare the hell out of me. What I need is to try to stay in one place until I turn eighteen. And money. Somehow I don't see Denise as the type to want to shuttle me everywhere or pay for my expenses when I'm out of the system.

"Actually, I need a job. Do you know any place that's hiring?"

"Really?" she asks, her mouth full. She swallows and looks at me steadily. "What kind of job do you want?"

"I don't know, something that pays decent money. Maybe waiting tables?"

She presses her lips together, studying me. "Where do you live?"

"Not far. On Green Valley Drive."

"There's a restaurant over there called Slice of Happy. They may be hiring. Oh, hey, Z, it's about time. You have to meet our new friend," Sam says as the strange guy from this morning sits next to her. He was in my second period English Lit class, too, though he didn't pay me any more attention than he did in Computer Science. At closer view, he's really not bad-looking. The black-rimmed glasses seem more trendy than nerdy. His lips are full, the corners slightly lifted in a wide pout, almost a smirk. His wheat-blond hair is plastered back, making me think his hair is longer in front. He kicks back in the chair, considering me for no more than a couple seconds before his attention shifts to Sam.

"Seriously, Sam?"

Um, rude much?

"This is Z," Sam says to me. "He's not as big of an ass as he seems. Z, this is… Can I call you Liv?"

I nod as Z's eyes rake over me. Suddenly I'm very aware of my hair pulling away from its ponytail, my too-tight shirt and expensive but worn shoes. My face heats up under his scrutiny and I cross my arms over my chest.

Sam smiles at me. "You were awesome in class today. I know you're easily going to be one of the best in the class." I feel a warm glow inside at the compliment, which is extinguished when I catch Z rolling his eyes. I glare at him but he just smirks back.

Sam continues. "She was just telling me about her foster home."

Shut up, Sam. I know it shouldn't be that big of a deal, but it's my business, not hers. It apparently interests Z, though. He stares at her for a moment, then turns an unsettlingly softer gaze on me.

"Foster home? That's cool." His voice changes to a smooth, almost melodic tone.

"You think?" I ask icily, pretty sure he's making fun of me.

"Yeah. Sam and I are also...unattached."

My mouth opens and closes stupidly, but I can't find anything to say. So two of the first people I meet are orphans like me. What the hell?

"She's looking for a job. Needs to make money," Sam tells him.

He looks at her and something seems to cross between them. The corners of his mouth curve up slightly as his eyes take me in again. Good Lord, you'd think I'm the first person to ask about a job. Maybe no one else works around here. I mentally scan through commonly used phrases, trying to find something useful to say.

The *hiss-pop* as he opens his can of soda makes me jump. He takes a sip. "So what kind of job are you looking for?"

"Sam referred me to Slice of Happy. I'm going to give that a shot."

He doesn't say anything, but the puckered expression on his face clearly says that he'd rather work in hell.

"Do you have a job?" I ask Sam.

"Sure. With computers."

"Really? Doing what?"

"Programming, for the most part."

Her eyes slide toward Z, but he's still watching me. I shift in my seat and try to focus only on Sam, because seriously—a job in computer programming for a kid in high school? I'd feel like I died and went to heaven.

"Does the company you work for need any more help?"

She grins. "Maybe. I'll let you know. They'd have to test

you first to see if you're a good fit."

"Oh, okay." A job like that would be so much better than waiting tables, and I'm confident enough in my abilities to know I can pass whatever tests are required.

Z's eyes are still on me, so I turn to look at him directly. "So is Z your real name?"

"Maybe."

"Maybe?"

His Cheshire Cat smile unnerves me. "Sure."

I'm mystified and more than a little put off by his attitude, which doesn't seem to fit his boy-next-door appearance. Makes me think of what they say about a wolf in sheep's clothing. Worse, he seems to be enjoying my discomfort.

"I just remembered, I need to go to the office for something." I stand up and offer what I hope is a warm smile. "Nice to meet you."

"Mmm-hmm." Z's lips twitch. What is *wrong* with the guys in this school?

I back away and bump into a chair, skidding it sideways into a girl at the next table. "Hey, watch it!" She glares at me.

"Sorry," I mumble, scurrying away as fast as I can. I find a deserted hallway and stop to lean against the lockers. Damn Sam and all her questions, taking me off guard. As much as I like her, I hate that she felt she could snoop around to find out my business, much less tell that Z guy.

The day finally ends without further glimpse of either Z or Sam. I get off the school bus quickly, almost running in an effort to avoid Tyson. I have a feeling he's going to try to find out where I live, and I don't exactly want him coming over to play.

The cool darkness of the house envelops me as I walk

through the front door. Derrick had mentioned they wouldn't be home until after five. I walk through the house, flipping on every light I can find and opening some of the blinds. Being in the dark reminds me of every horror movie trailer I've ever seen. I toss my backpack on a dining room chair and sit at the PC in the corner. It looks like it's a few years old. Great. There's got to be a way I can get my own damn laptop back.

A search for Slice of Happy Pizza shows the location only a couple of blocks from the house. The manager answers the phone when I call and tells me to stop by at four thirty to fill out paperwork and have an interview. That gives me almost an hour for homework.

Opening my folder, I take out the trig assignment and type in the address. At least they give homework online. I'm about halfway through it when the sound of a door opening makes me jump.

"Hey there," Derrick says, walking in with his briefcase and newspaper. "Thought you'd be home by now. Sorry I couldn't make it earlier; I got stuck at the office. How was school?"

"Oh, it was okay. Do you usually get home so early?"

He laughs. "Well, it's your first day of school. I didn't want you to have to come home to an empty house."

I can't find anything to say to that.

"Want a snack?" he asks, dropping his stuff on a chair and walking toward the kitchen.

"Sure." I sit back down and face the black screen. Damn it, the session timed out. All sections were saved except for the one I was working on. I grind my teeth in frustration and start the search through the temp files to see if it saved.

Derrick returns with a plate full of cookies in his hand. "How about joining me in the kitchen?"

"Thanks, but I have to finish this. Otherwise it'll time out again."

I reach for the plate but he pulls it away. "I'll put this on the table for you. Denise doesn't like people to eat anywhere but the kitchen or dining room. So how much homework do you have?" he asks over my shoulder.

"Just some trig." I purse my lips. I know he's trying to be nice, but I wish he'd just leave me alone.

"That's good. I need to log on and do a little work from home soon. I was thinking I could do this most days, you know. Leave work early to be here when you get back, that way you won't be alone."

"Oh, you don't have to do that." Translated: *Please don't do that.*

"I don't mind. I can work from here as easily as the office."

I want to scream out in frustration but have to satisfy myself with rolling my eyes when his face is turned. Although…

"Mr. Carter—"

"Derrick, please. Mr. Carter was my father."

"Derrick, don't you think it would be easier for you if I could use my laptop? That way you could have the computer when you come home. I would keep it out in the dining room so you know I'm doing my homework." I can't believe I have to talk him into something so stupid as getting my own laptop back.

He frowns a little. "I'm sorry, but Denise is very strict about those kinds of things. She'd get really upset if I gave it to you. Don't worry, you take all the time you want doing your homework. I can always go for a run if you're not done."

Cursing to myself, I finish up the homework. Derrick slides into the chair almost as soon as I vacate it, leaving me to find my way to the plate of cookies. I wonder how hard I'd have to fling the stupid dish at the wall to break it.

The clock shows that I have fifteen minutes to get down to Slice of Happy. I grab my backpack and head out the back door, shouting to Derrick that I'm going for a walk. I don't know how he'd feel about me working there, but the less I have to argue with him, the better.

Okay, so the word "restaurant" is a bit of an exaggeration when it comes to describing Slice of Happy. A glorified Domino's Pizza is more like it. There are only a few plastic tables crammed into the small space, with a couple more scattered outside and a handful of customers sitting at them. Mr. Bronson, the owner, is nice, though he seems a little too frazzled for the place being so slow. I wonder what he's like when the restaurant is full.

After completing the paperwork and talking with him for a few minutes, I'm hired. He only needs me on Saturday nights, Sunday afternoons, and some Monday evenings, with the opportunity to pick up an occasional extra shift. Judging by the looks of the place, the money probably won't be rolling in as fast as I'd like, but it's the only place within walking distance. Maybe I'll be able to at least get a down payment for a car so I can find something else farther away.

Denise is already home preparing dinner by the time I get back. She nods at me when I come in through the back door but she doesn't say anything. I'm okay with that, though the ongoing silence while she fiddles around the kitchen is eerie. Maybe she's one of those creepy Stepford Wives from Bernadette's favorite movie. That'd be something different, at least.

Over steak and potatoes, I deliver the good news. "I got a

job today."

Blank faces are my only response.

"At Slice of Happy. I'll be there Saturdays, Sundays, and Mondays."

Derrick glances at Denise, who looks mildly surprised but not too concerned. "Oh," he says. "Well, that's okay, but I wish you had said something to us before applying there. Will you need a ride?"

"No, it's only a couple blocks up, so I should be good."

He continues eating but seems disappointed, though whether it's about my not saying anything before or my not needing his help, I'm not sure. I know he didn't agree with me getting a job, but I don't really care.

I head off to my room after dinner. I can't take much more of the awkward silence. It's too *Twilight Zone*–ish out there. I'm convinced that at some point soon, Denise will sprout another head and reveal herself as a word-eating alien. The mental image makes me snicker.

For some reason, my thoughts drift back to Z. He's a friend of Sam's, so if I end up becoming friends with her, does that mean I'll be hanging out with him, too? There's something about the guy that I can't put my finger on. Something *off*, in both an exciting and frustrating way. It's like he knows something I don't, so I'm not really sure what to think.

And I'm not sure I want to know.

. . .

Z

"Slice of Happy? Really?"

Sam slams her car door with her foot as she tries to balance her latte, keys, and backpack. "Sure. Wait 'til she gets her first crappy paycheck. It'll be easy after that."

"I guess." I rest back on my bike, idly rotating the grip. I don't know if it'll be as easy as that, but I've got to hand it to her, it was pretty quick thinking on her part to refer Liv to that pit.

She stops walking when I don't follow. "You coming?"

"In a few. I have to find out what's going on with Jen."

Her face sobers. Even Sam gets it—you don't screw around with Bill. And I have to do this outside, as I don't want anyone else to hear the conversation. Right now, the kids in the house look up to me. It's the way I want to keep it, and no way can they think somebody I recruited can't handle the job.

"Wait," I call to Sam as she starts up the steps to the house. "Aren't you forgetting something?" I hold out my hand expectantly.

She grins. "Not until you admit it," she says, her voice teasing.

"Just give it to me."

"Nope."

"Sam…"

She reaches into her jacket pocket to remove the flash drive that contains Liv's school file. She flips it around her fingers as she walks toward me. "Admit it."

"Admit what?"

"That I found her." Sam's close to me now, waving the bright-green stick in front of my face.

I don't change my bored expression. "Fine. You found her." I reach up to grab the flash drive but she yanks it away.

"Admit that I'm better than you, and I didn't even have to rely on my sex appeal to get her."

Sex appeal? I grab her wrist and yank her close. Her eyes widen—does she think I'm going to kiss her? The thought almost makes me laugh. Talk about crossing the line. Sam and I don't work that way. Instead, I use my other hand to tickle her, making her squeal and jerk away from me. I grab the flash drive from her hand.

"I don't think so," I tell her, smirking.

She turns to go into the house in a huff. I pull the laptop out of my backpack and prop it on my leg, inserting the drive. I browse through the data, copying select information into my files. Current and past foster parents, date and place of birth, test scores. Everything that will give me background on this chick and anyone she's connected to. It's not hard to find talented kids; the complicated part is making sure there are no attachments that could interfere down the line. At least, as in my case, not on record.

Glancing through her file, I notice she's bounced around to a lot of different foster homes. Sometimes only six months or less between. Probably not very good ones, either, considering there are a couple of psychological evaluations noted. I remember the foster system very well. I hated it, and I have to admit that part of me hopes this works out just so she doesn't have to do it anymore.

Her picture from her last school is in the next folder. She's giving the forced "say cheese" smile for the yearbook. Her hair is as long as it is now, pulled over one shoulder. The corners of her eyes are creased, like she's actually happy. Surprising, considering the conflicting evidence in the file. My eyes are drawn to the gold heart-shaped locket she always wears. Like Sam, I'm curious about whose pictures she's hiding inside.

I can hear the engine spitting before the old blue pickup pulls into view. Jen's the only one who hasn't been able to upgrade her transportation yet, so she's stuck driving a dump that I could beat home by walking. I close the laptop and slip it into my backpack.

Jen slides out of the truck and doesn't notice me until she passes my bike. My arms are crossed, and my expression is as serious as I can make it. Her eyes harden when she sees me.

"What?" she asks, her voice steady despite her clenching and unclenching hands.

"You know what. Do you know what it means when Bill shows up in person to ask me about someone who can't even do her *job*?"

She shrugs. "I didn't think it was *that* bad."

"Not that bad?" I grit my teeth. "You're risking everyone here, Jen. You're screwing up and I'm the one who has to take shit for it."

Her face lights up, and I realize that I just said the wrong thing. She steps toward me now, a glint in her eyes. "You don't like me messing everything up? You're the one who left me on my own from the very beginning. Like I'm supposed to know how to do everything." She waves her arm around. "Maybe you should've stayed with me, at least until you showed me what the hell I was getting into. Maybe you still should." Her eyes soften slightly.

No. Way. She knew exactly what she was getting into. Oh, yeah, she's good at trying to make me feel guilty, but getting back together with this girl would be like stabbing myself in the eye with a fork. I can live with the guilt.

"You know that's never going to happen," I tell her.

"Then I guess you should free up time for more social calls from Bill." She swivels around to march toward the house, her hair whipping across her shoulder.

"Well, remember this," I say in a voice just loud enough to reach her ears. "Bill might blame me now, but do you think he'll let *you* get away with this? I'm valuable to him. You aren't. Keep that in mind."

Instead of going inside, I start up the bike to ride away, but not before I notice that Jen's smug expression has been replaced with a look of dismay.

CHAPTER FOUR

"Surprises, like misfortunes, seldom come alone."

—Charles Dickens, *Oliver Twist*

LIV

In the two weeks that I've been at this school, Z has said maybe five sentences to me.

And I'm okay with that. He intimidates the hell out of me, he's so damn smart. He makes the exercises in Computer Science look like first-grade work. Every time I finish one, way ahead of the rest of the class, I peek over my shoulder to see him with his arms crossed and eyes shut, as if he's done and now bored. I set a personal goal to finish before him on at least one thing, but I haven't done it yet.

Sam, on the other hand, never stops talking. She's funny and makes me laugh, but sometimes I feel exhausted after being around her at lunch. She seems to especially enjoy barraging me with questions about my past. I quickly realized that making up a whole lot of stuff was easier than telling her truths I'm not ready to share with anyone. Z doesn't seem to buy it. He occasionally glances at me with a raised eyebrow, but thankfully, he doesn't say anything. I wonder if he'll ever say anything.

I half listen to Ms. Walsh talk about Unix and Linux systems, stuff I already know. Sam is playing an online game, engrossed in a battle with weird-looking creatures. I tap a finger on the mouse, staring at the Explorer icon in the corner of my screen. Screw it. I click on the "e." The school's got to have information on Z, and it's too tempting to pass up. I use the secretary's password again, which works. I don't know anything about Z except that stupid initial. I put the initial Z in the field for first name and several pop up. I find the one that lists Z Z—*that's got to be a typo*—and open the file. There is an address and the name Nancy under contacts, but nothing else.

Pay attention.

I stare at the box that popped up on my computer, then quickly close out of the admin site, my throat going dry. *Crap.* I sit up straighter and glance over the monitor at Ms. Walsh. She's still going on with her lecture, not looking at me. Maybe she just has warnings scheduled to go off here and there on random computers to make sure we're listening. I wouldn't have expected something like that from her—she seems so disorganized.

The pop-up box appears again. **If you wanted to know something, you could've asked.**

If I… What? I look at Sam, who's engrossed in her game, then slowly peek over my shoulder at Z. His eyes flicker up once to meet mine, a tiny smile tugging the corners of his lips. Trying to look completely unaffected and doubting that I'm succeeding, I turn back to my computer, clicking on the "OK" button. Of course, no conversation box opens. That'd be too easy. I have a funny feeling he wouldn't tell me anything anyway.

Sam should attack.

I stare at the message on my monitor. Sam should attack? Sam's intent on her battle, looking like she's about to attack a goblin. Her elven character is brandishing its sword right and left as she gets closer to the creature. I notice what looks like a statue of an archer in the corner that moves slightly as she advances.

Okay, fine, hotshot.

I lean over to Sam, obstructing Z's view, and point to the archer statue. "He's going to kill you if you attack," I whisper.

She raises her eyebrows. Her character starts to walk toward the goblin, then turns and throws the sword at the archer statue. It collapses, and I can hear Z groan as his character dies. Sam turns to simultaneously give him the finger and me a quiet high five. I snort in laughter, but sober up when Ms. Walsh looks in our general direction. She goes back to her lecture like nothing happened.

Another pop-up box: **The statue was a weak link. So thanks.**

I click "OK" and glance over my shoulder to see a grin on his face. Typical guy to make it look like his idea.

The bell rings and Sam logs out of the game. Z walks by without stopping to say anything to me. His aloofness leaves me standing next to Sam, surprised and a little annoyed. He could've at least said hello.

"Hey Sam, does Z ever say anything out loud? I mean, other than 'yeah' or 'no'?"

"Sure. Well, not much, I guess, until you get to know him or if he wants to talk to you. He's a loner, really. Has been since

I've known him."

"So he doesn't date?" Now why did I ask that?

She smiles knowingly at me as I grab my backpack and follow her out of the room. "Oh, I wouldn't say that. But it's what I'd call 'dating with a purpose.'"

"What do you mean?"

She doesn't respond, but that he dates at all surprises me if he's such a loner. Which makes me wonder...

"Have you ever been out with him?"

She shakes her head. "I'm not really into the strong, silent type."

"So what's his story?"

"He doesn't have one. Not that he tells anyone, at least. In fact, I'll give you a hundred bucks if you can pry any personal information out of him at all."

A snicker escapes me. "Do you even have a hundred bucks?"

"Not on me, but I can get it."

She says it so casually, confidently, that I know she's telling the truth. Yesterday when I asked her again if she had checked about a computer programming job for me, she was pretty vague, simply saying they were looking into it. She won't tell me anything except that she figures out system weaknesses. Which to me translates into, *I'm a hacker for hire.* Something I've heard companies do to discover and fix their system issues. I could do it, too, if she'd just introduce me.

I switch subjects. "I thought you knew everything about everyone. You sure knew a lot about me on my first day."

She grimaces. "I can find out anything about anyone except him. He legally changed his first and last names to Z. He's got no known aliases, no past. All I really know about him is his current residence at Monroe Street and that he's a genius when it comes to…"

"What?"

"The social side of the net, I guess you could say."

Great, a social media junkie. Though he doesn't strike me as that type of guy. And his name… "So let me get this straight. His name really is Z…Z? Isn't that, like, snoring or something?"

She bursts into laughter at that. I laugh along with her, but now I'm even more curious. Who refers to a seventeen-year-old as someone with "no known aliases"? He dresses like a normal, smart kid—glasses, Polo shirt—but his demeanor is too confident, even arrogant. The word *asshole* occasionally comes to mind, until he smiles. Then my clueless heart skips a beat.

Like I said, he intimidates the crap out of me.

"Hey, check it out," Sam says, grabbing a purple flier taped to the wall. I read over her shoulder:

RAVE Friday night
7pm— midnight
It all goes off tonight

"What does that mean, 'it all goes off tonight'?"

Sam laughs. "It means it's going to be a kick-ass party. Wanna go?"

"Oh, no. I don't think so."

"Why not? You don't work on Fridays, and it's just a dance. Not some crack house meeting."

"I know, but…"

"That's why it's posted in the school, dork." She tries to smack me with the paper. "Come on, you need a little fun."

I snatch the flier away. "I don't know...maybe." I don't want to tell her I can't dance, don't drink, don't party, etcetera, etcetera. God, I'm so lame.

"Okay, you're in. I'll call you tonight to get your address." She slaps my shoulder and heads off to her afternoon class.

I open the crumpled purple paper to read it again. It doesn't say teens only or anything. But part of me does want to go. Beats going to bed after dinner to avoid weirdness with the Carters, anyway.

Screw it.

Sam's car is kick-ass. It's a red Chevy Camaro, shiny and new-looking, though she tells me she got it used.

"Yeah, but how could you *afford* this?" I ask. Kids who live in group homes just don't own cars like this, if they have one at all. "Did you have a huge trust fund or steal it or something? Or does that company pay you crazy money?" *Or are you doing something else you're not telling me about?*

Sam laughs but doesn't comment. I've hardly made anything at Slice of Happy, so it'll take me a good year or more to save up for a down payment on even the crappiest car. The thought makes me feel panicky, so I push it away

I run my hand across the butter-soft leather seat. "Do you take Z to school?"

"No. He drives himself."

"Is his car as nice as this one?" I need to know *something* about him. Anything. Then maybe I can stop thinking about him.

She snorts. "Not even close."

Her words make me breathe a little easier. Z must have an old car, which I hope means at least he's not doing anything illegal.

"So how'd you get them to let you out of the cage tonight?" Sam asks.

I grip the seat as she swerves around other cars like they're standing still. "I told Derrick we were going to a school function. He looked like he wasn't sure whether to let me, but then I smiled and told him thanks before he could think about it, and he said okay. Ugh, I had to give him the address 'just in case.' Like, what's he going to do, drive by every ten minutes to make sure I'm not getting plastered?"

"And what did Mrs. Pole-Up-The-Ass say?"

"I didn't ask in front of her. I'm not that stupid."

"Awesome!"

Sam pulls up to a warehouse building and swings into the packed parking lot, nearly clipping another car. I sink down a bit when its owner glares our way.

We park and walk to the building to join the line for the club. The thumping beat from within reverberates like an earthquake throughout my body, making me feel slightly nauseated. A quick scan of the line reveals that most people are our age, which is a relief, though I notice they're dressed far better than me in my jeans and long-sleeved black shirt. Z isn't in the line, which shouldn't surprise me, considering Sam told me this isn't his thing. I'm kind of bummed about that, though. I'm curious to see if he's as quiet outside of school.

We finally make it to the front and pay ten bucks to pass through the doors.

The club is dark and packed with people on and off the

dance floor. Strobe lights swirl around in drunken circles. I slide past a girl wearing what looks like a glorified bikini, practically strapped to some guy drooling all over her. Another girl is dressed in a slinky black dress cut up to the thigh, her hands all over her partner. I quickly avert my eyes.

Once we move to the center, I'm the klutz to Sam's cool moves, doing not much more than shuffling back and forth. Sam's really getting into it and a few guys start to notice her, one I recognize from my English Lit class. He starts to dance with us but only watches Sam. She swings closer to him and puts her hands on his chest, swaying her hips back and forth. Another guy I don't recognize moves in and when he grabs her waist, she swivels around and gyrates with him.

I try to step up my game, but it's stifling with so many bodies pressed close together. Dancing really isn't my thing. I squeeze through the sexually charged crowd toward the bar to get some water before I pass out. A whiff of stale cigarettes and sweat makes me gag. Someone's hands grope me as I pass, and I practically climb over the people in my path to get off the floor.

When I get to the cramped bar space, I wave my hand at the bartender, but he's already preoccupied with the dozen or so people who apparently all decided at the same time that they needed a drink.

"Hey there! I knew you'd come." I cringe at the familiar voice. Tyson is holding a plastic cup of something dark. "Here, take this. You look like you could use it."

"What is it?" I ask, frowning.

"Coke. As in Coca-Cola. That's all, I promise." He laughs when I shake my head. "They don't serve alcohol when it's teen night. You have to bring it in yourself." He flips open his jacket to reveal a silver flask in his inside pocket. From the way he's swaying, I'd say he's already enjoyed whatever's in there.

"No, thanks."

"Suit yourself." He sets the soda down on the counter. The bartender looks like he's nowhere near finishing his current orders, and he's completely ignoring me. I weigh the burning of my throat against the risk of spending time with Tyson.

Crap. Thirst wins. I pick up the glass and sniff it, then take a small sip. Plain Coke. I drink it, my throat clutching greedily at the liquid.

Tyson is saying something about how he really likes me. I roll my eyes away toward the dance floor. It's even more crowded now, and I can barely see the top of Sam's blond hair bobbing in the sea of people. I don't recognize many of the kids or even the couple adults, maybe chaperones? There's a guy from my history class, a girl from English Lit, and a guy who looks like my foster father from behind. I scan the perimeter and see someone sniffing something off a table. I laugh inwardly, imagining what Mr. and Mrs. Carter would say if they knew what was going on here. It's strange that this place is marketed to teens.

"So what do you think?" Tyson asks.

I have no idea what he's asking about, so I give him the universal excuse for *go away*. "Sorry, I need to find the ladies' room. Thanks for the drink."

I try to step away but get a dizzying head rush. The room is even hotter than before, and I realize I need fresh air. Reaching out to grasp the edge of the bar, I take a few deep breaths to steady myself.

"You okay?" Tyson asks.

"I think so." I rub my eyes to clear my blurring vision. "I'm just a little claustrophobic. Maybe some water?" Tyson orders water from the bartender while I fish out an ice cube from my nearly empty cup of soda. I flex my fingers to fight the weird tingling sensation in my hands.

"Hey," a soft voice murmurs in my ear. I whip my head around, fighting against another rushing sensation in my head, and gape at the hot guy in a black leather jacket leaning on the bar next to me. His blond hair hangs long over his forehead, and the kaleidoscope of colors swirling through his eyes cut deep into mine. I lower my gaze, despising the genes that cause the heat to rise into my face so easily.

He says something but I can't hear him over the throbbing beat of the music. I feel a nudge on my arm and twist slightly to see Tyson holding an unopened bottle of water, looking pissed about something. I try to take the bottle but it seems to blur and skip away from me. The blond guy takes it instead and opens it, handing it to me. Tyson glares at him before turning to storm away. I look back to the guy to see his eyes twinkling. Something about those dark hazel irises with flecks of emerald, the pouty smirk…

"Z? Is that you?" I gasp. *What the…?*

He leans closer to me and I catch an appealing scent of leather and spice. My knees tremble and I hold the bar to steady myself.

"Yeah, it's me," he says. "You here with Sam?"

"Um, yeah, Sam. She's out there on the dance floor somewhere." I throw my hand in the general direction of the dance floor, not taking my eyes off him. He looks out over the bobbing heads before his gaze wanders back to me. I'm so much more relaxed now, almost dreamy. He's got an intoxicatingly hot body, propped against the bar like some sexy model, and he's looking at *me*. And is that the start of a smile? I finger my locket and smile back at him, batting my eyelashes. Flirting like I know what I'm doing.

I have no clue what I'm doing. I can't help it. I start giggling.

"What?" he asks.

"Nothing. I'm just not good at this."

"At what?"

I wave my hand back and forth between us and accidentally pop him in the stomach with the water bottle. "Sorry. See? Point made."

He laughs. "Don't worry about it. I kind of like that you're not good at this."

In my mind, I scream, *What does that mean? What does that mean?* But all I say is, "Where're your glasses?"

"Contacts."

"Cool. I like this look." *Did I really just say that?*

He says something but the techno music sounds like it's been cranked up a few notches. I shake my head and point to my ear. The fact that I can't hear Z is really funny for some reason. I laugh out loud, then lean over to say something, but the floor seems to shift and I fall forward into his arms. His touch on my skin is burning, like me.

I put a hand on his chest to steady myself. His body is hard and muscular, even covered by the jacket. A sudden and unfamiliar craving grips me and I move closer to him, the only thing steady in a spinning room. I tilt my head and peer up at his surprised face.

"Sooo…Z. Wha's Z short for, hmm? Zipper?" I yank on the jacket zipper but it doesn't budge. Stupid zipper. My fingers won't work. Stupid fingers. I try to shake myself off.

"Are you okay?" the hot leather Z says in my ear.

"Sure." I giggle. The leather smells so good. I wonder if it tastes good. I lean forward to lick it and accidentally drop the bottle of water on his foot.

He winces. "Whoa, take it easy. Did you drink out of this?" He takes the empty cup next to me and smells it, like maybe he thinks it's roses or something. He frowns. "This is just Coke. Did you have something else to drink? Alcohol?"

"Nope. That's it. Coke." That's a funny word, Coke.

His eyes tighten. "Did you do any drugs?"

"Drugs, schmugs. I don't do drugs. Just like on TV."

"Who gave this to you?" he demands, his face crinkled in anger. Or maybe it'll be happy if I tilt my head…

"Is your frown turned upside down?"

"Who gave this to you?" He holds the cup in front of my face and shakes it to rattle the ice. I try to concentrate but my eyes keep slipping around to him. Hot guy is hot.

"Liv!" Z peers at me closer like he's trying to see inside my eyes. "Who gave this to you?"

"Ooh, him. Tyssson. He's sooo gross. Tries to sit on me on the bus. Or sit on the bus." I can't remember what I'm trying to say.

"Did you say Tyson?" Z looks around sharply before shifting his attention back to me.

I know he's asking me something, but I don't know or care. I only want to be in his jacket. I giggle again, then fall to my knees.

"I'm getting you out of here." He tugs my arm to pull me up. "Come on."

A tiny voice in the back of my mind screams that this is very wrong, but I can't focus on exactly why. I shake my head to try to clear the fog out of my brain, but all it does is make me dizzier.

"I need to lie down. Right now." I crawl to the edge of the dance floor and fall down flat, my cheek pressing against the cool, vibrating wood. Through heavy lids I can see the soles of many kinds of shoes sliding near my face. So pretty.

I feel a hundred arms pulling on me, but when they get me up, it's only Z and Sam.

"Hey, Sam. I don't feel good." I can see other people staring at me now. I wonder if they're sick, too.

She tucks an arm under my shoulders. She has to shout over the thumping music. "I know. You need to get out of here." She looks at Z. "Where do you want to take her?" I can't hear his response.

They're pushing me out into the cool night air. I want to protest, but I don't know why. Sam slides away from me and lets me fall across Z as she walks away. I feel his arms close around me as I fade into blackness.

. . .

Z

The window is stuck. I jiggle it, stick a pin in the lock, try everything to get it open. Judging by this window's small size, I'm guessing and seriously hoping it doesn't lead to the master bedroom. I drop the pin and pull out my pocketknife, jamming it underneath the wood. I wish one of the other kids were here, like Cameron. He'd have it open in ten seconds flat. A dog barks, making me almost drop the knife. *Damn it*. I'm glad Sam isn't watching. She'd give me hell for this.

Finally, I manage to pry the window open and struggle my

way through. For such a slender person, Liv is really heavy when she's passed out.

I lay her down in the bed and pull off her shoes, feeling kind of weird about the whole thing. Rubbing my sore shoulders, I take in the surroundings, lit up by a thick stream of moonlight. It's kind of blah for a girl's room, but maybe that's how she likes it. If this is even her room. Or her house. The last thought makes me laugh. If this isn't her house, then Sam is definitely slipping.

A small moan draws my eyes back to Liv, but she's still out. Bad dream, maybe. One thing's for sure: this chick is toast. I stare at the long brown hair draped over her face. She looked so different tonight—wearing makeup and her hair down around her shoulders. It's the thought of her in her usual ponytail that tugs at something inside of me, though, not this club look. On strange impulse, I reach down to brush the strands back with my fingers. Even though she's passed out cold, black liner pooling in the corners of her eyes, it's hard to ignore that she's pretty. I bet Tyson was thinking that, too.

Tyson.

I had pushed him to the back of my mind after leaving the club, since I was more focused on getting Liv home without her throwing up in Sam's car. But the thought of him now makes me want to pound a hole into the wall. I look down again at Liv's smooth face, a pang shooting through my heart at her innocence. She must be innocent to let herself get drugged at a club. Or just stupid.

I trace her cheek softly with one finger. I'll go with innocent.

As mad as I am, I feel slightly guilty about what we're involving her in. I shake it off and move back to the window.

First things first.

Sam takes me back to the club to get my bike. She's unusually quiet—both of us lost in our own thoughts.

"Who do you think it was?" she asks when we get to the parking lot outside the warehouse. It's the first time she's asked this, the first time I realize she has no clue. She turns to me, her face serious. "I didn't see anyone with her."

"It was that asshole Tyson," I tell her.

"Tyson?" Her eyebrows knit. "Oh, yeah. I saw him talking to her at the bar."

"He was trying to do more than talk."

She pulls on her earlobe. "Should we do something?"

"Yeah." I stare at the exit where a few people are leaving. "We should."

The anger simmering inside of me starts to boil as I recognize the spiky dark hair of the guy now staggering out of the club. He's waving to a couple girls and yelling something at them.

"Well?" Sam says. "What?"

I ignore her and step out of the car.

"Wait," she calls to me before I close the door. "Want me to screw around with his records or something?"

"No, I'll take care of him," I say, keeping my eyes fixed on Tyson. "I'll see you later."

I slam the door and hang out for a moment until she pulls away, but I don't get on my bike. Instead, I pull my jacket close around me and walk across the street, just in time to hear Tyson call out, "Hey, come back!" to the girls who are walking away. Preying on his next target. I start for him at a run, the anger finally bursting inside me like fire.

Tyson glances my way and I catch a look of surprise that turns to fear as I barrel toward him. He turns and runs to the side of the building, near the other parking lot. I'm faster. I tackle him to the ground, into the gravel, and flip him over. His cheek is scratched and bloody from the gravel, but I don't care. I raise a fist.

"What? What?" he squeals as he tries to push me off him.

"You know what, you asshole. Drugging girls the only way you can get your kicks?" I wrestle with his arms and let my fist fly into his face. The shock reverberates through my hand, but I raise my fist again. Before I can punch him, he grabs at my arms and flips me off of him, then shoves me away with his knee. The son of a bitch is stronger than he looks. He grabs a handful of gravel and chucks it at my face. One of the rocks hits my cheek hard, and I reach up to feel blood. I start after him again.

He scrambles to his feet, trying to run, but immediately trips on a concrete block, sending him flying to the ground, face-first. He groans in pain and rolls over, his face a gravel-beaten and bloody mess. I stare at the pathetic sight in front of me, the desire to hit him again fading. I point a finger at him. "Try that shit again and you're screwed."

I turn and walk back the way I came, slightly sick to my stomach. Nancy would be upset if she knew I was fighting again, but punching that loser felt good. Too good. I run through the events in my head. What would make me lose control like that? All I can come up with is Liv's face.

Am I buying into Sam's plan to twist Liv to our side now? That's got to be it. Makes sense—she's a foster, a loner, an easy recruit. Another pretty face.

I don't like picturing her face. All it does is make me want to go beat Tyson again.

No girl is worth losing control.

CHAPTER Five

"Through all these rapid visions, there ran an undefined, uneasy consciousness of pain, which wearied and tormented him incessantly."

—Charles Dickens, *Oliver Twist*

LIV

I awaken to the feeling of a thousand tiny fists trying to pound their way out of my head. Slowly I open my eyes and let them focus on the blue walls.

Blue?

My heart starts to pound hard as my eyes move about quickly, finally falling on an unfamiliar painting of flowers. *Shit, where am I?*

I push myself into a sitting position, my head as tight as an overfilled balloon about to pop. From this angle, I can see a lineup of small roosters along a shelf, and I breathe a little easier. Somehow, I ended up in the spare bedroom. How did I get here? I stumble to the door, leaning against the frame for a moment. The room isn't spinning like the club did last night, but I'm still unsteady.

Tylenol. Need Tylenol.

Last night—what happened last night? All I remember is Z showing up, looking incredibly hot, which was so surreal and even now makes me tremble. I remember feeling really weird, and Z putting his arms around me. And Sam leaving me with him. Everything else is a blur.

I walk to the bathroom, splash water on my face, and brush my teeth. The reflection in the mirror confirms that I look as good as I feel. I'm still wearing the clothes from last night, minus the shoes. My fingers get stuck raking through my tangled hair, so I tie it into a makeshift bun and trudge to the kitchen to search for medicine.

"I'm telling you, Derrick, we need to call the police. We don't know what kind of trouble she could have gotten herself into."

I freeze.

"Take it easy. They don't consider it a missing persons case until she's been gone for twenty-four hours."

"Then what? They'll find her dead in a gutter, and what kind of people will we be labeled as? And I can't believe you let her go to some dance with a girl we don't even know."

"I was trying to be a cool dad."

"You're a moron."

Crap. I chew on the inside of my cheek for a few seconds, then realize I have no story to tell, real or made-up. I walk around the corner into their view.

"Olivia! Where have you been?" Derrick rushes over to me and tries to take my hand, his face concerned, but I quickly shove it behind my back.

"I just woke up."

"Really? We checked your room this morning and you weren't in it."

"I know. I was in the spare room."

"What? Why didn't you sleep in your own room?"

"I don't know. I guess I was confused last night." Seriously confused.

Derrick flicks a quick glance at his wife, who's glaring with arms crossed. He switches his gaze back to me. "Well, how come you're wearing the same clothes you had on at dinner last night and smelling like an ashtray?"

I sniff my shirt. Yuck. "I guess I slept in my clothes. But I promise, I woke up this morning in the spare room."

"Did you sneak in through the window last night?" Denise asks, the tone in her voice telling me that no matter what I say, I'm screwed.

"I...I guess. I don't remember."

Denise looks accusingly at Derrick. "Well, obviously she was drunk. This is what comes of letting teenagers out on their own to do who knows what. Never again. If she stays in this house, she abides by *my* rules."

"I'm right here, you know," I say, rubbing my temples. Her loud voice is making the throbbing in my head worse. "I didn't drink anything, but I know you won't believe me. I think I remember something about—"

Whoops, don't need to go there. There's no way I can make her believe anything other than I was smoking crack or something. "Can I have two Tylenol, please?"

Denise sets her shoulders and glares at her husband, the look clearly saying, *See, hangover!* But she does get me a couple tablets.

I return to my room to lie down. Derrick follows me. "Are

you really okay, Olivia?"

"Yes, I think so."

"Do you remember anything that could've happened to you? At all?"

"A friend of mine showed up and we talked. That's when I started feeling…sick."

I suddenly remember feeling something else when Z showed up and hope Derrick doesn't notice the heat spreading across my face.

"Okay, well, I think you should be home at nights now. No more partying, you got it?"

I nod and he walks away. No worries there. I have no intention of doing any more clubbing in the near future.

Lying back on the bed, I close my eyes and try to sort through the foggy memories. And, oh God, I was with Z, of all people. Touching him. A lot. He must think I'm a complete idiot. So much for my plan to play it cool. And he looked so different. My mind tries to slip around the word *hot*, but it's hard not to admit it. Strangely, the way he was dressed at the club fits his personality more than his prep-school look during the day.

I don't know how I'm going to be able to show my face on Monday. But someone had to have drugged that drink.

I jerk up, trying to ignore the stabbing head rush. Of course, Tyson. He gave me the soda and I drank it all; he must've slipped something in it. Maybe I should call the police, but I don't know what they'll ask. It's probably too late for that, anyway.

I wander back out to the living room. Denise is nowhere to be found and Derrick is watching TV. I boot up the computer and Google "drugs at club." The results display information about GHB, ketamine, and a slew of other things. I've heard of some of these before, but for some reason, it didn't click until now that something like this could be what was slipped into my drink. Tyson was trying to put me out so he could…rape me?

My hand falls away from the mouse and I stare at the screen, numb. Why would he do that? He's a jerk, for sure, but I never thought he would be capable of something like that. In all the many horrors of my life, no one has ever tried to drug me.

"Everything all right?" Derrick speaks up from the couch. I don't say anything. I can't tear my eyes away from the screen. If it wasn't for Z showing up exactly when he did…

"My God, what are you looking at?"

Startled, I try to switch screens, but it's too late. He's already gotten a full view.

"Olivia," Derrick says, his forehead creased. "If something happened, I need to know about this."

I bite the inside of my cheek hard to keep from crying. "I don't know. I think someone slipped something in my drink." I clear my throat to steady the tremors in my voice.

"What? How'd you get home last night, then?"

"Sam gave me a ride. She saw me before I passed out, and I remember her taking me to her car." I don't tell him it was Z I ended up with before passing out.

He stares at the screen for a moment. "Do you know who gave you the drink?"

"No," I lie.

"Okay, well, I want you close to the house from now on, okay? And I'll be coming home early from work each day to make sure you aren't here by yourself."

Crap. "Um, you don't need to do that, Mr. Carter."

"Derrick, please. And I think I do. You don't want

something like this to happen again."

He moves back to the couch and I shut down the computer. Great. Now I'll never have a moment alone.

Derrick takes me to school on Monday with the promise that he'll be waiting for me when I get home. Wonderful. It won't surprise me if he insists on walking me to work, too. But part of me is glad that I won't be on the bus with that slimeball Tyson. I don't think I'd be able to stop from ramming my backpack in his face.

I get to school and approach my locker with no sight of Tyson. My thoughts are so jumbled by the time I get to Computer Science that I'm honestly not sure if I'll end up screaming, punching him, or ignoring him. Or maybe all three—in that order. At the door, I take a deep breath, square my shoulders, and walk in the classroom.

More than half the students are there already, but Tyson is missing. Z is typing and doesn't make eye contact when I pass in front of him toward my seat. He's dressed in his usual school attire—Polo shirt, glasses, hair slicked back—but there's an addition of what looks like a small red scratch etched into the side of his cheek. I sit down and catch him in my peripheral vision. He's still not paying attention to me, which I'm used to. But after Friday night, I'd hoped for a glance at the very least. Maybe the whole thing was all a drug-induced dream and he wasn't even at the club.

"Hey, girl, how're you doing?" Sam asks, slinging her backpack over the chair and sitting down to face me.

"I'm okay, but I've got a ton of questions."

"I'll bet. I tried calling you a couple times but your foster dad said you were busy."

"Yeah, apparently I'm three years old all of a sudden. They're really pissing me off."

Sam smiles at that. Then her eyes rise above my shoulder and widen in shock. The rest of the class gasps, and I follow the stares to see Tyson walking to his chair. He slumps down, not looking at me. I clamp my mouth shut and face forward as Ms. Walsh starts the class, but I can't help but peek at Tyson. His face looks like it was pummeled in the boxing ring. The top of one cheek is swollen, an eye is black and blue, and his skin looks like someone took sandpaper to it.

"What happened to you?" Kelly, the girl on his other side, asks. He glances at me, then back to her. "Nothing," he mumbles.

I turn to catch Z's eyes on me—probably the only eyes in the room that aren't on Tyson. His head is tilted slightly as he considers me with pursed lips, then his focus shifts back to the monitor.

What the hell?

Z beat up Tyson. I saw it in his eyes. How did he know? I kind of remember saying something about Tyson giving me the drink.

Damn it. Or good? I'm not sure what to think.

Tyson spends the entire hour not talking or looking anywhere but at his computer screen. Even Ms. Walsh seems stunned. She doesn't call on him at all. When the bell rings, he's the first one out the door.

"Z?" I say quietly as he walks by, but he doesn't stop.

I nudge Sam. "Did Z do that?"

Her eyes follow him, seeming genuinely unsure. "I'd say the less we know about that, the better."

I should be happy, but the whole thing doesn't seem right. Okay, so maybe I pictured it over the weekend, someone whipping the crap out of him, but I didn't think it would actually happen. It seems so...odd for Z to do that. He never even gives me the time of day.

Z completely ignores me in English Lit, showing up right as the bell rings and looking especially interested in whatever the teacher is saying. I stretch my arms out and glance at him, but he keeps his eyes focused on the front. I even resort to the childish move of dropping a pencil near his feet. He picks it up and places it back on my desk without looking at me. I'll have to corner him at lunch.

On the way to the cafeteria, Tyson intercepts me. He waits until a couple other kids pass by before cornering me next to the water fountain. I grab my backpack in my hands, planning to shove it at him should he even think to touch me.

"Why'd you send that guy to beat me up?" His voice sounds warped through his puffy lips.

I hold my glare. "What are you talking about?"

"Oh, come on. He was talking to you at the bar."

At the bar? He has no idea Z is the one who beat him up. Z did look very different that night.

"I don't really know him. Not really." Boy, that's the truth. "But why the hell did you try to drug me? I'm not stupid. I know what that drug is for."

Tyson stares at me for a moment, his eyes wide. "Wait, you really think I did that?"

I take a breath to steady my anger. I don't want to lose it in the middle of the hall at school. "You gave me the drink, you drugged it. It's not that hard to figure out. You're lucky I didn't call the cops."

His mouth drops open. "I didn't. All I did was hand you the drink like the guy asked me to."

"What guy?"

"He said he was a friend of yours. I was kinda drunk, so I don't know. Actually, come to think of it, I'm pretty sure it was the same one you were all over at the bar."

"The same…?"

"The same guy who gave me the drink. Yeah, that was him."

His casual observation cuts through me like cold steel. The same guy? Why would Z beat Tyson up if he were the one who gave me the drink? And why would I believe Tyson, anyway?

"Trust me, I didn't do it," Tyson says again. "I wouldn't do something like that."

Trust him? I almost laugh at the stupidity of it. "*If* that's true, which I don't know if I believe, you were an asshole to pass me a drink someone else gave you."

"I know. I'm sorry." He backs away to join his friends.

I take a deep breath and push the doors open to the cafeteria.

. . .

Z

Sam starts her bitching before she even sits down. "Z, you're an idiot. Why did you have to go beat up that dumbass?"

I sigh. Nothing I can say will make Sam happy. The worst part is I'm still not sure why I did it myself. Maybe because

Liv's wide-eyed innocence played heavy on my mind the whole night. If I hadn't been there to rescue her from that jerk... Even now, looking at his battered face, I feel strangely vindicated. Maybe that's why I don't tell her the gravel did most of the work on him, not me.

"I thought you liked Liv," is all I say. "The guy drugged her."

Sam rubs at her temples. "I do like her, and you know that's not the point. You're risking all of us, you know? What if he figures it out and presses charges? They'd come after you, and then we'd all be screwed. You should've let me handle it."

"They won't come after us. And maybe she'll like us more. We did save her from a major f—"

Sam pokes me as her eyes lift over my shoulder. "Hi, Liv!"

I turn to see Liv staring at me, frowning. Sam pulls a chair out for her but she doesn't move.

"So, I was thinking about going to the mall after school today. Want to come?" Sam asks, acting like she doesn't notice that Liv's still standing.

Liv's eyes are still on me. "Can't. I have to work."

"Tomorrow, then?"

"Maybe. Well?" She directs the question to me.

"Well, what?"

"Tyson's pretty messed up."

I shrug and take a bite of my apple, curious to see where she's going with this. Sam gives some lame excuse about getting water and leaves.

Liv sits down on the edge of a chair. "So you beat him up?" Her voice is low, her tone accusatory, and she seems upset...at me? I take another bite and don't say anything.

She twists her necklace around her finger and her eyes

drop to my collar.

"He looks really bad. Why did you do that?"

"Liv." Her eyes lift to meet mine. "You were drugged. He gave you that drink. He admitted it."

"He actually told you he put something in it?"

"No, he denied that, obviously. But he admitted to giving you the drink."

Her forehead wrinkles as she considers this, fiddling with a sugar packet on the table. "But what if he didn't put the drug in it?"

I stare at her for a moment. How the hell did she end up at that conclusion? "Are you serious?"

"I ran into him in the hall. He said someone else gave him the drink to give to me."

"Uh-huh."

"He might not have been lying. The person who slipped something in my drink could've been someone else."

"Okay, so, who do you think it was?" I'm sure my voice sounds patronizing, but I don't care. How could she believe *Tyson*, of all people? And I thought she was smart.

She looks away, her face flushed. "I don't know."

I can't help it. I laugh. "You sure are naive for a foster kid."

She jumps to her feet, her face screwed up in fury. "My personal life's my own business, not yours. And I can take care of myself."

I can't help laughing as she walks away. Take care of herself? Sure, and maybe she should call Tyson to see if he wants to go hang out later, just as friends. Give me a break.

Liv stops abruptly and turns back to face me, her jaw sticking out slightly in defiance of my laughter. I tilt my head to watch her as she moves slowly, deliberately back to me.

Her sudden switch from an open Pandora's box to this quiet, contained anger is fascinating. She rests one hand on the table next to me and leans in close—an intimidating move a girl's never made on me before. I'm stupidly nervous and intrigued at the same time.

Liv's ponytail falls forward enough for me to catch the soft, clean scent of her shampoo. There's nothing else soft about her right now, though. She pierces me with her eyes, like she can see into me. "I don't know what you're up to, Z," she says slowly, quietly. "Or what happened that night. But you don't intimidate me like you think you do."

She pushes away and walks out of the cafeteria, leaving me staring after her in undeniable awe. I would never have expected *that* from her.

"What'd she have to say?" Sam asks, startling me as she sits down. "And why are you staring at the door with your mouth open?"

I clamp my jaw shut and turn to her. "She doesn't think Tyson drugged her. She's only mad at me for beating him up. And I'm not sure, but it sounds like she thinks *I* might have done it."

Saying it out loud, it sounds even more ridiculous. How could she believe that? I notice the faster pace of my heartbeat, normally only triggered by meetings with Bill. *Shit, do I actually care about this?*

Sam's mouth drops open. "What the hell? You?"

I laugh out loud but cringe inside. If she thinks I'm just some bully beating up people, or that I'm capable of drugging her, she'll never trust me. Or Sam. And we may as well drop the whole idea of twisting Olivia Westfield.

CHAPTER SIX

"'Once let him feel that he is one of us; once fill his mind with the idea that he has been a thief, and he's ours—ours for his life!'"

—Charles Dickens, *Oliver Twist*

LIV

"Here, this will give you an energy boost before we start shopping." Sam offers me one of the Styrofoam cups and hands some bills to the woman at Nature's Table. She lost a bet on who could find the freakiest person outside the mall—I spotted a huge guy in a muscle shirt walking his cat on a leash. So she bought me the smoothie.

"Thanks." The food court is crowded, but we soon find a small table and sit down. At first, we chitchat about school, homework, stuff like that. She's so easy to talk to, and funny. She's got me cracking up with her impression of Tyson drooling over me. The women next to us throw us dirty looks for being so loud, but I don't care. I've had friends before, of course, but none who make me laugh as much as Sam.

The one thing we don't dwell on is the night at the club. She does tell me that there's no way Z would've drugged me. "He wouldn't pull a jerk move like that. I live with the guy, remember? I should know."

I don't want to talk about Z. I'm still pissed at his attitude toward me yesterday. The conversation with Sam turns to computer programming, and when she asks if I've ever done any hacking, I realize the perfect opportunity to ask, "Sam, what exactly do you do at that company of yours?"

She tilts her head, a tiny smile on her lips. "What exactly do you *think* I do?"

I fiddle with the straw in my drink, trying to figure out how to phrase it just right. "Well, obviously you make a lot of money to afford that kind of car. If I had to guess…maybe someone pays you to hack into their security systems?"

She considers that for a moment. "Hmm…well, I'd say that's pretty accurate."

I exhale lightly. "So did you get any response from your boss? I mean, do they need an extra hacker?"

Her grin widens. "Oh, I believe they're interested, yes."

"Awesome. How do I contact them?"

"They'll contact you." She laughs. "Liv, stop worrying so much. They'll get a hold of you when they're ready."

I laugh with her, but I hope it's not one of those "we'll call you" things where they never do. I take a sip of my smoothie, my thoughts slipping to Z. I can't seem to stop thinking of him, even when I try. He bothers me at the same time that he thrills me—his dark hazel eyes that light up when he smiles, the way his cocky attitude dissolved when I told him off. I've played the moment in my head a thousand times. Confronting someone the way I did isn't like me at all; I don't know what got into me.

The goose bumps tickle my arms as I picture his eyes widening in surprise and, most especially, the smirk melting from his lips. I have to admit, I felt pretty kick-ass at that moment.

I still don't trust him, though I don't know if it's because of what happened the other night or something else I can't quite put my finger on. He's such an enigma; how could I ever be friends with him?

"Hello?" Sam snaps her fingers in front of my face, startling me.

"Sorry, what?"

She shakes her head. "Okay, again, what's the worst thing you've ever done?"

She's already tried a couple versions of the same question, always disappointed in my answer. "I told you, the time I took money from my foster mother's wallet."

She snorts. "Yeah, twenty bucks to buy new shoes. Big freakin' deal. I'll bet it was because your shoes had holes in them or something."

I take another sip and watch a tired-looking woman shuttle her kids through the crowds. I don't tell Sam that yes, that's exactly why. Carla wouldn't buy me new shoes, new clothes, or even old ones. Whatever money she got to take care of me, she spent on her five bratty kids. Everything I had when living with the Grays I borrowed or bought with money I took out of Carla's wallet. It was a version of stealing, I guess, but I didn't have much of a choice.

I change the subject. "So what are you looking for today?"

She waves her hand in a vague gesture. "Oh, you know, whatever's good. Sometimes I find things, sometimes I don't. But I love to shop, so it doesn't matter. I can help you find tops that won't make you look like you're wearing kids' clothes anymore."

Well, that's direct enough. We throw our cups in the trash before taking the escalator to the second floor. The line of apparel shops caters to various extremes of women—heavy, thin; rich, poor; old, young.

"That's the loser store," Sam says, grabbing my arm when I make a right toward Penney's. "You don't want to be caught buying stuff in there."

"Oh, yeah," I say, like this is my area of expertise. Bernadette loved Penney's. "So where do we go?"

"Here," she says, pulling me toward a store where red satin lingerie and feathers are draped over bone-white mannequins. I jerk to a halt and Sam laughs.

"Just kidding! Over here."

She leads me to a trendy store called M. Young women in crisp pin-striped suits nod to her without acknowledging me. Of course, her confidence shouts out *I belong here*, while mine whispers, *Haven't got a clue*. I watch in amazement as she quickly sorts through jeans, shirts, and skirts and heads toward the back of the store with a small armful.

"You need to start with these," she says, pushing me into a large dressing room and latching the door behind us. She flips through the clothes and hands me a multicolored chiffon top and dark-blue jeans.

I face the wall and quickly remove my shorts and tee. I pull the new clothes on and turn to check myself out in the mirror. *W-o-w, wow!* The jeans are too tight for my taste, but the airy top floats over me in a flattering way. The reflection is of someone who knows about fashion. Someone who might be thought of as cool.

Someone who is *so* not me.

"That's awesome!" Sam says.

"It's a little see-through, isn't it?" I cover my top half with an arm and she laughs.

"It's supposed to be. You can wear a black bra or cami under it. Speaking of that, who bought you such a grandma bra?" She lifts the shirt to get a better look, but I push her hands away, my face burning. "Seriously, you should donate that thing to a retirement home."

"Cut it out. What other shirts do you have?" I ask.

"Try this one." She hands me a black nothing of a top and a black-and-white flare skirt, and I slip them on. The style is alien on me, like I'm headed out for a night in New York. Way too chic and definitely too clingy. It makes me think of the outfits some of the girls wore at the club the other night. That's reason enough for me to pull the tiny shirt back over my head and toss it on the bench.

"I like the first one better." I finger the light, airy material and find the price. Seventy-five dollars! "Oh. Never mind." I drop the tag and move to the next shirt, a plain black tee.

"Wait, what's wrong with this one?" Sam says, going back to the chiffon. She glances at the tag. "I thought you said Denise gave you money to buy some new clothes."

"Yeah, but not that much." Denise gave me fifty dollars, which I was grateful for. But in this store, it might buy me a pair of socks.

"What about tips from Slice of Happy?"

I snort. "Please. I couldn't afford the sleeve with the money I earn."

She holds the shirt out. "You know, this looked really good on you. Try it on again."

"I can't afford it."

"I know, but I want to see it again."

I slip the shirt on. Sam walks around me and tugs at the bottom, pulls at the sleeves.

"I think you should get it."

"I just said I can't buy it."

She puts an arm around me and leans close to my ear. "I didn't say you should *buy* it."

"What? No way, Sam."

"Come on. Denise didn't give you enough money for one thing, let alone a wardrobe. What does she expect, that you're going to wear those shirts that are too small forever?"

It was only one shirt that didn't fit, but Sam makes it sound like my entire closet. Still, my clothes are pretty worn out. "Maybe she'll give me more if I ask for it."

"Uh huh. You know what she'll say? 'Olivia, you should go to Walmart. It's good enough for me, so it should be good enough for your sorry ass. They introduced a new line of granny polyester to go with your Playtex bra.'"

Okay, that's funny. And probably true. I laugh in spite of myself.

"Hang on, I know what'll help. Stay right there." She disappears, returning with a couple of black lacy camis, so tiny they may as well be bras. "Try these and see if one fits."

She turns her back while I remove my bra and slip my arms through the holes of the cami. The clingy, lacy fabric is much more grown-up than anything I've ever owned. I pull the chiffon top over my head and look in the mirror, turning slightly to see the effect from the side. I swear I'm like one of those *What Not to Wear* victims, transformed from drab to... *damn.*

"Wow!" Sam says, whistling sexy-like.

"I can't wear this to school." Or anywhere else, for that matter.

She laughs. "It's not really meant for school. Promise me you'll get a new bra, though. Really. And toss that one in the garbage on the way out." She picks my old bra up with an empty hanger and flings it around in an exaggerated way.

I twist again to view myself. The clothes do fit nicely.

"Where's your T-shirt?" Sam whispers. "Put it on over this, and my sweater over that."

"I don't know, Sam…" But she's already pushing my T-shirt over my head. I look in the mirror at the shirt clinging for dear life to the thin fabric underneath. If I don't do this, I risk alienating the only friend I've made since moving here. Besides, I've behaved my entire life and look where that's gotten me.

"It's just a little thing, Liv," she says, her expression serious. She leans back on the wall, crossing her arms as she watches me. "You need new clothes and your foster parents aren't providing for you. It's not like I'm asking you to break open the cash register. When you make better money, maybe you can come back and buy something for real. Come on, Miss Thang…"

It's that pseudo-twang in her voice, the tone that reminds me of Bernadette, that makes up my mind.

Screw it. I put my arms in Sam's sweater, imagining the tiny conscience fairy on my shoulder getting beaten to a pulp by a little guy with horns and twisted tail.

...

Z

I take off my glasses and wipe at my eyes. Page after page of information about Brownlow, Inc., and its founder and I'm coming up with crap. From the endless number of articles on his charitable contributions, Carlton Brownlow is a pretty major benefactor. The money he's donated to United Way alone makes my take on most of these accounts look like a kid's allowance. This doesn't make me feel bad about cracking the bastard's accounts in the least. The wealthy try to impress by giving huge donations and starting foundations, but it's mostly tax-deductible shit that makes them feel less guilty about getting rich at other people's expense.

Micah sails through the open door and drops into one of the chairs, kicking his feet up on the desk. "What's up?"

"Took you long enough," I grumble.

"I was busy. Anyway, here it is."

He tosses me the flash drive, which is hot pink and covered in yellow flowers. I gaze at it, then him. "Really?"

He shrugs. "You don't like it? Create your own program then, jackass."

"Whatever." I pick up the silly thing and flip it around my fingers. "How long will it take?"

"Depends. This one starts out slowly, then builds to flood their system without alerting their IT. At least for a while. But you'll have to be ready. If his system is as advanced as I think it is, you won't have long. How are you going to get it installed? I doubt you can set up a fake page or pop-ups or anything that they'll recognize."

"Still working on it. Might end up having to take a pretty banker out for drinks."

Micah woo-hoos and smacks my hand. It's a tactic used by Bill, and one he wants me to try. It'd probably be easy—meeting a woman "by chance" at a bar, getting her tipsy enough not to notice me slipping a loaded flash drive in her bag. For some reason, even though the idea once excited me, I'm not really looking forward to it.

"Z!" The singsongy voice pierces the doorway. Of all the kids in the house, Sam is the one I can always count on to interrupt me whenever I'm working. "Guess what? She's in!" Sam says, bouncing on her heels like she's twelve instead of seventeen. Micah jumps out of his chair and grabs her hands; the two of them start hopping around like idiots.

"Do you mind?" I ask acidly. "Some of us are trying to work."

"But I did it! I got her to steal something! A shirt at the mall. It was ea-sy. Easy, easy, easy." She does a hip-bump with Micah to emphasize each "easy."

"Congratulations, sweetie," he says, kissing her cheek. He probably doesn't have a clue of what she's talking about, but that doesn't matter to Micah. He's a hound for a good time. "Gotta go, though. Party later?" He salutes us and leaves.

Sam frowns at me, her hands on her hips. "Well, don't break a sweat congratulating me or anything, Z."

I wave my hand at her. "Fine. Good for you. Now go away."

She grabs the arm of my chair and pulls it out from the desk. "Come on. Even you have to be excited about this. She's in!"

I stand and yank the chair away from her. "No, she's not.

You bullied her into stealing a shirt, which has nothing to do with us."

"Ha, so you say," she replies smugly. "But at least we know she *will* do it."

"So what're you going to do now? Have her steal a car? Or hey, maybe bring her on over and see if she'd like to rob a bank. How about that? You're an idiot if you believe it's that easy."

Sam's eyes darken and she punches my shoulder. My skin smarts, but I don't rub at it. I turn back to the computer and ignore her.

"I thought you'd be happy about this. Besides," she says, her voice rising angrily, "I'm the only one who's trying here. You're not doing shit. Exactly what is your problem, Z?"

"I don't have a problem."

"Yes, you do."

I sigh and swivel the chair back to face her. "Look, she thinks I'm an asshole. So what's the point?"

"Yeah, well, she also thinks you're hot. You should be doing more with that."

Yeah, some hot guy she thinks drugged her. "Good-bye, Sam." I turn back to the monitor, dismissing her. I don't have to turn around to know she's flipping me off before she heads out the door, no doubt to bitch to Nancy about how I'm not doing my part.

CHAPTER SEVEN

"*Such is the influence which the condition of our own thoughts exercises even over the appearance of external objects. Men who look on nature and their fellow men, and cry that all is dark and gloomy, are in the right; but the somber colours are reflections from their own jaundiced vision.*"

—Charles Dickens, *Oliver Twist*

LIV

After getting home with the stolen blouse from M, the realization that I took something really started to eat at me. I hung it in the back of the closet, not intending to wear it or the lacy bra. The fact that Sam persuaded me to steal makes me nervous about hanging out with her, so I don't chat with her during class as much. I make my lunch at the house every day so I can bypass the cafeteria completely to eat alone on the grass outside. Sam seems confused at first, then pissed off when I keep making excuses.

It's not just her, either. Avoiding her means avoiding Z. The more I obsess about it, the more I wonder if it really was him who drugged me. Why else would he show up at the bar at that moment and offer to take me home when I started feeling so strange? The only thing I remember is putting my hands all over his body and him taking me outside before I passed out. I remember his arms around me and his lips near my face. Sam says they both took me home. But then, he did beat up Tyson. Why would he do that?

Thinking about it all makes my head swim.

A couple other girls invite me to sit with them, but after a few lunches of listening to them gossip about pretty much everybody who walks by, I start making excuses to them as well. Tyson now completely avoids me.

Okay, well, that part's not so bad.

The solitude doesn't bother me that much, but I liked Sam. I even liked Z, I guess, so though it's me avoiding them, it does hurt a bit when they were the only friends I had here.

Z ignores me, too. Although a couple times I've caught him watching me. I try not to look at him, try to act like I don't care, but I can tell by the tiny lift to his lips that he knows better. *Freaking weirdo jerk of a guy who drives me insane.* I've mentally called him every name in the book, yet every nerve in my body stands at attention, tickling under my skin when we're in the same room together. *Stupid clueless body.*

Sam is waiting for me at my locker after my last class. Her arms are crossed and I can tell by her narrowed eyes that I better not move past her.

"What's up?" I ask for lack of anything better to say.

Her mouth drops open. "Seriously?" Then she laughs. "A week of not talking to me and you ask what's up?"

I fight a smile. "Yeah, I guess."

"I'm sorry I got you to steal that shirt. Sorry but not sorry.

Does that make sense?"

I shake my head. She sighs and wraps an arm around my shoulder. It's such an honest, friendly gesture, I don't pull away.

"Look, I've spent a lifetime in foster care. I know how it works. My parents died so long ago that I don't remember them. I bet you went through a lot of crap yourself. Am I right?"

I don't say anything. I don't have to. By the way she's nodding, she can read my expression like a road map through hell. Even though part of me is still pissed that she talked me into stealing, I miss her friendship too much to stay angry. Most of the other kids in my classes are nice—friendly, even. But their carefree smiles and casual chatter represent the normalcy of their lives that's missing from mine.

Sam, on the other hand, understands me. She gets it—the crap we go through being lost in a system that cares as much about us as stray dogs on the street. I can be myself with her, which is why I'm suddenly smiling back at her as if nothing's happened. Stealing that shirt was wrong, but it's not worth losing my friend over.

After school, I skip the bus and stand on the footbridge to the parking lot, waiting for Z. I'm just going to suck it up and confront him about what happened that night. Sam encouraged me, too, suggesting that I'd feel better if I talked to him. He walks up but stops when he sees me. Other kids slide past us, oblivious to the tension.

"We need to talk," I say, trying to sound as cold and distant as possible.

"Yeah?"

"Um, I need to know what happened that night." Damn it, my voice doesn't sound as strong as I need it to be. I try to summon whatever forces turned me into the girl who had no problem telling Z off the other day, but they seem to be asleep.

He takes off his glasses and crosses his arms, scrutinizing me with those damn sexy eyes. "Why don't you tell me what *you* think happened that night?"

I stare him down, trying to look braver than I feel. "Tyson told me a guy gave him that drink. The same guy who was at the bar with me."

Nothing.

I falter for a moment, then take a deep breath. "You were at the bar with me when I started feeling weird. You helped me out of the building."

He raises his eyebrows. I didn't really, truly believe it was him, but now I'm not so sure. It's like he's waiting for me to say it.

"It was you, Z, wasn't it? Not Tyson. What happened when you took me out of there? What did you do?"

Z uncrosses his arms and moves toward me, his eyes suddenly worried. I take a step back and he stops. "I took you home. Sam and I both did," he says.

"I only remember you. I remember how I... I remember your arms around me. That's all. It was you." My voice cracks at the last word, and my hands start to shake. I bite my lip to keep the tears pressing against my eyes from falling.

"Wait, what?" he starts, breaking off when I step back again. I take one more step and slip off the small footbridge into a muddy hole, twisting my ankle and falling on my butt. I try to get up but wince as a searing pain shoots from my ankle.

"Are you okay?" Z asks, reaching down to help me. I shake my head and slap his hand away. He steps back and waits until I manage to get on my feet. My ankle is screaming but I try not to let it show. I shift my weight to my left foot and do my best to ignore the cold, wet mud plastered to my clothes and skin. At least the threat of crying is gone. Now I'm just mad.

"Just tell me, Z, what did you do that night? Where else did you take me before my house?"

"I didn't take you anywhere. Sam was with us; she drove her car. We took you home."

"Why are you lying? I remember Sam walking away from us. And why wouldn't you have driven your car?"

He laughs. Really? Laughing? I scowl and hobble away toward the school.

"Hey, wait, you're hurt. Let me take you home."

"Get away from me. I've already called my foster parents and they'll be here any minute."

I keep walking as best as I can—*damn, this hurts*—hoping I'm not screwing up my ankle even worse. When I reach the building, I sneak a glance back but he's nowhere to be seen. *Good riddance.*

I hobble to the office and use the phone to call Derrick, but groan when he doesn't answer. I forgot that he's supposed to be in a meeting and won't be home until later. Denise never gets back until after five, and I can't stay here for two more hours. Most people in the office have already left for the day.

I massage my temples with my fingertips, trying to think. When Derrick drove me to school I was surprised at how close we actually live from here, since the bus takes a roundabout trip. It'll hurt, but I know I can grit my teeth and make it home by walking. I'll keep my foot on ice the rest of the weekend if I have to. I take off my right sock and wrap it as tightly as I can around my ankle, then stand up and hobble back out of the office. It's only about two or three blocks to the first light. I can do this.

A block later, my ankle screams that this is going to be a lot harder than I thought. I stop for a moment, debating whether to go back to the school and beg a ride off someone or continue walking. It scares me a little to think of hitchhiking, but maybe the horror stories only happen on the highway.

The low growl of a motorcycle closes in, startling me when it stops next to me.

"Want a ride?"

Oh, crap. "No, thanks." I keep moving without looking over, trying to ignore the images of abductions filling my mind.

"Liv, hey!"

I glance over as the guy takes off his helmet and brushes his no-longer-plastered blond hair to the side. *Oh, no. Not Z.* Looking at the bike, now at least I get why he laughed when I asked about him not taking his car that night.

He pushes his glasses up higher on the bridge of his nose. "C'mon, let me help."

"No." I continue limping toward the stoplight a couple blocks away, the knives slicing up my ankle into my entire leg. He moves the bike to the sidewalk and rides slowly alongside of me, balancing the growling beast with his feet.

My mind blurring with the pain, I finally stop. "You're going to get arrested for having that thing up here."

He cuts the engine and crosses his arms. "So come on, let me give you a ride home. I don't see that you have any other option, unless your foster parents are planning to pick you up at the corner."

I look toward the light at the corner and twist my ponytail around, thinking about what happened at the club. Is it possible Tyson made the whole thing up? Or that it could've been someone else? Is it stupid to give Z the benefit of the doubt? He certainly couldn't have taken me somewhere on a motorcycle. And once again, why the hell would I believe Tyson?

The questions fade away as I realize he's right. I can't make it home, and at this point, I probably can't even make it back to the school. I'll have to cross my fingers and assume he's really going to take me home. I limp toward the back of the bike. He reaches an arm out to help me mount up behind him.

"So you have a Ducati and Sam has a Camaro," I say. "I thought you guys live in a group home."

"I'm impressed. How'd you know this is a Ducati?"

"My last foster dad had one. It was his favorite thing in the world. He let me ride it." I don't add that I only rode once and it scared me so badly that I never got on the bike again. This one seems bigger, maybe, but not enough to keep me from hating the idea of getting on it.

"Cool."

"I guess. I live on Green Valley Drive."

"Yeah, I know. Here, put this on," he says, swiveling around to hand me his helmet. "I don't want to be responsible for killing you. Just kidding," he says, laughing at my expression.

He starts the engine up and idles it for a moment before turning to shout over his shoulder, "Hold on."

I wrap my arms around his waist and close my eyes, burrowing into his jacket as he throttles the engine. We bounce off the curb and he takes it slow down the street to the light.

I start to think that my memory of the motorcycle ride is exaggerated, until he makes the right turn. Then he kicks it into high gear and the bike almost literally flies down the street. I close my eyes and clutch at him in terror, but soon the rumbling of the machine and the wind against my skin kick-starts my adrenaline. I open my eyes and loosen my death grip a bit.

The houses fly by in a blur until he starts to slow down and make the left onto my street. He pulls to a stop in front of the rooster mailbox and idles the engine. I stay where I am for a moment, my body shivering against him.

He peers at me over his shoulder. "You okay?"

"Yes," I gasp, removing the helmet and handing it to him.

"Anyone home?"

"Yes, Derrick is home," I lie. In fact, I'm pretty sure Derrick would give me a lecture if he saw me right now on the back of a motorcycle.

I push myself off the bike, balancing by holding onto Z's shoulders. He puts his arm around my waist and helps me hobble to the front door. Even with the throbbing pain in my ankle, I am very aware of his closeness, the warmth of his body heating me all the way through. I fumble around my purse for the key and wobble on the step, one hand on the doorknob. "Thanks for getting me home."

"Sure." He takes his glasses off and gazes at me for a moment, his hand still positioned on my waist. "Do you still believe I spiked your drink?"

"I don't know. Maybe. I don't know what to think." The deep gold and green colors shift in his eyes. I wish he'd stop looking at me like that.

"Look, it's not my style to do something like that. If I

wanted to chill out with a girl, I'd just ask."

"Do you ask a lot?"

The corners of his mouth lift slightly and he puts his hand on the door, leaning in toward me. "Not lately."

I back against the doorframe, but his eyes don't relent their grip. My heart is running a marathon through my chest. Despite everything, I feel this weird, scary temptation to kiss him. I wonder what he'd do.

"I have to go," I say weakly.

He finally backs away. "See you Monday."

I manage to get the key in the lock with my shaking fingers and open the door. The engine revs to life, and he peels out of the neighborhood as I collapse into the first chair I find. I have got to get control of myself. Even if he really didn't drug me at the club, getting involved with this guy is *so* not a good idea.

0 1 0 0 1 0 0 1 0 1 1 1 0 1 0 0 0 0 0 0 0 1 1
1 0 1 1 1 1 1 0 1 1 1 1 0 0 0 0 0 0 0 0 1 1 1 1
1 0 1 0 0 1 0 0 1 0 1 0 1 0 1 1 1 1 1 0 1 1 0 1 0
0 1 0 0 0 1 1 1 0 1 0 0 1 1 0 1 0 0 1 0 0
0 1 1 1 0 0 0 0 1 1 1 1 0 1 1 1 1
1 0 0 1 1 0 1 1 1 1 0 1 1 0 0 1 1 0 1 0 1 1 0
0 1 1 0 0 1 0 0 0 1 0 0 0 1 0 0 0 1 0 1 1
1 0 0 1 1 1 0 0 1 0 0 0 0 1 0 1 0 0 0 0 0 1 0
1 0 0 1 1 1 1 0 0 1 0 0 0 1 0 1 1 0 0 1 0
0 0 0 0 0 1 0 0 0 1 1 1 1 0 0 1 0 1 0 1
1 0 0 1 1 0 1 1 1 0 0 1 1 0 1 0 0 1 0 1
0 0 1 1 1 0 1 1 1 1 0 0 1 0 0 1 1 0 1
1 0 0 0 1 1 0 1 1 1 1 0 1 0 0 1 1
0 0 1 0 0 0 1 1 1 1 0 0 0 1 1 0 1 0
1 0 1 0 0 0 1 1 1 0 0 1 0 1 0 1 0

CHAPTER EIGHT

Oliver: *And you Dodger, you're my friend.*
The Artful Dodger: *Huh! A friend's just an enemy in disguise.*
You can't trust nobody.

—a film adaptation of *Oliver Twist*

Z

Liv is speaking to Sam and me again. I'll admit I'm glad about that. Girls don't usually ignore me, but it's more than that. Her comeback at lunch that day has been stuck in my head. For as shy as she seems, she's got a fire in her that intrigues me. Part of me wants to push her buttons just to watch that fire ignite again, but that would definitely put me in the ultimate jerk category. Our plans would be for nothing if she pushed me away. Though she still might when she realizes what I've done.

At least she seems to have dropped the ridiculous idea that it could've been me who drugged her. I don't know why she'd believe that ass in the first place.

Speaking of…

"Hey, what the…" Tyson's mouth drops open to see me

sitting in his chair.

"Sorry, but I have to sit closer to see," I tell him, adjusting my glasses. He looks at the teacher.

"You can have Z's chair," Walsh says, pointing to my previous desk. "He does need to be able to see the board."

I return Sam's grin as Tyson grumbles and moves around to sit behind me. Just in time for Liv to walk in and stop short when she sees me.

"End-of-year seat change?" she asks, sliding past and setting her backpack on the desk next to me.

"Sure, why not? I need to sit closer for my eyesight."

"But you wear glasses."

"I know."

She shakes her head, though I can see the corners of her mouth fighting to lift.

"How's the ankle?" I ask.

"It's fine. I can't run on it, but at least it's not sprained."

Walsh starts the class by giving us what she believes is a complex design. It's stupid easy, though. I'm the first one who finishes, as usual, although a quick glance at Liv's monitor shows she's not far behind. Not that I'd tell Sam this, but she was probably right that Liv's worth a shot.

Liv squints at her computer, tapping away. So serious an expression for something so basic. Her hair falls forward as she looks down at her keyboard. I combat the urge to sweep the dark waves over her shoulder so I can see her face.

I open the Windows command prompt and input her computer's name, obtained as soon as I came into the classroom this morning. I quickly type out the prompt and watch as the message pops up on her computer: *Time's almost up.*

Her head jerks as she stares at Walsh, who is at her own computer, typing away. I almost laugh out loud and type in the next message: *Go for a ride after school?*

Liv cuts her brown eyes over to me, her lips slightly parted in surprise. A strong desire to taste those lips ripples through me, the intensity almost overwhelming. She faces her computer again to type her response, a tiny dimple forming in her cheek as she smiles.

No.

I frown at my monitor. *Why not?*

Have to go home.

Why?

She doesn't respond at first. Her fingers move to the keys, then away, then back again to hover as she frowns. *Just something at home*, is all she types. She closes the window and switches back to her assignment.

She's a bad liar. There's nothing she needs to go home for—she doesn't trust me. Not that she should. But still.

"You're not done?" I tease in a low voice as she taps out code for the assignment.

"Shut up, I'm almost there," she snaps. Unfortunately, her voice isn't so low.

"Miss Westfield?"

"Yes, ma'am?"

Walsh shakes her head. "See me after class, Olivia."

Liv's face flushes pink and she drops her gaze. I turn back to my screen, trying to brush off the speck of guilt I have from knowing what's coming.

. . .

LIV

The rest of the period lags on until the bell finally rings. After everyone files out, I walk up to Ms. Walsh's desk. Sam gives me a sympathetic look as she leaves the room.

"Miss Westfield, I've noticed you've been inattentive in class lately. Is everything okay?"

I clear my voice. "Yes, ma'am. I guess I've been tired." Stupid excuse. What am I supposed to say, that having Z next to me makes it hard to focus on anything?

"Well, you need to get better sleep at night if that's the case, but I don't know…maybe this class is a little more advanced than the ones you took at your old school?"

I stare at her. Is she serious? My last school's computer programming class makes this one look like first-grade work. "What makes you think this is hard for me?"

"Well, your low test score, for one. Tests are worth so much in this class. A low C is still passing, of course, but it can easily slip to a D. I don't want to see that happen."

I grow cold. "A C? I shouldn't have gotten a C on the test."

She sighs and pulls up my grades. "A seventy. Like I said, I'm concerned because I have nothing else to base this on."

I start to argue that there's no way I have a seventy on such an easy test, when Z walks back into the class. "Ms. Walsh?"

"Yes, Z?"

"I overheard what you said to Olivia. If she's having a hard time, I could help her out."

Is he kidding me?

Ms. Walsh smiles and claps her hands together. "Really? That'd be wonderful. Olivia, this will be perfect! Let's see…" She peers down at her agenda.

I scowl at him, receiving a smirk in return. "I don't think so, Ms. Walsh."

"Now, now, Z is the best. You two can meet here after school in my classroom, starting tomorrow. Z, will this be okay with your—?"

"Absolutely. No problem there."

I start to shake my head and say again that I don't need a tutor, least of all him, but Z seems to anticipate it. He looks at Ms. Walsh. "You'll probably want to let her parents know so they won't be worried when she shows up late after school."

"Of course I will. Thank you."

"Yes, ma'am." The smug vibes radiating from him make my blood boil. I elbow him hard in the ribs as soon as we walk out of the classroom.

"What's that for?" he asks, rubbing his side.

"Seriously? What the hell was that, making Ms. Walsh think I needed extra help? I don't know why she said I'm making Cs. There's no way."

"You don't like it? Do something about it, then."

"What's that supposed to mean?"

"Show me how good you are."

I'm tempted to smack the stupid grin off his face. "Look, let's get something straight here. You might think you're clever with the *basic* hacking trick you pulled on me earlier, but I'm not going to entertain you with everything I know. And I don't need you getting all cryptic on me. If you have something to say, say it. Otherwise, I'll see you tomorrow."

I walk away quickly, forgetting that he's in my next class

and feeling stupid when he walks into English Lit behind me. He's super friendly during class and at lunch, carrying on lively conversations with Sam and smiling at me as if I'm not staring at him with an evil expression. He knows I'm pissed, and I hate that he doesn't even acknowledge it.

After school, I take the bus home and log on to the computer as fast as usual to do my math work, until I remember that Derrick said he's going to be late today. I lean back and take my time, enjoying the privacy of doing my work without Derrick's constant attempts at conversation.

Damn it. Starting tomorrow I'm going to miss out on the only time I have to do my assignments before Derrick gets home. Thanks to Z, who I'll be stuck in a room with, alone, after school...

I forget where I'm going with that.

The computer whirrs and gives an error message when I try to open Internet Explorer. Damn it. I wish Denise didn't care if I could download a better browser. She's so worried about me getting viruses and going on sites I'm not supposed to. I've even caught her looking through the computer history. Which, of course, is the simplest thing to erase if I really wanted to go on "questionable" sites.

I slump heavily in my chair but jerk up when I remember the other computer in the house. After grabbing the Wi-Fi password from the user accounts menu, I move to the front windows to make sure that Derrick's car isn't pulling up unexpectedly, then slip into their bedroom, feeling more than a little uncomfortable. Denise would have a hundred fits if she knew I was in here.

Derrick and Denise share a large walk-in closet, occupied by hanging clothes, a neat row of shoes, and plastic boxes of, well, stuff. I sigh. This may take a while.

I open the first box to find purple and pink plastic flowers. The next box contains smaller boxes with cell phone accessories. The box under it—various computer and economic publications. I flip through them, mildly interested, until I see a magazine sandwiched among them featuring a woman flashing her boobs on the cover. I immediately drop the other magazines on top of it and close the box. *Yuck.*

There are more boxes stacked on the shelves above the hanging clothes. A stepladder is conveniently tucked in the back of the closet, so I open it and climb to the highest step, looking around until I spot my black laptop bag in the very back. I grab it but slip off the step, falling sideways into Derrick's suits. I try to regain my footing, but instead land on shoes and boxes. A couple of the boxes are turned sideways, their contents sliding out. I set my bag down and hurriedly try to sort the shoes and papers into their appropriate boxes.

As I put the last paper back into the large box, my eyes land on a folder labeled OLIVIA WESTFIELD. I open it to see a small picture of me stapled to the top of the first page, which lists my basic information. My foster paperwork. The documents Derrick and Denise had to fill out are here, too. I guess Julia gave them copies. It's pretty generic—statements about why they want to be foster parents and a list of references and stuff. I'm pretty impressed, actually. Derrick must have been the one to fill out most of it, since it appears to be a guy's handwriting, but there's information about Denise, too. And questions about their childhoods. The answers are all about wanting to show love for the foster child and crap like that. I flip through the pages, but one response catches my eye, mostly because I can tell it's Derrick's handwriting, though it's

Denise's form.

Have you been in a previous marriage or long-term relationship? Previous marriage to Alejandro Santos. One child, age two years. Both deceased via car accident.

Denise was married before and had a child who died? No wonder she's so withdrawn. How did she get together with Derrick, then, and why did she tell me she couldn't have kids?

The rest of the page is also filled out in a slanted version of Derrick's handwriting. It looks like he tried to fudge Denise's writing on almost the entire questionnaire. I wonder why Julia didn't notice. He lists out the strengths of their relationship from "her" perspective as loving, expressive, open communication, etcetera.

I somehow doubt that, if she had filled out this page, she would have said the same things.

A glance at my watch reminds me that Derrick will be home any minute. I stack the papers to put back in the box carefully, but one more thing catches my eye: a CD without a case is sitting at the bottom of the box. I pull it out and flip it over. There are no marks, no labels. I start to toss it back inside but change my mind and slide it into my laptop bag. It would be interesting to see what else child services says about me and my past. Quickly closing the box and placing it back under his clothes, I tuck the stepladder against the wall and leave the closet.

I run out to my room and hide my laptop bag in my closet, just in time to hear Derrick whistling in the house. My heart is hammering. Maybe I should've checked the plush carpet to see if any imprints of my shoes were left behind?

Before Derrick even asks, I offer to help him make dinner, mostly to overcome my guilt. He shows me how to cut the vegetables his way, on the slant, and talks the whole time about marinating steak and stuff. I try to show interest, and he seems thrilled about it. Actually, I feel pretty happy myself. I have my laptop back and can do my homework tonight from where I should have been doing it this whole time—in my own room. I can enjoy surfing the net and forget all about the fact that I'm stuck with Z tutoring me after school tomorrow.

Though I somehow doubt it'll be that easy to forget.

CHAPTER NINE

"There is no remorse so deep as that which is unavailing; if we would be spared its tortures, let us remember this, in time."

—Charles Dickens, *Oliver Twist*

LIV

Z is so damn smug. He's looking forward to making me feel stupid while "tutoring" me this afternoon, I know. I decide to ignore him completely. At lunch, I choose to sit with Steph and Kori, a couple of girls I've talked with a few times in my biology class. They notice Z watching me and spend the entire time speculating on whether I should go out with him or not.

"I don't want to date him," I tell them. "I don't even want him tutoring me after school."

This sends them into a round of giggles and inappropriate comments about his "lessons." The period finally ends, but it makes me even more irritated at Z that I had to spend an entire half hour listening to the ridiculous conversation.

The rest of the day ticks by slowly enough for me to obsess about what I'm getting into, as (1) Z will be hovering over me for an entire hour, (2) I'll probably look stupid in a subject I'm not at all stupid in, and (3) I'll be looking stupid while Z hovers over me for an entire hour.

Maybe I can head to the bus stop early to avoid Z. When the last bell rings, I pick up my books and walk toward the main doors of the school as fast as I can. I'll just pretend I forgot when I see him tomorrow.

"Trying to escape?" a low voice says from behind me. I groan inwardly.

"No, I was just getting a drink." My chin lifts in defiance of his arrogance as I move over to the wall and take a few sips of the disgusting lukewarm water from the fountain. I follow him back to the classroom and stand by the door, watching as he walks around the desks to the computer.

"You see, the way it works is that you have to come sit at the computer. The computer won't walk to you."

"Don't be an ass." I drop my backpack on the floor and trudge over to sit next to him. I start to boot up the computer but he puts his hand over mine. I jerk away and scowl at him.

"Easy." He holds up his hands. "I was only going to suggest that you use my computer. I have it all set up."

I sigh loudly but change seats. He plops down into my chair

"So, what should we start with? Algorithms? Arrays?" he asks in a cheerful voice.

"Look, I appreciate the offer to help, but trust me, I don't need it. I've never had a problem with this class or any like it."

"Really? How'd you get a C, then?"

"How should I know? Ms. Walsh must've confused my grade with someone else's."

"Well, why don't you go in and look at your scores to see why?"

"I can't access the student portal from here."

"How about through the admin site?"

I try to maintain my patience. "Um, because you have to be an administrator to access the administrator site."

"Yeah. I guess you wouldn't even know how to go about getting into the admin site." He chuckles as if he made some private joke.

"I already did, remember?" He's got to remember—he gave me a hard enough time about looking him up.

"I mean, other than using some password you stole from the secretary."

Crap, how does he know about that? I didn't say anything to Sam. Maybe it's just a guess. He doesn't look at me, seemingly intent on the screen in front of him.

"Why would I even want to hack in?" I finally ask.

"Never mind. It's hard to do. You could get caught."

Caught? This guy, worried about getting caught? "Have you done it?"

He fiddles with the keyboard. "Obviously. It wasn't hard. For me, at least. Just… Never mind."

He sighs and keeps tapping away at the keys. I don't look at his screen to see what he's doing; I know he's trying to bait me. I *know* it. But my pride takes over. "I can do it just as easily as you can."

He snorts. "I doubt that."

"I can do it right now." I don't care that I'm falling into his trap. I can't help myself.

He raises his eyebrows expectantly. "Prove it."

I stare at the monitor. There's no way I'm going to try the secretary's password. Not after what he said.

In my last school, a few of us would meet for computer

club. For some reason—probably because it didn't have close teacher supervision—we spent most of our time talking about how to hack accounts. And much of that time we discussed different ways to break into the school's site. Various methods were considered, but the one that made the most sense was the simplest.

I execute my shell script and wait. I have Z's full attention now but he doesn't say anything. I've never actually tried this. I'll be totally embarrassed if it doesn't work.

I create a bogus user name, Columbus1492, and a user password—"password."

Z snorts. "The user name I get. Clever. But 'password'? The most overused password ever?"

I glare at him. "I don't give a damn if this bogus account is hacked. I'm just proving a point. And I don't even know why I'm doing that."

He holds his hands out. "Sorry, do what you want."

I face the computer again.

"It's not what I would do, though." He can't seem to help getting in the last word.

I keep tapping at the keys, gritting my teeth and ignoring him. I log out. "There."

"There what? How do you know it worked?"

I sigh loudly but go to the admin site and type my bogus name and password. It works. I stick my tongue out at Z, who's grinning.

"Not bad. You may as well check your grades, since you're there."

I click around until I find "Student Grades" and enter my student ID number. All A's and a C in Computer Science. I scowl at the screen. "Impossible."

"What's impossible?"

"That I got a C. That I got a seventy in this easy class."

"What are you going to do about it?"

"What do you mean? About what? The test was online."

"Your grade. How are you going to improve it?"

Is he kidding me? "If you think I'm going to say, 'study harder,' forget it."

"Ah, well, maybe I should've said 'change it,'" he says, reaching over to the mouse. He clicks on the button for adjusting grades. He drops his hand and fixes his gaze on me, his eyes intent. "How are you going to *change* your grade?"

I stare at the cursor that is flashing over the 70. "What the hell, Z?" I whisper, my throat dry. "They'll catch us."

"They won't." He moves behind me and leans over my shoulder. "Trust me. Walsh is so oblivious to everything." I can't help but wonder if he's done this before. He places my hand on the mouse.

I shake him off. "I can do this, you know. I'm not stupid."

He doesn't move from behind me. "Then do it," he says calmly.

I know I didn't earn a C. I know it. But all I can do is stare at the screen, unmoving.

"Go ahead," he says in a low voice near my ear. His words wrap around me like a deceptively gentle embrace. "If it's not right, change it."

I bite my lip and change the seventy to a ninety-five. It's like I'm in a bad remake of the movie *WarGames*.

I did not earn a C. I click on the save button. As the computer whirs, I lean back in my chair with a mix of new emotions welling up in me, most surprisingly exhilaration. I don't know if it's because my grade is now what I think it should've been or because I broke the law. Remembering the shirt I stole at the mall, I swallow hard. I'm turning into a regular criminal.

Z sits back down in his chair, a triumphant smile playing on his lips. "Perfect. The grade you actually deserve."

"Wait a minute." My eyes narrow to slits as it finally sinks in. He's too sure of himself, too cocky. "You changed it, didn't you? You gave me the C. Why the hell did you do that?"

His smile grows wider. "I wanted to see if you'd change it back. You had an A. Actually, a ninety-five, exactly what you thought."

I jump to my feet and shove my chair at him as hard as I can. "Screw you, Z."

His laughter follows me as I stomp toward the door.

"Hey!"

I don't turn.

"Sorry, I know that was a shitty thing to do."

I don't answer.

"I was just seeing if you'd do it. I'll tell Walsh to check the test again, that she must've read it wrong. She makes mistakes all the time. She won't even think about it."

Nothing.

"Come on, come back. No more, I promise." He steps in front of me so I'm forced to look at him. "Or do you want me to take you home?"

"Yes. Straight home."

I walk out in front of him, never turning back. He doesn't try to talk to me. It's better for him that he doesn't—I really feel like kicking his ass. When we get to his bike I shove the helmet on my head and climb on behind him.

"Sure you don't want to go for a longer ride?" he asks,

smiling widely at me.

"Straight. Home."

The motorcycle drowns out his laughter as it rumbles to life. When we get to the house, I push myself off his bike, refusing his hand, and throw his helmet back at him. He runs his fingers through his windblown hair.

"So tomorrow, then?" he asks.

My only response is to turn my back, walk up the steps, and slam the front door behind me. I flip him off behind the door as the roar of his bike fades into the distance. *Jerk.*

"Everything okay?" Derrick asks, walking into the room.

"Um, yeah. A friend dropped me off early."

"Good. How was the tutoring session?"

"Fine."

He waves toward the kitchen. "I was just about to start dinner. Want to test out your culinary skills?"

Derrick is obsessed with this culinary thing. I should break it to him that I'm not interested in being a chef, but all I manage to say is, "Sorry, I have to get ready for work."

His shoulders droop in disappointment as I head to my room. I'm so pissed that Z thought he could manipulate me into changing my grade, when he's the jerk who changed it in the first place. But mostly I'm angry that I hardly even hesitated to break in to change it back, just like I so easily stole that top. I storm to the closet and grab the shirt from the back, slinging it on my desk and vowing to return it to the store at the first opportunity.

The worst thing is that I'm stuck with Z tomorrow afternoon, unless I want to come home and be Derrick's assistant chef. I have a feeling Z would tell Ms. Walsh, too, or do something to get me into worse trouble.

I refuse to acknowledge the adrenaline that flooded my senses when I changed my grade. *Damn him.*

After a while, I get up to put my neon nightmare of a uniform shirt on and head out to make crap for tips at Slice of Happy. Mr. Bronson introduces me to the newest addition to the Slice of Happy family, a woman named Jeanette. Why he felt the need to hire someone else when there's hardly any business in the first place is beyond me. Jeanette's nice, but very shy, even more so than me. She seems comfortable until a customer walks in. Then she freezes up. I'm patient with her, taking all the customers myself and letting her shadow me. Of course, I'll still split the measly tips with her.

I grab one of the newspapers a customer left behind and put it in back near my bag, intending to start looking for another job tomorrow.

I'm in the process of showing Jeanette how to work the register when the bell over the front door clinks. My breath catches to see Z, looking very much like he did in the club: leather jacket, dark jeans hanging low on his hips, blond hair falling over his forehead. He smiles at me as he sits down at the counter, placing his helmet next to him.

"He's all yours," I tell Jeanette, not bothering to keep my voice low. Jeanette is clearly frightened to death by the idea of waiting on her first customer. She walks over to him and stammers out an introduction.

Z is nice to her, asking for a Coke and a slice of pepperoni pizza. She seems relieved by the easy order. While she writes out the ticket, I move toward him slowly, sliding my hand along the counter and reminding myself that he is, in fact, a jerk and not to let the fact that my heart is still lodged in my throat influence me.

I muster up the rudest voice I can manage. "Why are you here?"

"Heard they had excellent pizza." His eyes twinkle, and the ridiculous comment almost makes me laugh. The quality of the pizza matches the quality of the tips.

"You still mad?" he asks.

"Yes."

"I'm sorry. Really. Can I make it up to you?"

"How would you do that?" I ask.

"I'll think of something. What time do you finish here?"

"Nine o'clock. Why?"

He leans forward slightly, his eyes holding mine. "Thought maybe you'd need a ride home."

"No, thanks. It's not a far walk."

"Somewhere else, then?"

I swallow hard. He doesn't give up easily, and I hate to admit that I kind of like that. I must be the biggest glutton for punishment that ever existed. "Seriously, it's not that far."

"I know, but do you really want to be out in the dark with the crazies on the loose?"

I snort. "Crazies? In this neighborhood? The worst that happens is someone's grill is out of propane. Is that really why you're here?"

He smiles at me without responding.

"Fine. Whatever." I flip my hand at him and move away to help the women who just walked in. Even as I take their drink orders I can sense Z's eyes on me, and I'm sure my face is turning several variations of red under his gaze. I have to ask the ladies twice what they want to order because I can't hear over the heavy whooshing of my pulse in my ears.

Throughout the rest of the evening it's the same—almost

becoming a game. I smile at the few customers and deliver their food, occasionally locking eyes with Z. His smile is soft as he leans on his elbow, watching me. The only time his smile fades is when I stop to chat with a couple of good-looking guys wearing University of Richmond T-shirts. I would normally never act flirtatious like this—not with Z, and not with these guys, as nice as they are. That's abandoning my comfort zone for Sam's. But he's scowling now, and his expression propels me into easy laughter, almost like flirting is second nature for me. Considering his asshole move from earlier, this is strangely satisfying. *Scowl away, Z.*

Finally, I say good-night to Jeanette and Mr. Bronson and walk out with Z to his motorcycle. He hands me a different helmet, red with gold swirling designs.

"Figured if I'm giving you rides, the least I could do is keep us both safe," he says. "I picked it up today."

Giving me rides? My heart flips but I try to keep a straight expression even as I strap the helmet on my head and slide on behind him. He takes off down the street, not too fast. Slowish, even. I find myself wishing that the short distance to my house were a lot longer. Maybe I should've taken him up on his offer to go out.

I dismount when he stops at the rooster mailbox. "Thanks for the ride."

"No problem," he says, removing his helmet to study me for a moment. "So how'd you do tonight? Good tips?"

"That's a laugh. At this rate I'll be able to afford a bicycle by the time I graduate."

"I might be able to get you a job that pays more. If you're interested, of course."

"Obviously. Is it Sam's company?"

His eyebrows shoot up in surprise. "Sam's company?"

"Yeah, she was going to get me a job with the company she works for."

Z crosses his arms, his eyes tightening slightly at the edges as he considers that. "What did she say she does, exactly?"

"Hacks security systems. Like testing weaknesses for companies and they pay her for it. Why, do you do that, too?"

His laugh is brittle. "Hack computers for the benefit of large corporations? No."

"Oh. Okay, well…" He looks so annoyed, but not at me. At Sam? "I'll see you tomorrow. But no more screwing around in the administrator's site, got it?"

The tension on his face dissolves as he grins. "Sure, got it."

I hand the helmet back to him and run up the low steps, glancing over my shoulder to see him watching me before he speeds away. I lean against the door, exhausted physically and mentally. I'm not sure how I feel about Z. He irritates the hell out of me, confuses me, but at the same time, my attraction to him is out of control.

Take a deep breath, Liv. Use your head. He's trouble, and you know it.

Yeah, well, someone needs to tell that to my body.

. . .

Z

"Little late, aren't we?" Sam gloats as I hang my jacket on the coatrack and set my helmet down. Jen glares at me from where she sits on the couch, but I ignore her.

Sam follows me to the kitchen.

"So what?" I ask her.

"So what? So you've been with Liv, right? Right?"

I pour myself a glass of water and take a sip. Why did I get stuck with the most hyper chick in the house for a partner? "Maybe."

"I knew it! Were you at her house? Or did you go up to Slice of Happy?"

"Slice of Happy."

"Ooh, I bet she was excited to see you. What'd you guys talk about?"

In my entire life, I've never known anyone nosier than Sam. It used to amuse me, the way she'd finish one question just to start another, but now it gets under my skin. I don't know what she was accomplishing by telling Liv she works for corporations, but now I realize I don't care. She wants to play games and not clue me in, fine. I can do the same.

"We talked about you," I tell her. "And some *very* interesting things came up."

"What? What came up?"

I dump the rest of the water into the sink. "Good night, Sam."

"Wait! What came up? What about me?"

Sam's words bounce off my back as I head up the stairs. Liv's starting to come around, I can sense it. She's gone from actually being mad at me to pretending to be mad. It's a total chick thing, and I've seen it enough times to know what happens in the end. She'll soften toward me, even start to like me, then I can gradually pull her in. It may take a little longer with her than the others, but she'll get there. And she'll be grateful for us getting her out of that dump of a pizza place.

Although, I have to say, she did look damn cute, bouncing around the place in that ugly orange shirt, ponytail bobbing. Cuter than anyone has a right to look in neon. And the way she lit up when she laughed with some of the customers, even those college guys she pretended to flirt with... Takes a player to know one—I knew exactly what she was doing. I didn't like the effect it had on me, though. Damn adorable girl actually made me feel a twinge of jealousy.

No matter. Everything is working out as it's supposed to.

As it always does.

CHAPTER TEN

"Everything was so quiet, and neat, and orderly; everybody so kind and gentle; that after the noise and turbulence in the midst of which he had always lived, it seemed like Heaven itself."

—Charles Dickens, *Oliver Twist*

LIV

Z is nicer, not as cocky over the next few days. Although the tutoring sessions evolve into nothing more than showing off, in my opinion. Every time I write a script, he shows me a better way to do it. Though I've been able to one-up him on a few tasks, I'm more than slightly annoyed by how good he is.

"Yeah, I know you know a lot more than me," I say as he takes over my keyboard to type. "I do things my way, you do them yours. Whatever."

He smiles. "How's Slice of Happy?"

"It's okay. Didn't you say you knew of a job that pays more?"

"Maybe." His eyes stay focused on the screen. "So how much hacking—serious hacking—have you done?"

"What?" I pinch my fingers together nervously. First Sam, now Z? He already tried to convince me to run a script on Ms. Walsh's computer to shut it down every time she logs on, and on Tyson's computer to create rude pop-up messages, but only laughed when I told him to do it himself. It's not really the hacking that bothers me, since most kids with a brain like his love to pull those pranks. It's the fact that he seems only interested in pushing *me* to do it. "Are you trying to get me in trouble again?" My attempt at laughing him off sounds fake even to my ears.

He smiles. "Come on, I know the school's admin site wasn't your first go at it. So?"

I study the monitor. "A bit," I admit. "Mostly Facebook accounts, security systems, stuff like that. Just for fun."

I can feel my face turning red under his scrutiny. Okay, so it wasn't always just for fun. Jessie's pinched face resurfaces in my memory.

Jessie was in my eighth-grade class and made my life in middle school a living hell. She was the epitome of a mean girl. She took a picture of me changing in the locker room and posted it all over the Internet. The image will always be seared into my brain—my too-small fraying striped panties, boobs practically falling out of an old bra that bordered on the training size. Reality of life in a family that didn't provide for me at all. Not to mention the small roll around my middle that popped out from the way I was bending. So many nicknames were given to me that year—Betty Boop, Pretty Panties, Jelly Roll. I hated that year.

But I made Jessie pay. She was always on Facebook and used to brag about how many hundreds of friends she had. I hacked into her account and slowly, painstakingly messed up her social life—first by changing her attributes, then by posting random comments on other people's pages. I found information about her, including guys she was crushing on, from her private messages and shared them with the world. When she finally figured out what was going on, she canceled the account. But not before getting a taste of what she had put me through.

I cringe a little at the memory. It was a mean thing to do to her, even if she did deserve it. But all I say aloud is, "Hacking is really the only way to learn, not from this crap they try to teach in school. You already know this. I know you do it." I pause for a moment, thinking about what he convinced me to do with my grades. "Do you get paid for it, like Sam?"

He snorts. "Like Sam. Please." He stops typing and looks at me, his face serious. "Would you?"

"Would I what?"

"If you could make a ridiculous amount of money with hardly any effort, would you?"

Oh, no, I was right. "Z, how'd you afford that motorcycle? What do you do, anyway?"

"You'd really like to know that, wouldn't you?"

I hesitate. Do I really want to know what I already suspect? "Yes."

He stands up. "Let's go, then."

"Where?" I ask, not moving.

"You'll see."

"Well…"

He leans down, his hands balanced on the desk on either side of me. My breath catches. "I know you're interested to see where I live. You only mention it all the time to Sam. So come with me." He straightens and extends his hand.

I stare at it, giving myself a second to think about this. He's more than smart, he's devious, arrogant, and not exactly someone I trust. On the other hand, this could be my only chance to figure him out. And I'm really curious now.

"Okay, but just for a little while."

His eyes light up as he grins. He seems charming, less devious when he smiles, which sends up the familiar warning flags in my head. I ignore his offered hand and stand, slinging my backpack over my shoulder. I don't want to appear like some girl who's only going to his house looking for a good time. His lips twitch at my distance, but he doesn't try to take my hand again. We don't talk much on the way to the bike, but I can sense his excitement to take me back to his home.

He takes his bike faster than usual, weaving around cars like they're standing still. At least I'm not putting the death grip around his waist anymore. I'm kind of proud of that.

He makes several lefts and rights until I get totally confused. No way I could find this place on my own. We end up in an almost rural part of town. Z turns onto a driveway under an elaborate gate arch inscribed, MONROE STREET HOME FOR BOYS AND GIRLS.

The leafy canopy of the large trees blocks the view of the house from the street until we get closer, and then it's like, *wow!* The gray stone house is really more of a mansion. It's almost castle-like, with everything but the moat. Large beveled glass windows reflect the golden lights from within, and what look like spires are even peeking out of the top. I wouldn't be at all surprised to see a knight riding out through the oak doors. This is a *group* home?

Z pulls his bike to the side and cuts the engine. Several nice cars sit in the driveway, including Sam's red Camaro and a huge black Hummer.

"This is where you live?" I ask, unable to hide my amazement. "It's like a fairy-tale castle or something."

He laughs and dismounts, taking my hand to help me. His arm slides around my waist as we walk to the front door of the house, and though I try to clear my head, my awareness is tuned in to the position of his hand on the curve of my middle, the heat of his body spreading into mine. Almost as soon as he opens the door, a young, round-cheeked boy with a brown mop of hair rushes up to Z and throws his arms around Z's waist. "Dodger!"

Z returns the embrace. "How's it going, buddy?"

"Dodger?" I ask, trying not to laugh.

"It's a nickname. Some people here like to call me that."

"Why?"

"I like the Dodgers. Great team." He grins.

"I've been practicing," the boy says happily. "The algorithms aren't tripping me up anymore. I can break through now!"

I glance sharply at Z. What exactly is he teaching this kid?

"That's awesome! I'm proud of you, Dutch."

Dutch grins and smacks hands with Z, then looks at me and winks. The gesture is so unexpected, so mature, that I can't help but laugh.

"So have they started yet?" Z asks Dutch.

He rolls his eyes. "Yeah. Jose is ahead. Sam's mad that you weren't here."

Z ruffles his hair fondly. "Well, you keep practicing. Soon, Sam will be looking for you instead of me." Dutch's answering grin would light up an entire room. It's obvious that Z is like a big brother to him.

We walk down the steps into the main area of the house, Dutch chattering a million miles an hour at him. Z doesn't seem to mind. There's apparently more to him than the guy who acts all cool at school, who hacks into computers, who makes me crazy in so many ways.

"Well, well, well, is this the young lady I've been hearing so much about?"

A pretty woman with a long cascade of red hair approaches us, smiling. She's older, maybe in her thirties, and the way she lightly hugs Z and kisses him on the cheek prompts a memory of my mother snuggling me and reading *The Little Red Hen* in one of the many shelters we stayed in.

"Liv, this is Nancy. She's kind of like our house mother."

Nancy takes my hand. "It's so nice to meet you, Liv."

"Nice to meet you, too," I say. She's kind, offering me something to drink, asking polite but not probing questions.

Loud cheers erupt from somewhere in the back of the house. "Is there a party?" I ask Z.

He laughs. "Nope. But there's a pretty cool competition going on right now. Want to check it out?"

"What kind of competition?"

"You'll see. I think you'll find it very interesting."

He leads me to a large room in the back of the house. A few computers line the far wall, but in the middle of the room, four laptops are set up around a large round table. There are two guys and two girls sitting at the table, one at each computer, and a bunch of kids are behind them, yelling back and forth at one another. A couple of people smack Z's hand in welcome, but no one seems to notice me.

"What's going on?" I yell to him over the rowdy crowd. They're getting louder, and the four around the computer are fixated on their screens, their eyes moving back and forth and fingers typing frantically.

Z leans close to speak in my ear. "It's a hacking competition. They're seeing who can get in the fastest."

"Into what?"

"Not sure. It's different each time."

I peer over a shoulder at the girl nearest me as her fingers tap the keys so fast they almost blur. The excitement in the room is reaching a fevered pitch, when the guy on the opposite side of the table punches the button on a small silver bell and yells, "Done!" I take a deep breath to try to slow my racing heart. I've heard of these before, or maybe I saw it in a movie, but I never knew anyone who actually participated in one.

Sam appears from within the throng of people to peer closely at his screen, and other people press in closer. I guess she's the moderator, which is interesting because she doesn't seem serious enough for that.

She grimaces. "Jose is the winner."

Everyone cheers, with the exception of the kids who lost, and papers begin switching hands with lightning speed. Not paper—money. Betting on the winner. The theme song from *Dr. Who* is playing while the transactions take place. I've never been to Vegas, but I imagine it's a lot like this.

"Sometimes these are tougher than others," Z says. "Jose wins a lot. Never when I'm playing, of course."

The girl in front of me, whose display I'd been watching, leans forward, head in her hands. I'd be upset, too.

"I could do that," I tell Z. Of course, I'm speaking much louder than normal to be heard over the crowd, and it's at that exact time that the noise dies down so everyone can hear my bold words. The other kids turn and stare at me, and I can feel my cheeks turning red. *Crap.*

The guy named Jose huffs and looks me up and down as if I'm a child who got misdirected in the search for the playroom. "Really, *niña*? You think you could take me? Ha."

Oh, no he didn't just say that. "Doesn't look like much of a challenge to me."

It's quiet for the space of a heartbeat, then the shouts start up again, even louder than before. Several hands push me forward and the girl at the nearest laptop stands up, half smiling as if she feels sorry for me. I sit in her chair and wait as the people place their bets. My stomach starts to churn.

"You can do this," Z leans down to murmur in my ear.

I feel incredibly shaky—whether it's from the anticipation, the fear, or the excitement of Z's warm breath tickling my skin, I'm not sure. I look across at Jose, who's running his hands through his long black hair. He doesn't look nervous; in fact, he grins at me like we're just talking about school or something. Cocky. I just nod shortly without smiling.

"Game on," I say loudly.

Sam takes a deep breath and focuses on me. "This one appears simple, but it's all about mining information."

She pauses and flicks a look over my shoulder, maybe at Z. I swear, if I didn't know better, I'd say she's nervous about me competing. "Anyway," she continues, "the person to get the right password and break into the account wins."

I sit up straighter. Mining information. Easy enough. Sam hands me a pad and pen, then a slip of paper with the first and last name of the victim—Samuel Calderon—and the name of his bank, one I've never heard of.

A bank?

I stare at the paper in my hand as the reality of what

they're asking us to do sinks in.

They created a fake bank account for this contest. This isn't a real person.

I wish I were more naive. I think of Z's Ducati, Sam's Camaro. The job she has breaking security systems.

Oh, God.

I look over at Sam, who's watching me carefully. I can tell by her worried expression that she thinks I'm going to back out. Jose is snickering. The room is quiet now, waiting. Z is staring intently at me. *Don't quit now*, his expression seems to say.

I know I shouldn't do it. But I also know that I have to. I can't walk away from this. Not with everyone staring at me and Sam thinking I'll quit and Z so sure that I won't. I have to hope they're not going to use this information.

It's just a competition, I remind myself. *Just for fun.*

I sit up straight in my chair and nod tersely at Sam, my hands poised over the keyboard.

Sam nods. "Go!"

I start with a basic search on the bank first, since it sounds like a smaller, local one. Sure enough, it's a small bank out of Rockford, Illinois. There are a couple of Samuel Calderons there, but one is eighteen, the other thirty-six. I pick the thirty-six-year-old. I find the years he attended high school and a LinkedIn page with scant information. Not much to go on. This Samuel Calderon doesn't even have a blog or much of a web presence at all. My eyes rise over the screen to see Jose busy scribbling things down on his paper. *Crap.*

My heartbeat almost matching the quick tapping of my keystrokes, I do a quick search for his high school yearbook and find a few images someone posted to Facebook. I find

Samuel Calderon's name and scan over to look closely at his face—skinny, full lips, high cheekbones. Weird-looking guy.

Finally, I find a mention of a Samuel Calderon in his high school alumni records—and an AOL address. Part one is complete, but that's usually the easiest anyway.

I open a separate window for the bank and paste the e-mail address, then press the button to request a password reset.

Error message.

Damn it. Old e-mail address. Of course it wouldn't be that easy. I go back to the LinkedIn page and peruse it again but of course, there are no e-mail addresses. I scan down. No mention of any companies he's worked for, but several organizations and groups are listed. I know most, but there are two—NCTE and HRC—that I don't recognize. I enter the letters into Google.

Wha—?

Organizations for transgender people? Holy cow! A giggle threatens to bubble up inside of me, but I suppress it. I look over the monitor, but Jose's face is scrunched in concentration. I'll bet anything he hasn't noticed this yet. I sit back for just a second and look at the name again. Samuel Calderon. He could go by another name altogether, of course, but Samuel = Sam = Samantha. I lean forward and type "Samantha Calderon Rockford" and click on the images.

Immediately, there are a few pictures displayed of a blond woman with similar features to that yearbook picture of Samuel Calderon, down to the large teeth. I wonder briefly why he didn't go all the way and get the teeth fixed.

I switch over to the bank account. I go back to the results and find a Facebook page for him—and an e-mail address using his new name. I glance at Z, who's now sitting in one of the vacant challenger chairs, eyes intent on me. He raises an eyebrow and I give him a small smile. He nods, looking way too confident in me. I swallow hard and turn back to input the e-mail into the bank account. It accepts it, but I can't reset the password until I figure out how to get into the e-mail account.

The password for the e-mail account—these can be so simple to figure out, since people can be really stupid when it comes to security, but there's usually a limited number of attempts. And I'm guessing since this is a competition, it won't be something so obvious as "password." Instead, I go to the security question for e-mail password reset. "Who was your best friend in high school?"

Okay, so back to Facebook. I find "in a relationship with Philippe Martinez." I type various versions of the first and last name into the security question but it doesn't work. The Facebook page has a few pictures posted—mostly Samantha with friends, but there is a cute little schnauzer in two of the pictures. The comments mention it by name: Espanol. Why couldn't that be her security question? I try it for the actual e-mail password, but it doesn't work, either.

I go back to Calderon's Facebook page and look at her friends. There are only about seven hundred of them, and I have to figure out which one was her best friend in high school. I scan through the pictures posted but don't see any from high school. Impossible. Maybe I should just keep trying the password instead.

I read down her news feed and notice some light conversations with various people. Then this as a status update:

Thank you to everyone for supporting my debut today!

And a picture of her book, *Making the Change*, with a link to Amazon. An idea occurs to me. I click on the link and open the preview pane, scrolling through the pages until I get to the dedication:

Thank you to Jenny for always encouraging me to believe in myself, to make the change and start a whole new life. Forever in your debt.

My blood is pounding in my ears so hard that I can't hear the chatter around me. Jenny sounds pretty important. *Jenny, please be the best friend from high school.*

I cross my fingers and switch to the screen with the security question. I type Jenny into the box and the CAPTCHA code, then enter date of birth and zip code as second verification and click the next button.

And I'm in! I reset the password and open up the e-mail account. I almost bounce up and down in my seat, but Jose is starting to look a little too confident. Instead, I scrunch my eyebrows together and try to look worried as I go back to the bank site and request a password reset for that account, too. I tap my fingers on the keyboard, impatient for the e-mail to come through. Finally, a new message appears in the window. My fingers are flying now for the last steps.

Hacked.

I smack my hand down on the bell so hard I'm sure there's a hole in my palm. Sam moves quickly behind me to review my screen, along with the throng of kids. I can't help but grin at the shocked expression on Jose's face.

"Winner!" Sam calls out gleefully, and the room erupts into deafening cheers. Everyone's patting me on the back, laughing, passing money around.

There's one person not shouting or saying anything at all. Z just looks at me with a huge grin and pride shining in his eyes. No smirk, and none of the arrogance that usually marks his face. Only a kind of pure joy that makes me want to jump up and down like a child.

The energy from all the excitement makes my blood pound through my veins in double time. All the other noise is just background as Z reaches out a hand to help me up. This time, I accept. For an exciting second, we're so close that I wonder if he might kiss me. But other arms quickly pull us apart, congratulating me again on the victory. I lose track of who's who as the other kids try to introduce themselves, one speaking over the other.

A light touch brushes my elbow, making me jump. Z is next to me, nodding toward the door. As he steers me out of the room, Sam runs up to us, her face glowing.

"Hey, girl! You don't want to forget this!" She shoves a handful of bills into my hand.

"What's this for?"

"Duh, it's for winning the challenge. You kicked ass, you know that?" She leans closer to my ear. "And kicked Jose's ass, which is always a good thing." She tosses a triumphant grin Jose's way, like she just showed him up. She links her arm through mine to walk with us into the main area of the home. "So Z finally convinced you to visit us, huh?" she says. "Great timing!"

Finally? I suppress a grin. "Yeah, I guess so."

"Want to come up to my room?" Z asks me.

Sam seems surprised at this for a moment, but then grins. "Oh, well, if we're showing off our rooms now…" She grins at Z, who scowls at her. She turns to go back to the party after congratulating me again.

I follow Z up the stairs. It's so quiet here, though my ears are still ringing with all the noise from the competition. He leads me to a room down a long hallway of doors. The room is more like a suite, with tall columns, a TV that covers most of a wall, and a plush leather sofa. There's even a small kitchen, with refrigerator and microwave. I'm not sure how much I like that Z is into the flashier things. Reminds me of a pimp or something, which is weird because I don't get that vibe from him. He opens up a small fridge and tosses me a can of soda.

"What do you think?" he asks, eyeing me closely.

"It's big."

"Yes, it is. Do you like it?"

"Well, it's…it's not my style, really. This is where you actually sleep?"

He laughs out loud, the first real non-sarcastic laugh I think I've heard from him. "No, I don't. Come on."

He escorts me out of the suite and across the hall to a very modest-sized room, about a quarter of the size of the monstrosity across the hall. I can tell it's his room by the trace scent of his cologne, which never fails to set my heart racing. There's a simple twin bed, a shelf overflowing with books, a laptop, a small fridge, and an electric guitar plugged into an amp.

"You play?"

He shrugs. "Occasionally, and not very well. Nancy went through a music phase a few years ago and made us all take lessons. She thought it'd help us deal with life better."

"Did it help?"

"For some, maybe. You like this room more?"

"Yeah." I look at the titles on the bookshelf. There's a mix of new fiction and classic literature. "You have real books."

"Yeah, what'd you expect? Computer manuals?"

I don't say it but yes, that's exactly what I expected.

He laughs and presses a button on his cell phone, hooking it up to small speakers on his desk. A gentle guitar riff fills the room. I recognize the song—"Whiskey Dream Kathleen."

"You like the Spill Canvas?" I ask nervously. "Kind of a romantic song for a guy."

"I like some of the ballads, yeah. I'm surprised *you* know them, though."

"Don't be," I snap at him. "I'm not that clueless."

"I didn't say you were." He disappears into an adjoining bathroom.

Damn, he's infuriating.

He returns, changed from his school clothes into a pair of faded jeans and black T-shirt. He's still wearing his glasses, but his sandy hair has fallen forward over his brow.

And hot. Crap.

He sits on his bed and pats the space next to him. I sit down on the edge, more than a little anxious about his intentions, but he leans back, hands threaded behind his head. The music builds to a crescendo, and I imagine Z following along on his guitar. The thought sends an electric charge over my skin.

"So you bring girls here a lot?" I ask, shifting under his gaze.

"No, you're the first I've invited to my room."

"And the other room?"

"More."

I look down at my hands and pick at my cuticles. I'm dying to ask him how many is more, and what does that mean, though I wonder if I really want to know.

"You're uncomfortable," he says. "Why is that?"

"I'm not sure if I trust you."

"That's probably smart. What else?"

My cheeks warm. "Well, it kind of feels like you're hitting on me." I can't believe I said that. I try to recover. "Not that you are or anything, it just—"

"I'm not arguing with you." He sits up to move closer to me, and my heart does a little happy dance that I hope doesn't show on my face.

I clear my throat. "So that's how you make your money, huh?"

"How's that?" He tilts his head like he's really interested in what I'm going to say. I open my mouth to state the obvious, "hacking competitions," but then close it without saying anything when I see the slight smirk on his face. Like there's something else.

Something other than competitions.

I try to meet his gaze without flinching. "You do a lot of these, um, competitions, and…" I can't bring myself to say anything other than that, though. To say anything else would mean he's a criminal.

"I'd say you're almost right."

"Almost?"

"Almost." He curls his hand around mine and leans closer. His lips are so close to mine, we might breathe the same air.

A knock at the door makes me jump. "Yeah?" he says, without looking away from me.

Sam opens the door and peers in, looking from me to Z with a raised eyebrow. Her expression isn't happy, but it doesn't seem like a jealous thing, either. I know I should be more concerned with whatever's got her worried, but my thought at the moment is that I wish she had waited a couple minutes before knocking.

She steps in and closes the door behind her. "We have company."

0 1 0 0 1 0 0 1 0 1 1 1 0 1 0 0 0 0 1
1 1 1 1 1 0 1 1 1 0 0 0 0 0 0 0 0 1 1 1
1 0 1 0 0 0 1 0 0 1 0 1 0 1 1 1 1 1 1 1 0 1 0
1 0 1 0 0 1 1 1 0 1 0 0 1 1 1 0 1 1 0 0
0 1 0 0 0 0 1 1 1 0 1 0 1 0 0 0 1 0 1 1 1 0 1
1 1 1 1 0 0 0 0 1 1 0 0 1 1 0 0 1 0 1
0 0 0 1 1 0 1 1 1 0 1 1 1 0 1 0 1 1 1 1
0 1 0 0 0 1 0 0 0 0 1 0 1 0 0 0 0 1 0 1
1 0 1 0 1 0 0 1 1 0 0 0 1 1 0 0 0 1
1 0 0 1 1 1 0 0 1 0 0 1 0 1 1 1 1 0
0 0 0 0 0 1 0 0 0 0 1 0 1 1 0 0 1 0 1 0 1
1 0 0 1 0 1 1 1 1 0 0 1 0 0 1 0 0 1 1
0 0 1 1 0 0 0 0 0 0 0 0 1 0 0 1 0 1
1 0 1 0 0 0 1 1 1 0 0 0 0 1 0 1 10 1
0 0 1 0 0 0

CHAPTER ELEVEN

"Bless the bright eyes of your sex! They never see, whether for good or bad, more than one side of any question; and that is always, the one which first presents itself to them."

—Charles Dickens, *Oliver Twist*

LIV

Sam directs an intense look at Z, slowly enunciating her last word as if to say, *I don't want Liv to understand what I mean.* His expression doesn't change, but his hand tightens around mine, squeezing so hard I have to pull away before it goes numb.

"He'll want to see you," she says when he doesn't respond.

"Shut up, I'm trying to think." He jumps to his feet to pace around for a minute, then stops to face Sam. "Stay here with Liv," he tells her. "Don't come downstairs until he's gone."

"What…" I begin, but he's already out the door.

He turns back at the stairs and holds up one hand when he sees me following, mouthing, "Stay here."

"What's going on?" I ask Sam, trying to peer over the

railing as Z reaches the first floor. She puts a finger to her lips as she pulls me out of view. It's not long before the conversation from below rises to my ears.

"Z," a man's deep, gravelly voice says.

"Bill." Z's voice is quiet, barely audible. I yank my arm away from Sam and move toward the stairs, trying to stay in the shadow of a potted tree.

A tall, black-haired man in a dark business suit stands in the foyer. His back is toward me so I can't see his face, but I do see Z and the others. Judging by their expressions, no one's thrilled about this visit. Nancy is standing next to the guy, twisting her hands together, her eyes moving back and forth from him to Z.

"How far along are you?" the guy asks Z.

"Getting there." Z's tone is curt. I lean closer, jostling the tree and almost knocking it over. Z doesn't even flinch at the movement, though I'm sure he knows I'm there.

"Well," Bill says, "you better finish soon. I need you on this case and I don't like to wait."

"I know."

The front door opens and a young woman walks in. She's pretty, with dark curls spiraling around her face and long slender legs extending beneath a short pink skirt.

"Maggie?" Z says, almost choking on the word. His eyes seem fixed on her. Uh-oh. I take a second look at her. From what I can see, she seems maybe a couple years older than me. Ex-girlfriend? She's got to be.

She twists her hands together and mutters something I can't hear.

"I told you to wait in the car," Bill says without turning.

"I wanted to see them," she says, a catch in her voice. I

feel someone nudge close to me and catch Sam peering over my shoulder, her eyebrows pinched together. Bill walks to Z and grabs his arm, yanking him closer and saying something in his ear. Z shakes his head, his face tight. Bill releases him and turns to Maggie, nodding curtly to the door. They leave, and the entire room seems to exhale.

"Who the hell was that?" I ask Sam.

"Bill Sykes," she says. "And don't ask anything else. I don't know."

She pushes past me down the stairs and takes Z's elbow, pulling him aside. Nancy approaches me. "Everything okay?" She's as kind as before, though it seems a little forced. Her eyes are focused on Sam's and Z's backs as they talk.

"Yeah, thanks. I think Z's taking me home." I want to ask her what the hell just happened, but she's not the one who owes me an explanation.

"Ah, well, if you ever need anything, as a friend of Z's, you should feel free to come to us. We're here for you." Her cheerful tone is so strange after such an intense moment.

Z gestures to the door and I follow him out. He exhales heavily, rubbing at the arm where Bill grabbed him. "Crazy, huh?" His attempt at a smile doesn't erase the tension in his eyes.

"Yeah. What was that about?" I ask.

"Just some weirdness. It wouldn't make that much sense to you, anyway. Bill owns the house, but Nancy runs it, so we don't see him that often. He's kind of intense about things, so we humor him."

Humor? "Who was the girl? Maggie."

His hesitation before he responds with "Just a girl" is probably no longer than a millisecond, but in that instant the twinge of his eyebrows makes me realize there's more to Z and Maggie than he'll want to tell me. He moves quickly to the bike and tosses me the helmet.

"Wait, I haven't finished."

"Later, okay?" he says. "I've got things I need to do." The bike roars to life and he looks at me expectantly.

I jam the helmet on my head a little too hard and climb behind him. As we pull away from the house, I'm pretty sure he's hoping I'll drop the subject.

Think again.

• • •

Z

After dropping Liv off, I head to the house on Lindler Drive, my nerves on edge. Maggie should be back by now. Access to the grounds is restricted, of course; it's the house Bill keeps most secret to avoid getting busted. I don't know much about this side of his business, but as close as it is to Washington, DC, and plenty of lonely politicians with deep pockets, I figure it's pretty busy. I bypass the security gate and turn the bike down the next road to ride alongside the house. I can see the black roof through the trees. Moving along a gray stone perimeter wall, I find an area where there is a thick growth of oaks, with branches low enough to use as a ladder. I maneuver along the branches and cross over the wall.

The dense thicket spreads all the way up to the house. I move out of the moonlight to the shadows, pressing my back against a tree trunk as a man gets into a sedan and drives away.

I wait a few minutes, then text Maggie: *Outside.*

A couple minutes later, I see Maggie, now wearing black jeans and a T-shirt, illuminated on the front porch. She looks around quickly before walking down the steps. I whistle and she heads toward me, the dark clothes on her thin body making her appear almost specter-like.

"What are you thinking, coming here?" she whispers when she reaches me in the cover of the trees. She flings her arms around me, though, and buries her face in my neck. A sickly sweet smell floats about her, like cotton candy and roses. I almost choke but let her cling to me.

Finally, she backs away. Her face is still pretty—high cheekbones, flawless light-brown skin, full lips—but her once bright and happy eyes have lost their smile. Maggie's only a year older than me, but she looks like she's aged twenty since I last saw her.

"I don't get why you did this," I tell her. "You didn't have to go with Bill. You could've stayed at Monroe Street."

Tears flow down her cheeks, but her voice is strong. "You know why. I couldn't be there, not with you around. Not with Jen, who I know would continue to rub it in my face every chance she could."

"I'm not with Jen anymore."

She stares at me, her eyes wide. "You're…not with Jen?"

Uh-oh. "But there's somebody else," I say quickly to head off the thought I'm sure is swirling in her head. I don't have those feelings for Maggie anymore, if I ever really did.

Her shoulders slump. "You dumped Jen for a new girl? Why do you keep doing this?"

I rub at my forehead with one hand, wishing today would just be over. "Because I have to."

"You don't give a shit about anyone, do you?"

"That's not true." I hold up my hands in defense. "I never would have brought you in if I'd known you were going to end up…" I can't bear to finish the sentence.

She backs away, as if being an asshole is contagious. The tears continue to stream, and she wipes at them with a fist. "So what? You would've been fine with how everything worked out if I'd stayed at the house? You'd be content to keep slumming around with every girl who crossed your path. You don't care about me, you never did. Or Jen. Or whoever the hell this new girl is. None of us matter—just the business. You stand there, judging me for what I do, and you think you're so different? Go away, Z. Go whine to someone else about how guilty you feel about poor Maggie. I don't need to hear any more."

She runs to the house without looking back and I collapse against the trunk of the oak. Why did I come here, anyway? Instead of talking Maggie out of here, I pushed her away even more.

Liv's sweet face is as clear as if she's standing in front of me. The thought of someone like her ending up in a place like this makes me sick. Damn it. After I'm done screwing up her life, too, I'm going to let Sam do the recruiting. I can't take this anymore.

I jerk to my feet. Liv won't end up here—she's not like Maggie. And she's a good hacker. She'll fit in at Monroe Street.

She will.

I take one last look at the house before turning back into the darkness of the woods.

0 1 0 0 1 0 0 1 0 0 1 1 0 1 1 0 1 0 0 1 0 1 0 0 0 0 1 1 1
1 0 1 0 1 1 1 1 0 1 1 0 0 0 1 1 1 1
1 0 1 0 0 0 0 1 0 1 0 1 1 1 1 0 1 0 1
0 1 0 0 0 0 1 1 1 0 1 0 0 1 1 0 1 0 0 1 0 0
1 0 1 1 0 0 0 1 1 0 1 1 0 1 1 1 1
0 0 1 1 0 1 1 1 0 1 1 1 1 0 1 0 1 0
0 1 0 0 1 1 0 0 0 1 0 0 0 1 0 0 1 0 1 1
0 1 0 0 1 0 0 1 1 1 1 0 0 0 0 1 0
1 0 0 1 1 1 1 0 0 1 0 1 0 0 0 1 0 1
1 0 0 1 1 1 0 1 0 1 0 1 0 1 1 0 0
0 0 0 0 0 1 0 0 0 1 1 1 0 0 1 0 1 0
1 0 0 1 1 1 1 1 0 0 1 0 0 1 0 1 1 0 1
0 0 1 1 0 0 0 0 0 0 0 1 1 1 0 1
1 0 0 1 0 0 1 0 0 1 1 0 1 0 1 0 0
0 0 1 0 0 0 1 1 1 0 0 0 1 0 0 1 0 1 0 1 0

CHAPTER TWELVE

> *"'There is no pursuit more worth of me: more worthy of the highest nature that exists: than the struggle to win such a heart as yours.'"*

> —Charles Dickens, *Oliver Twist*

Z

It's not long before the so-called "tutoring" morphs into more personal conversations. The girl I once thought shy is definitely not, especially when she's after information from me. *Relentless* is a better word to describe Liv. She reminds me of Micah's program that strikes at all points of a system to weaken it. I know she's trying to get information about Maggie, but that one I refuse to talk to her about. If she knew the truth about Maggie, she'd never trust me.

It soon becomes a strange kind of game for us. I ask her a question, just to have the question turned back on myself, just for me to turn it back on her. It annoys and fascinates me at the same time.

"But why did you change schools?" she asks after I tell her

I've only been in this school since the beginning of the year. "I mean, did you get kicked out of your last school or what?"

"Of course not. It's not easy to explain. I finished what I needed to do and decided to move on."

"What do you mean, what you needed to do?"

I don't answer the question. She doesn't need to know my reputation in my last school. She doesn't need to know that Jen told everyone I used her and dumped her, which was true. She definitely doesn't need to know how big of a jerk I can be. I came to this school to start fresh.

Liv's studying me now, and I wonder what it is that she's able to read on my face.

"So did you make many friends in your past schools?" I ask her.

She shrugs. "Here and there. I moved around a lot, so there wasn't really time to make strong friendships. What kind of friends were you and Maggie?" she asks, going back to her first line of questioning.

I groan. Damn, she's persistent. "Why does it matter? We don't see each other anymore."

"You looked upset when you saw her."

"I just wish she'd made different choices, that's all."

The corners of her eyes wrinkle in frustration. That doesn't bother me at all—she can stay frustrated. No way I'm getting into a conversation about Maggie. "Don't you have any homework to do?"

She shrugs. "Nothing that can't wait."

I open my backpack and pretend to be busy with something in it, though I can feel her eyes on me. "What?" I ask.

"You do a lot of hacking competitions, huh?"

Ah, finally. I set my backpack aside and look at her. "Why do you ask?" I keep my expression innocently curious, though I know exactly why she asked. Like Sam said, a week of working at Slice of Happy can't be anywhere near the pay she made in minutes of hacking. And Liv has got to be questioning why we chose to break into a bank account during the competition. She's got to know something's not legit. Now I just need to see what she does with that knowledge.

"Well…" She looks at me, biting her lip as she waits for me to fill in the blanks. Of course, I won't. I raise my eyebrows, waiting patiently as she fumbles around for the words.

"I wouldn't mind doing another," she finally blurts out. "Hacking competition, I mean."

I stay cool on the outside, but inside I'm whooping and giving myself high fives. I *knew* it. "Big bucks compared to Slice of Happy, huh?"

She nods, her eyes bright and eager. I wonder now if it's more than the money that she's after. I'll bet she's addicted to the rush. I know that feeling very well—it's something that was lacking in Jen and Maggie. They only did it for the money. I pull out my cell and text Sam. "Don't feel bad," I tell her. "It is pretty addictive." I slip the phone back into my pocket and stand, extending my hand. "Come on."

"Where?"

"I think I can arrange something."

Her eyes alight with curiosity, she lets me pull her up, her hand soft and warm in mine. On impulse, I carefully loop my fingers through hers, expecting her to pull away like she usually does when someone touches her. But she doesn't. Instead, she closes her fingers around mine, her lips curving upward in a tiny smile as she lifts her backpack to her shoulder with her other hand. It's such a small, simple gesture, and one that certainly shouldn't cause all the blood in my body to rush to my head. But as I stand staring at her like an idiot, I realize I want nothing more than to pull her to me, to taste those strawberry-kissed lips and tangle my fingers in her long hair. The desire isn't what shocks the hell out of me; it's what I don't do about it.

For the first time in my life, I don't take what I want.

Instead, we walk out to the parking lot, our fingers linked as if it's just a sweet middle school crush. I release her hand at my motorcycle with a twinge of regret, but the feelings reignite with a vengeance when she slides onto the bike behind me, her arms wrapping around my waist, her body pressed against mine. I shake my head to get control of myself and start the bike to head to Monroe Street.

...

LIV

Something is different. Back in the classroom, it wasn't Z's usual confidence and cocky attitude. It was genuine... something. I don't know. Something softer. Whatever it was, it sent my heart reeling in ten different directions. Even sitting behind him on the bike, something I've done a few times now, seems so much more intimate. I want to rip off this helmet and rest my cheek against the leather of his jacket as we fly down the streets. I want to run my hands under his jacket, under his shirt. I want to let my hands curve around his waist, explore the warmth of his skin.

I squeeze my eyes shut, trying to block these feelings that are starting to freak me out.

Z takes the bike back to his house at Monroe Street. There aren't as many cars in the driveway this time, though I do recognize Sam's red Camaro. She appears in the foyer almost as soon as we walk through the large oak doors.

"Hi, Liv!" she says brightly, throwing her arms around me for a hug.

"Hey, Sam." I hug her back.

"Ready?" Z asks her.

"Of course," she says, taking my other hand and leading us to the back of the house. A few kids look up from where they're playing cards at the dining table. One of them—a pretty girl with long wavy blond hair—jumps to her feet, her blazing eyes moving from Z to me, then to our entwined hands. A younger girl pulls on her arm to try to get her to sit back down, but she shakes her off. I glance at Z but he doesn't appear to even notice her. *Great.* Another ex-girlfriend, I'm guessing.

Sam opens the door to the same room where the hacking competition was held, but it looks different without the wall-to-wall crowd of people that was here last time.

"Where is everyone?" I ask Sam.

She laughs. "There's nothing going on today," she says. "Although that's not true anymore, is it?" She leads us to a table in the center of the room. Two laptops are set up, back to back. I know what this is for, and my stomach twists.

He wants to hack…against *me.*

There are whispers behind me, but I don't turn around.

"This isn't a show for everyone, Sam," Z says, jerking his head toward the door. Sam moves to shut it as Z's fingers deftly type passwords into the laptops. While they boot up, he leans against the table, arms crossed, eyes fixed on me. "Well, what do you say?" The softness of earlier has been replaced with the cunning look that I'm more familiar—and more comfortable—with.

I fidget with the hem of my shirt for a moment. Sam said Z is easily the best at coding, and I can't beat him in anything at school. Hasn't it been something I've wanted to do? He appears so confident right now—I ignore the word *sexy*, which is printed in bold letters in my mind—and I'd love to wipe that cocky look off his face.

I cross my arms and stare back at him just as intently. "What are the stakes?"

The smile spreads across his face slowly, almost leisurely. I try to keep my gaze cool, to not let him know my knees are shaking.

"Well, money seems to be what you need most right now," he says.

At this particular moment, I'm not sure that's exactly true, but I nod anyway. "And for you? I don't have much money."

His eyebrow works its way up almost suggestively.

My breath catches. "No."

He laughs. "I'm not suggesting what you think. But how about you go for a ride with me today."

I shift nervously. "A ride where?"

"My choice."

"Where?" I repeat firmly.

"Don't worry, just a ride. I promise."

I know it's stupid to agree to something so open-ended like this, though the idea of heading into the unknown, gripping his waist as he flies down the highway, makes me want to concede the game right now. Still, I nod. Conceding isn't in my nature. No way am I letting Z win.

"You guys want to get to business now and stop flirting?" Sam asks, and it's only then that I realize she's been standing here, listening. My cheeks burning, I sit in the chair across from Z. His eyes are still fixed on mine—smiling eyes, the kind that make my skin tingle with excitement.

Sam snaps her fingers between us. "Seriously, you guys are making me sick. Okay, you're both going to be given unique links to your own YouTube videos. Whoever gets the most hits within fifteen minutes wins. That's all—get people to your video. Easy."

She hands us earbuds to plug into the computer so we don't hear each other's videos, then holds out a paper bag. "These are the links. Get people to it. You have a total of fifteen minutes, starting now."

Z and I reach in the bag—electricity snapping my skin as our fingers brush—and both grab a slip of paper with a link printed on it.

I type in the address that takes me to a video of a Japanese man reenacting a popular hip-hop song—very badly. I copy the link, then think for a moment. Various options run through my mind for getting people to the site. I don't have a Twitter account—not even a Facebook account, because what's the point if you don't have friends to keep up with? Hacking one wouldn't make much of a difference. There's always a place like eBay, where I could list it as an item for sale, but that might not have much payoff either.

I stare at the video—the man circling his hips around comically—then peer over the monitor at Z, who's focused on his own screen, his eyes tightened slightly but otherwise relaxed. I can hear his fingers flying over the keys. His eyes slide up to meet mine for a moment, lips curving just enough for me to realize he thinks he's got it made. I want to win this now, more than anything. I want to steal his thunder.

And his viewers.

I focus again on my monitor, noting the date my video was created, and click on the creator's name: SG3241. I scroll down the list of videos created on the same day, clicking on them at random to check the number of hits. One video is of a woman sitting in her bathtub and screeching out the national anthem. I notice the number of hits rising at each refresh—quickly, so it must be Z's.

A few months ago at my old school, some of us were screwing around with YouTube and found an XSS exploit to get user data. Unless it's been fixed, this could work. I enter a bogus comment to inject JavaScript into the page that will redirect users from Z's video to mine.

By now, his has over 300 hits. I don't know what he's doing, but I know if I hadn't figured this out, I'd be in trouble.

I switch back to my video to watch and refresh the page to watch the numbers rising. *Yes!* I glance at Sam's timer. Three more minutes. I look over the monitor to see Z's eyebrows knit together, confused. I drop my eyes to my screen and tap a random key nervously, praying he doesn't figure out why his hits have stopped until it's too late.

I refresh my page. Almost a thousand hits. I suppress the urge to giggle. I don't want to let Z catch on too early. But as I hear him cursing, I can't help it. I start to laugh. Z stares at me, his eyes wide.

"One minute," Sam says.

He jumps up and walks to my side.

"Hey, cheating!" Sam calls out, but he ignores her as he leans over to look at my page.

"Redirected," he says, groaning. "So simple." He stands up again, palm to his forehead. "Forget it. She won."

Sam looks at both monitors and bursts out laughing. "Simple for sure. What made you choose that?"

"I didn't think I could beat him any other way," I say, now a little embarrassed. Maybe they were expecting me to be cleverer. "I thought he could do all the work and I could just steal his numbers."

She claps my shoulders. "Brilliant, my friend. Brilliant!"

Z returns to his chair, leaning back to consider me, his lips flirting with a smile. "You have such an interesting way of looking at things, don't you?"

I grit my teeth. Interesting meaning easy? Maybe I shouldn't have said I couldn't have beat him otherwise. "Yeah, well, it's the easy ones that are hardest for geniuses like you," I say, probably a little more snappish than I mean to.

Z's smile grows wicked as he hooks his ankle around the leg of my chair, pulling it closer. He leans toward me, one hand on the side of my chair. I try to keep cool, though I'm melting inside as his thumb grazes the outside of my thigh. The way he's looking at me could be considered illegal in certain circles.

"My idea of genius is a little different than yours," he says in a low voice.

"Guys," Sam says in exasperation, making me jump and effectively breaking the tension. "Take it outside or upstairs or something. And pay up," she says to Z, her hand extended.

He sighs but reaches into his pocket for his wallet, pulling out a couple hundred-dollar bills for me and a twenty for her. She slips it into her pocket, then grins at me. "I bet him you'd win."

"You carry this much money on you all the time?" I ask. Nothing should really surprise me about this guy anymore, but still.

"Not always. I thought you might have a chance, too." His smile seems genuine. He takes my hand and we head out of the room. The girl who was at the dining table earlier isn't anywhere to be seen, but other kids I pass welcome me warmly as they slap Z's hand in greeting. He introduces me to them— Micah, Cameron, Cara, James, Drew, Em—but so quickly I know I won't remember who's who.

"Do you have to go home now?" Z asks as we walk out of the house to his bike. He hands me his helmet. "There's something cool I want to show you."

"You lost the challenge," I remind him.

"I know, but…"

He purses his lips, his eyebrows pinching slightly, and his sudden lack of self-assurance is strangely adorable. "Okay, okay. I'll go for a ride. But I need to be back by five."

He grins.

Z takes the bike in the opposite direction of my house. The rush of adrenaline flows through me as we fly down an unfamiliar two-lane road with no traffic and nothing but fields on either side of us. We spend about fifteen minutes or so riding through the countryside before he finally turns onto an avenue leading to a picturesque wood, with large oak trees canopying the road. We cross an old wooden bridge over a rushing river and Z pulls to the side. He takes off his helmet and cuts the engine.

While he hides his bike in dense brush, I walk to the edge of the river to watch the water rushing along its wide path, swirling around and sometimes over the giant rocks set here and there. I have an urge to kick off my shoes and let the cool water rush across my feet at the shallow bank.

I can sense Z behind me, watching. I pivot around to smile at him. "This is awesome."

"Actually, there's something else I wanted to show you." He takes my hand in his and pulls me along the riverbed, steadying me a couple times when I slip on the rocks. Very soon, he turns onto a small path leading up into the woods. I hesitate for a moment, having that feeling of *oh, crap*, when I realize I'm going into the woods with the only person who knows where I am. I hate that, even now, my suspicious nature extends to him.

The path gets narrower and the climb more precipitous, the trees pushing closer until we're ducking under limbs and skirting around fallen branches. Despite the cool spring weather, I start to sweat under my shirt. Finally, the trees break and we emerge from the dark forest.

"Oh, wow," I say softly.

A sheet of crystal water cascades over jagged rocks that form a sort of staircase through the trees, ending in a sparkling pool of water. A slender stream continues from the pool into the forest, where I assume it ends its journey in the river below. And of course, a rainbow shimmers across the mist of the gentle waterfall. Too perfect. It reminds me of a painting in Bernadette's house—Manet or Monet, I forget.

"What do you think?" Z asks, still holding my hand, his eyes fixed on me.

"It's beautiful! I didn't know anything like this was around here. How did you find it?"

"I like to explore sometimes. I found the path one day

and followed to see where it went. I come here when I need to clear my head."

I let go of his hand to walk across the emerald carpet of grass at the edge of the pool. I can understand why he escapes here. I'm suddenly jealous of his freedom.

"You know, your skills are pretty major."

"Oh?" I turn to see him lounging back on his elbows in the grass, the muscles of his arms flexed and defined. The intensity of his gaze makes my stomach flip.

"Yeah. You have such a different way of looking at things."

I frown. "What exactly is that supposed to mean? I can only do the easy stuff?"

"Obviously not. It's like your mind processes the quickest, easiest way to get things done, that's all. I don't know anyone who would've thought about redirecting my hits. Most other hackers would've tried to show me up with mad skills. And last week—I mean, you shocked the hell out of Jose."

"Does Jose live at Monroe Street, too?"

"No, he's at a different one, like some of the other kids who were there that day—Damon, Lindsey. We're all affiliated, though." He laughs. "You should've seen Sam's face when you hit the bell. They went out once but he was an ass. So she's loving you right now."

"Ah." I can't figure out any response to that, but it does give me the opening I've been waiting for. I take a deep breath. "Z, what did you guys do with that bank information?"

He raises an eyebrow. "I'm curious. Did you just now think about that? Or did it occur to you while you were hacking into the account?"

I look down at my feet for a moment. Yes, I did think about that. But it doesn't matter what they intend to do with it; I'm the one who broke in. Peering up again, I catch Z's grin.

"That one was just for the competition, Liv. Just for fun—like today. Don't worry about it. Come on, sit down," he says, patting the ground next to him. His lips are raised slightly in his flirty half smile, causing the butterflies in my stomach to take flight.

"Oh, I, um…I need to get going soon. You know, homework. Derrick said he'd probably be back early today." *And just being around you makes me nervous as hell.*

"You're fine. Don't worry about it."

My excuses sound ridiculous, even to me. I walk over and sit facing him.

"Relax." He curls my hair behind my ear with gentle fingers. One trails down my neck, my skin quivering in its wake, but I don't pull away. "Who do you have in here?" he asks curiously, balancing my locket on a finger.

I insert a fingernail to pop open the locket, revealing the heart-shaped photos inside. I don't have to look at it to know where my mother's picture is. "The one on the right is my mother. She died a long time ago. The other one is of my grandparents, I think."

"You think?"

"Yeah, my mom didn't talk about them except to say they never helped her when she needed them."

His eyebrows pinch slightly as he studies the picture.

"What?" I ask.

"Nothing," he says. "The man—your grandfather—looks kind of familiar, but I can't place him."

I twist the heart around to peer at it.

"Have you ever tried looking for them?" Z asks, taking the locket back to study the pictures again.

I shake my head. "My mother said she thought they died. I was never sure if that was true, but if she ran away, something must be wrong with them."

His lips are pursed as he studies the picture. I take it from him and pinch it shut. A conversation about family is a buzzkill for me. But then, turnabout is fair play. "What about your parents?" I ask him. "Your mother?"

His face grows very still, but there is a flash of something like anger in his eyes. "She died. When I was a kid."

"Oh. I'm sorry. And—"

"Look, I don't want to talk about it, okay? Not right now." He runs his hands through his hair. Not wanting to talk about the past is something I'm familiar enough with to not press him.

"Okay," I say softly. I touch his cheek with my fingers, and the hard features of his face soften.

"Anyway," he says. "I've been in foster care before. It sucks being bounced around."

"Yep, it does."

"How many homes have you seen?"

I hesitate. "I don't know. I lost count around ten. Some sucked bad, but most of them were okay, I guess. I mean, for transitional homes. Nothing special."

Nothing except the last one. I don't know if I'll ever understand Bernadette and Marc's decision not to adopt me. I wonder almost every day what I did wrong to make them leave me behind.

I glance at my watch. "It's getting late. Derrick will be pissed if I don't show up by five."

"You really care what he thinks?"

"No, but having to sit through one of his lectures is so

painful that I try to avoid it whenever I can. Anyway, he would never let me out again, and I kind of like hanging with you."
Ugh, that sounds so stupid.

"Well, don't worry about it. He won't miss you for at least another half hour, since he got an e-mail from the school saying you'll be out late for chess club."

"Chess club? What the...?"

He grins, but I don't return the smile. "You need to stop messing with the school. They're going to catch you. Besides, I didn't say you could."

"You really mind?" he asks, sitting up and leaning toward me. His face is so close. Just a little farther and his lips would be touching mine. I shut my eyes, aware that my heart is thrashing around in my chest.

He doesn't kiss me, though. Instead, his cheek brushes mine as he murmurs, "I don't think you do. I think you like living on the edge." His soft voice sends tremors through me, like tiny earthquakes underneath my skin.

I open my eyes and look away, trying to shake off the spell. Something about this isn't right. He's too persuasive for a typical seventeen-year-old guy. And his moves seem almost calculated. The softness I saw in his eyes in the classroom isn't there. I pick a tiny purple flower growing in the soft grass and twirl it around in my fingers. "I've been meaning to ask, why do you look so...I don't know...smart at school and so badass outside?" I bite my lip. I didn't mean to say it like that.

He gives me a sly smile. "I used to dress like that for school, too. But I got tired of the attention. And I almost got arrested once. It was too easy for the cops to believe I was guilty when I was dressed like that. I thought when I transferred that I'd try to change my image."

I remember what Sam once said about how Z dates "with a purpose" and wonder if the way he dresses when not in school is part of his plan. He's so smooth, so manipulative. Why is he even hanging out with me? Guys like him are into girls who are…not me.

"How many girls have you brought here?" I ask. "Truthfully."

"Including you?"

I nod, my throat constricting.

"One."

He tilts my chin up so my gaze meets his, his thumb brushing lightly across my lips. I close my eyes. I know Z is trouble. I know that being with him is going to get *me* into trouble. I don't care. At least at this moment, I don't care.

"Liv," he says. I open my eyes to see him frowning, his eyes seeming both reluctant and yearning. A hint of vulnerability is there, hiding beneath the swirling colors. "I need to tell you something."

"What?" I whisper. "I know you're a hacker. What else could—"

He presses his mouth against mine, effectively cutting me off. The pressure of his lips starts out as a light touch, then slowly changes, deepens, sending a sudden and intense shiver through my body. Whoa, this is not the first time he's kissed a girl, that's for sure. I relax into the kiss, my body responding with a building fire as his lips part mine, his tongue just touching the inside of my upper lip.

"That was nice," I whisper as he pulls back.

"Nice?" He chuckles. "That's a funny thing to say." He touches my cheek with his fingertips. "You okay? You look scared."

"Not scared. Just…that was pretty amazing."

"It's like you haven't been kissed before."

My cheeks are burning now. "I haven't."

He's already leaning in toward me again but stops about an inch away from my face. "What?"

"You're the only person I've ever kissed." At least willingly.

"The only one?" He jerks away and stares at me with shock on his face. "Why me?"

"Why? You're the first guy I've ever wanted to kiss. What's the big deal?"

"What's the big deal," he mutters, his forehead creasing as he looks away. This isn't going the way I thought it would. He actually looks upset and I have no clue why.

"Why does it make such a difference to you?" I try to reach for him, but he stands up and backs away like I'm some sort of rabid animal.

"It doesn't. It's fine. Come on, it's time to go." Z offers his hand to help me up, then heads into the trees, leaving me to gawk after him. I shake myself out of the daze. I don't know what's bugging him, but I can't be sure that he won't ditch me if I don't follow.

Before long I find myself strapping my helmet on and struggling to slide behind him as he starts the motorcycle's engine. The bike moves as soon as I sit down. The trip back to town seems shorter, almost like he takes a closer route to get me home faster. I don't even have time to process what just happened.

When he drops me off at the house, I try to talk to him but he doesn't even remove his helmet or cut the engine. I finally back away and trudge up the steps to the house. The bike growls behind me, and I don't have to turn to know there's probably a big cloud of dust from his fast exit.

I know he was into the kiss, too—I know it. So why would he reject me now? Why would he turn my very first kiss into something terrible? Well, I'm not up to head games, so if that's how Z wants to be, then fine. I don't need him. I don't.

I swallow hard past the knot in my throat.

I don't.

. . .

Z

"What's your problem?" Sam asks as I tread up the stairs. She follows me to my room but I slam the door in her face. She knocks, knowing better than to barge in. "Z, what's going on? Is it Liv? Did something happen?"

I sit on my bed and pull off my shoe, throwing it hard at the door. No response from the other side. *Good.*

What the hell? Who *is* this girl that she's never even been kissed? She can't be *that* innocent. She knows I'm up to something, and she wants to be with me. She's a hacker, for God's sake. She's broken into a bank account. Redirected my hits. Changed her grades. And she did these things knowing it was wrong.

Damn it!

If she's telling the truth and I'm the first guy she's kissed, what now? I'm supposed to bring her into our world, turn her into a criminal, then dump her? Watch her become as screwed up as Maggie or as jaded as Jen?

I grab my guitar, my fingers picking over familiar riffs.

Over and over. Why am I so irritated? I shouldn't be reacting so stupidly. It was just a kiss, that's all. She's just like any other girl.

Except that she's not.

Oh, I am *not* falling for this chick. I force a laugh out loud. Stupid. That wouldn't happen. That never happens.

So why am I so upset?

I can picture Liv's face: wide-eyed, trusting. Her smooth lips that tasted like strawberry Fanta. The way my heart races when she's near. The emptiness I feel when she's not.

I set the guitar aside and rub my temples.

I can't let this happen.

CHAPTER THIRTEEN

*"Joy and grief were mingled in the cup; but there were no bitter
tears: for even grief itself arose so softened, and clothed in such
sweet and tender recollections, that it became a solemn pleasure,
and lost all character of pain."*

—Charles Dickens, *Oliver Twist*

LIV

Z carefully avoids me at school. In the two classes we share,
he is suddenly very interested in what the teachers have to say.
He skips out on our tutoring session, making me too late for
the bus and forcing me to walk home. At first I was depressed
about it, but now it pisses me off. He nods at me in passing but
won't let me talk to him. I soon stop trying. He's acting like a
stupid jerk, and I'm starting to believe he is one.

But my heart still aches every time I see him. I work my
shifts at Slice of Happy and help Denise around the house, but
the entire time my thoughts are on him. I keep an ear out for
the phone, hoping he'll call, but it never rings.

I hate this. I almost hate him.

Today, as usual, Sam and I are the only ones at the table for lunch.

"What's going on between you two?" she asks as soon as we sit down a few days after the kiss. "Z won't tell me anything."

"Nothing," I say, fixing my eyes on a tiny crack in the table.

She places a sympathetic hand on my arm. "You've fallen for him. Girls always do."

"Great. I'm one of many," I say dully.

"No, not really. Not at all, actually."

"What do you mean?"

Sam takes a sip of her soda. "Well, I've never seen him avoid a girl. Never. He's broken quite a few hearts but mostly by playing the friend card after he's done with them. I mean, it's really weird. He actually seems affected by you. Like how he watches you all the time."

"He watches me?" I look hard at Sam to see if she's teasing, but she's considering me with her lips pursed, uncharacteristically serious.

"Liv, you know I'm only saying this as a friend, but you don't want to get *too* serious with him. Z's smart, great to hang out with, and yeah, I get that he's hot. But he's not the kind of guy you should be taking home to meet Foster Mom and Dad. He knows that, too, which might be why he's trying to avoid you."

"Yeah, well, considering he's not talking to me at all, that's not going to be a problem."

"He likes you. Give him some time. But…" Her lips twist as she seems to struggle with her words. "Just don't get your heart all caught up."

I sigh. I don't want to admit it to her, but it's far too late for that. Something else occurs to me. "Sam, what exactly does Z do for all that money? I mean, outside of those competitions. I'm pretty sure they don't pay enough for a Ducati." *Or a Camaro,* I want to add.

"What's he told you?"

"A bit."

Sam looks skeptical. I roll my eyes. "Okay, nothing, really. I think he was going to tell me the day I went out to your house, but then…"

"You'll have to ask Z. It's his job to tell you that."

"His job?"

She starts to say something in response, then seems to change her mind. "So speaking of jobs, how's yours? Going okay?"

She hasn't mentioned the job that was supposedly interested in me and I've pretty much given up on it. "Yeah. It'd be nice if we actually had customers, of course. The money from the hacking competitions is more than I make in a month at Slice of Happy." That's for sure. A few of those and I'd be able to afford that car.

She nods as if she can read my mind. "And how's everything at home?"

"Fine. The usual."

"Well, if you ever want a change, you can always stay with us."

"Thanks." Yeah, that's a great idea. I'm sure Z would love it.

. . .

Z

"You're lucky to have me in the middle here," Sam says. "Now's your chance."

"What are you talking about?" I ask.

"Come on. It's obvious that Liv is totally into you," she says. "So why are you acting like an ass and ignoring her? You should, you know, kiss and make up." She waggles her eyebrows.

I look at her in disgust. Just one minute earlier and I would've been on my bike and not standing in the school parking lot, listening to Sam's constant blabber. "Is your mind ever *not* in the gutter?"

"Not really. But I'm trying to figure out where *yours* is. She thinks you hate her, and I happen to know that's not true." She tries to poke at me but I step back. "You like her, she likes you. So go for it already."

"I thought you were friends with her," I say, irritated.

"What's that supposed to mean? Of course I'm friends with her."

"Then why do you have to act like we're in some covert operation? I've done fine on my own so far."

I step around her to get to my bike, but she follows me. "Wait. Why are you acting like this?" She grabs my arm and studies me with wide eyes. "Oh my God, you like this girl. Like, *really* like. Holy shit! Someone actually cracked that hard shell." She laughs and bounces on her heels as if she's three and I just offered her a cookie.

"Shut up, Sam." I yank my arm away and get on my bike.

Of course, she doesn't shut up. "This is a first—Z actually falling for a girl." She stops laughing and crosses her arms with a frown. "Seriously, though, you better not screw this up."

"I don't know what you're talking about."

"Yeah, you do. Don't try to turn this into a real relationship thing. You're going to end up hurting her, or she's going to get mad and end up just like Jen. I like her too much for that. And what about Bill?"

"What about him?"

"You're going to have to twist Liv soon or he'll get pissed, and then we'll both pay. So keep your heart out of it."

"I can handle it." I say the words with confidence, though I cringe inwardly. She's right about that. Bill has his own expectations and if I fail…

Forget it. I start the engine and put my helmet on, drowning out Sam's attempts at continuing this conversation. I can focus on my job like I've always done. I'll crack that account Bill gave me, and he'll be so happy, he'll overlook everything else. No big deal. No failure.

No worries.

• • •

LIV

After several days of Z avoiding me, I can't take it anymore. I refuse to let this consume me. I forgo the bus and corner him on his way out to the parking lot after school. He's walking behind a large group of kids and can't see me, which is perfect. I let the group pass by and step out in front of him. He looks up, surprised, then wary.

"Not right now, Liv. I'm in a hurry."

"Really? You're never in a hurry. And we need to talk."

He frowns, but I couldn't care less that my demands irritate him. He tries to walk around me, but I move over to block his path. He finally gives up and looks straight at me. "Look, I'm sorry. I just…I don't think this is going to work out."

"What? All we did was kiss, and you act like I popped the tires on your bike or something." If I weren't so pissed off, it'd be funny how much I downplay my first kiss. Even the thought of it makes my skin tingle, despite what happened after.

He looks away, but one corner of his mouth tugs up at my ridiculous analogy.

"Come on, talk to me. I've missed the bus now anyway because of you. So the way I see it, you owe me at least a ride."

He taps his fingers against his leg for a moment, but then shrugs. "All right, I'll take you home. That's it, okay?"

"And we can talk?"

"Maybe."

Z takes me on the short ride home, stopping at the rooster mailbox. I push myself off the bike, gesturing toward the house. "Come on." He reluctantly cuts the motor and follows me up the path.

Inside the cool, dark house, I lead him to the kitchen and pour some glasses of iced tea.

"I'm guessing they like roosters," he says, looking bemused at the decor.

"Denise does. She's from the country and says they remind her of her childhood. Pretty creepy at first, but I've gotten used to them. Though I do have to turn them around when I change clothes; that way they don't stare." I laugh at his expression. "I'm kidding."

I hand him a glass with a couple sugar packets and a spoon and we sit at the table in awkward silence for a couple minutes.

"Why have you been avoiding me?" I finally ask.

He wrinkles his forehead and takes a sip of the tea. "I don't think… You're not my type, I guess." He's not looking me in the eye.

"That's not it. What is it?"

"I'm not right for you."

Is he kidding me? I want to tell him he's not my father, but instead I say, "Why? Because I said I've never kissed a guy? That's stupid." It's hard, but I manage to keep my voice level.

His expression is hard, unrelenting. "Is this it? I need to get going."

I scoot the chair until our knees are almost touching. I'm going to have to change tactics. "Okay, I do have one more question." I cross my arms. "Do I disgust you?"

His eyes pop open wide. "Disgust me?"

"Yeah. We kiss, then you avoid me, don't look at me, don't talk to me. So either my breath grossed you out, you find me totally repulsive, or there's something else going on. I deserve to know. No more games."

He stares at me in silence, a conflict of emotions playing across his face. I start to worry that it really was my breath, when his eyes soften and he leans toward me. I don't relax my posture, although my insides start spinning around violently at the change in his expression. He stops a couple inches from my face.

"You are the exact opposite of that for me." He gently

places his hand around my head and removes the remaining distance between us. This time, the kiss is soft, quick, almost a whisper touch against my lips. My spinning insides come to a complete halt; my heartbeat is the only thing racing now. He rests his forehead against mine. "This isn't a good idea."

I lean back slightly to catch his gaze. I have him now. I can see in his eyes that he's fighting himself, not me. "I know you're trying to tell me I shouldn't get involved with you because you think you're a bad influence. I know you have…things…going on. But I'm not a little kid, you know. I can make my own choices."

"You don't understand…"

I touch his lips with a finger, my heart skipping a beat when he closes his eyes. "Maybe I do. I may not have gone on dates and kissed and stuff, but I'm not new at this whole life thing. And I'm not into games, so stop playing them."

He cradles my head again as he crushes his mouth hard against mine, for such a long, desperate moment that I wonder if I'll ever breathe again. Or if I'll even want to. His fingers slowly trail down my arms to tuck into the waistband of my jeans, tugging me to his lap. My arms slide across his shoulders as his lips move slowly, leisurely down my neck, resting at the hollow of my throat. I sigh and tilt my head back as he works his way back up to my mouth, sizzling my skin with his kisses.

My entire body is on fire…

"Olivia? What is going on in here?"

I jump off Z's lap to see Derrick standing in the kitchen, mouth turned down in disapproval. *Shit.*

"Um, Derrick, this is Z. He's in my class at school."

"Z, huh? You're the one who's tutoring her?"

"Yes, sir." Z stands up and stretches out his hand, which

I'm not surprised Derrick ignores.

"And *this* is how you tutor? I think this is the end of the sessions. You need to leave now," he says, his jaw twitching furiously.

Z looks at me and I nod briefly, my heart sinking. I walk him out the front door in silence and pull it shut firmly behind me, which I know is going to irritate Derrick even more. I walk Z down the path to his bike.

"Sorry I got you in trouble there," he says, fingering my locket and sending shivers through my body at his touch.

"I'm not. I'm glad you were here."

"So I'll see you at school Monday. Or can I pick you up?"

I sigh. "I would love that, but Monday's probably not the best day to start. Maybe after Derrick's cooled down a bit."

Z glances at the door, then draws me closer to give me a tantalizingly slow kiss before getting on his bike. The front door opens and I turn to see Derrick watching the bike rev to life and peel away. I smile, knowing he's going to be super pissed at me…but not caring one bit.

CHAPTER FOURTEEN

*"The dew seemed to sparkle more brightly on the green leaves;
the air to rustle among them with a sweeter music; and the sky
itself to look more blue and bright. Such is the influence which
the condition of our own thoughts, exercise, even over the
appearance of external objects."*

—Charles Dickens, *Oliver Twist*

LIV

"Olivia, you don't know boys."

I grind my teeth. It's the third time Derrick has said this, and I can't take any more of this stupid lecture about how boys only want one thing, and do I know what that is, etcetera, etcetera.

"Do you have birth control?" he asks suddenly.

I almost fall out of my seat. I couldn't have heard that right. "What?"

"Birth control," he says in a tired voice. "To prevent pregnancy. You do know about condoms and stuff, right?"

My chin drops and I stare at him, heat rising in my face.

This is definitely a first—I've never had a foster mother, let alone a foster father, try to explain sex to me, much less ask me if I use birth control.

"Um, Derrick, I really don't need that—"

"If you're going to act like a grown-up, you need to take certain precautions to make sure you don't end up pregnant. You do know about *that*, right?"

"I... Yes, of course, but I don't do that... I don't...you know..." I can't believe I'm actually sitting here having a sex talk with my foster father. Totally. Ick.

"So you're still a virgin?" he asks skeptically.

"Look, can we please be done with this conversation?" I can feel my face burning. Can't he see how uncomfortable I am? Doesn't he have a clue?

"All right, then. I won't say anything about this to Denise. She won't be as understanding as I am."

I practically fly to my room. Understanding? The last half hour ranks in the top ten worst moments of my life, and believe me, there have been a lot. I shut my door and fall face-first into my pillow, screaming into the foam as hard as I can.

But was it worth the kiss with Z to have to endure the painful lecture? Hell, yeah.

My body tingles when I think of his hands around my waist, his lips against mine. There are still warnings in my mind that remind me something is off about him, but it's easier to shove them to the back of my mind. I know how he feels about me, and I simply don't care about the other things.

The weekend drags by with nothing going on. Mr. Bronson only scheduled me for a few hours on Saturday, so I'm bummed that I can't even work more. It's not that great of a job, but it's a lot better than helping Denise weed the small flower bed in the front yard and studying for tests. I manage to sneak in a few hours on my laptop, mostly listening to iTunes and scanning the Internet to find information about Z and Monroe Street. There's nothing except the address.

True to his word, Derrick doesn't say anything to his wife, but he also doesn't let me go anywhere except work, even when Sam calls to invite me to a movie. He won't let me use the phone and hovers over me like a hawk. He does ask me to watch television with him. Joyous. I might actually go crazy if I have to suffer another weekend like this.

On Monday, I get on the bus eagerly, counting the minutes until I see Z. Tyson doesn't bother me at all anymore, just looks away when I glance at him. I'm pretty convinced the only thing he did wrong that night was to take a drink from a total stranger and deliver it to me, which wasn't a good choice but didn't deserve the beating he got from Z. That being said, I'm not at all disappointed at the lack of attention from him.

I hurry from the bus to my locker, then wait outside the Computer Science room for Z, feeling a little too much like a kid looking for the ice cream truck. Z soon appears, and I notice he's wearing dark jeans and his hair isn't plastered back. He's wearing his black-rimmed glasses, though. He grins and walks straight over to me, getting as close as he can, eyes teasing mine.

"I like this look," I whisper. It's all I can do not to throw my arms around his neck and kiss him.

"You don't want me to pretend anymore," he says, running a finger down my arm to my trembling hand and bringing it to his lips. "So I won't."

He pulls me into the classroom, never letting go of my hand until we sit down.

A quick glance around the room reveals several surprised looks, including Tyson, whose mouth is hanging open at us, and Sam, whose eyebrow is raised. I take my notebook out of my backpack as Ms. Walsh starts the class. Z, of course, looks attentive as usual, answering Ms. Walsh's questions without effort while snaking his foot around mine under the table.

Our desks in English Lit are individual and farther apart, so there's little opportunity for covert affection. At lunch, though, he pulls me to his lap, his hands curving around my hips. I press my hands against his cheeks, loving how he closes his eyes at my touch.

"Oh, give me a break. Get a room already." Sam's voice cuts in, startling us.

I pull away from Z and sit back in my own chair. "Sorry, Sam," I say sheepishly. She sinks into her chair and stares at Z.

"What?" he asks testily, even as he drapes his arm around me.

Her frown deepens. "Seriously?" she asks him. She looks pointedly at me. "So you two are a thing now?"

I can feel the blush creeping up my cheeks. I don't answer, but Z does. "Shut up, Sam."

"Bill called," she says, her fingers playing with a straw on the table. Z's arm stiffens around my shoulders. "He talked to Nancy this morning. Wants to know how we're coming along on our project."

"I said, shut up."

"I told Nancy it looks like it's going to end the same as your other projects." She flips the straw across the table and smiles at me. "How are you doing today, Liv?"

"I'm…" Confused? Yeah, definitely that.

Z's arm disappears from my shoulder as he leans closer to

her. "We'll talk later," he says, his voice quiet but strained.

"No worries." She smiles brightly at him even as she stands to leave. "I just wanted to check in with you."

She winks at me before walking away, leaving us alone in awkward silence. Z sits back and takes a long drag from his soda, not looking at me.

I don't know where to begin. Actually, I do. "What project are you guys working on together?"

He smiles, and it shocks me that he looks so calm after the way he responded to Sam. "Just a project for the house. It's top secret, though."

"Does it have to do with me?"

He laughs, but it seems too casual of a laugh for him. Forced. He takes my hand. "What makes you think that?"

He says it like the answer is no, but I don't believe that for a second. I jerk my hand away and stare him down. "I'm not an idiot, you know."

The laugh lines in his face smooth as he grows serious. "I know. I'm sorry. There're some things going on right now at the house that I can't talk about. Can you just trust me?"

It's not like me to put trust in something I know nothing about. It's not in him, either, so I doubt he expects it. "Why's it such a big deal that Bill called Nancy?" I ask instead of answering his question.

He shrugs. "Bill gets a little intense about things, that's all. None of us likes to be on his bad side, but he's a pretty decent guy. He pulled us all out of bad situations—almost everyone in that house was either on the streets or close to heading that way when he intervened."

I stare at my hands. I wish my mother had found someone who could've intervened for her. My life might've been so different.

"What are you thinking?"

"Just wondering when you're going to tell me your real name, because I know it's not Z."

He takes my hand, kissing my fingers again. "Someday."

"Today?"

"Someday," he says more firmly, chuckling. "You want to go for a ride after school?"

"I'm supposed to head straight home. Derrick will be there waiting on me, I know it."

His thumb traces a path around my palm, eyes holding mine. As usual, I melt into jelly.

"Okay," I say simply. His mouth curves into a devilish grin. "You knew I would, anyway."

He laughs again and kisses me lightly before standing. "I'll see you after."

I watch him walk away, almost glad I have the afternoon classes without him. He distracted every single one of my senses during the morning classes so I have no idea what I was supposed to learn. I don't exactly want to fail.

After school, on my way to the footbridge, I spot him and Sam arguing heatedly but am too far away to catch what they're saying. Sam's gesturing wildly and yelling, but Z is standing with his arms crossed, shaking his head. Every once in a while it looks like he's trying to say something but she cuts him off. When I get closer, Sam's eyes slide past Z to me.

"Hey, Liv! Come join us."

Z turns around, scowling as I walk to them, but Sam is smiling widely. The contrast in their expressions makes a pit form in my stomach. *What the hell?* Z turns back to her, saying something I can't hear.

"Yes, it is," Sam says to him. She turns to me. "So the company I told you about is ready to offer you a job."

That's the last thing I expected to hear. "Really? That's awesome, because I really could use…" I stop as I take in Z's stance. His hands are clenched and he's shaking his head at Sam, who's ignoring him. "What's going on, guys?"

Sam raises an eyebrow, turning her attention to Z. "Well? Tell her about the job."

He looks at me, the muscles in his face relaxing slightly as he takes my hand. "Let's go," he says.

"Wait a second, what job? You said you didn't work with Sam."

"Really?" Sam drawls. "Interesting."

Z's glare is murderous as he pushes past her, pulling me with him. "Come on."

"What was that about?" I ask when we get to the parking lot. I stop and yank my hand from his. "What the hell is going on?"

He removes his glasses to rub at his eyes. "I'll tell you. Just not here."

I stare at him. I worry that if I give him time to think, he'll come up with something that skirts the truth.

"Please," he says. "I promise I'll tell you."

"Fine. Where?"

"The waterfall?"

The memory of kissing him at the waterfall surfaces in a way that makes my body ache, but I try to ignore it. I'd get completely distracted there, which is maybe what he's hoping for. "No, that would make me at least an hour late, and that's pushing it with Derrick. I think he's probably capable of sending the cops after us if I stay out too long."

"Gotcha. We'll go somewhere closer." We walk to his bike. "Liv, I promise, it's not that big of a deal. Trust me." *Trust* him? He tries to wrap his arms around my waist, but I grab my helmet and hold it between us.

"Do you work with Sam? Hacking? Just tell me."

"Yes, but it's not that simple. That's why we need to talk." He climbs onto the bike, looking at me expectantly.

I jam the helmet on my head and slide behind him, my heart heavy. Whenever someone says, "We need to talk," it's never a good thing. Never.

Z takes us out of the suburbs into another countryside, this one filled with pasture after pasture of cows, horses, and barns. He speeds up so fast that my adrenaline kicks in full-throttle as the fences and trees fly by in a blur. Slowly, I let the bundle of nerves from the conversation earlier be whipped away as the wind slashes at my skin. I close my eyes and lose myself in the sensation of flying, until a loud whirring sound breaks rudely through the rumble of the bike.

In my peripheral vision I can see a police car pulling off the road onto the highway after us. Z must hear it, but he speeds up. As the car closes in on us, I try yelling at Z to pull over, but my words get lost in the helmet and roar of the motorcycle. The police sirens scream behind us, not far back now, and I grip Z's waist as he pushes the speedometer harder. He hasn't gone this fast with me before. I'm not the praying sort, but I'm praying now as I hold on for dear life. What is he thinking? We're definitely going to jail—if we don't die first.

The car is right behind us now. As we approach a bridge, he careens off the road and down a grass ramp, completely freaking me out, then angles a sharp left under the bridge before speeding up again. The police sirens grow dim, then fade away completely. I try to catch my breath, both relieved and angry. Stronger than those emotions, however, is a strange sense of excitement, of danger and escape. An absurd feeling of exhilaration that reminds me of the way I felt after I'd been drugged in the club. I want to hit Z or kiss him—neither an option at the moment as he zips down the winding dirt road.

Z finally pulls into a weed-choked drive. The dilapidated house at the end looks deserted. He cuts the engine and removes his helmet.

I slide down from the bike and yank my helmet off to hit him. He ducks away, laughing.

"What the hell was that? You could've gotten us arrested. Or killed."

"Relax, I knew we were almost outside the county. Those guys don't try to follow when you pass over the county line."

"Still…" I have nothing else to say. Especially because I'm mad at myself for being so excited by the whole thing.

He shifts slightly and wraps an arm around my waist, pulling me to him. He pats the console of the bike and I slide to face him, lifting my legs over his. A fluttering of nerves tickles within me as his fingers run a trail up the length of one of my blue-jeaned legs to my thigh, and then the fluttering of nerves turns into an all-out war in my body.

I grab his hand, holding it firmly. Derailing me would be oh so easy to do right now, but I need answers. "What are you and Sam pulling? Obviously it involves me, and it has to do with this company that she—well, that you both work for, apparently."

He sighs. "Sam and I work together, yeah. In a way. We're hackers, but probably not quite what you're thinking."

"Okay, so what does that mean? You don't hack security

systems?"

He smiles a little. "Well, I wouldn't say that."

I remember back to when I first rode in Sam's Camaro, when I briefly wondered whether she stole money to pay for it. I had been embarrassed of the thought at the time. I grow cold inside as the truth dawns on me. "So you're hacking for your own profit?"

"Pretty much."

I'm stunned. Here I am sitting on his bike with my legs propped up over his, listening to him admit he's stealing money. All the desire that he stirred inside my body is gone as I think of the house—the mansion—at Monroe Street. All the expensive cars lined up outside. The group home full of insanely rich orphans.

"Wait a second, you and Sam and who else?" I narrow my eyes as he glances away. "Z, what exactly goes on at Monroe Street? How does everyone have such nice cars and motorcycles and stuff?"

He frowns. "Monroe Street is a really good home, and all of us are either unwanted or orphaned. Nancy is the best mom any of us could ever have."

"I know, but…"

"It's also a place of business."

A cold knot pulls tight in my belly. The entire house? "What kind of business?" I'm guessing they don't sell Tupperware.

"Well, we all have one thing in common—we're experts in computer programming."

I snort. "Programming? Or hacking?"

"Well, depending on how you look at it…"

More answers in circles. I resist the urge to shove him off

the bike. "Z, I'm going to ask you a few direct questions, and I deserve some direct answers. No more bullshitting. Okay?"

He sighs. "Fine."

"Is everything that you and Sam do illegal?"

"Yes."

"Is that how you make all your money?"

"Yes."

I try to keep my voice even. "Large or small scale?"

He pauses for a second. "Large."

"And is the whole house involved?"

"Yes."

Oh. My. God. I push myself away from him, sliding off the bike. "Are you saying every person in that house is a cybercriminal? Even little Dutch? Does Nancy know?"

His laugh is short, almost brittle. "Of course she does. How else do you think we can afford all those cars, motorcycles, even the house? We're hackers. We target banks, corporations, even governments."

"You're not hackers, you're crackers. Hackers do it for the challenge. You're stealing from people." But I did it, too. I hacked that account. I was an accomplice. The knowledge twists my insides until I can't breathe.

His mouth drops open slightly at my choice of words. "Only those who can afford it, Liv. Kind of like Robin Hood, if you see it from our perspective."

I can't believe he's trying to justify this. Robin Hood? I'm not five years old. As if on cue, a roll of thunder sounds in the distance, harmonizing my growing anger. "It's still stealing. You're like...organized crime. And why didn't you tell me this before? Why didn't you tell me you all were a bunch of criminals?"

He glares at me. "And what would you have done? Called the cops? Told me to screw off? Why do you think I didn't want to tell you?"

"You're going to end up in jail."

"Wait a second," he says, his voice sharper. He swings a leg over the bike and walks toward me. "You're bothered about us taking a little money from those who don't do shit for anyone else, but you don't care that that house saved all of us. Some of us would be on the streets now if it wasn't for that home. We make a lot of money from people who would never give us the time of day. I know this for a fact. Some of these people…you have no idea."

His jaw clenches and he closes his eyes, his face screwed up like he's in pain. *Damn it.* I don't want to feel bad for him.

"What?"

His eyes snap open to meet mine—his expression angry and sad and something else I can't put my finger on that cuts deep into my heart. "Let's just say I know for a fact that these people shit on everyone else. My own father was one."

He trails off again, staring up into the gray clouds. "Before you go judging us, stop and think about it. Has anyone ever cared about *you*?" He gazes back down at me, his voice quieter. "What have you gotten from the homes you've been in but heartbreak?"

The pain so apparent in his eyes softens me. He knows. He's gone to hell and back himself. "It hasn't all been bad. Bernadette and Marc loved me." I falter at my own use of the past tense.

He steps close to me, one hand sliding down my arm to thread his fingers through mine. His lips brush my forehead. "No one gives a damn about us," he murmurs. "You know that.

The only people we can rely on are ourselves."

His other hand slides behind my neck, tilting my face up slightly. "Monroe Street is a family. We help each other out. And we make a lot of money, sure. How else could any of us survive? Think about it—what do foster kids get after we graduate? Tuition for college? Great. But what are we supposed to live on?"

I hate that what he's saying makes sense. It's exactly what I've been worried about this whole time. Why I need a good job. I always wanted to go to Princeton, and Bernadette said she and Marc would support me. She told me she'd be there to help me.

And now she's gone.

I swallow over the lump in my throat. I promised myself not to cry about this anymore. She's gone, and I have to move on. I have to do what I need to survive.

Z's thumb brushes down my cheek to skim over my parted lips. The dark look in his eyes gives way to something that stirs the butterflies of desire inside me again.

"I didn't make the world this way, Liv. I just try to live in it."

He leans in, his lips pressing mine apart in a gentle caress. All the words I want to say—all the coherent thoughts that once made sense—dissolve at his touch. But as hard as it is to pull away from him, I lean back and look directly into his heavy-lidded eyes. "I don't think I can do what you do. I mean, I don't know."

"It's okay. Just think about it. All right?"

"But what if I decide not to?"

He teases my lips with a light kiss. "Then I guess I'll just have to take you to the movies or mini-golf like every other boyfriend out there."

The word "boyfriend" makes my insides melt, thought it's pretty hard to picture Z playing mini-golf. I wrap my arms around his shoulders and we kiss for a while, minutes or hours, doesn't matter. In the entire world, there's nowhere I'd rather be than here. With Z, who doesn't care if I join his gang of hackers or not.

Thunder cracks directly overhead as the sky lights up. Several large drops skim my face. "We need to go. I don't want to get caught in this."

We run to the bike and I shove the helmet over my head while he starts the engine and pulls out of the yard. The darkening sky taunts us as Z speeds toward the blue patch hovering over the skyline of Richmond. I close my eyes and huddle into his jacket as large drops spatter against us. Then the sky opens up and all hell breaks loose, drenching us before he's able to pull off the road into an old abandoned barn.

I dismount from the bike and remove the helmet, shaking out the one dry part of me. The downpour is loud, crashing against the metal roof of the barn, and I shiver. Even though it's late spring, the rain makes the air especially chilly.

"How long do you think this will last?" I ask, rubbing my hands up and down my arms. Derrick is probably already foaming at the mouth at my being late.

Z joins me to look out at the white sheet of rain. "Not long. It's a short afternoon storm, no big deal. Will you get in trouble?"

I snort. "Y-You think?"

He glances at my soaked clothes. "You need to take off your shirt."

My mouth drops open but I manage to croak out, "Excuse

me?"

"No, really. You're freezing. Here," he says, sliding out of his jacket. "Don't worry, I won't look." He turns his back to me.

I manage to pull the soaked shirt over my head, all too aware that I don't have a tank on underneath. I had thought with the warmer spring weather I would only need the one layer. Stupid, stupid. I slip my arms through the dry sleeves and pull the jacket tight around my body. It smells deliciously masculine, giving me goose bumps despite the warmth. "Okay, you can turn around."

His arms circle my waist, and I rest my head on his chest. It's a surprisingly comfortable feeling, considering I'm practically naked under the jacket. I wonder what I'd do if he were to slip it off my shoulders. The thought of his hands moving across my bare skin sends a sharp spasm through my body that borders on frightening. I push the image from my mind and concentrate instead on the rain. We stay like this for a while until the torrential downpour becomes a light drizzle.

"I guess we should be heading back," I say reluctantly, caressing the smooth leather of the jacket. "I shouldn't let Derrick see me in this. He'd blow a gasket, and I really don't feel like sitting through another lecture on birth control."

Z gapes at me, such a foreign look on him that I start giggling. "Derrick talked to you about birth control? Are you serious?"

"Yes, and it was the worst half hour of my life. Don't even get me started."

He starts to laugh but then stops, tilting his head to look at me seriously. "Wait, a half-hour conversation about birth control? Didn't that creep you out?"

I shrug. "I guess he's just against teen sex. Come on, let's go already so I don't have to sit through a lecture on how rain can magically give a person a cold."

He laughs at that.

I pick up the sad-looking waterlogged shirt off the ground. This will be a cold, uncomfortable ride back to town. "Let me put this on so I can give you back your jacket."

He takes the soggy shirt from me and slings it over his bike. "Keep the jacket. You can bring it to school tomorrow."

Because of the wet roads, Z drives slower back to my neighborhood. He drops me off in front of the house and I kiss him quickly before running up the steps to the front door, wet shirt in hand. Unfortunately, when I step inside, Derrick is standing at the window, watching Z pull away.

"Again, Olivia? Do you really have no care at all for what we ask? And look at you. Out for a ride with the bad boy?" Disgust is plain on his face as he glares at Z's jacket.

"He's not a bad boy. He's a friend, and you can't tell me what to do," I say sharply, turning to walk to my room.

He catches up to me and grabs my arm. I whip around. "Don't touch me."

"Look, all I want to know is that you're safe. You're kissing all over this guy who's supposedly your tutor, then the next thing I see is you pulling up on his motorcycle, wearing his jacket and carrying a wet shirt. What do you think I'm supposed to say? I know I'm new at this parenting thing, Olivia, but help me out here."

"Okay, I get it." I sigh. "Sorry I worried you. But you can't expect me not to hang out with my friends."

"Just respect our rules. That's all I ask." His eyes rake over my damp jeans and waterlogged shoes. "Go change. We're having a get-together tonight with some of my coworkers. I expect you to help Denise out. I don't want any drama from you, all right?"

"Sure, no problem. No drama here."

He nods curtly and I head to my room. "Oh, and Olivia?"

"Yes?"

"Straight home tomorrow. On the bus. Got it?"

The way he says it means there's only one possible answer that will avoid a lecture. "Sure. Got it."

I get into my room and slam the door, knowing I'll be on the back of Z's bike again tomorrow afternoon, and every afternoon after that. I hug the oversized arms of the jacket around me and breathe in the familiar warm scent. Being close to him like this makes every cell in my body sing.

· · ·

Z

I don't go back to Monroe Street. Instead, I ride around on the bike for a while, ignoring the damp chill that slices through me without the leather to block it. For the first time, I'm letting myself be stupid-happy and not thinking about what's going to happen next. I don't care about Bill, about Nancy, Sam, or anyone else who would disapprove. No longer does it bother me that Liv's face fills my thoughts all the time. It doesn't even matter that she's hesitating to join us. She'll come around eventually. And if she doesn't, screw it.

I throttle the engine and speed down the lonely country road.

Nothing matters anymore. Just her.

0 0 1 0 0 1 0 0 0 1 1 1 1 1 0 1 0 1 0 0 0 00 1
1 0 1 1 1 1 1 1 1 1 1 0 0 0 00 0 0 0 1 1
1 1 01 0 0 0 1 0 0 1 0 1 0 1 1 1 1 1 1 01 0 1
1 0 10 0 0 0 1 1 1 01 0 0 1 10 1 0 0 1 0
0 0 1 1 1 1 0 0 0 0 1 0 1 0 11 1
0 1 00 1 1 0 1 1 1 0 1 1 10 1 0 1 1
1 0 01 0 0 1 1 00 01 0 0 0 010 0 0 010 1
1 1 1 0 1 0 0 0 1 0 1 1 100 1 0 00 1
0 0 10 0 1 1 1 1 1 00 1 10 0 0 01
1 1 0 1 0 1 0 0 01 01 1 1 110 0
1 0 00 0 0 0 1 0 0 0 1 0 1 1 1 0 0 101 0
0 1 1 1 0 0 1 1 1 1 0 0 1 0 1 00 1
0 0 10 0 1 1 0 0 0 0 1 0 1 0 1 00 0
0 0 0 1 1 0 1 1 0 0 0 1 1 0 1
1 1 01 00 0 1 1 100 0 10 1 10 1

CHAPTER FIFTEEN

"He stood for a moment with the blood tingling through all his veins from terror, that he felt as if he were in a burning fire; then, confused and frightened, he took to his heels."

—Charles Dickens, *Oliver Twist*

Z

Sam must have said something. Not only is everyone in the house coming out of every room to look at the guy who's always pulled together—now a windblown, chilled mess—but their emotions are written all over their faces: disapproval and misplaced concern from Nancy and Sam, surprise from Micah and Cameron, though they bump my fist as usual. Bitterness from Jen, though that's nothing new.

What bothers me is how Sam felt she could so blatantly discuss my business with everyone at Monroe Street, not to mention put me on the spot with Liv. She looks as if she wants to talk to me, but I head straight to the office and slam the door behind me. I refuse to let the high I'm on from my afternoon with Liv be punctured by Sam's ranting about how

I'm neglecting my job, how I'm screwing things up for her, too. How I'm going to break Liv's heart.

My lips tug up at the memory of kissing Liv, holding her as we watched the rain—and God help me, the way she looked wearing my jacket. Sam has no clue; breaking this girl's heart is not in my plans.

Needing a distraction, I sink into the chair and pick up the file I'm supposed to be working on for Bill. He's going to start asking about it soon, and I've only looked into the business and charitable dealings for background. I start with some of the leads I pulled for personal information that could help me break his password.

Most of the results again focus on the various deals of Carlton Brownlow and his company. Pictures of him as an old man are scattered through various articles. His face looks so familiar. I glance at the black-and-white image stapled to the paper in front of me. Maybe I've seen him on TV or in the *Wall Street Journal*. I know it was recent.

I get his place and date of birth, early family life, parents, brothers, sisters, aunts, uncles—recording everything I can find that could be used for a password. It can't be easy if Bill's team already tried. Looks like he was married with one child—a daughter named Agnes—and both wife and daughter are listed as deceased.

In an old newspaper clipping, I find a picture of him and his wife in a society paper. They look young and happy, maybe in their forties. The background includes a welcome sign for Niagara Falls, and the caption reads, "Mr. and Mrs. Carlton Brownlow revisit Niagara Falls for park rededication." Brownlow is obviously quite a public figure, which helps.

I open an article about some arts foundation and scan

through it. A close-up of an older Brownlow and his wife and daughter appears at the side of the article. The daughter looks to be in her mid-teens, with dark hair and large brown eyes that seem familiar somehow. I zoom in and stare at the picture for a moment. The caption underneath the smiling family reads, "Carlton Brownlow and his wife, Olivia, are featured benefactors of the arts at this weekend's event."

Something snaps inside my head like a trap that finally catches the elusive mouse. I can't take my eyes off the picture, off the familiar heart-shaped locket the woman in the photograph is wearing.

Shit.

• • •

LIV

At six o'clock, I shut down the laptop and slip it under my bedspread before joining Denise in the kitchen to help her put together the appetizers for Derrick's party. She runs through her list with me: deviled eggs, sausage balls, fruit platter with strawberry cream cheese, chips and dip. I peruse the list and decide that since Denise is so picky, I'll chop the vegetables and fruit. I'm slicing strawberries when Derrick walks through.

"Oh, Olivia, it's so nice that you're helping Denise put together the appetizers. Isn't that nice, Denise?"

I look at him. Does he not remember telling me I had no choice in the matter? He walks over to me with an arm stretched out, but I quickly slide away to the other side of the island. He acts like he doesn't notice, but I wish he would.

The guests begin to show up at six thirty, and an eclectic group it is. It looks like the only thing they have in common is that they work together. Derrick opens up the liquor cabinets and begins acting as bartender for the group, having me take a Bloody Mary to the vamp-looking woman, a rum and Coke to the guy who's obviously gay and comfortable with it, a beer to the ex-football-player-turned-salesman. Derrick and the wanna-be-a-football-star guy spend a lot of time talking about their glory days on the high school football team. Bor-ing.

Derrick makes a special martini for his boss, who politely accepts and sips at it, but then slogs it down when he doesn't think anyone's looking.

Okay, then.

Derrick himself holds a drink of one kind or another all night, as does Denise. Her usual vodka and tonic in hand, she starts getting loopy pretty early on. I'm starting to see a new side of Denise—one that looks nothing like the withdrawn, mopey woman who barely says two sentences to anyone. She's making stupid jokes about sausage balls and hanging on Derrick. Derrick has his hands all over her.

Ick. I can't take any more of this.

Though he had insisted I stay out and help with the party all night, I head to my room. My guess is that Denise will crash soon and Derrick will probably be pissed that she didn't fulfill any of her promises.

I pull out my laptop and do searches for Z and Sam and Monroe Street Home for Boys and Girls instead. I know it won't show me anything except generic information—and absolutely nothing on Z—but now that I know what they do, I'm interested in finding any possible hint of information. I find Sam's birth records in Washington, DC, but nothing else.

It doesn't make any sense. There was tons of information on me—the proof is sitting in Derrick's closet in that little box. Which reminds me of the disc in my laptop bag. I reach over to fish around the inside of the bag until my fingers feel the smooth round disc. I pull it out and slip it in the CD slot of my laptop.

The computer whirs for a while, then iMovie opens up. I had assumed the files would be PDF files, not a video. Did they record their responses, too? Curious, I click the play button.

The video is black and white and seems to be from high above in a room. I watch, but nothing is moving. I peer closer. It looks very much like…my room.

I gasp. It is my room. I can see my *Believe* poster on the wall, over my bed. Why is my room being recorded? Nothing happens for a minute, then I watch as I walk through the door, kicking off my shoes and pulling my Slice of Happy polo over my head. I'm in my bra, searching in my closet for a T-shirt.

I'm in my bra!

I stare at the screen, my throat suddenly constricted so badly that I can't breathe. Why are they recording me?

Not "they."

He.

As soon as the thought enters my mind, I know it's true. The memories of the seemingly kind touches and fatherly gazes flood through me like pinpricks all over my skin. Derrick has been watching me. He's a pervert of the worst kind.

My stomach churns as I watch myself slide out of my pants and slip on some shorts—and between, a clear shot of my panties—then grab my homework folder and lie down on the bed. I force my eyes up from the screen toward the ceiling, and there's what seems to be a small hole where the ceiling meets the wall.

The door bursts open suddenly and I slam the laptop cover down. My hands are shaking, but I slide them under my legs and fight against the bile rising into my throat as I face Derrick.

"'Livia, you're not supposed to have that," he slurs. "You're gonna get in trouble with the missus, but don't worry, I won't tell." He holds his finger to his lips. His eyes are glassy and unfocused.

"You should knock," I say, my voice raspy. The words register in my brain only after they've left my lips. It's a little late for knocking.

"Oh shhure. Come on out. I need help cleaning up; everybody's leaving." He stands there for a moment, lurching on his heels, then shuffles away.

I slip the laptop under my covers and pull my knees up to my chin. As if on fast replay, my mind shifts quickly through memories of helping Derrick in the kitchen, trying to avoid his casual hugs and touches.

Oh, God.

Maybe I should go to Sam. Maybe Z…no, not Z. He'd go ballistic.

Maybe the video is just to see if I'm doing drugs. Maybe this is a ploy of both Denise and Derrick to see what the bad foster kid is doing. I close my eyes and pray that's all it is.

I hear my name being called. I grit my teeth and step out to the living room to get this over with. Maybe I can convince Derrick to go to bed so I can clean up in silence. He doesn't drink often, but from what I've seen from the few times he's had too much, he gets riled up easily.

There are only a few people left now. Denise is nowhere to be seen, so I assume she's already crashed. The vamp lady is running a hand along Derrick's chest as she leaves. He slaps her on her ass and she winks suggestively at him.

I look away before I lose whatever's in my stomach.

Another couple guys stumble out the door with Vamp Lady, apologizing for having to leave early, since she's their ride. Last to leave is his drunk boss, who slurs about how grateful he is to have such a great employee.

I pick up the cups off the floor and stack them on top of dirty, discarded plates. I offer to Derrick that I'll clean everything.

"Nooo, 'Livia. I made the mess; I help clean it up." He gets a black trash bag and puts the paper items into it, clean and dirty, whistling the whole time. I give up and head to the sink to wash the serving dishes. As I dump what's left of the salsa down the drain, I sense Derrick watching me. I cut my eyes over to see him tilting his head at me, smiling. My gaze switches back to the sink as I rinse out the bowl, my mouth suddenly dry.

"Okay, I'll clean the rest in the morning. Let's call it a night," I say, turning around with bowl in hand.

"Olivia, you're so pretty," he says, moving closer to me. My heart pounding in my ears, I try to slide around the island but slip in a puddle of something and fall forward onto the tile, smashing the salsa bowl and cutting my hand.

"Crap!" I pull a large shard of glass out of the oozing red gash on my hand and press it against my stomach to stop the bleeding.

"Oh, no, let me help you," Derrick says as he crouches to push me up. I try to move around but he's gripping my injured hand, making me wince in pain. "You're bleeding. I need to have a look at that."

"It's okay," I gasp as I stand and try to wrench my poor hand away. "I'll go wash it off. Why don't you sit down and I'll be right back." Sometimes the quickest way to get out of a bad situation is to pretend to go along with it. It's always worked for me in the past.

"No, no, lemme help you. You're in so much pain, Olivia." He pushes me back against the sink, crooning, "Poor Olivia," and I shove at him with my good hand, as hard as I can. He doesn't budge. His hand moves under the hem of my shirt but I push it away. He laughs but moves toward me again.

"Derrick, get off me. You're drunk. You don't want me. Go wake up Denise."

"Denise is a cold, frigid bitch. Not like you."

"Get off me. DENISE!" I scream as loud as I can, trying to squirm out of his strong grasp. He shoves one of my arms behind my back, pressing his body against me hard to trap it. He grabs my wrist and pushes it up against the cupboard. It shocks me how strong he is for a drunk. The stabbing pain in my hand doubles as it's crushed behind my body.

"None of that," he rasps, leaning close. The stench of stale alcohol sends a wave of nausea through me. "You're not so innocent. I've seen you together—in the kitchen and at the club. I know you've been screwing that guy."

"At the club?" *Oh my God.* A dim memory of someone who looked like Derrick from the back flashes in my mind. "Why?"

He laughs hollowly and presses closer. "Your little friend got in the way. You didn't need him. I would've taken care of you."

Derrick drugged me. His admission makes me more terrified, if that's even possible. I try without success to wriggle away, my knees shaking so badly that I can barely support myself.

He works his leg between mine and moves his free hand up to my chest, forcing his way under my bra and squeezing me hard. I start to cry, my whole body trembling uncontrollably, but he doesn't stop, doesn't care. He releases my wrist and moves down to fumble with the button of my jeans as his mouth presses hard on mine. I try to shove him away, but my muscles seem to have forgotten how to move. He grabs my hand again and holds it above my head, against the cupboard. I try to scream but my throat is so tight that nothing more than a squeak comes out.

I can't let him do this.

My senses come reeling back to me and as hard as it is to do, I relax for a moment, just long enough for him to believe I'm going to comply, then turn my face and sink my teeth into his arm. He yelps and yanks it away. The distraction allows me to thrust my knee up into his groin, making him double over in pain.

I shove away from him and run on quivering legs to my room, slamming the door behind me and looking around for something to place against it, since none of the stupid doors in this house have locks. Oh, why didn't I run out the front? I manage to move the desk chair underneath the knob and sit with my back flat against the door, breathing fast, shaking violently, tears pouring down my face.

"Olivia? I'm sorry. I didn't mean to…" Derrick's muffled voice sounds on the other side. He tries to push it open, but the chair holds, blocking his entry. "Come on, let's talk about this. I want to help you."

"Go away!" I scream as hard as I can, quaking even more

at his wheedling voice. "Go away! Go away!"

Nothing but silence. I pull my shirt over my face and sob into it.

The throbbing in my hand soon reminds me of my other problem. I look at the gash and the blood everywhere. There's no way I'm going back out there, but I remember a half-empty bottle of water in my backpack. I stumble over and use my good hand to unzip it, grateful to see the bottle still there. I manage to open the cap and pour the water into the wound. It doesn't do much, and the liquid makes it sting, but I have no other options.

I wrap the hand in one of my clean older shirts, tying the knot with my teeth. Terrified that Derrick may try to break in again, I grab Z's jacket and slump down in front of the door. I wish I had a cell so I could call Z or Sam. Or the police. But what would happen then? I could climb out the window, but it's pouring rain, and I have no idea where to go. I crawl on my knees to the alarm clock and fumble with it to set it at 6:00 a.m., so I can get out of the house before Derrick and Denise are up.

My broken thoughts tumble over one another as I crawl back to the door and clutch the jacket to me, rocking back and forth, never forgetting the camera that must be filming everything.

0 0 1 0 0 1 0 0 0 1 0 1 1 0 1 1 0 0 0 0 00
1 1 0 1 1 1 1 1 1 1 1 0 0 0 0 0 0 0 1 0 1 1
1 0 1 0 1 0 0 1 0 0 1 0 1 0 1 1 1 0 0 1 0 1 0
0 0 1 1 1 1 0 0 0 1 0 1 0 1 1 0 0 1 1 1
0 1 0 0 1 1 0 1 1 1 0 1 1 0 1 1 0 1 0 1 0 1 10
1 0 0 1 0 0 1 0 0 0 1 0 1 0 1 0 0 0 10
1 1 1 0 1 1 0 1 1 0 1 1 0 0 1 1 0 0 0 0
0 0 1 0 0 1 1 1 1 0 0 0 1 0 0 1 1 1 01
1 1 1 0 0 1 1 0 0 1 0 1 0 1 1 1 10
0 0 0 0 0 0 0 1 0 0 0 1 1 1 1 0 0 1 0 1
0 1 1 0 1 0 1 1 1 0 0 1 1 1 0 0 1
0 0 0 1 1 0 0 0 0 1 0 0 1 0 1 11
1 1 0 1 0 0 0 1 1 1 0 0 0 1 0 1 1 0

CHAPTER SIXTEEN

"Morning drew on apace. The air became more sharp and piercing, as its first dull hue—the death of night, rather than the birth of day—glimmered faintly in the sky. The objects which had looked dim and terrible in the darkness, grew more and more defined and gradually resolved into their familiar shapes."

—Charles Dickens, *Oliver Twist*

LIV

I am wearing a veil of flowers against my white satin wedding dress, gazing with love at Z, who walks down the aisle and stands next to me. "You look so beautiful," he says, curling a tendril of my hair around his finger and making my heart soar. He kisses me on the cheek, then moves to the side and looks down the aisle expectantly. I'm confused at the distance between us, but turn to follow his gaze. Derrick is walking toward me wearing a blood-red suit, his eyes black. I shake my head and back away in fear, but he grabs me and pulls me to him hard. "Now you're mine," he says harshly. I look to Z for help, but he's laughing. "Show him how you kiss me. Show him how you

want me," he says, his voice taunting. The wedding bells start to
chime, morphing into a clanging sound that fills my head.

I startle awake, confused, before realizing the alarm is
going off. My back and legs ache like I've been beaten with a
baseball bat, and it's a struggle to crawl to turn the obnoxious
sound off. I pull myself up and rub the sand from my eyes,
trying to make sense of why the alarm is set so early. A shadow
of the chair against the door is reflected in the darkness,
triggering the memory of last night. I shiver and cradle my
hand, the pain throbbing from the gash. My head feels like it's
stuffed with cotton, and my eyes are on fire from crying.

Knowing that Derrick doesn't usually wake up until almost
seven o'clock, and who knows what time after he's been
drinking, I take a deep breath and pull the chair away from
the door. The bus gets here at seven fifteen, so I'm counting
on him being so hung over that he won't bother chasing after
me. I tiptoe out into the dark hallway, aware of every sound in
the still of the morning. In the bathroom, I pull the door shut
quietly, then flip on the light and throw my arm over my eyes
at the brightness.

After a few moments, I open them to see a horror movie
reflected in the mirror. Eyes puffy and bloodshot, hair a
mess, face streaked, not to mention the red-stained torn shirt
wrapped around my left hand and the large bruise forming
on my other wrist. I grit my teeth and remove the homemade
bandage from my hand. The dried blood pulls painfully away
from the gash, reopening my wound and making my hand look
like it got mangled in a shredder.

I open the cabinets and find a brown bottle of peroxide,
which I pour liberally over the wound. It stings and bubbles
up as it washes out the dirt. There aren't any bandages in the

bathroom, so I settle for a small clean towel to wrap around my hand. It's not great, but it's a lot better than nothing. I brush my hair, my fingers quivering like mad, and splash water on my face. It refreshes me slightly but doesn't do a thing for my puffy eyes.

I change into jeans and pull a sweatshirt over my thin tank, slide my arms into Z's jacket, and tiptoe with my backpack to the living room. The darkened room is silent except for the sound of light snoring, which stops me in my tracks, my heart racing madly. A faint outline shows Derrick passed out on the couch. I look at the front door and chew on the inside of my cheek, thinking for a moment. I could try to slip out quietly, but if he heard me he'd come after me. Instead, I head back to my room, carefully pulling the door shut and putting the chair under the knob again. Maybe it will buy me some time if Derrick wakes up and thinks I'm still hiding out in here. I walk over to the window and lift it, welcoming the shock of cold morning air against my battered skin.

At the bus stop, I'm the first one. I know it's not even seven o'clock yet, so I sit on my backpack and wait, facing the direction of my street in case Derrick comes looking for me. I don't know what I'd do. Maybe run the opposite way.

The other kids gradually appear, starting with Tyson. For the first time ever, I'm glad to see him, though I hope he doesn't ask me why I look like crap. I take a notebook out of my backpack and hide my hand under it.

"Hey, how's it going?" I ask as he approaches, hearing my own voice sound in a much higher pitch than usual. He looks surprised that I'm speaking to him.

"Good. You?"

"Pretty good."

His eyes rake suspiciously over me, eyebrow raised at Z's jacket, and he puckers his mouth, probably hoping for Candy and the others to show up so he's not alone with a red-eyed psycho. They finally appear, acting their usual snobbish selves. Candy starts making out with Tyson, cutting her eyes over to me occasionally. I don't glance away from them like I usually would. It's like my eyes crave the normalcy of the situation.

Finally, the bus pulls up and I take one last look in the direction of my street, grateful that either Derrick slept in or he decided it wasn't in his best interest to follow me.

"What happened to your hand?" Candy shrieks, pointing at my homemade wrap, already red-stained.

"I cut it." I shrug my backpack over my shoulder and step up to the open door of the bus.

"With what? A machete? What's with the towel?"

"No Band-Aids." If she only knew.

As the houses slip away, so does the threat of Derrick chasing me to the corner. The adrenaline fades and my body starts to relax a little. I can feel tears stinging the backs of my eyes. I shake my head to force them away and sit up straight.

Don't let him get to you, Liv. You've been through hell before. You can do this.

You can do this.

You can do this.

The bus finally pulls up to the school and I get out to walk over to the parking lot. Z's bike is in its usual spot, and the sight of it makes my stomach flip over in anticipation and impatience. I follow the stragglers to school, biting my trembling lip fiercely.

I can-*NOT* cry at school. I can't.

I move woodenly through the crowds of students and

manage somehow to find my first class, but stop at the door. What if the teachers call on me? What if someone asks me about my hand? What if someone can tell what happened?

I can't go in there.

I stand in front of the door, quaking as other students pass by me, oblivious to my dilemma. Someone calls my name, I think, but I don't turn.

I can't!

I flee to the girls' restroom and head straight to the last stall, the disabled one, and fumble with the broken lock before giving up, collapsing on the floor in tears. The stall door swings open again.

Get up, Liv, get up.

But I don't. I sit there, sobbing and shaking, knees pulled close to my body, head buried in my arms. Someone walks in and says something in a faraway voice, but I can't understand anything. I shrink away when she touches my shoulder, never looking up. I don't know if she's still here. I don't care. I heave with racking sobs, my body ripping in half.

Voices sound again. Someone puts hands on me. My body jerks and I hear my voice croak out, "Go away!"

"Liv!" The familiar voice finally reaches me. I open my eyes and peer through the thick veil of tears to see Z kneeling next to me, his eyes wide with shock. The sight of him releases a fresh wave of tears, but I let his arms wrap around my shaking body. "It's okay. It's going to be okay."

I can't raise my head, just sob even harder into his chest, gripping his shirt. I hear him say something to the other person in the bathroom about getting me out of here. I recognize the owner of the second voice—Sam. She dampens a paper towel and offers it to Z, and he places it on my cheek. It's cool against my skin. He asks me to breathe deeply and slowly, but my body still shudders with dry sobs, turning into hiccups.

"Tell me," he says in a deadly quiet voice. "Was it someone here at school? Another kid?"

I shake my head, wanting to tell him but not finding the words. I start crying again. He pulls me back to him and strokes my hair.

"I don't know about the bike," he says to Sam. "I don't think she'd be able to hang on."

"It's okay, she can ride with me."

I want to ask where they're going to take me, but decide I really don't care. As long as it's not to class and not back to that hellhole.

"Come on, girl. We're getting you out of here," Sam says in a soft voice.

Z keeps his arms around me, helping me into a standing position. He touches the towel covering my gash but doesn't say anything about it. My body still shakes, but I've got no more tears left.

Sam wraps an arm around my waist from the other side. "Let's get her out front and I'll pull my car up," she says quietly as they walk me out into the deserted hallway.

As soon as we're through the front doors, Sam leaves us. Z wraps his arms around me to steady me, leaning against one of the columns.

"I-I-I'm sorry." I choke the words out, but Z just holds me, stroking my hair and whispering gentle, calming words. Soon, Sam's car swings into the parking lot and I climb into the backseat, Z next to me. I'm sick to my stomach now, and my eyes burn so much I can hardly open them. I lay against him, my body ice cold, despite the warm jacket. His hands move up and down my back to warm me.

The next thing I know, Z is shaking me gently awake. "We're here," he says softly. I step out of the car, trembling and unsteady on my feet, and see Sam holding something steaming in a to-go cup. She offers me some but I shake my head. Z puts an arm around my shoulders to guide me into the house. Nancy meets us at the door, brows furrowed in concern.

"I got Sam's text. What's going on?" she asks.

"Don't know," he says shortly. "Taking her upstairs."

"I'll put on some tea."

Z escorts me up the stairs and down the long hallway to his room, where he tucks me into his bed.

"Don't go," I say drowsily as he pulls the blanket over me. Blackness dances around the rims of my eyes, beckoning me into the soft world of dreams.

"I won't." He sits next to me and smooths my hair with a gentle hand. I know he's worried and upset. I can't bring myself to talk about it. Not yet.

I let the sweet darkness envelop me.

. . .

Z

I don't know how long I've been sitting at the foot of the bed, watching her shoulders rise and fall with every breath as she sleeps. Minutes? An hour? My body and mind are still numb with shock for this strong, seemingly resilient girl who completely fell apart this morning.

What the hell happened? I've asked myself this question

a hundred times. She said it was no one at school, ruling out that creep Tyson, not that an idiot like him would be capable of bringing her down like this. That leaves Derrick or Denise or someone else. She mentioned a party that the Carters were having, so it could've been someone there. And she did tell me yesterday that Derrick had a talk with her about…

I can't finish the thought. I clench my hands so hard I'm sure I've drawn a trench in my skin.

Someone knocks softly at the door. A sober-faced Sam peeks her head in. "How's she doing?" she asks softly.

"Still sleeping."

"Here." She sets a cup of water and two tablets on my desk. "Nancy said we should give her Tylenol as soon as she wakes up because she'll probably have a raging headache from crying so much."

"Thanks."

"What do you think happened?" Sam whispers. "The asshole she lives with?"

"I don't know. She mentioned they were having a party…"

I stop talking as Liv moans and rolls to her side, her eyes still closed but her face pinched. I move over and carefully adjust her bandaged hand so she doesn't put pressure on it.

Sam steps up and touches the bandage. "Nancy did a good job," she observes quietly. She glances at the bloody towel in my trash can, shaking her head.

I run my hands through my hair for the hundredth time, hating this sense of helplessness. Sam looks at me, chewing on her bottom lip like she does when she wants to say something.

"Just spill it," I tell her.

"This makes it easier, right? I mean, she's here now."

I frown. Yeah, she's here now. This doesn't mean she *should* be here. I was up all night last night trying to figure out what to do with the information I found. This morning I had decided to simply tell her, to show her what I had discovered and see what she wanted to do about it. I should still do that.

I don't know.

What the hell happened?

"Z?" Sam's voice startles me. She's frowning slightly, like she can tell what I'm thinking. "Nancy wants us downstairs—she wants to talk about our next steps."

"Next steps?"

"Yeah, what we're going to do now."

"Sam…"

"Don't," she says. "Don't say you don't know what to do. I…"

I put a hand up to stop her as Liv stirs again. "Outside," I whisper.

We step into the hallway and I pull the door shut behind me.

"Where are you going?" Sam asks as I start toward the stairs.

"Downstairs. If I have to say anything, I may as well say it to Nancy, too." Although exactly *what* I'm going to tell them isn't yet clear to me. One thing's for sure, Liv can't stay here.

And I'll stick to that.

0 1 0 0 0 1 0 1 1 0 1 0 1 1 1 0 0 0 1 1 0 0 0 0 1 0 1 1 1 1 1 0 1 0 0 1 1 1 0 0 1 0 1 0 1 1 1 1 1 0 1 0 0 0 0 0 1 1 1 0 1 0 0 0 0 1 1 1 0 0 0 0 0 0 1 0 1 0 1 0 1 1 1 1 0 0 0 1 0 1 0 1 0 0 1 0 1 1 1 1 0 1 0 1 1 1 0 1 1 1 0 0 1 1 0 0 0 1 1 1 0 0 1 1 0 1 0 1 1 0 1 1 1 0 0 0 1 0 0 1 0 1 0 1 0 0 1 0 0 0 1 1 0 0 1 0 0 1 0 1 0 0 1 0 0 1 1 0 0 1 1 1 0 1 0 0 1 0 1 1 1 0 0 1 1 0 0 1 0 0 1 1 1 0 0 1 1 0 0 0 0 1 0 1 0 0 0 0 1 0 0 1 0 0 0 1 0 1 1 0 1 0 0 0 0 1 1 1 0 0 1 0 1 0 1 1 1 1 1 0 0 1 1 0 0 0 1 0 1 0 1 0 0 1 0 0 0 1 1 0 0 0 1 1 0 0 1 0 0 1 0 1 0 1 0

CHAPTER SEVENTEEN

"The cares, and sorrows, and hungerings, of the world, change them as they change hearts; and it is only when those passions sleep, and have lost their hold for ever, that the troubled clouds pass off, and leave Heaven's surface clear."

—Charles Dickens, *Oliver Twist*

Z

"Why do you keep asking him what he thinks?" Sam addresses the question to Nancy, whose fingers are pressed to her temples. I have a headache, too. Thirty minutes of arguing, Sam won't get off my back, and we're no closer to a decision. "He's not going to change his mind. He doesn't care that the timing is perfect."

I take a deep breath. Losing my temper will only cause Nancy to tune me out and Sam to win. "She's... It's complicated. She's just not ready."

"She's ready. You're letting this thing you have for her get in the way and it's ridiculous. Nancy, he's not objective anymore, you can see that. His head hasn't been in this for a while now. It's just like I've been telling you."

"It's not like that," I say, throwing Sam a nasty look. "After Sam threw me under the bus, I had to tell her. And she wasn't ready for it. If I could've been left to do it my way, another week or two and she would've fit right in."

"Another week or two that we don't have now, dumbass."

"Let it go, Sam. You've said enough," Nancy says firmly. "She stays. And Z, I understand your feelings, but you do need to pull it together, okay? Especially before Bill gets here."

Anger and dread churn in my stomach. "She's definitely not ready to meet *him*." I'm barely able to say the words. Nancy's face is set; Sam's is triumphant. I turn to storm out of the kitchen. Right now, I just want to go for a ride on my bike as fast as I can to blow off this anger before I put a fist through the wall.

I round the corner and almost run into a wide-eyed Liv. *Shit. How long has she been standing here?*

"Hey," I say, forcing a smile to my lips and letting my anger dissipate. "How are you?"

She smiles and I relax, taking her hand. "I'm okay, I guess," she says. "Just a little weirded out."

"I bet." I curve my hand around her waist and pull her to me, pressing my lips to her hair. She smells of flowers and me, a startling combination that makes me want to never let her out of my arms.

She looks up into my eyes. "What was that all about?"

"I'll tell you later," I murmur. "Right now, I want to know what happened to you."

Sam and Nancy appear from the kitchen and Liv holds up her bandaged hand. "Thanks for this," she says.

"Of course, you poor girl," Nancy says. "Come sit down and tell us what happened."

"I don't think so, Nancy." My arms tighten around Liv, but

she pushes away.

"It's okay," Liv says. "They can hear. It's probably better, anyway." She peers up at me from underneath her lashes, knitting her eyebrows slightly, and I know exactly what she's thinking. Something she's going to say will make me want to beat the living shit out of someone. I can feel the fury burning in the pit of my stomach already.

Nancy leads us into the living room, sitting in an armchair with Sam perched next to her. I sink into the black leather sofa, keeping my arm around Liv's waist. She is silent for a couple minutes, apparently lost in thought as she draws some random design around my knuckles with her unbandaged hand. Sam and Nancy lean forward, intent on Liv as if she's about to recite a Grimm's fairy tale.

"So, after you dropped me off yesterday, Derrick was pissed. That's an understatement. It was the second time he saw me with you, and I guess he assumed we had been..." She trails off, her cheeks turning pink. "Anyway, he told me they were going to have a party for his work people. It wasn't that many people, but they were weird, so I went to my room. I mean, I was supposed to be helping but I couldn't stay out there and watch them get drunk and stupid. So I got on my laptop and remembered a disc I had found with my foster paperwork weeks ago."

Her fingers have stopped their movement around my hand and are now pressing into my skin. "You okay?" I whisper as her face pales. "Want to stop?"

She shakes her head in a jerky motion. "Anyway, I put the disc in the computer and...and so it was my room...and I got upset but then I had to go back outside."

She mumbled everything together so fast I couldn't have

understood that right. "Wait a second, back up. What did you say?"

She looks at me, her large brown eyes rimmed in red, though there are no tears. "It was my room. They...he was recording me—a camera—in my room."

Like a flipped switch, everything stops. There are no sounds, no movements, no breaths. I am shock-frozen in a block of ice, screaming and pounding my fists on the inside but unmoving on the surface.

"Everyone left and I started to clean up, but I slipped and fell and sliced my hand on a piece of a broken bowl. Derrick..." She hesitates, clearing her voice. "BasicallyDerrick attackedmeandwouldn'tletmegobutIgotaway."

It takes me a moment to piece together the rushed words. She mumbles something about him drugging her at the club then doesn't say anything else. She doesn't have to. Freed from paralysis, I slowly look from the hands that are gripping mine to the eyes that are squeezed closed. Her chest is rising and falling faster, but as she opens her eyes to fix on mine, she's not crying. She's not crying. She's not even...

I jump up and start pacing. Nancy and Sam scramble to their feet at my reaction but I keep my eyes on the ground. Only one thing I know. One thing.

Derrick is going to pay.

"Stop and look at me," Liv says, her voice high-pitched, but I can't. "It happened to me, not you. Z, look at me!"

"Z, take it easy." Nancy tries to take my arm. I yank it away. "Breathe. Count to ten. Now."

Her unusually firm voice brings me back to years ago when she took psychology classes to learn how to help me deal with my anger; self-control techniques she thought could help the angry boy who wanted to destroy everyone who'd hurt him. It used to help. I close my eyes. *One, two, three…*

Liv's sweet, innocent face fills my mind.

Four, fivesixseveneight.

I head to the door, pausing only to grab Sam's keys from the foyer table. Somehow Sam and Liv get to the door first, though, blocking my way with linked arms. Nancy is calling to me from behind. I ignore her.

"You can't do this," Sam says. "You'll get caught and no one will care about why you did it."

"Get out of my way." I step forward, staring through them at the door. It'll take me fifteen minutes to get to the scumbag's house.

"No!" Liv steps forward, unlinking her arm from Sam. "I won't let you get in trouble on my account. He's not worth it."

"Move, Liv," I snarl through gritted teeth.

"No," she says firmly. She reaches out to cup my fist in her small hand, unwrapping my clenched hand to thread her fingers through mine. The touch is a gentle breeze to my raging storm, softening me.

"No," she whispers, slipping her bandaged hand around my neck. My hands automatically wrap around her waist; she feels so small in my arms. She stretches up to press her lips against my ear. "You have to trust me. You can't go. Not now. I need you here."

And that's it. I know the fight is lost with those words. "Liv," I choke out, hating how weak I sound, "he can't…"

"It's okay. We'll figure something out." She loops her arm through mine and effectively moves me away from the door and toward the staircase. Nancy and Sam gape at us.

"Well, you were right about that," Nancy says to Sam, who shakes her head. I ignore them.

As soon as we get inside my room, I turn to Liv, who's watching me cautiously. "That asshole can't get away with this."

"I know. Don't you think I know that?" Her voice starts to rise. "Since when did this become *your* problem? It's up to *me* what we do about this. Me. Not you. *ME.*"

"Shh…it's okay." I try to take her in my arms but she pushes away.

"No! I'm not a child." She glares at me, which doesn't bother me at all. Anger is good. Anger turns into action. "Promise me you won't do anything to him. *Promise!*"

What?

I stare at her, sure she's joking.

She's not.

I sink to the bed and rest my head in my hands. I do *not* understand her at all. "Why? After what he did…"

"Because if you go beating him up or whatever, you'll get caught. He's not worth that." She takes a deep breath, ending in a sigh. "You're all I have. I don't want to see you in jail."

I lie back on the bed, tugging her with me. Her head rests on my chest.

"Your heart is beating so fast," she says, drawing circles over it with a finger.

I run my fingers through her tangly hair, afraid of the feelings I have for this sweet girl. How could anyone hurt her? And I don't understand why she's letting Derrick get away with this. The rage begins simmering again within me. *One, two, three…*

She glances up at me, her eyes narrowed as if she can read my mind. "Maybe we should just call 911."

I thread my fingers through hers, tenting our hands over my stomach. Anyone who cared about her *would* call the police. But it would alert them to Monroe Street. "That's just it. We can't. They wouldn't believe you, anyway, and besides…"

"What?"

"Nothing," I mumble. "It's complicated."

"Too bad we can't just put him on the sex offender registry ourselves," she says. "That way he wouldn't be able to mess with any other kid's life."

I flip on my side to face her, almost laughing out loud. "That's perfect."

"What?"

"Putting him on the registry. We have a contact—a detective at the station who can help me hack in."

"Not you. Me," she says firmly.

"You?"

"Yeah. Like I said, this is my problem, not yours. I want to do it."

I smile. She's not incapable of action after all. She's pretty kick-ass. "Tonight, then."

. . .

LIV

The longer I stay here, resting in Z's arms, the calmer I feel. Now that we have a plan, and now that I'm more confident he's not going to go all berserk on Derrick, I can start to push the bad memories to the recesses of my mind. Z cares for me, for real. And I'm falling so hard for him. There's only a thin, fragile wall left to protect my heart, and the thought is frightening.

We stay in his room for another hour, holding each other

and talking very little, until a voice outside the door announces that it's time for dinner. Dinner in the new house and a chance to meet the other kids. I don't want them to know what happened, but judging by the sympathetic looks everyone keeps throwing, they already know. It's uncomfortable at first, but it's not long before I'm treated as another member of the house.

There are about fifteen kids or so, anywhere from middle to high school. Some I've already met. Little Dutch is there, immediately finding Z and sticking to him like glue. He hangs on every word Z says.

I met Cameron the first time I visited the house. He makes a pretty distinct impression, since he's about six feet tall and built like a defensive lineman. He's soft-spoken and super nice, though, smiling at me and asking how I'm doing. He stands to pull out Sam's chair for her when she arrives at the table. Sam smiles at him as she does everyone else, but by the wistful way Cameron looks at her, I'd say he likes her more than a little.

Most of the kids' names blur—they're friendly, but it'll be hard to remember who's who. With the exception of Micah, who totally cracks me up doing impressions and poking fun at everyone. He's so hyper that every once in a while he jumps to his feet to talk.

Another who stands out is Jen, for a much different reason. I can almost feel the daggers cutting into my face, the way she glares at me from her seat farther down the table. The same glare she gave when she saw me holding Z's hand the last time I was here.

I lean over and whisper to Sam. "What's with her?"

She smirks and puts her hand up to cover her mouth. "She was in love with Z. Big-time. They always fall for him. Like you did."

She winks at me and turns to talk to someone else, but her words reverberate through my head for the entire meal. *They always fall for him.*

Like you did.

Throughout dinner, I sneak glances at Jen. She looks over at Z a lot, sometimes angry, sometimes longing. The fact that he might've used and dumped her makes me see him in a new light, and a part of me I can't seem to ignore worries that he'll do the same to me. When he catches me watching him, he smiles and takes my hand, kissing my fingers.

After dinner, everyone splits to do his or her own thing; some hang out in the living room to watch TV, some go back to their rooms, and a couple of the older ones decide to go out for the night. I want to talk to Z, but Nancy approaches us before I can manage to get him alone.

"Olivia, I've got a room ready for you for tonight, and for as long as you'd like," Nancy says. She turns to Z. "Bill will need to know she's here now."

His hand clenches around mine and his jaw tightens. "No, he doesn't. Not yet."

She shakes her head. "You know that's not a smart idea. You can't keep this from him."

He doesn't respond. She sighs and looks at me. "Come, Olivia. Let me show you where your room is."

I nod and follow her, knowing I should care more about Bill finding out I'm here. But now I'm worried about something else: Derrick and Denise. I hope like hell they don't report me missing. I almost don't care what Z and Sam are up to right now and why it's a big deal if Bill finds out I'm here. The sound of the rain beating against the windows reinforces my need to feel safe. Protected. At least for a little while.

Nancy and Sam walk me upstairs and turn down the hallway opposite of Z's. "This is the girls' wing. The younger girls share a room; the older ones get their own. You're right next door to Sam, and she can help you settle in." She opens the door to reveal a lovely decorated room, painted a soft, creamy white. Graceful ballerinas moving through large black-and-white framed paintings hang over the bed and desk. The twin bed is covered with a light-pink comforter. "Feel free to personalize the room however you'd like."

The way she says that makes me think she's planning for me to stay forever. Considering the illegal operation of the house, I'm not sure how I feel about that. But this is my only option right now, so I step inside. "It's beautiful, thank you."

Nancy beams. "Of course. Let Sam or me know if there's anything you need. Toothbrush, hair dryer, whatever. We don't have many house rules. There's no curfew, you're free to come and go whenever you'd like, do whatever you'd like. The only thing we insist is that you do well in school and manage your share around the house, including some things that Z or Sam will show you. That's it. Sound good?"

"Sure. Thanks, Nancy. I don't know what I'd do if…"

She saves me the trouble of finding the words by giving me a warm hug. "You're part of our family now." She turns to leave, Sam following.

"Hey, wait a second, Sam." As soon as Nancy is gone, I pull Sam back into the room. "I don't have any of my things, my clothes, personal stuff. My laptop is back at the house, too. Inside the bedspread. I can't go back, and there's no way I'm sending Z. Do you think…?" I look down, embarrassed that I have to ask such a huge favor.

"Of course," she says. "Leave it to me. I'll take care of it."

I exhale and smile. "Thanks."

She gives me a hug. "I'm glad you're here. I mean, I hate what happened to you. But it's good we could bring you here. You're safe now."

"Thanks. I'm glad I'm here, too."

She smiles at me, and I follow her out of the room and down the stairs. She grabs a confused Cameron at the bottom and drags him with her, saluting me before pulling the heavy door shut.

"What was that about?" Z asks, walking over to me and wrapping his arms around my waist.

"Nancy showed me my room. It's nice."

"Mmm…" He nuzzles into my hair. "Maybe you should give me a tour."

His voice is sultry, sexy. Too sexy. I stiffen and pull away without thinking. He raises an eyebrow, but his arms loosen around me. I try to cover with a laugh that ends up sounding more like a choke.

"You understand there are no expectations here, right?" he asks softly, caressing my cheek. "None at all."

I nod and lean forward until my head is against his chest. Why did I react like that, pulling away from him? I trust him. But it's only been a day since… So maybe it's to be expected. Hopefully.

. . .

Z

Liv and I stare at the TV without really watching it, waiting for Sam and Cameron to return with her stuff. Liv's eyes flick to the door often. I guess I know why she sent them to get her things instead of me, though it's frustrating that she didn't even tell me. Of course, I might've figured out a way to go along, just in case I could run into Derrick by "accident."

She glances at me. "You know Derrick will be looking for me. Even with what we're going to do, do you think he'd figure out where I am? Alert the police?"

"I doubt it," I tell her. "And it doesn't matter. As soon as he goes to the cops, they're going to see his record and then his ass will be in serious shit."

She smiles and leans back, then sits up again, frowning. "I've been meaning to ask you. I keep hearing things I don't really get."

"Like what?"

"Well, like Jen, for one. She's in love with you?"

Of course, it's at that moment Jen walks in, making a sharp U-turn when she sees us on the couch. Liv glances at my face, her expression tight. Oh, wonderful fun this is going to be—once again, the ex jealous of my new relationship. I wish Jen would find someone else, like Cameron. Cameron would be perfect—he's the type who'd be completely devoted to his girlfriend. If he weren't so into Sam, who doesn't give him the time of day.

Sam and Cameron soon return with Liv's stuff. She jumps up to meet them, thanking them over and over.

"Hey, it was kind of fun," Sam says, handing a laptop bag to Liv. "I haven't done that kind of break-in in a while. Cam's the best at it. The window was locked, so I guess they shut it after you left. He broke the lock and we sneaked in to get everything. I wanted to go find the jerk and kick his ass, but Cam held me back. That's the only part that sucked. I was looking forward to it."

Liv frowns at me as if she can read my mind. Oh, yeah, I

would look forward to it, too, if she didn't have such a hang-up about violence. Passive-aggressive is not my thing.

The darkened house is quiet at this hour, and most of the kids are asleep. After a brief introduction, Liv has done most of the talking with Jim Rush, our contact at the police station. Bill would be pissed if he knew I had contacted Jim, as he's the only one who's allowed to, supposedly. But Jim's cool, and I'm grateful that he agreed to keep this to himself.

Jim gives her the address and password so we can hack in through our proxy sites without anyone tracking us. She uploads a picture she grabbed from his Facebook page, reworked in Photoshop to Jim's approval, and makes up names and incidents. I watch her as she works, fascinated that she's so focused. For as much as she didn't want me to hurt the guy, she sure is set on screwing up his life.

It was almost too easy. Liv leans over to touch the monitor and select the pen, using a finger to draw a red X over his disgusting face. I click refresh, keeping my eyes fixed on the second monitor, until his name pops up on the registry. Perfect.

She leans back against me and sighs. "Done."

Good luck with that, Derrick Carter.

CHAPTER EIGHTEEN

Oliver: *Dodger, it's not a game anymore.*
The Artful Dodger: *[sadly] It never was a game, mate. You just
thought it was.*

—a film adaptation of *Oliver Twist*

LIV

My new room is comfortable, spacious, and way too quiet.
I toss and turn for a few hours, my mind fighting a whirlwind
of images I'd rather bury. I finally sit up in the darkness and
swing my legs to the side of the bed. I know where I want to be,
but what will he say? And will he take it the wrong way? He
promised there are no expectations.

I decide to take my chances and tiptoe through the dark
and silent hallways.

I slowly turn the knob and slide into Z's room, closing the
door softly behind me. He's asleep, his profile serene in the
quiet moonlight. His blanket is on the floor, and my face burns
as I realize he's wearing boxers and nothing else. I watch his
bare chest rise and fall evenly, all the while knowing I should

go back to my room and not wake him, but my body moves forward almost of its own accord and slides into the twin bed with him. I wrap an arm around his waist and press my cheek against his arm. He startles awake, then relaxes when he sees me. His arm curves around me and I snuggle into him, warm and comfortable, his lips against my hair. Remembering the blanket, I reach down to the floor and snatch it up to drape it across us.

I don't dream at all. Z's presence keeps all the nightmares away.

The sun streaming through the window awakens me in the morning to a lonely bed. Z is sitting in his desk chair, dressed in shorts and a T-shirt and watching me.

"Hey." I smile shyly and pull the blanket up to my chin, which is probably silly, since I'm wearing a cami and shorts. "You're up early."

He laughs. "Not really. Do you usually sleep past nine?"

I jerk upward. "Nine? No way."

He moves over to the bed and kisses my forehead. "You can sleep as late as you want. Doesn't bother me at all."

"But we're missing school."

"Do you really want to go?" he asks, his expression amused.

"Well, no, I guess not." I look down. "I hope you didn't mind my sneaking in here last night. I had a hard time going to sleep."

"Are you kidding? It was nice having you next to me.

Tempting, but nice."

Heat rises to my face, my expression making him laugh.
"So what do you want to do today?" he asks. "The waterfall?
Or maybe you want to stay here and rest?"

"No, the waterfall is perfect." I head to my room to change
as Z goes downstairs to pack a few snacks. The house is quiet,
since the others are in school. I wonder what Nancy does
during the day.

"Sleep well?"

I almost trip over my feet. Jen is standing in her doorway
with her arms crossed. I try to recover and act casual. "Aren't
you supposed to be in school?"

"Aren't you?" she asks, her lips pinched in a sneer. She
glances over toward the boys' wing, her eyes narrowed. "He's
using you. I hope you realize that."

"Whatever." I start toward my room again but she steps
in front of me, blocking my path. I step back automatically,
wondering if this is the part where the ex-girlfriend tries to kick
my ass and wishing I knew karate or something useful.

"Relax," she says, holding up her hands. "I'm not going to
fight with you. But if you're going to live here, there are some
things you should know."

"Okay, fine. What things?" I don't try to keep the
exasperation out of my voice. She may not want to fight me,
but I know this is definitely the part where she's going to say
something to try to split up Z and me.

"How much has Z told you about why you're here?"

Why I'm here? "Everything," I lie.

She shakes her head. "Everything meaning nothing, right?
He's trying to bring you in quietly, just like he did me. And
then you're here and you get stuck in their game. And you can

never leave because you're too involved."

I don't even try to make sense of whatever she's saying. I attempt to sidestep her but she moves with me. "Did you know Z knew everything about you from the very beginning?" she asks. "Probably before he even spoke to you."

Now I laugh. "You have the wrong story, Jen. I met him at school."

"Yeah, but he's had all the details on your past for a long time. I know that for a fact."

"Okay, so how?"

She smiles a secret kind of smile. She's baiting me, but I hate to admit I'm curious. Even more, I'm worried. She looks too confident.

"Why don't you, ah, change first." She looks at my pajamas, her mouth twisted in contempt. "Meet me in the office downstairs in two minutes and I'll show you the file they have on you."

She flips her hair around as she saunters down the stairs. I turn toward my room and shut the door behind me, my heartbeat picking up speed. They have a file on me?

I change quickly and head downstairs to the office. Jen is already seated at one of the computers, her hand poised over the mouse. I move to her side and watch as she opens a strange database and clicks a file called "Olivia Westfield." Just the sight of my name makes my breath catch.

She leans forward to read from the monitor. "Julia Winters, age fifty-seven. Caseworker. Current foster parents: Denise Carter, née Anderson, age forty-three. Previously married to Alejandro Santos, one daughter, deceased. Derrick Carter, age forty-three, no children—"

"That's no secret," I interrupt her. "Anyone can get this

1214   Vivi Barnes

information."

"You mean *all* of this?" She leans back in the chair so I can have a closer look. Listed are my previous foster home addresses and Julia's information, plus Derrick and Denise are listed with their pictures and occupations. Basic information.

The next entry makes my heart stop. My mother's name, along with a picture.

What the…

I grow cold as my eyes sift through the data. My history with my past foster care is listed. Along with the reasons I was pulled from each home. Including…

Jen recites it aloud as my eyes fix on one section. "Incidents requiring removal from home: age ten, physical neglect—failure to provide adequate clothing and shelter. Age twelve, sexual abuse—offender Frank—"

"Shut up," I say, my voice no higher than a whisper. I'm frozen in place. This information was here the whole time? Z knew *everything*? This whole time, he's known? I can feel the heat rushing through my body, warming my cheeks, numbing my arms, my legs.

"So you see how it is," she continues. "He's a recruiter. Goes after the sweet foster girl to bring her into our world. He's good at his job, I'll say that much for him." She stands and places her hand on my shoulder, as if in sympathy. I can't even move to brush it away. "He's playing you, Liv. Like he played me."

"No." I can almost feel Z's arms around me, holding me after Derrick's attack. She's got it wrong. I don't know why he has all this information, but it doesn't mean he's using me.

"Z's a jerk of the worst kind. Has he told you his real name?" She nods when I don't respond. "Exactly. He won't tell anyone. I don't even think Nancy knows. And he has no file here, so nobody knows anything about *him*." She backs away toward the door, eyes still on me. "You're just another one of his projects. Don't trust him. You'll thank me later—I wish someone had clued *me* in."

The word "projects" makes my stomach flip. Jen pulls the door shut behind her, leaving me with nothing but a file full of sorrow and questions I'm not sure I'll ever find answers to.

Laughter from outside startles me from my reflective thoughts. Jen conveniently left me logged in to the computer, so I do a quick search through the files of the database. I find a file on Z, but every space is filled with the same word: *Classified*. With the exception of the comments field, which contains a simple line: *If you're that desperate to know something about me, close this file and get a life*. I press my lips together to suppress a grin, despite everything. He's such an ass. I just wish I knew what he was planning.

You're just another one of his projects.

Jen's words join hands with Sam's from days ago: *I told Nancy it looks like it's going to end the same as your other projects.*

I grow cold as the realization of exactly what this project is sinks in.

Z is outside starting his bike. His smile seems genuine as he sees me walking toward him. "What took you so long?"

"Nothing. When did you get the bike back?" I ask, trying to keep my voice light.

"Early this morning. I caught a ride to school with Sam while you were sleeping. I figured you'd be out for a while. Here," he says, handing me a cell phone. "This is for you. From Nancy. We all have one."

A cell phone. I should be happier about it, feel like I belong somewhere finally. It's just that I don't know where "there" is. I do make a mental note to call Mr. Bronson later and quit Slice of Happy. I won't be going anywhere near the Carters, that's for sure.

Z puts his helmet on and revs the engine as I climb behind him. As usual, the sensation of flying down the road behind him sends my adrenaline pumping, my heart racing. The way people describe the "thrill of the road" totally makes sense to me now. Today, the cool wind brushing against my skin is especially cleansing, though it can't do anything to erase my suspicions.

Z drives the bike slowly over the river, bouncing on the old slats of the wooden bridge. He pulls off and conceals the bike in the thick of the brush. We walk hand in hand up the path until we finally reach the waterfall.

I follow him along the narrow path between the small pond on the left and the ravine on the right to reach the cascade of water bouncing playfully off the rocks. The cool spray of mist from the falls is refreshing after the long, hot climb. We take off our shoes and wade carefully into the cold water, climbing onto a large, smooth, flat rock in the center. I lie back on his jacket as Z starts telling me about the people in the house. He's unusually talkative, and before long I'm caught up in the details of each person—their personalities as well as what they bring to the house.

"Micah acts like a big goof, I know," Z says. "He's a

prankster. But he's the best at creating and debugging software, proxy sites, pretty much everything. The best part is that no one outside our house takes him seriously. He can get away with anything and no one would know."

"And Dutch is the youngest, right? Is he in middle school?"

"Sixth grade. He's a genius, though. You can ask him any algebraic question and he'll give you an answer almost without thinking about it."

I prop myself up on my elbow to look at him directly. "Jen doesn't seem to like me very much."

"I'm sure you can guess why," he mutters without looking at me.

"But exactly what kind of relationship did you have with her? I'm sure she's not just crushing on you."

"She was never really my girlfriend."

"But you did have a relationship."

He doesn't have to say anything; his eyes answer my question. "Z, just tell me, what happened between you two?"

He exhales as his hand moves to stroke my side, but I brush his fingers away. I won't let him distract me this time. "I brought Jen to the house a year ago. She might have... misunderstood my intentions. I was too friendly with her, I guess."

"Friendly? The same kind of friendly you are with me?"

His eyebrows rise at that, but his voice remains steady. "Jen was different from you. She was really into the fact that I had a motorcycle, that I had a lot of money, that I was the 'bad boy.' That's one of the reasons I changed the way I dressed. I was tired of attracting the shallow end of the pool."

It bothers me that he can so easily blow her off. "So it was all her, huh? You didn't do anything to encourage her?"

"Relentless, aren't you? Okay, so maybe I made her think she was more special to me than she actually was. I guess I should feel kind of bad about that, especially since it's making her hate you so much. But she was never that nice, believe me."

I lean back and rest my arm over my face. Would he do the same to me? Is he just using me? He shifts slightly, tugging my arm away from my face. "What are you thinking?"

"Just feeling bad for her. What you did was terrible, and I can't imagine…" I can't even finish that thought.

His eyes are wide, worried. "You know it's not the same with you, right? I wouldn't do that to you."

"I don't know."

"Liv, please." He wraps his hand around mine, his eyes intent on me. "I swear it's not the same. You and I…we're real."

I shouldn't believe him, considering his history, most of which I don't know. But I'm not sure. Maybe it's the intensity of the promise, the anxiety in the eyes of this normally cool and self-possessed guy. Until I know the truth, though, I can't trust him a hundred percent, and that knowledge sucks. Still, I smile a little and he seems to relax. I put a finger over his lips as he leans toward me. "I'm not done."

He groans, resting his forehead on my chest. "I didn't think you were."

My thoughts move quickly now. Despite everything, I don't really want to throw Jen under the bus just for showing me my file. "I've heard people say you're a recruiter, and I've heard the word 'project' thrown around a few times. What project are you working on, Z? A new recruit?" I keep my voice innocently curious, my eyes fixed on him.

His head snaps up, his expression very still, stone-like. My heart sinks—Jen was right about that, at least.

"Let's see, you recruited Jen, right? And Maggie."

I tick them off my fingers as I say their names. Maggie was just a guess, but by the way the corners of his eyes twitch nervously, I know I'm right. I continue, keeping my voice calm though I'm dreading the next words. "I thought so. Then, let's see, you also recruited...*me*."

He pushes himself up to his knees, jaw set. But he still doesn't say anything.

"You recruited me, like you recruited Jen. You knew everything about me. *Everything.* All tucked away nicely in a little file. And I'm going to end up like her, aren't I?" Though it'd be a cold day in hell before I'd stick around to be bitter while he brought home other girls.

"No!" His voice is firm, but there is no regret in his expression. "I told you, you are *not* like Jen. Not like any of them."

"You lied to me." I say it like I'm talking about the weather. Calm and simple.

His mouth opens and closes but nothing comes out. He shakes his head as I stare him down. "I didn't lie."

"Yes, you did. You preyed on me from the very beginning, trying to make me feel special, but the whole time..."

"So now I'm a criminal and a liar, right? Yeah, my plan was to invite you to Monroe Street. I thought you were perfect for us. Thought we could help you get out of the system. And I did try to let you off the hook when I realized how much I... when I realized you weren't cut out for this. Which is why Sam is pissed at me, too."

Off the hook? "You tried to let me off the hook? I didn't see a whole lot of that going on, Z. Or, I don't know, was making out with me your way of letting me off the hook?"

He swings around and slides down into the water, making his way to the shore. Wait, he thinks *he* has the right to be mad? I follow him to the bank, wincing as the icy water bites into my skin.

He turns to face me as I scramble up the slippery bank. "You think I played you? You think this is all some game for me?"

"Isn't it?" I step forward but slip and fall on the slick grass. He offers his hand, which I slap away. He reaches down to pull me up by the arms. His chest is rising and falling faster as he glares at me. Then the emotion in his eyes turns from anger to something different, raw and hungry. The sudden shift in his expression makes my body ache, but I try to ignore it.

He kisses me hard, his lips slipping over mine in the soft spray of mist, shocking me. I push against him until I break free, then slap him in the face. Hard.

He looks as stunned as I feel. He opens his mouth as if to say something then closes it. "I'm sorry," he says, rubbing his cheek. "You're right. I didn't mean to drag you into all this. I mean, I did then, but now…" His eyes drop to my feet. "I get why you're mad, but this isn't a game for me. Not anymore."

He turns to walk away. I almost let him go, but something inside me stirs as the memories flood over me like a wave—the concern and anger in Z's eyes after Derrick's attack, the gentle pressure of his lips against mine, his arms warm around me, making me feel safe. His eyes telling me what his words don't.

I'm furious that he knew everything and kept it from me, but at the same time, I know he's not trying to hurt me. When he told me about the operation at Monroe Street, I didn't run from him. So why am I so angry now? Because he didn't tell me he knew about my shitty past? That information is pretty much a matter of public record.

My head hurts. In my mind I know it'd be stupid to stay with someone I can't fully trust. But my heart disagrees. I can't deny this—whatever *this* is. Right or wrong, I stretch my arm to take his hand in mine and pull him back to me.

His eyes widen in surprise as I reach up to twist my fingers into his damp hair and pull him down to me, to press my mouth against his. This time it's me driving the kiss, forcing his lips apart with mine, locked with an intensity that's frightening. His hands slide down my body to rest on my hips, then around to pull me closer until we're melded together. My leg slides up against his and my body goes limp as he wraps his hand around the outside of my thigh, hitching me up until I'm lifted off the ground. The warning bells clang in my mind but the pounding of my heart drowns them out. He sets me back on my feet, his breathing as labored as mine.

"Come on, you're getting soaked." His voice is rough but his eyes are shining. I let him lead me away from the falls, across the narrow path to the clearing. We lie down on the warm, dry grass and listen to the sound of the rushing water as the sun's rays soothe my damp skin.

Z leans over and traces the outline of my face with his finger. "I'm sorry I got you mixed up in this."

"I don't agree with what you guys do," I tell him. I'm going for total honesty, and I'm hoping he does the same. "But I know that I have nowhere else to go."

"You know you're going to have to do it, too."

I don't know that I can steal like that, no matter how easy it is or how much he tries to justify it. But I refuse to go back into foster care. I can do whatever I have to do to stay out of the system until I turn eighteen. "Just promise you'll stop keeping secrets from me."

His eyes shift away. "Okay."

I put a finger under his chin and tilt it toward me. "Promise?"

He nods. His lips meet mine, then slide down my jawline to my neck. A pleasant tingling sensation moves throughout my body at his touch.

"When are you going to tell me your name?" I ask, since we're speaking of not keeping secrets. Even more, I want to see how much he trusts *me*.

"Mmm…?"

"Your name?" I push on his shoulders until he looks up at me. I touch a fingertip lightly to the slight pink blotch on his cheek where I slapped him. "Your real name."

"My legal name is Z."

"Yeah, yeah, I know, and there's no record of you. No, I want to know your *real* name. The one you were born with, the one not even Sam knows." *Or Jen.*

He doesn't say anything. The warmth inside me begins to chill. "If you don't trust me with that, how can I trust you enough to stay at the house?"

He bows his head, the blond hair falling forward so I can't see his eyes. "It's important to you, isn't it?"

"Obviously."

"I promised myself I would never tell anyone. Never." His voice is barely audible. I get the feeling he's trying to convince himself more than me.

"What are you afraid of?"

"Everything," he whispers. It's a strange admission, coming from him, but one that I kind of get. To tell me his name is to trust his entire life to me. Maybe he's not ready for that. Am I?

I brush his hair back and he gazes at me, his eyes a deep well of painful memories. I'm not the only one who's gone through hell. I touch a finger to his lips. "Don't tell me right now. Tell me when you're ready." I want him to do it because he wants to, not because I guilt-tripped him into it.

He nods, his face serious as he fans my damp hair across my shoulder. "I promise."

Interestingly, for the first time in my life, and regardless of all the crap Z is involving me in, I'm starting to trust my feelings. I really like him. I almost feel like I could trust *him*.

Even though there's still a part of me that warns against it.

CHAPTER NINETEEN

"She was not past seventeen. Cast in so slight and exquisite a mould; so mild and gentle; so pure and beautiful; that earth seemed not her element, nor its rough creatures her fit companions."

—Charles Dickens, *Oliver Twist*

Z

My life has always been so easy when it comes to girls. I've never had a problem manipulating their emotions. I know how they react to me—to my looks, my attitude, my money. I know what they want, and I give it to them in order to get what *I* want. There's never been a time that I haven't been in control.

Until now.

Liv is different. I tried treating her like all the rest until I accidentally fell... I choke on the word, even in my thoughts. I don't want to be in love. Love causes nothing but trouble, and it gets in the way of business. I've been fine with my life so far. Why would I want to screw it up?

Liv stirs next to me. She's a restless sleeper. In all three nights that she's been here, she hasn't spent a single one in her own bed. Sharing a bed with a girl just to sleep is new for me. Girls I've recruited in the past, like Jen, were always very quick to let me know they were interested in much more. It was too easy.

I wince at the thought of Jen. I admit, I let that one go way too far. Like with Maggie, it's my fault she's so bitter.

In the stream of morning light through the window I can see the corner of Liv's lips turn upward, and I smile. Must be a good dream. I touch her cheek with one finger and kiss her forehead as she sleeps. I wish I could protect her from the world, because the world sucks. I'd do anything to keep Liv from having to go through more hell.

She shifts slightly toward me, her gold locket sliding down her neck. I stare at it for the longest time, remembering my promise to tell her everything. But she's been hurt so many times. How do I know this time would be different?

I reach a hand over the side of the bed to the windowsill and feel around for my glasses. Using a fingernail, I pry the little heart open and peer closely at the tiny pictures within. On the right is a young woman, not much older than Liv and so like her in the face, with the same large brown eyes. The picture on the left is of her grandfather and grandmother. I stare at the man's smiling face. Smiles can hide everything and tell a person nothing. I press it closed, just in time for Liv to sigh and slowly open her eyes, focusing on me.

"Good morning," I say, brushing her hair back over her ear.

"Mmm…good morning," she says, her voice thick with sleepiness. "What time is it?"

"Six forty-five. Time for school."

She stretches, catlike. "Mmm…don't want to go."

"I know. But there are only a few days left."

She frowns. I know what's on her mind, though she won't admit it. There's a possibility Derrick could be at school, waiting for her. Nancy's nervous that he'll have the cops on us here, but I know that scum like him are usually too afraid to involve the police until they get their own story straight. And if he went to the police...the thought of that makes me laugh.

There is something else that worries me, though. Starting this afternoon, Nancy says I'm to get Liv involved with our cyber activities. We haven't talked about it since the waterfall, though I'm sure she knows it's coming. I just don't know how she's going to react.

"I have something for you." I reach back to my nightstand and lift the small blue box. Her eyes widen as I open the lid to reveal a thin gold bracelet.

"Oh, Z, it's beautiful." She lifts it up to gaze at it.

"It was my mother's," I whisper as I watch the gold strand flex through her slender fingers. "It's the only thing I kept of hers."

I take it and gently fasten it above her hand, then kiss the inside of her wrist. The one thing I have that means something to me now rests on the only person who means everything to me.

Her hand strokes my cheek. "Thank you," she says softly.

I lean down to press my lips to hers, then her chin, her jaw, her neck, loving how she tilts her head back to give me better access. I let my fingers trail down her side to pull her closer to me.

A noise from outside brings me back to myself. Keeping my self-control around this girl is not easy.

"Come on." I pull her up and kiss her lightly before she

heads back to her room to change. I go into my bathroom to splash cold water on my face—thank God for whoever invented cold water—brush my teeth, and slip on a pair of jeans. I head downstairs, making it out the door before Nancy has a chance to remind me about this afternoon. Liv meets me at the bike and we head to school.

As we turn into the school parking lot, Liv's arms tighten around me. I pull into a space and take my helmet off to look at her, but she's buried into my back, not moving.

"What's wrong?" I gently unfold her arms from their grip around my waist.

"Hey!" A shout echoes across the parking lot. The devil himself, Derrick Carter, is standing outside his car, pointing at me. Unlatching Liv's trembling hands from my jacket, I slide off the bike, ignoring her faint protests. My focus is only on the asshole who doesn't know what's about to hit him. I can barely hear Liv shouting at me as I first walk, then run to my target, my anger breaking over me like a storm. The bastard's eyes get wide as he backs away, just making it into his car when I reach him. He locks the door and shakes his head as I pound on the glass with my fist.

"Get out, you son of a bitch!" I back away a couple feet and stand to watch him with my arms crossed, daring him to step out.

He rolls down his window an inch. "I've called the police," he says, holding his cell. "You have no legal right to her. I'm her legal guardian, so she has to come with me."

Ha. I shake my head and walk back to Liv. Perfect. Let him figure it out. Let him explain to the cops why the system shows she's emancipated, why there's no record of them being her guardians. Then let him find out that he's now a registered sex offender who's in the parking lot of a high school. *Yeah, let's see you squirm out of that one, scumbag.*

Liv is still sitting on the bike, her wide eyes focused on the car. I put my arms around her trembling body. "It's okay. He won't hurt you anymore."

I expect her to start crying, but she shrugs me away and slides off the bike.

"What are you doing?" I ask.

"I'm not dealing with this anymore," she says, her voice shaking but her face set. "I'm sick of being scared." She heads toward Derrick's car.

"No, Liv, wait." She ignores me, instead walking faster toward Derrick, who is still in his car. I can hear sirens growing louder as they get nearer. Shit, he really did call the cops.

I get on the bike and start it up, riding over to stop in front of Liv. "Get on. Cops are coming."

Her face is a storm cloud. "Z, get the…" She stops, staring as a police car pulls into the parking lot.

"Get on. Now."

She slides behind me and I pull away just as Derrick gets out of his car to wave the police down. Her grip around me is like steel, though it loosens as we get farther away from the school.

Liv is visibly calmer once we reach the waterfall. She doesn't say anything about what happened in the parking lot, but at least she's no longer angry. I flip on my side in the grass to face her, brushing her arm with my fingertips. She flinches, then relaxes. I hate when she flinches. It's like there are secrets so deep that I'll never be able to uncover them. "Tell me about your past."

"My past? You already know."

"No, I don't." I look her straight in the eyes. "I only know what's on record. I know Derrick wasn't the first person who abused you."

She jerks away from me, standing up and walking to the edge of the pool. I wonder if I've gone too far.

"Derrick was the worst, but there was another time with a foster brother. He used to touch me. A lot." She shivers and crosses her arms. "Most of my homes weren't as horrible as that. I just wasn't in them long enough to get to know them. And some really sucked. I remember at one place, the kids thought it was funny to pull pranks on me. They drove me out to a haunted cornfield on Halloween and left me there. I could hear them laughing as they drove away. The last straw was when they locked me out of the house in my thin pajamas in the middle of winter. A neighbor called the police for me. Julia moved me every time there was a problem, but the problems never seemed to end."

She sighs. "To be honest, I've never really loved anyone or trusted anyone since my mother died. Bernadette's the only one I got even a little close to, but I didn't love her, either." She pauses and her forehead wrinkles. I know she's not telling me the whole truth on that one, which makes me dislike Bernadette even more for leaving her and breaking her heart.

"It's funny, you know?" Liv continues, walking back over to sit next to me. "I'd see all these kids with their parents and when I was little, I'd wish that were me. And I was pretty angry at my mother for getting hooked on drugs and running away from home to live on the streets. But that's the weird thing. When it was just the two of us living on the streets, that's when I felt the most loved. When I got older, I figured I didn't need love, just a place to sleep and eat, really. That's all I felt toward most families, like the Carters."

Her story isn't unusual. At Monroe Street, there are too many stories like this, though the kids who eventually find their way to us are the lucky ones. But it still breaks my heart. I can't believe she's made it this far without getting mixed up in the trouble that typically plagues kids with that kind of past.

I touch the gold locket just under the hollow of her throat. "What would you do if you ever found out you had family? I mean, say you had an aunt or an uncle or something."

"I don't know. I guess it depends on the circumstances. What would you do?"

"I'd probably run the other way." I say it without thinking.

She laughs. "You realize you left me with the perfect opening to ask *you* now, right?"

"I guess. What do you want to know?"

She raises her eyebrows. "Really, you have to ask? Okay, so let's start with how you came to Monroe Street. What made you decide to start doing, you know, what you do?"

What *I* do. She can't say the words, a red flag that I decide to ignore for now. "I came to Monroe Street when I was around eleven. I'd been in a lot of trouble before that, even got sent to juvie. But Nancy found me when I ran away. She took me in, then told me she was starting up a home for kids who needed a place to stay. I'd have to earn my keep, but I'd like the freedom of the place. I was skeptical at first, but she was good on her word. It started out as simple jobs until I really got involved. I guess you could say I founded the online division."

"You didn't do any hacking before Monroe Street?"

"Well, not like I do today. I did a lot of malicious stuff, though. Viruses, bots, things like that. Nancy made me stop when I came to live here." I frown at the memory. "Poor Nancy.

She had a seriously angry kid to deal with while trying to start up the business. I can never repay her for everything she did for me."

"Why were you so angry?"

"It doesn't matter. Life just sucked. But like I told you, Monroe Street saved me. Saved all of us."

"Is Nancy a computer genius, too?"

"No. Nancy got her start a different way. Very different. She was a pro."

"A pro at what?"

Her innocent, wide-eyed expression makes me laugh. "A pro—a prostitute."

Liv gasps, throwing her hand over her mouth. "*Nancy*—a prostitute? What the hell?"

"Well, more of a high-class escort. Not on the streets like you're probably thinking. That's how Bill…" I stop for a minute, my thoughts going back to Maggie. Escort or prostitute, I can't understand why anyone would choose that life.

"So have you ever been caught?"

"Nope. It's not like we pick pockets. Cyber crime is totally different."

"Like how?"

"Well, it's not like in the movies or on TV. Actually, what they do isn't even close. And we don't go into banks dressed in our best suits to get a briefcase full of money or have cool holograms projecting into vaults."

I smile at the thought. It's one of the first things I have to tell new kids—our way of hacking accounts usually consists of password cracking, SQL injection, or social engineering. Maggie actually thought we'd be going all Bonnie and Clyde on banks. I think she was disappointed when she found out how unglamorous the business is.

"So you go after easy targets. Do you prey on little old ladies with cats, too?"

Her tone drips with sarcasm. I can't believe that she would even think that about me. "No. I've told you this before—we're not evil. We go after big targets, not people who can barely afford to feed themselves, let alone their cats."

"Ah…okay." Her lips twist and I know she's not convinced. I'm not sure what else to say to make her understand. It was never this hard to convince the others, not even Cameron, who thought we were being watched all the time. Although he's still pretty paranoid. Maybe that's why Sam flinches at the idea of dating him.

Liv takes my hand and draws idle circles around my knuckles with her thumb. Her hands are small, her fingers so slender. I'm caught up in staring at them, which is probably why her next question, "How did your mother die?" takes me off guard.

I jerk away from her. "What?"

She stares at me. "I'm sorry, I know I shouldn't…"

"My mother died when I was seven. It was pretty bad. She just…" I yank on the grass next to me, throwing it aside. It doesn't make me feel any better. "She just couldn't handle life."

It's the main thing I remember about my mother—the bleak depression that eventually led to her suicide. I shove the memory behind the wall in my heart.

Liv takes my hand again. Her touch is warm. "What happened to your father?"

Anger washes over me with the other memory I never let surface. I don't say anything this time.

"He's still alive, isn't he?"

She's too perceptive. But I can't tell her. Can't tell anyone. I'm sweating now, though it could just be the heat of the sun. I want to crawl to the edge of the pool and sink into the cold water, swim away from this girl who asks too much.

"It's okay," Liv says quietly, as if reading my mind. "You don't have to tell me."

I take a deep breath and stare into her soft brown eyes. This is it, the ultimate test. Do I open myself up to her and bare my most painful truths, or do I blow her off and lie?

"I've never told anyone. No one except Nancy knows about him." I manage to keep all emotion out of my voice. "He's a hedge fund manager. He's a billionaire, living the life in New York City."

Her mouth drops open in shock.

"Yeah, I was pretty surprised myself," I tell her.

"How did you find out?"

"My mother told me, right before she died. She gave me a letter he once wrote to her, telling her how much she meant to him, promising to leave his wife for her. He had an affair with her while he was married and refused to claim me as his son. Yep. Dear Daddy is still alive."

It's hard to talk about him without using every possible curse word I can think of. His denial of me, of us, was the reason my mother was so depressed.

"Did you ever try to contact him?"

I thread my fingers behind my head and concentrate on the needles of the pine trees, my heart constricting. "Yes, three years ago. He acted like he didn't know me, but I could tell he was lying. I look exactly like the son of a bitch. It's okay. He's unknowingly been providing more than enough payback for abandoning us. I've seen to that." Although money will never, never make up for what he did.

We sit in silence for a while. Then she asks, "Have you ever wished your life was different? More honest?"

I look away. "No. I like my life the way it is. I've never thought twice about it." *Until now.*

"Really?" Liv's eyes reflect doubt, but she still smiles—sunshine piercing through my dark clouds. Being with her is like being with the best part of myself, a fragment remaining from my innocent childhood. She makes me want to go out and give all my money to the homeless, feed stray dogs, kiss babies, and all sorts of stupid shit. Sometimes I feel like riding my Ducati away from Liv as fast as I can; at the same time, I want to hold her and never let her out of my arms.

"Z?"

Liv frowns, maybe because I'm staring at her like an idiot. I smile and curl a stray lock of hair around her ear, letting my fingers trail along her jawline. She closes her eyes at the touch and tilts her head up for the kiss I won't give her.

Not yet.

"Jack." The word feels strange coming from my mouth.

Her eyes flicker open. "What?"

I brush my thumb over her parted lips, craving the taste of them. "My name is Jack."

It's a relief to finally say the name I've hidden for years, ever since Nancy found me and helped me get rid of my identity. She knew Bill would never stop using me against my father if he knew about my association. And once I picked the name Z, Nancy never called me Jack again.

Liv stares at me, wide-eyed, those lips I desire curving up slowly. "Jack," she whispers.

I close my eyes. "Say it again."

Her soft hands lightly press against my cheeks, igniting fire inside of me. "Jack."

I slide my hands along her arms to the hands touching my face, tugging them around my neck. My lips skim hers at first, just enough so I can breathe in the softness of her.

"Jack," she whispers through a sigh, the word falling so naturally from her lips. Why the hell did I wait so long to tell her? I press my lips to hers again, coaxing them apart to taste her mouth, then pulling away to tease her into saying my name again. "Jack," she says, smiling softly without opening her eyes.

This time, I don't hold back. I let my mouth consume hers as my hands slip down her waist and over her curves.

We slowly lie back on the grass, never breaking the lock on our lips. God help me, she tastes of sunshine and roses. She tilts her head back as I explore the lines of her jaw with my kisses, then the length of her neck. I want to dip farther, to know every inch of her. But as my hand moves over her stomach, I can feel the muscles underneath tense. I glance up to see her eyes squeezed tightly closed.

I sigh and press a kiss just above the V of her T-shirt, mentally shouting every possible curse against Derrick. Liv's eyes flicker open and a mix of relief and disappointment flashes through them as I tug her shirt down.

"You're not ready for this," I tell her, caressing her cheek. "It's okay."

"I want to, Jack. I'm just…I just have to deal with what's in my head first."

"Totally understandable." I kiss her lightly and rest back on my elbows, watching her. She's got something on her mind, the way she's staring at the sky, biting her lip. I hope she's not overanalyzing this. "What are you thinking about?"

"Maybe we should just run away together. We could be on our own, start a new life, put all the demons behind us."

I wasn't expecting this answer. Run away to start a new life? The thought is exhilarating, tempting, and scary as hell. Possibilities that aren't possible for me. Still, I ask, "What would you do if you left here?"

"Well, college, for one. I'd love to go to Princeton. Have you applied to any schools yet?"

I shake my head and cringe inside as she keeps talking about what life outside of Monroe Street could be for us. It's not that I haven't thought about it. She's *made* me think about it. But hearing her talk about college makes me feel sick. *Possibilities that aren't possible.*

I shake that thought off. She hasn't even started yet. She'll come around once she gets that first paycheck. Everyone does.

• • •

LIV

"So what exactly are we going to do with this account?" I ask, my hand poised over the keyboard.

I can't bring myself to hit enter. It's my first transfer, and I can't do it. I know I'm frustrating Jack, who's morphed from the sweet, sensitive boy who opened his heart to me at the waterfall into the hacker who's all business. I can tell he's trying to maintain his patience, but it's not that I don't know how. When it comes down to it, it's really not that hard. Once you're in, it's almost scary how simple it is to transfer money into the ghost account. But I can't get away from the biggest problem here: this is major, throw-your-butt-in-jail theft.

Jack takes a deep breath, his eyes focused on the blinking cursor. "Not we, Liv. You. This one's easy enough. The password cracker got you in; now you just have to complete the transaction. It's not a large enough amount to raise an alarm, especially from this company. You never want to transfer a huge amount of money at one time unless you're planning to do a dump-and-run. It'd alert the authorities right away." He speaks so casually, like all I'm doing is looking up my account balance or something.

"What's a dump-and-run?"

"It's Bill's term for taking a huge sum and cutting ties after. He does it sometimes with large accounts. The rest of us don't."

"Oh." I drop my hand to my lap and stare at the monitor.

Jack groans. "You have to do it, you know. It's required if you live here. And you'll be given your own accounts soon."

"I know, but…"

"Look, don't you want to be here?" His voice sounds desperate, almost pleading now, strange from someone like him. I can't help thinking his question isn't if I want to be here, it's if I want to be here with *him*. Obviously, I want to be with him more than anything, but…*damn it.*

He runs his hands through his hair and tries a poor attempt at his old easy smile. "Just type in these numbers and click here. Easy enough. Then you get a piece of that."

"Where does the rest go?"

He hesitates for a moment, not meeting my eyes. "The home, things, you know."

Yeah, I know—Bill. He's the one pulling all the strings here, like a pimp. You just don't want to admit it. I try a different tactic. "So these people who work for this money never notice it's gone. But doesn't it ever bother you that everything you have is bought with stolen money? Or do you always do whatever Bill tells you to do?"

He jumps to his feet and heads for the door.

Oh, jeez. "Wait," I say, following him. He stops as I slip my hand into his. "I didn't mean to make it sound like that. I'm just not ready yet, I guess."

He pulls me to him and buries his face in my hair.

"Jack?"

His grip around me is tight. I push on his chest, noticing his heart pounding quicker than usual under my hands. He releases me and turns back to the monitor. "Don't worry about it," he says in a softer voice. "I'll finish this, then you can do one tomorrow." He types the information and presses enter to activate the transfer. It takes him all of ten seconds. Then he leaves the office without looking at me.

I collapse into the chair and stare at the screen. I hate to disappoint him, but I don't think I can do this. And the fact that he can so easily makes me worry that this is just one more situation in my life that isn't going to work out.

CHAPTER TWENTY

"'But tonight he's a thief, and a liar, and all that's bad. Ain't that enough for the old wretch, without blows?'"

—Charles Dickens, *Oliver Twist*

JACK

In my room, I slam the door and take a deep breath. I sink onto my bed and rest my head in my hands. Liv's hesitation is not about ability, as this was one of the easier transfers. It's the act of stealing that's bugging her. And I really, really wish it wasn't, because she's making *me* think twice about it.

I didn't ask for this!

She's not like Jen or Maggie, or any girl I've known. Liv isn't impressed with the bike, the money, the *show*. She likes me for me.

At the same time, I know I can get her to do this. She doesn't like stealing, but she'll do it for me. On the surface, she's an easy target, the perfect recruit, but damn if her questions don't make me wonder why I'm getting her involved with this life. Or why I'm even in it myself.

I squeeze my eyes closed and try to shut out my inner voice. The fact that she might not go through with this worries me. The fact that she might bugs me even more. Sam was right—I'm in way over my head.

I know Bill will blame me if she doesn't perform. After Jen's issues, he won't forgive me if Liv fails, too. And I know he won't let her go, either. Not now. He'll realize how I feel about her. He finds everything out eventually. He might even transfer her to another house. I try not to think about what happened to Maggie. Bill knew I cared about her, too, and that was nothing compared to Liv. The very thought of that happening again makes me sick.

But Liv has a real choice now, even if she doesn't realize it yet.

I open my desk drawer and take out the file on Carlton Brownlow. Should I give this to her like I planned before she got attacked, let her decide what to do with it? Or finish the job and toss it? She's been hurt so many times, I don't want to take the chance that it'll happen again.

I drop the file on the desk and head downstairs to seek out Sam, who I find playing the Xbox with Jen. Jen glares at me with the usual hate-filled eyes, but I ignore her. Sam sets the remote down at my gesture and follows me outside.

"What's up?" she asks, her blond hair bobbing around as she bounces on her heels impatiently.

"Bill is supposed to be coming by soon. Have you heard anything?"

"Not really. Nancy mentioned it was sometime this week, but I don't know when. Why?"

I hesitate for a second, not looking forward to her reaction. "I've changed my mind about Liv. I don't think she can do this.

You know he doesn't have any patience, and if she doesn't perform, he may put her somewhere else."

"What? You've got to be kidding me. You're saying this *now*?"

"And if I try to cover for her, he'll find out. I don't want her to have to deal with him."

Sam snorts. "Look, Z, stop thinking with your dick. Whether you like it or not, she's going to have to meet Bill. Everyone does. And she'll probably fly right under the radar like the rest of us. You're his golden boy. He doesn't have much use for anyone else."

"Really? What about Maggie? Remember her, or have you forgotten where she ended up?"

Sam's face clouds over. "I don't think that'll happen to Liv. Besides, you know Maggie was more street-smart than Liv. She was glad to do anything for an extra buck." Sam's voice is slightly subdued. Of course it is. Sam was friends with Maggie.

"And look where that got her. I can't take a chance. Liv's got to get out of here."

"Wait, what do you mean by that?" Her eyes narrow. She steps closer and lowers her voice. "You will leave her right here. She's both of ours, not just yours. What will you tell Bill when he asks where she is? What will I say? You know what he's capable of. We can't let her go."

I grab Sam's arm. "Please."

She shakes me off, looking disgusted. "You're losing your edge, Z. She's turning you into a marshmallow. I warned you not to fall for her, and this whole time, you didn't listen to me. But she's here now, so deal with it. Help her adjust or something, but don't send her away. She's probably a lot stronger than you give her credit for, anyway."

Sam yanks the door open, then stops, her expression hard. "Besides, it's mostly because of you that she's here now. You're the one who got her to trust us. *You.*"

She slams the door behind her, leaving me stunned. I sit on the step and rest my head on my arms, hating Sam, hating myself. She's right; it's my fault. Liv is in this mess because of me.

A low hum turns into a familiar rumble as I look up to see a long black car headed straight for the house.

Shit.

I yank open the door and run through, calling for Nancy. Others stop what they're doing to stare at me. Nancy appears from the kitchen.

"Bill's here." My voice sounds higher than usual.

The emotions on her face are a conflicting mix of anxiety and excitement. As much as she knows he's just using her, she's still in love with Bill. It's disgusting to me; she's such a great person, and he's such a—

"Z?" Liv appears next to me. I'm relieved she remembers to call me Z in front of everyone else.

I grab her hands. "You need to get up to my room. Now."

Her eyes widen, and I realize I must look completely out of control. I try to get a hold of myself. "Bill's here. You're not ready to meet him face-to-face."

But it's too late as the front door opens. I pull Liv behind me. The entire room goes silent except for the sounds of brutal war emitting from the Xbox. Dutch moves next to me.

"Nancy?" Bill calls in his gritty voice.

Liv shifts slightly behind me, and I try to see him from her perspective. He may have been decent-looking at one time, with his ice-blue eyes and dark wavy hair. But the perpetual scowl on his scarred face and the pallor of his skin could easily cast him as a movie villain. Usually, he doesn't get to me. I try to steady my breathing and look disinterested.

"Yes, Bill, I'm here," Nancy says, rushing forward, twisting her hands together. She touches his arm and stretches up to kiss his cheek. He doesn't push her away or say something rude, so at least he's in a good mood. I notice a folder tucked under his arm.

"Z." He nods at me then raises an eyebrow when I don't respond. Great. Now he knows something's up. "What's going on?"

"Nothing." I try to keep my voice level.

"Where is she?"

I squeeze Liv's hand behind my back, hoping she gets the hint. "She's not—"

"She's right here, Bill," Jen calls out, walking over to grab Liv's arm and pull her to the front. I really do wish looks could kill. She'd be ashes.

Bill tilts his head toward me, then narrows his eyes and walks around the two girls, appraising Liv like she's cattle for slaughter. "Olivia, right?"

"Yes," she says. Her voice is strong, and her chin seems to tilt up a bit. Despite everything, something in me stirs—pride, maybe. She's not one to be intimidated by someone like him.

"Got any family?"

"No."

"Any old ties? Foster parents?"

She doesn't say anything. Sam speaks up from the side. "She came from a foster home. It didn't work out. They're not in the picture."

Bill flicks a look at Sam, who retreats a step. *Shut up, Sam.*

Better to stay in the shadows than to tell Bill things he already knows. He wants to hear it from Liv. I grit my teeth to stop myself from moving to her side.

He turns his head slightly toward me. "Well, Z? Is she ready?"

"Almost, but not yet. She just got here."

Sam rolls her eyes but doesn't say anything. Bill catches the look, however. My stomach lurches. He knows.

"Something going on here?" he asks, taking a couple steps closer to examine Liv. He cocks his head at me.

"No." I look him straight in the eyes. He doesn't believe me, I can tell. He rubs the stubble on his chin, watching me, then her.

"Very pretty, isn't she?" His gaze cuts through me. I don't say anything, hoping like hell he can't see the faster rise and fall of my chest. "I'd like an assessment of her myself. See how she handles an account of her own."

I don't even blink, but I'm thinking as fast as I can. I need to buy time. "Sure, no problem. A week. She'll be ready by then." As soon as I say it I know I'm screwed. No one gets that long.

His lips flatten into a sneer as he hands Nancy a folder. "Now. Here's her target, and it's not a tough one. I want to see the account cracked within the next two days. I'll come back then for my own assessment." He turns to leave. Everyone lets out a collective breath when the door closes behind him. No one ever wants to attract Bill's attention.

I catch Liv's confused look and try to smile, failing miserably. "Come on." I lead her to my room. I know she'll have too many questions.

"What the hell was that about? What does he mean by

'assessment'?" she asks, moving to the window and peering out through the shades.

I glance at the other folder on my desk, the one for Carlton Brownlow. Bill hasn't asked me about it in a while. "He's giving you an account as a test, but we need to talk about—"

A knock on the door interrupts me. "What?"

"Hey, Nancy wants you," Sam says, peeking her head in.

"Not now."

"Now, Z." She looks at Liv. "I'll be back in a sec. Nancy wants me to show you how to do the research on this file from Bill." She tosses the folder to Liv, but I intercept it.

"That's my job."

"Just the research. Not the transfers."

"Fine." But when Sam turns around, I switch the file Bill gave her with the one on my desk and slip the other under a magazine. I hand Carlton Brownlow's file to Liv, then brush past Sam into the hallway. "This better be good," I mutter.

Sam follows me out, leaning against the doorjamb with a superior look on her face. "Oh, give me a break."

"I'm not kidding. If anything happens to her…"

"What? You'll do what? The only thing I did was exactly what you've done for every new recruit you've brought to this place. Every last one of them. Including Maggie. You've screwed yourself into this corner, Z. Now deal with it."

She goes back into my room and leaves me at the top of the staircase. Nancy is pacing at the bottom.

"What do you want?" I ask as I descend to her level. I know my voice is harsh, but after what Sam said, I'm not in the mood for a friendly chat.

"Come with me," she says quietly, leading me to the study and pulling the doors closed. "What exactly are your intentions here?"

"I don't know what you're talking about."

"Stop it. I know you're planning something with that girl. I saw your face. You don't intend on letting Bill anywhere near her. What are you going to do?"

I remain still.

Nancy takes my arm. "Come on. You and I go way back, further than anyone here. You know you can trust me."

"You're his girlfriend…," I start to say, but she waves a hand at me.

"Yes, but don't think I'm stupid. I know him, and you're like a son to me. So if my kid's in trouble, I want to know about it. But I also need to warn you, if she refuses to do this or tries to run, Bill will have questions. And he'll be after you for the answers."

I pace the room in frustration. "Don't you think I know that? Damn it, I can't give her over to Bill."

"Stop blowing this out of proportion, Z."

"Stop making light of this, Nancy."

She shrugs. "I don't know why you're getting so worked up. He's just going to have her hack into some accounts, see where she's strongest. No big deal. Standard stuff."

"She can't."

"Of course she can."

"No. I mean she *won't*. Not even for me."

Nancy's expression turns from curious to concerned. "Well, she will with Bill standing over her."

"I doubt that. She's got it in her head that what we're doing is wrong. Damn it." I continue pacing.

"Oh, God, Z. How could you have slipped like this?"

I stop pacing, shocked at how pale she looks. "What do you

mean, slipped?"

She lifts a hand to her forehead, closing her eyes in exasperation. "How many times have I told you how careful you need to be about bringing people in? After the disasters with Jen, with Maggie—why didn't you make sure she'd work out before bringing her here? Bill knows that she knows about us. He'll never let her go, you know that."

"I know that." I almost choke on the words. It's my fault she's here, and now, thanks to me, she only has two options: join us or run.

"That's not the only problem, is it?" she asks in a tone that reminds me of so long ago, when she would comfort me after the never-ending nightmares. "Sam's right. You've fallen for her." Her eyes are sympathetic, but I want none of that.

"So what? It doesn't matter. This isn't for her. She doesn't want to be a thief." I try a different tactic. "You know she could put our whole operation in jeopardy."

Nancy's mouth forms a grim line. "Okay, so then what are you planning to do?"

"I'm getting her out of here."

"She doesn't know how to disappear like you do, Z."

My eyes fix on the tattered first edition of *The Adventures of Huckleberry Finn*, set on a gold stand in the bookshelf. The book was once my favorite, the story of a runaway. "She won't have to."

Nancy doesn't say anything, but then her eyes widen. Her hands clutch my arm in a panic. "Oh, God. No, you don't. You aren't running away with her. You can't."

It's not that I haven't thought about it. I didn't think it was possible before. But now that she says it—now that it's come down to it—I realize it's exactly what I want to do. But all I say is, "I can get her far from here, change her name, set her up in college…something. I can do that for her. If you're really my friend, you won't stop us, and you can't tell Bill. You know what he would do. Think of Maggie."

Nancy's shoulders sag. "Maggie was a different story. She wanted to be transferred there."

"No, I don't think so. Bill saw an opportunity because she was pretty and she couldn't hack. Look what became of her." The last words come out in a choked whisper. I still hate myself for not having the balls to stop her from leaving Monroe Street, or to get her to come back. Liv is better at hacking, of course, but if she refuses to do it—

I clear my voice. "Anyway, I'm not going to let this happen again, Nancy. You should know better than anyone what that life is like."

Nancy looks offended, as she always does when we reference her past. "Maggie knew what she was getting into. And the chances of something like that happening are slim. You're overreacting. He's going to put Liv through his usual crackerjack tests. Nothing else. Then he'll leave her alone and we can go easy on her."

"Just promise me you won't say anything to Bill."

"It's not Maggie's fate you're worried about, is it? You think Liv's too good for us?" Her expression is more hurt than angry. She sits on the sofa, her head down.

I sit next to her and take her hand. Nancy has been like a mother to me for so much of my life. The last thing in the world I want to do is upset her. Well, the next to last thing… "Please promise me."

She touches my cheek. "I won't say anything. But please, please think about what you're doing, what you'd be giving up if you join her. As good as you are, Bill's better. If he finds you, he'll kill you. And I can't protect you."

"I know. I'll have to take that chance. There's no other way to get her away safely."

I walk out of the room, pulling the door shut with a *click*. The lie is easy. In my mind, at least, there's no alternative that I'm willing to consider. Nobody needs to know about Brownlow.

For the first time in a while, I'm not worried. I can run with her. It will work.

· · ·

LIV

I stare at the monitor, stunned, the file Z handed to me loose in my fingers. Ever since my mother died, I'd believed I was alone. No cousins, aunts, uncles, siblings—nobody. But here, in the millions of people in the state, in the billions of people in the world, I find out I'm not alone.

I have family.

Not just any relative, but a grandfather. My mother's father.

And of all things, I find him this way—as my first target. My eyes move back and forth from the enlarged picture on the screen to the tiny picture in the locket to the square picture on the file that Sam gave me. Exact same long nose, same serious gray eyes, same dark, wavy hair. If there was any doubt, the name of his deceased wife—Olivia Westfield Brownlow—put an end to that.

My stomach turns as I stare at the images. I didn't know he

was even alive. I remember asking my mother about the people in the picture when I was little, and she told me her parents died. She told me she had no family left. And I think she looked sad. Of course, she always looked sad, so I don't know.

How am I supposed to deal with this information? One thing is for sure, I can't do this to someone I'm related to. I can't steal from him. Not that I can steal from anyone.

The click of the door handle behind me interrupts my thoughts. Jack slams the door and drops into the chair next to me. His eyes are blazing. "Do you still want to leave?" he asks. "With me, I mean?"

Whoa. Something happened. "Yes, definitely."

He nods shortly. "Fine."

What? "Wait, are you serious?" My heart does ten leaps over the moon. "Where would we go?"

He shrugs. "Doesn't matter. We'll figure it out. I just need to get enough money without drawing attention. Here," he says, nodding at the open file. "I'll handle that for you."

My heart falls from the moon like lead. He wants to handle this account? My grandfather's account? I know I can't do it. Can I even let him?

"No." I nod at the image of my mother with her parents. He stares as I point to the caption: *Carlton Brownlow, pictured with wife Olivia and daughter Agnes.*

I lift the locket up on my fingers. "Agnes was my mother's name."

A shadow seems to cross his eyes as he stares at the picture.

"It's my grandfather," I supply quietly.

He closes his eyes for a long moment, then opens them to stare again at the picture on the screen. "Your eyes are just like your mother's." His voice is hoarse, barely recognizable.

"I know," I say, staring at the wide brown eyes that crinkle slightly with her grin. "It's weird to see her looking all happy in this picture. I don't remember her as happy."

"How come you never knew he was alive?"

"My mother's last name was different. She must've changed it from Brownlow to Westfield, her mother's last name, when she left. I never found anything on her the few times I looked."

Actually, I never really spent much time looking up my mother, except for a quick search for her name, which provided no results. If I had spent time looking for her, maybe I would've found this. Maybe if I had even looked up myself, I would've discovered my grandmother. The thought is a little disturbing.

Jack looks at me intently. "What are you going to do now?"

"Nothing, I guess. But I'd rather not work this account. Please don't tell anyone."

"Don't you want to meet him, though?"

I shake my head firmly. "No. He's never been in my life, and I don't need him now."

Jack nods, frowning at the monitor.

"So, what did Nancy want?"

He doesn't say anything right away, lost in thought as he considers the picture of my grandfather. It makes me wonder if any of the kids here ever found family members this way or if I'm the first.

"Jack?"

He sighs. "Nothing. Just stuff about some accounts."

• • •

What are the odds?

The minutes blur as I shuffle through marriage records of Carlton Preston Brownlow III and Olivia Margaret Westfield, then the funeral announcement of Mrs. Olivia Westfield Brownlow, survived by her loving husband and teenage daughter—my mother.

I sort through the files I printed off the Internet, spreading them over my bed. I barely recognize this happy girl from the tired, sad woman who trudged through streets and shelters with me.

Someone taps on the door. I quickly gather the papers into a stack and shove them under my pillow. "Come in," I say.

It's Nancy. "I just wanted to check to see how you're doing," she says, sitting in my desk chair to face me.

"I'm fine," I say nervously. I wonder if she normally meets with new kids or if she has another agenda. Or if this has something to do with Jack running with me. I don't know if he said anything to her, but mostly, I hope he didn't mention my grandfather.

"That's good. You know, we're all glad you're here. Sam and Z think so highly of you, and you're a wonderful addition to our family."

I don't know what to say to this, but I try to smile. To me, this translates to, *You're going to be a wonderful thief.*

Nancy continues. "I know you're wondering why I'm here. The meeting with Bill must have made you a little uncomfortable."

A little?

She clears her throat. "You know, he's very careful about who lives here, for obvious reasons. He doesn't know you yet, so he is a little rough around the edges until you get to know him better."

She pauses, maybe to wait for my response, but what can I say? Bill scares the crap out of me. I can't imagine being comfortable with him. Plus, there's the way even Jack reacts when someone mentions Bill's name.

"What are you thinking?" Nancy asks. Her voice is pleasant enough, but her smile is tight.

"Just…um…Bill was kind of intense."

Nancy laughs. "Yes, he can be. Everyone finds Bill intimidating when they first meet him. But you know, he's responsible for all of this." She waves a hand around. "Did you know it was his idea to take kids in from the streets in the first place?"

I shake my head.

"Well, it's true. I know it's hard to see his good intentions under his tough exterior, but he's not that bad. He got me out of a tough situation." Her voice trails off and she looks down for a moment, making me wonder if *she* sometimes has a hard time seeing his good intentions. Or maybe she thinks she owes him something for getting her out of that "tough situation." She clears her voice. "And yes, as Z has explained to you, we use this house as a business operation. We're hackers. But only for the purpose of making our lives better, especially the lives of those kids who might otherwise be living on the street."

I stare down at my hands. I don't see how she can convince me that Monroe Street is anything more than a way to make easy money.

"There's more to this place than you know," she says softly, as if she can read my thoughts. "Like Micah. He was on his way to a boot camp with a very bad reputation when we discovered him. He'd been messing around with the computer files at his old school, screwing with the school's budget. They expelled him, of course, and his so-called adoptive parents decided to send him away, saying they couldn't put up with him any longer. We rescued him right before they sent him off. They were all too happy to give him up."

She steeples her fingers together and touches them to her lips. "He's one of the most intelligent, funny kids you'll ever meet. But if he had gone to that camp...can you imagine? And then, of course, there are even younger kids like Dutch who just fall through the cracks of the system after enduring terrible physical and emotional abuse. Trust me, Olivia, if it weren't for this home, these kids would be so much worse off, if even alive."

The thought of anyone abusing little Dutch—who clings to Jack as if he's his big brother—tugs at my heart. "I know. You've done a lot for these kids. And I'm really lucky that you took me in, too." I *am* grateful, even if I'm not sticking around.

She nods. "I'm glad you appreciate it. Just remember, it takes hard work to keep this place going. Everyone does his or her fair share, Z included. Without him, this place would fall apart. And if that happened, all these kids would end up back in the system. I'm sure you can imagine how traumatic that would be."

I go cold inside, thinking of Derrick. Yes, I can certainly imagine that.

Nancy stands up. "Just remember, we're all here for one another, just as a family should be. If you ever need help with these accounts, don't hesitate to ask."

"Thanks, Nancy."

After she leaves, I fall back on the bed, throwing my arm over my eyes. What the hell? This place depends that much on Jack? After being here even a little bit, I can kind of see that.

So what am I supposed to do now?

CHAPTER TWENTY-ONE

"'I am chained to my old life. I loathe and hate it now, but I cannot leave it. I must have gone too far to turn back—and yet I don't know.'"

—Charles Dickens, *Oliver Twist*

JACK

While the rest of the house is sleeping, I'm glued to the computer monitor, my stomach churning. For the hundredth time, I zoom in on the familiar gold heart-shaped locket the woman in the photograph is wearing. And her daughter—the same large brown eyes, same serious expression as Liv. I was right—she has her mother's eyes.

You switched the file on purpose. You gave it to her, hoping she'd figure it out, I have to remind myself. I want a better life for her. Carlton Brownlow is rich enough to afford the finest universities. He could help get her into any Ivy League school she wants. She deserves that. If we ran, we would always be running.

So why am I so upset?

I wish I'd never seen this file.

Do the right thing, Jack. For once.

My heart sinking, I dial the private number for Carlton Preston Brownlow III.

Liv stares at me, her burger untouched. It was easy enough to get her to think we were just stopping at a café in this little town on our way out of Richmond. I shove my sweating, trembling hands under my legs. She doesn't need to know how sick to my stomach I am right now at having to tell her the news this way.

"What do you mean, my grandfather's coming?" she asks.

The waitress brings our check and places it next to me, but I don't take my eyes off Liv. "He'll be here soon. He lives in the next town, outside Norfolk." The town that is two hours from Monroe Street. From Bill.

From me.

The tears begin to roll down her cheek. "Wait, why are you saying this? What happened to our plans?"

"You belong with him. He's your family."

"I don't have any family. Just you."

Her words tempt me to drop this whole plan, but I only shake my head. "You deserve so much more than a life with someone like me—a criminal."

"No, Jack, that's not—"

"Yes, it *is* true. Think about it. You want college. I want the easy life. It's not going to work. And he'll be here soon…"

She jumps to her feet and storms out of the café.

I open my wallet and toss some bills down on the table before heading out to follow her. I make my way across the street to the park, where Liv is staring at the lake, her long dark hair whipping about in the wind.

She doesn't turn when I approach her. "That's why you wanted to take Sam's car instead of your bike, isn't it?" she asks. "To bring my stuff here. I should've known. You never planned to run away with me."

Her voice is so bitter. I'm just another person in her life who's let her down. Hopefully for the last time.

"If you ran away with me, we'd always be running. Always. If you stayed with me at Monroe Street, you'd become a thief, just like the rest of us. That's not in you."

She doesn't say anything.

"Liv, talk to me."

She doesn't move, though I can see her hands shaking. "About what? How you're dumping me with some stranger? I told you—I don't have any family. I don't *need* any family."

"I'm not dumping you."

She whips around. "Bullshit. You still think I can't fit into your life, don't you?"

"Look, I'm doing this for…" I break off as my eye catches a long black Mercedes sedan pull up to the curb next to the café. A man in a black suit and cap gets out to open the back door.

"Don't you dare say you're doing this for me," she says, her voice loud but shaky. "What are you, my father? If you care for me at all, you'll run away with me. But that's it, isn't it? You don't want to leave Monroe Street."

She almost spits the last words out. Damn it, she's so stubborn. But now it's clear what I have to do.

A tall, elderly businessman steps out of the back of the Mercedes, buttoning his suit coat and speaking with his driver. They are looking at the café. My eyes move back to Liv's teary ones. At that moment, I take every happy memory I've had in my life—all spent with her—and shove them down. Deep, deep down inside of me where they won't interfere. I harden my eyes, my posture.

My heart.

I tuck my thumbs into my jeans, assuming that cocky look I'm most familiar with. "You're right. I don't want to run away with you. My life is at Monroe Street. You don't fit in there."

She tilts her head, her eyes narrowing slightly. "Wait a second, this doesn't sound like you at all, Jack." She reaches for me, dropping her hand when I step out of reach. I can't let her touch me, or I'll fall apart.

"Nancy and I agreed. We can't take the chance that you wouldn't follow through. Bill would eat you alive if he saw you hesitate even a little."

"But…"

I cross my arms and release an exasperated breath. "Look, I like you a lot. You already know that. But I also like being a thief. You don't. And your grandfather *wants* you. Do you know how many of us would give anything to have a family member actually want us?"

Her eyes soften and I silently curse myself. I slipped there. I didn't mean to bring up my own history—it weakens me. I look back at the Mercedes. I'm not lying; she is lucky. "You know how important this is to me. You have an easy way out that anyone would take. So this is it, okay? You have your family and I have mine."

"So that's it? That's all?" She shakes her head. "I'm sorry, but I just don't believe you."

I keep the hard exterior while my insides evaporate into nothing. "Monroe Street's my family, my life. Knowing that it's not yours is what makes me a good recruiter. And whether you believe it or not, a good friend."

She believes me now. I can see the hardening in her eyes when I said *recruiter*. *Why would you believe this, Liv?* But I'm relieved. It's the right thing; I know it. Doesn't matter if it makes me feel like absolute shit.

She swipes her hand across her eyes to brush away the tears and straightens her shoulders. "Fine. Get my bags. I don't want to see you ever again, *Z*."

I wince as she turns abruptly to walk toward the Camaro. I follow her, wondering what I'm supposed to say or do now. I don't want it to end like this.

I open the trunk and Liv grabs her suitcase, shrugging off any help from me. She starts toward the café, then turns back to me, dropping the bag. She removes the bracelet and throws it at me so hard I barely catch it.

"You'll want this back to give to the next sucker," she says. "I'm sure the story about it being your mother's is just one more lie you told to screw with me."

She picks up her bag and walks toward the car. Her grandfather and his driver are staring at us now. Liv's steps slow as she approaches them. I catch up and walk next to her. I want to check out this guy again for myself before I abandon her.

His liquid gray eyes are fixed on Liv's face. "Carlton Brownlow, this is your granddaughter, Olivia Westfield," I say quietly.

"Olivia Westfield," the old man says, his voice hardly rising above a whisper. "Your grandmother's name. You look like her, like your mother."

His eyes drop to her neck, his Adam's apple bobbing as he swallows. "May I?" he asks.

Liv drops her bag and unlatches the locket from around her neck, handing it to him. He opens the clasp and draws a quick breath, his eyes filling with tears. "Agnes."

He pulls a worn photograph out of his wallet and unfolds it. It's the same picture of her mother that's in the locket. Liv glances once at me, her eyes filled with tears. I can't even force myself to look away.

Brownlow returns the locket. "Olivia, I know you have a lot of questions about why Aggie…why your mother left. I have a lot of questions about what happened to her. When she ran away almost eighteen years ago with her boyfriend…" He trails off, wiping his brow with a handkerchief.

Liv's face pales. *Oh, shit, don't make this sound like her fault.*

He folds the handkerchief into his pocket, sighing. "I'm sorry. She swore I'd never hear from her again. I looked everywhere for her. I didn't know anything, not even that she was pregnant. My wife had just died…" He clears his throat and smiles. "You were named after my wife. I think—I hope— Aggie planned for us to find each other."

Liv doesn't say anything. Maybe she's still in shock. Maybe I should've told her first thing this morning. Or yesterday, when I made up my mind.

"Thank you, Jack," Brownlow says, turning to me. But my eyes are fixed on Liv, who's staring at me now. I gave Brownlow my real first name hoping she'd realize I still care about her. Her attention moves back to her grandfather. I don't think it makes much of a difference to her. Not now.

"I'm in your debt for bringing Olivia home," Brownlow continues. "I've started the process to change her last name, as you asked. And if there's anything I can ever do for you—"

"Yes, there is," I interrupt. "Forget you ever saw me. Forget everything you think you know about me."

I intend the last as a warning to both of them. It's probably a little dramatic, but I'm pretty much past caring. I can't have him looking for Monroe Street. My eyes are starting to burn, and I know I need to go now or I'll lose it. I turn to walk back to the Camaro, stopping for a moment when I pass her. She doesn't look at me.

"Bye, Liv." I barely manage the words without choking on them.

My feet carry me forward, my chest constricting so much I can't breathe. I'm straining to move against a rubber band that wants to snap me back to her. I want to turn around, to say the words I was always too afraid to say. I want to grab her hand and run, getting us the hell away from everything and everyone.

I almost do it.

Instead, I slide into the driver's seat of the Camaro and watch as Liv gets into the car with her grandfather. She won't ever think of me without hate. The realization makes me sick.

As the Mercedes pulls away with my heart inside, I rest my head on the steering wheel. For the first time since my mother died, I allow myself to cry.

. . .

LIV

The car is too quiet. Maybe the fancier the car, the more it blocks out sound. It sucks that probably for the first time in my life, silence bothers me, allows me to dwell on Jack's words and go over and over our conversation until I feel like screaming.

This man who is my grandfather tries to start a conversation, but I can't talk to him. The only one I could talk to isn't here and never will be. All I can do is stare out the window, forehead pressed against the cool glass, willing myself not to cry.

I don't understand what happened. Jack seemed eager to leave town with me, telling me he couldn't care less about the life he was leaving behind. Said the kids at Monroe Street would be fine with Nancy and Bill. Said they didn't need him at all.

He lied to me.

I want to punch something or someone. I can't exactly hit the gentle old man next to me, so I just pinch my hands in my lap. I'm sure I've drawn blood by now. How could Jack do that to me? I know he was falling for me. Or I thought he was, anyway.

That's why he's a good recruiter. Jen was right. I couldn't do the job, so he got rid of me.

I know he'll be back at school in the fall, preying on some innocent girl, getting her to fall for him and then dumping her once he gets her to Monroe Street. Just like Jen. Maggie. Me. The list goes on.

I hate him. More than I ever despised Derrick or Bernadette or anyone else in my life who hurt me. Jack crept all the way into my heart and then smashed it.

Carlton Brownlow clears his throat. "The school is the same your mother went to. It's private, one of the best in the country. What do you like to study?"

What do I like to study? Computer programming. I swallow hard and say "English lit" instead. My voice sounds weird, squeaky.

He starts talking about how he minored in English lit in college, but I don't hear most of what he says. My eyes are now drawn to the neighborhood we're driving through. Massive houses are set back from the road with long driveways and almost unnaturally green lawns, some with fountains, all with wrought iron gates.

The car slows and turns into the driveway of the last home. It is closer to the street than the other homes, flanked by huge oak trees.

"Olivia?" the old man says kindly. "This is my home. Your home."

This is my new home? When the car stops, I stay frozen to the seat for a moment. I thought Bernadette and Marc's house was huge. I thought Monroe Street was like a castle. But this obscene display of wealth can't be real.

The driver opens my door as I take in the hulking mansion. The pristine white columns stretch up three stories. It's like one of those pictures of the old Southern plantation homes in the history books, minus the horse and carriage.

"You live by yourself?" I ask.

He laughs. "Well, sort of. There's a wing in the house for the servants."

Servants? Who calls people servants? I guess old men with a buttload of money can call people whatever they want.

The driver takes my suitcase from the trunk and smiles at me. "Olivia, this is James."

Oh, well, of course he'd have a chauffeur named James. I'm convinced now that I'm in a really weird dream. Maybe Jack will be there when I wake up...

I follow James and the man who is my grandfather into the house. I'm prepared for a huge entryway, so I'm not completely shocked by the extravagant foyer.

I am, however, blown away by the grand marble staircase leading up to the next floor, then the one that climbs above it. I feel so insignificant in this massive house. If I lived here, I'd go insane.

Of course, I do live here now, so maybe I will go crazy.

A short, round woman appears from nowhere, her plump face one big smile. "Olivia," she says in a surprisingly deep voice. "I'm so happy you're here."

"This is Mrs. Bedwin, our housekeeper. She's been with our family for a very long time," Carlton Brownlow says.

Mrs. Bedwin wraps her arms around my shoulders in a big hug. I'm too surprised by her familiarity to pull away. She is warm and friendly and smells of rosemary and cinnamon. Okay, I'll go with it, since I'm dreaming anyway.

"Oh, she looks just like her mother did at that age," Mrs. Bedwin says to the old man. He nods.

"I wouldn't know," I mutter, but no one seems to hear me.

Mrs. Bedwin takes my bag from James and offers to show me to my room. I follow her up the wide staircase, as out of place as Alice in Wonderland.

Down a long hallway, she stops at the fourth door and turns the handle. "This is your room. I didn't have much time, so it's a little plain, but I thought you and I could sit down to look at paint and fabric to come up with something that is more you." She pushes the door open.

The room is about three times the size of my room at Bernadette's. In fact, it's about the size of some of the foster homes I've stayed in. I walk over to the four-poster bed and sit on the flowery comforter, taking in the mauve walls and floral print on the settee. Not my taste, but if I were to decorate according to how I feel right now, the room would be painted black.

Mrs. Bedwin is watching me closely, so I say, "Thank you. It's really nice." It's like déjà vu. I just did this a few short months ago at the Carters'. And again at Monroe Street.

Just another house, another place to sleep for as long as it lasts.

Mrs. Bedwin smiles and points to a door behind me. "Your bathroom connects to this room. Like I said, feel free to make this as comfortable as you'd like. It's been a while since I've had teens around, so I don't know what your tastes are. Paint it black, if you want."

She grins. Maybe she reads minds. That would make as much sense as everything else. "Thank you," is all I say again.

When Mrs. Bedwin leaves me to "get comfortable," I approach a set of French double doors on the other side of the room's sitting area. I turn the latch and pull the doors open to a balcony. A light breeze sweeps across my face as I walk to the railing and cross my arms over it, peering down. It looks onto the quiet street, semi-blocked by one of the huge oak trees. It's so peaceful here. It's perfect within the surreal confines of this dream.

But when the dream ends and I wake up, what will I have?

Not Jack.

Not love.

Just myself and the longing for something that no longer exists.

CHAPTER TWENTY-TWO

"The regret of no recent separation was fresh in his mind; the absence of no loved and well-remembered face sank heavily into his heart."

–Charles Dickens, *Oliver Twist*

JACK

During the next weeks, I move around Monroe Street like a zombie, not saying much to anyone. The times I don't spend working, I'm on my Ducati, trying to steer clear of the rest of my family. I can't take their sympathetic looks, their ridiculous attempts to cheer me up. Most of them think Liv ran. They have no idea I chased her away. Sam knows what really happened and makes several attempts to draw me out, to talk to me, but I ignore her, too.

A light tapping sounds at my door. I ignore it, knowing that whoever it is will eventually give up and go away like every other time.

"Z, open up," Nancy's voice calls, startling me. She never visits me here. "You can't stay in there forever."

I hear several clicking noises, then the door opens. I forget how good she is at opening locked doors. I swivel my chair around to face the window, laptop across my legs. The hot summer sun streams through the panes, baking my face. I don't care.

Nancy places a hand on my shoulder. "She's gone. It's what you wanted, what you needed to do. I know you miss her, but this has gone on long enough. Talk to me."

I remain still, withdrawn. "Jack," she finally says softly, touching my cheek gently. "Don't do this to yourself."

I don't know if it's the motherly touch or that she used my name for the first time in seven years, but I lean into her and let her stroke my hair as if I'm a small child. It's a feeling that's surprisingly more comforting than annoying.

"I made a mistake, letting her go," I manage to say, my voice cracking from disuse.

"You didn't, and you know you didn't. Liv doesn't belong here. She has family," Nancy says. I had told her about Liv's grandfather when I returned. And she helped me cover with Bill. "She should be safe. Bill doesn't know who she is. He believes she just ran away."

I know this, but I can't stop hating myself for letting her go.

"Come on," she says. "You look like hell. You need to take a shower and shave. And eat something. You're getting skinny."

I wait until she's left the room before I go into my bathroom and look at my reflection. She's right; I do look like hell. I run my hand along the whiskers on my cheeks and chin. Maybe I should switch to the grunge look. Fits my grunge feelings at the moment. I shake my head and start the shower.

Downstairs, the warm aroma of bacon and eggs is inviting for someone who's avoided eating much for so long. At the table, everyone except Nancy looks surprised at my sudden, and maybe clean, appearance. Not that I care what they think. I slouch in one of the chairs and Jen immediately sits next to me. Her hand is on my knee, slowly moving upward under my shorts. *Why not,* I think to myself, eyeing the deep line of cleavage beneath her tank as she leans over to get the salt. *It'd be easy, no strings attached.*

Why not? Because I'm not interested.

I push her hand away and move to the other side of the table, ignoring the daggers her eyes are casting my way. I have no idea why she still wants me, considering the way I treated her.

After breakfast, Sam corners me as I head toward my bike. She looks around to make sure no one is listening, then asks, "How is she?" in a low voice.

"I don't know. I haven't talked to her since she left."

Sam's eyebrows lift in surprise. "You haven't even texted to see how she's doing?"

"Have you?"

"No. Nancy asked me not to. But come on, I'm sure you've peeked in on her or something."

I run my fingers through my hair. She's so nosy. But then, Sam really did like Liv, even if she never approved of our relationship. At least she's stopped being angry that I let Liv go. "Yeah, I checked on her once. She's fine."

The one day I went to see her, I sat for a long time on my bike beneath the cover of a large oak across from the house. She was reading on her balcony, twisting her soft brown hair over one shoulder, as she tended to do when she was deep in thought. I watched her for almost an hour, feeling like a stalker. I knew it would only make things worse, but I didn't care. I just couldn't bring myself to call to her.

Sam sighs. "I'm glad she's okay." She cocks her head to one side. "Are *you*?"

"Yeah, I'm fine."

She nods, but I know she doesn't believe me. It's strange, but I get the feeling she misses me. Still, she drops it and lets me leave.

I get on my bike and ride around aimlessly for a while, almost surprised when I find myself at the river. I park and follow the path to the waterfall, stripping off my clothes and sinking into the cold, clear water. It's invigorating on my tired skin. I lie back in the water for a while, unable to clear my thoughts from the web of Liv. Her smile, her eyes, her kindness—everything haunts me. I've become useless— completely estranged from myself. And I can't stand it. It would have been better if I *had* used and dumped her.

I wish she'd never come into my life. I wish I'd never let Sam talk me into twisting her.

I wade out of the pool and pull my clothes on, not caring that I'm getting them wet. I've got to see her, if she's willing. I have to.

. . .

LIV

Three weeks and I still walk around in a fog, though mostly because I feel like a square peg in a round hole in this new life. Servants are always close at hand in case I need anything— new linens, lunch, even Starbucks lattes if I want. It's disconcerting to say the least. They're all polite and friendly, but they look at me like I'm some sad orphan from *Annie*. All except Mrs. Bedwin, who at least treats me like a member of the family, not whispering behind my back or tiptoeing around me like I might break.

My grandfather works most of the time, but we meet for lunch two days each week, more if he knows he'll be late for dinner. He says he can't stand the idea of me being alone all the time. He's tried taking me shopping, to a play, to dinners at his country club. He's tried introducing me to his friends' granddaughters, but even though they're polite, I haven't really made a connection with any of them.

He tries different conversation starters with me. I'm respectful enough to answer his questions about school and stuff, but I don't get into details about my past. I don't want or need to open up to anyone. Not now, and maybe not ever.

I admit that I'm growing to like him more, though. He's kind, the type of person who doesn't understand how people can hurt each other. I know my mother hurt him when she ran away, but he never says anything other than wonderful things about her.

"Aggie shut down when my Olivia died," my grandfather told me once. "That's when she stopped calling her friends, when she started associating with kids I didn't approve of. I made it pretty clear to her, especially about that one boy…"

He stopped short, flushing when he realized he was talking about my father. I didn't care. I didn't know my father, and since my mother ended up on the streets soon after she left, I'm guessing he sucked as a person. And I've kept the darkest side of his "sweet Aggie" from him. He doesn't need to know she was pimping herself out, that she died of an overdose right in the middle of the street with her own little girl watching.

Grandfather doesn't ask about my past, I'll give him that. He made a comment when I first moved in about believing in fresh starts.

I once believed that, too. If I had met him before Jack, it might've been very different.

Jack. I spend my evenings staring out into the distance from my balcony. Once I thought I saw him on his motorcycle. It was dark, though, and I couldn't be sure that it wasn't someone else. And even though my grandfather gave me a new cell phone, I keep the old one charged up. I don't have a clue as to why. It's not like Jack will ever call. It's not like I even want him to.

Mrs. Bedwin seems more understanding. She doesn't bug me except for general questions about my health and comfort. She did find out over dinner that my favorite foods were tacos and pasta with meatballs, and now they're on the weekly menu. Sometimes she tells me stories about my mother. The girl she describes sounds nothing at all like the sad, thin woman who never smiled.

I know my grandfather is disappointed that I haven't gone out of my way to fit in here, but I appreciate that he's trying to give me space. I can at least read in my room now without him hovering nearby like he did the first week, asking Mrs. Bedwin if I'm feeling okay. I could hear her through the door, telling him it'll just take time. I don't know about that. I guess I appreciate his effort, but a lifetime of shit can't be washed away with tacos and a few smiles.

A knock sounds at my door, and Mrs. Bedwin pops her head in. "Mr. Brownlow wants to know if you can meet him for lunch today," she says.

"I guess," I say without enthusiasm, my eyes returning to *Sense and Sensibility*. I've read this book twice already, but it's an easy escape without having to think.

Mrs. Bedwin sits next to me on the bed and smooths my hair over my shoulder. "You can't shut him out forever, you know," she says. "He loves you. He wants to get to know you."

She gently removes the book from my hands and folds it over on the bed. "Olivia, your grandfather is trying. He just needs a little help from you. I'm afraid I insist."

I gape at this usually quiet, unassuming woman. "You insist?"

She smiles, but her smile is of steel. "Yes. I don't like to see him sad. So you will go to lunch, you'll talk with him about something. Anything. Sports, music, art, theater, books, whatever you want. But you will talk."

I groan and bury my head in my blanket, but she's unmoved. "James will be ready in thirty minutes." She strokes my hair again. "I'm not going to pretend to know what you're going through," she says. "But I watched your mother spiral down into the black pit of depression before she left. I can't watch you do the same. Especially not at your age."

She stands up. "Your grandfather loves you, Olivia. All he wants in return is for you to start living your life."

She leaves, closing the door behind her. I hug my pillow close. Start living my life—a lifestyle of legitimate wealth and privilege—without Jack. Just like I'm sure he's doing without me.

I walk over to my dresser and stare at the cell Nancy gave me. It's plugged into the charger as always, with no incoming calls or text notifications. I unplug it and drop it into my top dresser drawer. I don't intend on recharging it again.

. . .

Lunches with my grandfather usually happen at stuffy cafés near his office. I've picked through my fair share of salads and am practically a connoisseur of cucumber sandwiches and salad dressings.

But today, James drops me off at a hole-in-the-wall Mexican restaurant, several streets away from his office in a shopping district. At first I question him, sure he's got the wrong place, but he says, "No, ma'am, this is where Mr. Brownlow said to meet you."

My grandfather is sitting on the bench just inside the door, reading a paper and looking completely out of place in his business suit and tie. Other patrons are wearing shorts and T-shirts.

"Ah, Olivia," he says, smiling and standing. "We're ready," he says to the hostess, who escorts us to a small wobbly table near the window.

"Well, this is different," I say, smiling slightly at the sight of the old man trying to look dignified as he slides into the red vinyl seat of the booth.

He laughs. "I wanted to find a place you'd enjoy. I think you've had enough of the business lunch spots, huh?"

I shrug. "I don't know, I was getting used to cucumber and dill sandwiches."

"Hey! I remember you ordering a hamburger or two, never a cucumber sandwich." He winks and I laugh. His eyes brighten at my response. I guess laughing isn't too hard to do if it makes him this happy.

The server approaches and takes our order. I ask for beef tacos and watch as my grandfather tries to make his way through a menu full of MSG. "They do have a salad," I tell him, pointing to the extremely short section in the menu. He orders a salad from the server.

We sit in silence, fingers fiddling with sugar packets and chips while the mariachi band plays in the background. He's made so many efforts before to draw me out that I get the feeling he's giving up trying. Maybe he's waiting for me. Mrs. Bedwin asked me to try harder.

"So I was thinking of going shopping for some clothes for school after lunch."

The words are out of my mouth before I even have a chance to think about it.

He looks up in surprise. "School is still another couple months away, right?"

"Yes, but I thought I'd get started on it."

He grins. "Let me give you my credit card." He reaches into his suit jacket for his wallet.

"You already did, last week," I remind him. The credit card he gave me sits idle in my purse.

"Oh. Perfect, then. Charge as much as you want. No limits, just have fun. Do you want to call Lisbeth or Elanor to go with you?"

"No, that's okay. I like to shop alone." Which is in itself a lie. I don't like to shop at all. I think back to the theft at the mall with Sam—it seems like years instead of months ago. Still, I like the idea of walking around without everyone watching me.

"Well, I'm just glad you're getting out. James will go with you."

"No, that's okay. I'll just get a cab to go home."

His brows knit. "Oh. Well, I don't know." He's such a

contradiction—wanting me to get out but worrying about everything. I wouldn't be surprised if he showed up at home tonight with a can of mace for me to take on future shopping trips. At the same time, his concern touches me.

I smile brightly. Smiling never fails to soften him. "Please, stop worrying. I'll grab a cab. It'll be fine."

He sighs. "Okay, go off shopping. Have fun. But promise me that you'll call James to pick you up if you need. Or call me. I'm never too busy for you."

I smile again, this time for real. He really is a kind man, someone I can see growing closer to over time. "Thanks, Grandfather." I use the name on purpose, since most of the time I don't refer to him by any name at all. It's a little awkward, I guess, but I can't picture calling this refined man "Grandpa." And he frowned the one time I called him Mr. Brownlow. It made me sad to see his reaction. I might not be comfortable with this situation yet, but I don't want to hurt his feelings. So "Grandfather" it is.

He grins and dives into his salad. It's not that hard after all, making him happy. Maybe eventually I'll be able to figure out how to make myself happy.

After lunch, he walks with me out of the café. "You sure you don't need James to drive you around?"

"Definitely. I'm good."

"Okay, well…" He stands there, looking awkward. I wonder if he's trying to decide whether or not he should give me a hug. I back away, waving slightly. "I'll see you tonight."

"This afternoon," he corrects. "But if you want to get together with Lisbeth or someone, just call and let me know."

"Okay. I'll see you later."

I turn to walk down the street and into a store a few doors

down, just to show that I'm interested in shopping in case he's still watching me. A large gold sign on the wall has one letter: M. Crap. I shouldn't be in here—I still feel so guilty about stealing that shirt from the other M—but maybe I should make up for it by buying a bunch of clothes now.

I'm randomly pulling out tops to decide if I want to try something on when I feel a light tap on my shoulder. "Liv?"

I turn, shocked to find one of the last people I'd expect to see. "Nancy! What are you doing here?"

She seems nervous, wringing her hands and looking around. For a split second, I wonder if she's shoplifting, but I push that thought from my mind. "Is everything okay?"

"Yes, yes. Sure. But…can you come outside with me for a few? I need to talk to you," she says.

"Um, yeah, sure." I slide the shirts I'm holding back onto the rack and follow her out the door. Her hair is pulled into a ponytail. I don't think I've ever seen it up that way before.

She turns back to me, and in the sunlight, I notice a red mark around one side of her neck. "Nancy, what happened to you?" *Let me guess—Bill.*

She pulls her ponytail around to cover it. "Oh, it's nothing. But I'm so glad I ran into you, Liv. I need your help."

"What's going on?"

Her eyes fill as she stares at me, but she doesn't say anything.

"Nancy!" My heart is suddenly lead. "Is Z okay?"

She shakes her head. "He's in trouble, Liv. Bad trouble. He needs you."

All the motion around me slows to a crawl. Nancy is a mile away from me, and I can't move. *Jack is in trouble?* "Why? What happened?" I grab her arm when she doesn't respond.

"Nancy! What happened?"

She's trembling now, her eyes wide. "His depression after you left got so bad that he wouldn't eat. Now he's sick. Really sick. You can come with me, right?"

I nod. Jack is sick—I don't care what happened before, all I know is that I need to be with him.

Her smile is a little unsteady as the tears slip from her eyes. "You're such a good kid, Liv."

"It's okay. I'll come with you. He'll get better." She doesn't move until I start forward. She walks alongside of me, staring at the sidewalk. She is so distracted, so different from the Nancy I knew before. But then, Jack is like a son to her.

"Where are you parked?" I ask.

"A couple of blocks down."

I walk faster and she keeps pace with me, though her speed seems dependent on mine. I glance at her. "Everything else okay?"

She nods but doesn't say anything. And that horrible Bill probably tried to choke her. I hope she figures out a way to be done with him once and for all.

We reach a cross street and she points to the right. We walk into a deserted alley, but halfway to the next street she grabs my arm, pulling me around to face her. "I'm so sorry, Liv."

"It's okay." She looks so upset now that it's starting to freak me out. "Where's the car?"

"It's right here, hon," a man's deep voice rumbles from behind me. A hand is clasped around my mouth and I'm pulled backward, unable to get my footing. I try to open my mouth, to bite his hand, but something is shoved over my nose, something sweet, and my arms and legs start tingling. My body goes slack as the world melts around me.

The last thing I see is Nancy's sorrowful face as she whispers, "I'm sorry."

CHAPTER TWENTY-THREE

> "'Well,' said the robber, grasping Oliver's wrist, and putting the barrel so close to his temple that they touched; at which moment the boy could not repress a start; 'if you speak a word when you're out o'doors with me, except when I speak to you, that loading will be in your head without notice. So, if you do make up your mind to speak without leave, say your prayers first.'"
>
> —Charles Dickens, *Oliver Twist*

JACK

I sit on my bike, trying to make sense of why the long black car is in the driveway. It's not Bill's day to be here, so why is he? It's not a good sign. I consider for a moment riding away as fast as I can. I have a sickening feeling he's here to see me, though, so it's best to give him whatever it is he wants and get him out rather than having him wait around for me to show up. He causes trouble if made to wait for long.

In the house, Micah, Jen, Dutch, and the rest of the kids are standing together, talking in low voices. The conversation breaks off immediately when they see me. Dutch's wide eyes tell me what I feared: Bill's waiting for me. I make eye contact with Sam, who looks more serious than I've ever seen her. Even scared. She shakes her head, but I turn away from her. Might as well get this over with. I square my shoulders and march to the office. The only thing I can hope is that he doesn't know where I sent Liv. I open the door and freeze, my heart almost stopping when I see the unexpected guest seated on the sofa. What the… *Shit!*

Liv's terrified eyes twitch from me to Bill and back again. I stare at her for a moment, unmoving, my body stiff with fear. My fingernails bite into my palms.

Bill is calmly seated across from her, holding a handgun in his lap, and Nancy is in the corner, holding her side with one hand, one of her eyes puffy and purplish red. Her lip is cut, and a mottled yellow-and-gray mark the size of a fist is forming on her cheek. Liv doesn't seem harmed—yet. *Shit. Shit. Shit.*

My stomach flips, but I keep my face as smooth as I can, breathing deeply and slowly so I don't look as panicked as I feel.

"Come on in, Z, and look who we found wandering around the streets with her newfound family." Bill's voice is quiet, a warning sign in itself. I step inside and pull the door shut. He stands to face me, his icy eyes burning into mine. I have never been more scared shitless than I am right now.

"So, aren't you glad to have your girlfriend back? I figured you would be, seeing as how she ran away. Or, wait, what was the real story, Nancy?" A sob escapes her but he doesn't turn. "He helped her find her dear grandpa, right? And you covered for them."

"What are you going to do?" I ask, keeping my voice steady.

He laughs darkly. "Do? Well, you're the genius here. What do you think? Come on, Z, tell me. She's got a rich grandpa who just happens to be a big-time investment fund manager. Who just *happens* to be the target you were supposed to be handling for me."

Bill stands and walks toward me, casual and relaxed. I force myself not to step back. "I wondered why you dropped that case so fast. This *uncrackable* account, right? Maybe you should've covered your tracks on your research instead of letting me find out exactly what you were up to." He tsks, waving a finger at me. "You're slipping, Z. Shows me that you've lost your focus. I'll help you find it again."

The back of his hand smashes against my jaw like fire exploding across my face. I fall against the door, the pain reverberating through my body. Liv cries out and starts to run to my side, but I shake my head. Bill wraps his hand around my throat and holds me against the door, his fingers pressing in to cut off my air. I grab at his arm but he's too strong.

"Bill, please," Nancy pleads.

"Shut up. Now, here's what we're going to do, Z. You and this pretty young lady are going to help me crack the old man's account. According to your girlfriend here, he checks his account every night. She's going to be *very* helpful to us in installing some special software on his computer. If not…" Bill's hand squeezes tighter. My arms and legs tremble as my vision blurs and little specks of black float in front of me.

"Bill, stop it!" Nancy yells, running over to yank on his arm. He shoves her away but releases me. I fall to my knees, my head pressing against the floor as I struggle to pull air into my lungs. Bill is saying something, I think, but my head is swimming and I can't focus on anything but oxygen and the blood pounding in my head.

There's the sound of a phone ringing, then Bill's voice

answering it. The pressure of Liv's arms around my shoulders. I finally sit back on my heels. Liv touches my tender jaw with a gentle finger. "Are you okay?"

I nod but don't say anything.

Bill finishes his call. "Let's go." He gestures to the door with his gun.

I put an arm around Liv's waist and walk with her toward the front of the house. The area is pin-drop still, everyone focused on us. I avoid looking at Dutch—I don't want to see the panic I'm sure is on his face. My gaze instead falls on Sam, whose angry eyes and bunched fists are clear indications that she wants to jump Bill. I narrow my gaze and shake my head slightly at her. This is not the time to lose control.

Bill's car is waiting for us. As we climb in and the driver pulls away, Bill keeps his eyes and barrel of the gun trained on us. My arm is fixed around Liv, my hand over hers. She's no longer shaking, but her body's tense. I want to talk to her, to reassure her and beg her forgiveness, but Bill's too close, watching us. Instead, I spend the time running through several scenarios in my head, trying to figure the best way out of this. Bill's smart, though. He'll catch us if we run, and then we're good as dead. I've never heard of him actually killing a kid but wouldn't put it past him at all.

"Give me your phone," he says to me when we get close to Liv's grandfather's house.

I reach into my pocket to hand over the cell, and he slips it into the interior of his jacket. I raise an eyebrow at Liv but she shakes her head. He took her phone, too. Of course.

When we arrive, Bill pulls a silver flash drive out of his jacket and hands it to Liv as the car slows. She takes it with her fingertips at the corner as if it's a germ-infested tissue.

"Now listen to me very carefully. Install the keylogger. Then back out, fast. Don't talk to anyone, don't leave any notes, don't make any calls. I have someone monitoring the lines. If there's even the slightest hint of a problem, the sound of a siren or anything, your boyfriend dies. Followed by you and your loving grandpa." He leans close to her. "And if this doesn't work, if I don't see the data tonight, or if there are any problems whatsoever, you're both dead."

He waves his revolver and she steps out of the car, her eyes catching mine before closing the door. There's no trace of fear there, only calm reserve. I know she's not the type to go down without a fight, but Bill isn't kidding around, and I know he'll kill me if there's any chance she calls the cops or runs away. I draw in a shaky breath and close my eyes to wait.

· · ·

LIV

My legs are so wobbly that I can't believe I actually made it inside the house. Mrs. Bedwin is walking from the kitchen, envelopes in her hand. She looks surprised to see me.

"Oh, Olivia. Your grandfather said you were going shopping. Do you need money to pay a cabbie?"

I force the corners of my mouth upward. "No, I caught a ride home with a friend instead."

Her quizzical eyes flick toward the window, as if trying to catch a view of my "friend." Of course, I don't have any friends, but I pray she believes I called one of the kids he's been trying to match me with.

"Um, he just dropped me off." Mrs. Bedwin's mouth puckers as she considers this. Damn it, I shouldn't have said "he."

"Okay," she says. "You might want to call your grandfather, though, just to let him know you made it home."

I exhale softly. "I will." I move past her quickly and up the stairs. When I look back over my shoulder, I'm relieved to see her flipping through the mail in her hands. Mrs. Bedwin has been nothing but kind since I've been here. There's no way I'm getting her involved with this.

In my grandfather's office, I boot up his personal computer and enter the password. It's easy enough—Aggie0225. My mother's nickname and birthday. It's strange how so many people choose family members or pets as passwords, though those can be the easiest to figure out. He's so weepy when he talks about my mother. It took me less than a minute to guess the password one day when I was bored and screwing around with it.

And he never knew she was pregnant with me. I wonder how different my life would've been if he'd known. I have no doubts that he wouldn't have stopped until he found us. His obvious love for my mother and his regret at her running away made me start thinking of him as my grandfather instead of just some old man I was related to.

But I never really let him get close to me. I wish I had now. I wish I hadn't pushed him away.

While the computer churns, I stare at the flash drive in my hands. I can't do this. I can't ruin my grandfather's life, let Bill have access to everything. I didn't want to do it when I hadn't even met him. How can I do it now?

I can just pretend to go along with this. Bill will never know. I can act like I installed the malware, and maybe it didn't run right or something. Maybe he never logs on and the passwords remain safe. Or maybe I can leave a note telling my grandfather not to use the computer.

There's no way. Bill will be expecting that. He won't let us go until he knows for sure that the spyware works. If my grandfather doesn't log on, he'll know I told. Then there's the question of whether he'll let us go at all, even if everything does work.

I place my palm on the handset of an antique-style phone. One call could alert the police.

One call and Jack will die.

His face flashes in my mind, and I swallow hard. I can't let that happen.

I shove the computer keyboard and fight the tears. There's no time for crying. *Damn it!* We're screwed either way, I know it. Why would Bill let us go, even if this works?

Think, Liv.

I stare at the welcome screen for Brownlow Inc. Bill will be able to see every page my grandfather goes to, every keystroke. But then, Bill doesn't know what his home screen is. I tap my cheek for a moment. I could have the landing page be a warning against hackers, or maybe information about keyloggers, but that would clue Bill in immediately. It'd have to be something that would alert my grandfather and not Bill. Something simple and clever, like when I redirected Jack's hits on that YouTube video.

I sit up. *So simple,* Jack had said. Now to come up with something that will get my grandfather's attention.

A couple days ago, I overheard a conversation between my grandfather and one of his associates about how the owner of a company called Keating Financial used to work for Brownlow Inc., and how they're planning to sue for using trade secrets.

My grandfather was so mad about it—I hadn't ever seen him that agitated.

I do a search for Keating Financial and assign it as my grandfather's home page. Then I redirect Brownlow Inc. to the same Keating Financial page. This should raise a red flag to him but not Bill.

I stick the flash drive in the USB port of the computer. As the file loads, I fiddle with the stack of Post-it notes on the desk. Writing a message—even a cryptic one—won't do any good; no one will know where I am. I don't even know where Bill's headed after this. Back to the home? To his place? Jack once told me that no one knew where he lived.

My eyes move to the phone again. If only I had my cell, then maybe I could generate a call at some point. It could be traced. But I gave my cell to Bill...

My cell! Bill has the phone that my grandfather gave me, but I have another—from when I first moved in to Monroe Street. *Please, oh please let it have a charge still on it.*

The software finishes loading and I remove the drive and shut down the computer. As fast as I can, I run down the hall to my room and yank open the top dresser drawer. The cell is sitting on top of my old school folders. I grab it and power it on. The battery indicator shows a low level, but at least it's yellow and not red. I breathe out. It's enough to get help. It's tempting to call the police right now, but I can't risk it—not with Jack on the other side of Bill's gun.

I slip the cell into the waistband of my shorts, where the outline is hidden under my shirt. I tiptoe down the stairs to avoid Mrs. Bedwin and quietly let myself out the front door, headed toward the black car and my uncertain fate.

CHAPTER TWENTY-FOUR

"And now, for the first time, Oliver, well-nigh mad with grief and terror, saw that housebreaking and robbery, if not murder, were the objects of the expedition."

—Charles Dickens, *Oliver Twist*

JACK

The fifteen minutes Liv was gone were the longest of my life. Bill kept the barrel of his gun pointed at me, never moving except to occasionally receive calls on his cell. My hands shook every time it rang, expecting to hear that Liv broke the rules, that she made a call, that she ran.

I wished she would run.

I start to breathe again when she walks back to the car and taps on the window. The doors unlock and she crawls in next to me, nodding once to Bill and handing the flash drive over. I clasp her shaking hand in mine, relieved that she doesn't pull away. Once we get back to Monroe Street, I can escape with her. I know it.

I watch the late afternoon sun drop as we head back west,

when the driver suddenly turns south. I sit up straight and stare at Bill. "Where are we going?"

Bill laughs shortly. "You didn't think I was just going to drop you off at home, did you? We're going to my office. I need to verify that it worked before letting you go."

My heart sinks. No one has ever seen Bill's office. There's a reason for that. Fear wraps its cold hand around me as I realize there's not going to be a return trip for us. I should've realized that the moment Bill found out we let Liv go, we were already dead. My brain starts working overtime to come up with something to get us out of this nightmare.

Liv is watching me. "What?" she whispers.

I shake my head and look out the window as we turn into an old, seedy neighborhood, stopping in front of an apartment building. Bill says something to the driver, who nods and tosses the keys to him. He waves his gun at us, not even bothering to hide it, and we step out of the car and walk ahead of him up the weed-choked walk to the entry. My eyes dart around, but there's not a single person in sight. In fact, it looks as though the neighborhood is abandoned. Probably why it suits him.

At Bill's direction, we climb the dirty, echoing stairwell to the fifth floor, emerging into a dark hallway that smells like wet soccer cleats left in the heat to mold. I can hear a TV playing through the walls and some guy shouting, and a woman yells back at him in another language. Bill unlocks the last door and motions us through. The smell of crisp computer equipment hits me before I even walk in, and now I can see why.

Bill types the number into the pad to disengage the alarm as my eyes take in the massive amount of computer equipment pushed up against the far wall, where a dining room would normally go. A black leather couch faces a television, but other than a computer chair and desk there is no other furniture in the room. This must be Bill's headquarters. I've heard he has multiple addresses. Why the hell would he keep this much expensive equipment in such a shitty neighborhood?

Bill gestures with his gun to a doorway just off the living room and we step inside a small, windowless bathroom. He flips the light on—"Keep your mouths shut"—before slamming the door. Liv's eyes stay focused on the door. I take her hand. She doesn't resist, but she doesn't meet my eyes, either.

My heart thuds slowly in my chest. "I'm sorry. I just wanted you to be safe. I know you hate me for getting you into this mess, and now everything's backfired." The regret eats into my stomach like acid. I've screwed everything up, again. Maybe for the last time.

She leans on me, her head against my chest. I wrap my arms around her, as tight as I can without hurting her. "I don't blame you," she says. "Not anymore." She pulls away and stares at the ceiling. "I guess it's too much to hope for a wide ventilation system that we can crawl through, huh?"

I laugh halfheartedly, but I glance up at the ceiling just in case. Other than the main door we just came through, there's nothing but a tiny air-conditioner vent in the room.

Liv moves closer to the toilet and lifts her shirt slightly. I turn around, my face heating up. If she has to go, I guess she has to go.

"Why'd you turn around?" she asks, her voice amused. I peer over my shoulder to see her standing, fully clothed. A cell phone is in her hand.

A cell phone! "Where'd you get that?"

Her grin deepens. "It's the one from Nancy. You gave it to me when I first got to your house, remember? I still had it in my room. Bill's pretty stupid not to realize there might be another cell in the house."

I laugh out loud, then clap my hand over my mouth. I move to Liv and grab her, kissing her hard. "You kick ass, you know that?" I whisper. I hold my hand out for the phone.

"What are you doing?" she asks, jerking it away.

"Calling Nancy. Why, who do you want to call?"

She looks at me like I've grown another head. "The police, obviously."

"What? No way. You call the police and they'll find Monroe Street."

"I don't give a damn about them finding Monroe Street," she says, her voice rising. "I don't want to *die*. Do you?"

"Liv, give me the—"

"You can call Nancy and warn her when I'm done. But I'm calling the police. Got it?"

Obviously she doesn't see the bigger picture here. They need to get the hell away from the house. I try to stay calm. "Nancy can get us out of this."

Her laugh is bitter. "You mean like how she handled Bill as he drugged me and dragged me back to your house? Or when he beat her up after he figured out how much she helped us? What makes you think she can handle this?"

I grit my teeth to control my irritation before saying, "Nancy could've handled it fine, but I'm sure her concern about the other kids in the house was pretty good persuasion." I grab again for the phone but she steps back.

"This is *my* phone. *I* will make the call. You figure out your own plan if you want. But I'm calling the police."

Bill's sudden and loud cursing cuts us off. I go to press the lock button in the handle while Liv taps furiously on the phone. The blood pounding in my ears, I can barely hear her giving her name and asking the police to trace the line. I run back to her as Bill tries the handle. She's whispering a description of the location. Bill bangs on the door, but we stay pressed against the far wall of the bathroom.

It is quiet for a moment, then a light scraping sound of metal on metal sounds from the door. Liv slips the phone into her pocket just as the lock clicks and Bill opens the door, a metal hanger in his hand. He throws the hanger into the tub, his eyes blazing.

"What happened to the account?" he yells, waving his gun at Liv's face.

"I...I don't know what you're talking about," she says. *Oh, shit, what did she do?*

"You alerted someone, didn't you?"

I hold my hands up. "Hang on a second, Bill. She didn't do anything. Something's just wrong with the system. Try it again."

He opens his mouth to speak, then lowers his eyes. "What the hell is that?" he asks, pointing at Liv's shorts.

"Nothing," she says, her voice shaking. She sucks at lying.

He holds the gun up to her face. "Don't make me ask again."

Liv dips a hand into her pocket and pulls out her cell. Bill's face is rage-purple. She drops it on the floor and kicks it away, toward him. He stoops to pick it up, never taking his eyes or the gun off us. He checks the display, his face paling, then presses a button on the top of the phone. He places the phone into his pocket.

"I see," he says, his voice an eerie calm. "You thought you'd call the police. How very clever of you." He raises the gun higher and points it at Liv, then me. I swallow hard and stare at the bullets turning in the barrel as he pulls the action back. "You can watch your boyfriend die now."

$$\cdots$$

LIV

I clutch at Jack's hand while the gun makes the ominous clicking sounds that only mean death. With the round iron glaring at Jack, I'm barely able to get the words out. "The police traced the call. You don't have time to drag bodies out of the building."

Saying the word "bodies" makes me queasy. But Bill's eyebrows pinch together slightly as he considers this.

"Well, aren't you the smart one?" he says softly, stepping aside and waving the gun toward the door. "If they've traced the line, they're on their way. Out, both of you."

We march in front of him. I wish I could ram him when I pass by, making him lose his grip on the gun, but that's a move I've only seen in movies and would definitely screw up.

At the door, Bill grunts at us to stop while he reaches over with one hand to tap something on his computer.

"I never warned them," Jack whispers, his face ashen. I know he's referring to Monroe Street. I do wish he'd been able to call them. I wish there had been time, though I hope he realizes we had to call the police first. Dutch's face flashes in my mind, and I can only hope they stay safe.

Bill marches us in front of him down to his car. No one is in sight, so he keeps the gun pointed at us. Maybe this is why he chose this spot for his office. From the distance, I can hear sirens. Bill obviously hears them, too. He curses, grabbing me and pressing the barrel of the gun against my head. My heart starts pumping double time. The sirens get closer, maybe only a couple blocks away.

"Get in the car and drive where I tell you, or she dies," Bill hisses to Jack, tossing the keys to him.

Jack catches them, giving me a nod and a small smile. I try, but I can't seem to force my lips up in response. The word "dies" is echoing in my brain. I have no doubt Bill will kill us.

"Wait," Bill says, his voice sharp. He yanks my hair back and says, "Give me the keys. She drives."

Me? Before I know it, Bill is pushing me into the front seat, his gun on me, then Jack. He tosses the keys to me and gets in the backseat with Jack. My shaking fingers fumble with the keys. I can barely get them in the ignition. I haven't driven since Bernadette tried to teach me last year, and I really sucked at it. I glance in the rearview mirror as I finally manage to get the car started.

Bill's gun remains on Jack, who is directly behind me. "No funny business. Got it?"

I nod and press the gas too hard. The car jerks forward. I can see blue and red flashes behind me as I approach the next street, but it looks like the police stopped at the apartment building. Another car with flashing lights flies by us, headed back toward the building as well. *We're here. We're here*, I scream in my mind, wanting to honk the horn to attract their attention. Instead, I follow Bill's instructions and take a right.

As I drive, the knowledge that we're done for hits me hard. I'm sure Bill's only plan now is escape, so once he's free of the police, he'll have no more use for either of us. As soon as we're out of range, we're dead. Our only chance is to somehow escape before we get to that point. As I drive, my eyes dart around the passing streets and buildings. Bill's finger is on the trigger. Slight pressure and Jack is dead. It'll have to be such a shock that he won't be able to think clearly enough to pull the trigger. Should I ram it into a building? A tree? It might kill us, too, though.

Jesus, I don't know how to handle this kind of stuff.

"Make a left and follow the bridge out of the city. Faster."

As I turn the car, I can see the bridge stretching over the James River. This is it. On the other side is nothing. We'll be free and clear.

And dead. Murdered, like abducted teens in some made-for-TV movie.

Like flipping a switch, an idea is illuminated as clear as if it were written on the bridge in neon.

"Z, you should put your seat belt on," I say. Jack looks at my reflection in the rearview mirror, his face incredulous. I narrow my eyes and I think I hear a latch click. I clench the wheel harder to keep my hands from trembling.

"Shut up and drive," Bill snaps.

I can't even swallow—it's like wads of cotton have been rammed down my throat. I press the gas pedal hard and the car jumps forward as we approach the bridge. The speedometer needle rises as quickly as my heart rate. I push the pedal harder, my eyes on the bridge railing that's under construction. It's our best chance out. Bill's not wearing a seat belt. Jack and I are.

This will either be the stupidest thing I've ever done or the bravest.

I'm counting on bravest.

I take a shaky breath as the click-clack sound echoes

beneath the car. Almost there.

I lower my window and Jack's, ignoring Bill's shouts for me to close them. Jack's wide eyes meet mine in the mirror, his mouth gaping open. My heartbeat pounds in my ears as the traffic clears in front of me. I almost change my mind.

We're going to die anyway.

I set my teeth together and cut the steering wheel hard, flattening the gas pedal. Bill starts to curse loudly but he's cut off as the car crashes through the construction barriers. The metal rails scream against the car as it careers off the bridge and plummets toward the river.

I close my eyes, praying we make it. Praying that I don't hear a gun exploding.

Somebody screams. It might be me.

Something thuds heavily against the front seat as we tilt forward.

The smash of the impact on the water triggers the airbag, which is crammed into my face and whooshes the air out of my lungs. I can't breathe.

I can't…

Darkness.

Hands. Hands are slapping me.

A voice. Soft. Urgent. "Liv!"

My name.

I open my eyes and cough. White powder puffs from my lips. I'm still alive.

The car is bobbing up and down like a rubber duck in a

tub. I cough again and rub powder out of my face. My head is throbbing; a wet trickle is making its way down my face. Jack is next to me, his hands unlatching my seat belt. He pulls me to him.

"Liv! Are you okay?" he asks, his voice trembling. "Answer me!"

He sounds so scared. I start to answer but end up coughing again. I nod instead, and he cries out in relief.

"You stupid, crazy girl," he says, his fingers examining my head, my face. "What were you thinking?"

"Saw it in a movie." I manage to choke out. "Bill?"

"A movie?" Jack's mouth drops open, then he shakes himself. "I think Bill's dead. We have to get out of here."

The car is already sinking. "We can't," I tell him. "The car will suck us down. We have to wait." I've seen this in a movie, too. I glance back over the seat and see blood on the window of Bill's side. Bill's slumped forward, unmoving.

The car tilts backward. "Jack!" The cold water starts creeping in, flowing faster as we sink. My breathing is coming faster and shallower.

Jack takes my hand as I start to panic. "Listen. Just take some deep breaths, okay? Wait till we're under and then crawl out the window. We're going to be okay. Just breathe until you can't anymore. Don't panic."

Too late. But he repeats the word "breathe" over and over. I get control of myself and squeeze his hand hard as the water slams into us. As the car sinks farther and the interior fills, we both take a last deep breath and descend into the cold, black depths of the river.

As soon as the car is submerged and the water surrounds us completely, Jack pulls my body over him to guide me out the window. His hands are shaking. I try to hurry so he can follow, grasping the window ledge and sliding out. I want to turn to help Jack but my body betrays me, my legs propelling me upward to get air. *Please let Jack be behind me.* Every second feels like an hour as the oxygen is expelled from my lungs.

My chest is so tight.

The light is getting closer.

I finally break the surface and gasp, choking as I try too hard to fill my lungs. I look around to see Jack treading water just a few feet from me, coughing.

He tilts his head toward the bridge. We swim for what seems like miles over to the support beams. My arms scream in protest, but I make them keep pumping.

We wrap our arms and legs around the closest concrete pillar, holding on tight as we catch our breath. Jack studies me, his eyes worried. I open my mouth to tell him I'm okay, but nothing comes out.

Lights are approaching, headed straight for the bridge and us.

"L-Look," Jack says through chattering teeth. "You need to get on that boat. They c-can't take me."

I shake my head. "N-no, you need to come—"

"No. Too many questions." He waits until the boat gets closer before turning to tell me, "Hold on as t-tight as you can and don't let go. Do you understand?"

I nod. Sirens are screaming somewhere. Maybe above us. I want to reach for Jack as he pushes away, but my body feels like it's frozen to the beam.

"You'll be okay now," he says as he treads water. He glances once more at the approaching boat. Then he's gone.

CHAPTER TWENTY-FIVE

"The persons on whom I have bestowed my dearest love lie deep in their graves; but, although the happiness and delight of my life lie buried there too, I have not made a coffin of my heart, and sealed it up for ever on my best affections. Deep affliction has only made them stronger; it ought, I think, for it should refine our nature."

—Charles Dickens, *Oliver Twist*

LIV

Hands reach down to pull me up into the boat. They have me sit on what appears to be an ice chest surrounded by fishing poles, nets, and buckets, and I'm freezing. It's hard to see much about my rescuers except they all seem to be men with beards.

A light is flicked on, the beam directed at me. I flinch and the beam is immediately directed upward.

"Sorry 'bout that, little lady," one of the men says. I can see him more clearly now, although it's hard to make out much of his face through the fluffy white beard.

I've been rescued by Santa Claus. The thought makes me

want to laugh, but the giggle is stuck in my throat. My teeth are chattering so hard I'm afraid they might break.

One of the men throws a large towel around my shoulders. It smells like fish. "You were in that car that flew off the road, right? Was anyone else in there?"

I shake my head, but I can't seem to make the words come out.

"She's in shock, I guess," someone says. "We need to get her to shore. I radioed for help."

Help? From whom, Santa's elves? I start to laugh now, and my body shakes. That makes me laugh harder.

"Whoa, easy there," Santa Claus says. He hands me a thermos. "Drink this."

My mind replays the club scene. No way. No more drinks from strange men for me. He puts the thermos down and mentions something about stubborn women. Which is something Z might say. Not Jack, though.

I sit upright, shivering underneath the fishy towel while the men do boat things. My feet have fallen asleep, but I can't seem to focus my mind on anything. And it is so cold out. Isn't it almost summer?

When the boat makes it to shore, an ambulance is waiting. They carry me to the hospital, checking my vitals in the back of the vehicle on the way. Somebody says my blood pressure is low. They slip an oxygen mask over me. When we get to the hospital, they take me to a room and insert an IV in my arm. I drift off to sleep, interrupted a few times by the sound of alarms clanging. In my sleepy fog I hear the nurse say something about dangerously low blood pressure. I just want to sleep.

When I wake in the morning, the clock on the wall shows

that it's eight thirty. A cup and pitcher are on the side table. I help myself and drink half the pitcher.

A nurse comes in and smiles at me as she checks the machines. "Your vitals are much better now," she says. "How're you feeling?"

"Fine, I guess," I say.

"Your grandfather is outside talking with the doctor. I'll get him for you."

"Wait. Is there anyone else?"

"No, I don't believe so. Were you expecting anyone?"

I shake my head. I guess I should be glad Jack didn't come here. Exposure to the home and all. It still sucks, though. "No. Just a weird dream I had, I guess."

She nods and leaves, but the door almost immediately opens again to admit my grandfather and a doctor. Oh crap, and a police officer.

"Olivia, are you okay?" my grandfather asks, moving to my side. He looks so messy from his usual perfectly pressed suit look—well, his shirt is wrinkled and untucked, and for him, that's messy.

"I'm fine. Just tired." My eyes move to the police officer. I'm glad it's a woman. Or maybe not. Women are more intuitive, and I have to be extra careful not to say too much.

He pulls a chair to my side. "How did you end up going over the bridge into the river? Mrs. Bedwin said you came home earlier but left again. What happened?"

I hesitate, glancing at the policewoman, who introduces herself as Officer Jenkins and smiles encouragingly at me. Why didn't I ask Jack what I should tell people? I have no idea now what to say.

"Um, I can't remember everything. This man took me off

the street and said he wanted me to help him steal from my grandfather. That's when he took me back to the house and made me put spyware on the computer. He was going to kill… me…if I didn't do that. Then he took me to an apartment where I called the police to trace the line, and then he made me drive him away. I turned the car over the bridge rails because I thought it was my only chance to escape."

"Yes," Officer Jenkins says. She's looking at her notes. "That's consistent with our reports. Our team is working with the FBI to handle the contents in his apartment."

"What contents?" my grandfather asks, but I know. I know exactly what they're going to find. I swallow hard, hoping there's nothing on Bill's computer that will lead them to Monroe Street. I look at the phone. If I could only get in touch with Jack, but I don't want to risk it. They're probably monitoring my calls.

What a mess.

"Was anyone with you when you called 911?" the woman asks.

With me? "Nobody, just me. And that man."

Officer Jenkins scratches something on her pad. She asks me more questions, but I answer vaguely, as if the details are confused. After we play another round of "I don't know, I don't remember," my grandfather firmly asks the officer to leave me to sleep. I'm grateful, as I don't think I can keep my eyes open much longer.

I fall asleep, thoughts of Jack soothing my weary mind.

...

JACK

The farmer stops his truck at a gas station, three blocks from home. I climb out of the truck bed and give a short wave.

The trek to the house is terrible. The night is cooler than normal for this time of year. My clothes are almost dry now, but I'm freezing cold. My body is moving on autopilot.

All the cars are still in the driveway. Damn it, I wish I'd had the chance to call Nancy ahead of time. My hands are shaking so badly I can barely open the door handle.

I barely register the shocked faces on the others in the house when I collapse just inside, the chill finally taking over my body.

Nancy rushes to my side. "Cameron, help me bring Z upstairs. Micah, get him some hot tea."

Cameron and Nancy help me up the stairs to my bathroom. It is the most painful climb I've ever experienced; my bones feel like they're going to snap at any moment. Nancy starts the bath, but before she leaves I grab her hand.

"He's dead. Bill's dead."

She doesn't say anything, just stands and stares at me. I try to tell her that Liv and I both escaped, but tears are in her eyes. Of all things—tears. We could've died because of Bill, and all she can do is cry about love lost or some stupid shit. Disgusted, I turn toward the bath.

"I'm so glad you made it," she says through her tears. She touches my shoulder but I don't turn around. "I feel responsible…"

She turns to leave, and I don't stop her. I'm not pardoning her part in all this. If she had fought against Bill more, if she hadn't helped him find Liv, we wouldn't have had to go through this tonight.

Of course, Bill might've killed her. Then me.

Cameron tries to help me remove my clothes, but finally gives up and has me get in the tub in my shorts. The water feels like teeth—biting hot, then icy, then hot again. I lie back against the tile wall and close my eyes as my body temperature slowly evens out. I hope Liv is somewhere warm right now, too.

Micah brings me tea. The hot drink and the bath make me feel a hundred times better and a thousand times more tired at the same time. I get out of the bath and change into jeans and a T-shirt, staring at my bed longingly. I could sleep for a hundred years.

I lean forward to stare at my jaw in the closet mirror. The spot where Bill hit me is turning weird blue and orange colors. I touch it gingerly. I wonder how long it'll take them to recover Bill's body, and if they'll trace anything back to Monroe Street.

Shit!

The fatigue evaporates as I remember the computers at his apartment. I run downstairs to find Nancy in the kitchen with Sam. Sam's arm is around Nancy, but she's not fooling me. I know Sam is glad Bill's gone, too. They both look startled at my sudden appearance.

"Do you have access to Bill's computer at his apartment office?" I ask Nancy.

She reaches out to touch my jaw, her eyes now full of concern. "Are you okay?"

I swipe her hand away. "Nancy, do you have remote access to Bill's computer?"

"Of course not. He never trusted anyone enough to give out that kind of information."

I nod. I figured as much. "We need to get away from here," I tell her. "Bill's apartment—a call was traced. Liv had a cell. The police are probably there now, trying to crack his computer."

The color bleeds from her face. Cursing softly, she presses the little-used intercom for the house. "Code Red. Front door. Fifteen minutes." I always thought it was a stupid code, but I guess it works for emergencies better than anything else.

Sam hands me a sandwich, then runs off to pack her own stuff. Nancy leaves, too. There's nothing upstairs I have the energy to take. Except…

"Sam, grab my guitar," I call out to her. "And my laptop. And the little blue box from my desk."

She nods from the top of the stairs and disappears. I follow Nancy to the office, watching her open the safe. She removes several papers and envelopes, then turns to hand me a flash drive imprinted with a skull. Her eyes are teary.

"I never thought we'd have to use this," she says. "I guess we should be glad we got away with it as long as we did."

I don't say anything—don't remind her that our safe house is set up for emergency purposes like this, ready to continue business as usual. Monroe Street has been home to me for so long, so I understand and feel her pain. "Come on, we'll be fine. Only difference is that we'll call it Briarcreek Avenue instead of Monroe Street."

She sniffs and wipes at her eyes. "Yeah, I guess so," she says, half laughing.

I take the jump drive to the workroom and start downloading the virus onto the iMacs. I feel like I'm murdering a pet or something. I almost want to apologize to them.

When I finish, I power them off and on again. Nothing. Just a blank screen.

Before I leave the room, I put in a call to Jim Rush to fill him in on Bill's death. The FBI has the computers now, but he hasn't heard anything as to whether it's cracked them.

I also ask him to check hospitals. He finds out Liv is in stable condition, to be released tomorrow morning. I breathe easier.

The kids are already in the foyer when I finish. They look like they're going on a long vacation with all the suitcases and laptops. Nancy is giving them a speech about breaking up and meeting at separate times at Briarcreek Avenue.

As the kids file out the door, Nancy turns to me. She looks like she's about to say something, then stops. She reaches up to brush my hair aside, a familiar gesture that seems somewhat sad. "You're going to her, aren't you?"

I nod. "Tomorrow night. After I help you guys get situated."

"Will you be back afterward?"

I don't have an answer.

0 0 1 0 1 0 0 1 1 0 1 1 1 0 0 0 0 0 0 0 0 0 1 1
1 1 0 1 1 1 1 1 0 1 0 1 0 1 1 1 1 1 0 1 0 1
1 0 1 0 0 0 0 1 1 0 1 0 0 1 1 0 0 1 0 0 1 0 0 1 0
0 0 1 1 1 0 0 0 0 1 0 1 1 0 0 1 1 1 1
0 1 0 0 1 0 0 1 1 1 0 1 1 1 1 0 1 0 1 0
1 0 0 1 0 0 1 0 0 0 1 0 0 1 0 0 1 0 1
1 1 1 0 1 1 0 1 0 0 0 1 0 1 0 0 0
0 0 1 0 0 1 1 1 0 1 0 0 1 0 1 0 0 1 1 0
1 1 0 0 0 1 0 0 0 1 0 1 1 1 0 0 1 0 1 0
0 1 1 0 0 1 1 1 0 0 1 0 1 0 0 1
0 0 0 1 1 0 0 0 0 0 0 1 0 1 1 1 0
1 1 0 1 0 0 0 1 1 1 0 0 0 1 0 1 1 0 1

CHAPTER TWENTY-SIX

"They were mine, by day and night; and with them, came such a rushing torrent of fears, and apprehensions, and selfish regrets, lest you should die and never know how devotedly I loved you, as almost bore down sense and reason in its course."

—Charles Dickens, *Oliver Twist*

JACK

The new home is much smaller than Monroe Street, but it's a place where we're safe. It's something I convinced Nancy to purchase a long time ago, keeping it off Bill's radar in case anything ever went wrong.

Man, did it go wrong.

My mind is a blur. A busy night and day of transitioning to Briarcreek Avenue after the events of yesterday exhausted me. But sitting on my bike here, at Liv's house, adrenaline—or maybe fear—has taken over.

I stare up at the darkened window behind her balcony for several minutes. What if this is a mistake? I can't bring Liv back to that life. Can I still run away with her? What if she asks? Or, worse, what if she doesn't? We were together once, the same. But I have no family and she has a loving, rich grandfather who'd give her anything, and can. It's the life I want her to have, but it turns me into a loner again.

Get a spine.

I summon up enough courage to get off the bike. The large, flowery vines conveniently creep up the side of the house, making the perfect ladder. Like Romeo, I carefully climb the wet rope vines. Aching with nerves, I pull myself to her balcony and swing my legs over the rail. I try the balcony door—it's unlocked. I open it but pause at the sight of her in bed, asleep. Peaceful. I guess I had expected her to be up, pacing the room, worried about this or that. Or me. But now, as my eyes trace the curving outline of her body, I realize she fits here, in this privileged world where all the possibilities *are* possible. She belongs to this life, not mine.

I love her too much. Can I find the strength to let her go?

. . .

LIV

A cool breeze strokes my face, stirring me from my restless doze. The digital display next to me says that it's almost midnight. I throw my arm over my face. Deep sleep is what I want most but it's out of the question. I consider going to the kitchen for some milk, but this house is so huge the mere thought of making my way across to the kitchen is exhausting.

Then it occurs to me that I was woken by a breeze. I look sharply at the door to the balcony—it's open. My heart begins its familiar uncomfortable pounding in my chest. Who is waiting for me outside the doors? Someone Bill was working with? I sit up and grab the alarm clock on my nightstand, hefting it in my hand. He's going to get a fight if that's the case.

I can see him now, watching me. In the shadows, I can just make out enough features to set my heart racing—fingers hooked in his pockets, blond hair falling over his forehead in that dangerous-sexy way that makes me want to explore my darkest desires.

I don't remember getting out of bed, don't remember moving across to him like a magnet drawn to its opposite. All I know is that I'm within inches of him, my heart pounding so hard I can't hear anything else. Jack's gaze is fixed on me, the swirling colors masked in the near-darkness. He slowly reaches out to touch my cheek, like a man unsure if the desert oasis is a mirage.

"Jack."

He pulls me to him, kissing me fiercely. I respond with a ferocity of my own, matching the pressure of his lips with mine. His hands start at my hips, curving around as I slip my arms over his shoulders to draw him closer. He tastes of wind and rain and tears, which may be the ones slipping down my cheeks. My sleep tee is hiked up around my thighs as he lifts me into the air, but I don't care.

After a minute or an hour, Jack sets me back on earth, whispering, "I'm so sorry about everything. Such a pathetic thing to say, I know."

"Shh...I get it. I understand." My hands move up to smooth back the long layers of his hair. So soft without the gel to flatten it back. I caress the stubble on his cheek—he hasn't shaved in a couple days at least. I kiss him again, then nestle into his neck, breathing in the wonderfully familiar leather and spice. I could stay in this position forever. "So what now?"

His fingers move to lightly stroke my arms, sending vicious tremors through the quietest parts of my body. "Specifically?" he asks, his lips moving in my hair.

"Well, you're not tied to that life anymore."

The mesmerizing motion of his fingers stops. I can feel him stiffen and pulling away, though it's probably only a fraction of a centimeter. My heart sinks. "Liv, I—"

"You're staying there, aren't you?" It's not really a question. I already know the answer.

He sighs, bowing his head and threading his arms through mine. "Yes."

I untangle myself from his embrace. "Jack, when are you going to realize that you're too good for that life?"

"No, *you're* too good for it. Not me. I can't just quit. Anyway, I need to watch out for Dutch and the others. I can't leave them. The place would tank without me there."

I don't even bother to fight against the tears building up again in my eyes, spurred on by sleep deprivation and physical frustration from his kisses. "But you'd leave me." I knew this was too good to be true.

He catches a rogue tear with a fingertip. "No, Liv. It doesn't have to be like that. We can still see each other. Like how normal kids date."

"Normal" has never been a word to describe our relationship. "We're not normal kids, though. Not even close. And I can't do what you do. I can't even approve of what you do. It's not in me."

His eyes twitch slightly as he considers me. I know he's surprised by my response. As much as I want to be with him,

I can't believe he really thinks a relationship like that could work. He turns around and splays his hands across the balcony railing, looking out over the soft lights illuminating the massive houses. "I know. You don't need me. You've got a good thing going here. A shot at a real life, with college and everything you've ever wanted. My past would get in the way of your future." His voice is bitter.

"Stop saying that. I know my grandfather can help you get out of that world. He'd do anything for me."

Jack shakes his head. "No."

I rest my forehead against his back. The "old" me might've agreed to dating, or maybe even trying his lifestyle. But I'm not the same person I was when I first met him only a few short months ago. I'm stronger now—and I know it's partly because of him. But knowing that doesn't make this any easier.

"I wish I could make you see that you're better than all that. You're better than 'Z.' You deserve more than a life of crime, and you can get out if you want to."

He shakes his head. "I can't. Not now."

I sigh. So much for happy endings. "I won't give up on you. Even if you find someone else…" I almost choke on that one. Maybe I'm getting carried away, but I don't want him to find anyone else.

He swivels around to cup my face in his hands, the intensity of his gaze overwhelming me. "There is no one else. Ever. I love you. For so long now."

Love.

The word I've longed for, dreamed of, desired my whole life. Given to me by the one person I thought would never say it. The world spins around me, and I'm wrapped in Jack's arms.

His *love*.

"I love you, too, Jack."

And I know I do. The words are so natural, so easy, I wonder why I was never able to say it to him before. The acknowledgment is bittersweet—a fairy tale gone wrong. If only he could see in himself what I see in him. If only he could leave that damn Monroe Street.

He removes his mother's slender gold bracelet from his pocket and fastens it around my wrist, kissing it. I slide my arms around his waist as his mouth meets mine. The kiss is different this time—desperate, even pleading. I know he wants me to ask him to stay. And I want to so badly. I toy with it in my mind—how it would feel to wake up in his arms, knowing without a doubt that he loves me. Banishing the bad dreams, the darkness. I want him so much it scares me.

But I can't. Not until he chooses me over that life.

And he knows it.

He murmurs another "I love you" in my ear as he slips a note into my hand and closes my fingers over it, kissing them gently. "I'd better go," he says hoarsely. His eyes travel up and down as if memorizing me, even as he backs away. In my mind, I reach out for him, pull him back to me. I almost do it.

Then he's gone, taking my heart over the balcony wall with him. I sink to my knees and press my tearstained cheek to the cold stone of the balcony wall until the rumble of the motorcycle fades into the dark.

"I love you, Jack," I whisper to the quiet night. "Always."

Epilogue

*"'I offer you the heart so long your own, and stake my all upon
the words with which you greet the offer.'"*

—Charles Dickens, *Oliver Twist*

LIV

Though it's early fall, the whisper of wind is surprisingly
sharp, cutting like an icy knife through my light sweater. I ask
Mel and Jess to stop while I take my favorite blue Princeton
sweatshirt out of my backpack and slip it over my head.

Mel's eyes are glued to her book. "Liv, what do you think?
Greatest impact on literature from the English Renaissance?"

"Huh?"

She laughs. "Seriously, have you looked at the material at
all?"

I sip my latte and toss the half-empty cup in the trash,
barely listening as the two go back and forth in their
debate about the impact of Marlowe and Shakespeare on
contemporary literature. Usually, I would join in, but today
I'm melancholy. Music from the Spill Canvas was playing in

the coffee shop. The same song from which Jack took the lyrics in his note on that evening long ago—bittersweet words that spoke of love and loss with no promise held for the future.

My fingers fiddle with his mother's bracelet on my wrist. I wonder what he's doing right now.

Mel continues to chat it up about class, when she stops suddenly and whistles under her breath. "Whoa-hoah, hello there. Holy hot guy on a motorcycle. Is he looking at us?"

I follow her gaze to see the hot guy in question leaning against his bike, arms crossed.

Waiting for me.

I suck in the cold air as my heartbeat revs up to the rusty but familiar staccato. I walk to him, Mel and Jess on my heels.

"You lost?" I ask, trying to sound as casual as possible while my insides are dancing madly.

He looks around before his kaleidoscope eyes settle back on me. "Maybe. I'm new here. Could use a guide. You volunteering?"

"Maybe. You really enrolled?"

"Yep. Nancy knows someone on the board. I thought college might be an interesting change. There's another incentive here, too, of course." His lips curve into a sexy smile.

I grin and gesture to my friends without turning. "Mel and Jess, this is…" I hesitate. Z? Jack? Who is he now?

"Jack Dawkins," he says, nodding to them. "Old friend of Liv's."

I barely hear the girls excuse themselves, barely notice anything except him, his black jacket, windswept blond hair hanging over his forehead. He looks older now, more serious. But then the familiar sparkle in his eyes draws a smile from me. He tucks his fingers through my belt loops and pulls me until I'm pressed hard against him. I inhale the familiar scent of spice and leather. I'm pretty sure he can hear my heart pounding.

I ask the one and only question that worries me. "Does this mean you're out? For good?"

He tucks a strand of hair behind my ear. "Yes."

I laugh and wrap my arms around his neck. Then something else occurs to me. "Is Dawkins really your last name?"

His voice is low and husky. "Maybe. Want to go for a ride?"

"Maybe," I say, caressing the length of his arms and tilting my head up to him. He brushes his lips against mine. "Mmm... definitely. But you knew I would anyway."

He laughs and swings his leg over the bike, pulling me behind him. I barely notice the cold air swiping at me as I wrap my arms around his waist and feel the warmth of his body against mine. Exhilaration builds up in me as it sinks in—he's left his life of crime behind, all for me. For love.

I get my happy ending after all.

ACKNOWLEDGMENTS

First and foremost, HUGE kisses and hugs and thanks to my kids, Jack, AJ, and Elaine. I'm sure you guys wish you had a dollar for every time you heard, "Shh…Mom's writing." Or every time you had to listen to me sing.

Learning to open myself up to the muse was a result of meeting with my amazing fellow Chicks—Peggy Jackson, Tracey Smith, and Eva Griffin. You guys helped me find myself, and I will always be grateful to have you in my life.

And my dear friend Peggy, you have forever been my confidante and partner in crime. I could write an entire book about how awesome you are.

Cheers to my fabulous agent, Pam van Hylckama Vlieg, my calm in the storm. You go above and beyond the expectations of an agent, and for everything, I thank you!

My incredible editors, Stacy Abrams and Nicole Steinhaus, who encouraged me to reach into the cobwebby depths of my mind and find just the right ways to "show this." The entire Entangled team, especially Kelley York for the amazing cover, Alycia Tornetta for your support, Erin Crum for your error-catching skills, Jessica Estep for the fabulous advice, and all the publicity efforts of Team Heather Riccio and Sarah Nicolas! You guys are the coolest!

Lots of love to my fabulous OWLS critique group that helped me become a better writer (and kept me laughing), especially Marlana Antifit, Joe Iriarte, Rina Heisel, Jan Eldredge, Christy Koehnlein, Jennye Kamin, Peggy Jackson, and Stephanie Becherer.

Virtual hugs to my critique partners who totally rock— Tara Kelly, Julie Bourbeau, and Kristen Lippert-Martin. You are amazing authors, and I'm in awe of you!

Thank you to my early readers—Lindsey Jackson and Leslie Fillip, who helped me with teen talk (though I still don't get "like a boss"); teachers extraordinaire Kellee Moye and Dawn Mincher; my sister, Patricia Taylor (that hat has a slimming effect on you); my fabulous mom, Pat Harris; the lovely Jen Woods (who realized that the Jen in the story was just misunderstood); Amy Parrish; Nancy Williams; and Marco van Hylckama Vlieg (master of all things technical!).

A toast to my entire work team for your incredible support during this entire journey and your patience during my freak-out moments, especially Jen Woods, Dina Kuhlman, Karen McClintock, Karla Salansky, Sarah Reed, Becca Dixon, Em Schaefer, and yes, even you, George Rowen.

Special thanks to all my Twitter, OneFour KidLit, Facebook, and SCBWI Florida friends who kept me sane throughout this entire process. And a shout out to my funny friend Wynn, who introduced me to my MacBook Pro. You know I love it!

To you, dear reader, thank you for taking this journey with Olivia and Z.

And finally, to my sweet, wonderful David, who dealt with all the home chaos (and all my "personalities") while I worked on this story. I could not have done this without your support. Scale of one to ten—I love you ten billion trillion!

Olivia Twisted Reading Group Guide

The Carters take Liv's laptop away and censor what she can view as soon as she first gets to the house. Why do you think they did this? Is censorship ever okay?

Z tells Liv that the Monroe Street family is what saved him, and that what they do is necessary because they'd be on the streets otherwise. Is there ever a time that it's okay to break the law?

Why do you think the author chose those specific quotes at the beginning of each chapter? Are there any that stand out to you as particularly fitting?

Liv ends up trusting Z even though he was not always honest with her. After being burned so many times by families in the past, why do you think she let her heart rule her head? Did she make the right decision by trusting Z again?

Denise is very cold throughout the book. Based on the background we are given about her, why do you think she is the way she is? Does it make you feel angry or sorry for her?

Why was Liv okay with hacking, but not okay with stealing? Aren't they both breaking the law?

Why did Sam test Liv by having her steal a shirt at the mall before bringing her to the house? Why didn't they begin with hacking?

What made Liv succumb to the pressure to steal the shirt?

How did your impression of the Carters differ from the beginning to the end? At what point did your impression of them change?

In what ways did Sam and Z manipulate Liv throughout the story? Why did she go along with them even though she knew something was wrong?

Why did Z erase his past? Why is he afraid to allow Liv or anyone else to know anything personal about him?

Why do Z and the other children stay dependent on Bill even though he is clearly not a good man?

What in Z's and Liv's pasts make it so hard for them to trust others?

Why didn't it ever cross Liv's mind to turn in the Monroe Street gang to the authorities? What would you have done in her situation?

If you are interested in learning more about how the characters connect in the two stories, visit www.vivibarnes.com.

Olivia Twisted Interview With the Author

Why did you choose to write a version of OLIVER TWIST?
My aunt introduced me to the movie musical *Oliver!* when I was going through a difficult time in middle school. I probably watched it fifty times that year ("Please sir, I want some more!"). I remember thinking, "Now there's a kid with real problems." Then I read the story and thought it'd be cool to have a book with a female protagonist and call it *Olivia Twisted*. So truly, that's how the idea began—with a title.

How does your book compare to OLIVER TWIST?
I wanted to keep the themes of abandonment, abuse, hope, desperation, and love that are prevalent through the original story. Wherever possible, I tried to parallel the plot lines of OLIVER TWIST. To update the story for contemporary times, I took license with certain story lines, such as making the criminals an underground ring of hackers instead of pickpockets and making the romance central to the story instead of an aside.

Oliver Twist is a passive child. Why did you choose to make Olivia more confident?
In the original story, society was more of a protagonist than Oliver himself. With *Olivia Twisted*, I wanted to have two strong main characters who weren't just victims of their world, but instead shaped their own destinies.

What type of research did you do for this book?

I'm convinced there's a special list the FBI uses for writers, considering the searches I've conducted. But I'm grateful to have experts with computer programming to help guide and review the hacking scenes. I also did extensive research on the foster care system, and though there are some amazing stories out there about people who truly care, there are also a lot of holes in the system. My hope is that someday, these deserving children will stop falling through the cracks.

Don't miss Christine O'Neil's snarky and feisty heroine in

CHAOS

Available online now!

My name is Maggie Raynard. After sixteen years being just plain me, suddenly, when I lose my temper, my fingers become weapons of mass destruction. Turns out I'm a semi-god, descended from Aphrodite. Sounds cool in theory, but when I accidentally put my ex-boyfriend in a coma, things go downhill pretty fast.

Now some new guy named Mac Finnegan has made it his mission in life to continually piss me off. I'm stuck learning how to use my new powers while also dealing with regular high school problems, and with this annoying—and super-hot—guy all up in my business, I'm about to flip out.

But it gets worse. I just learned there's this watchdog council of semis who keeps an eye out for any bad apples. They think I'm the baddest of the bunch and want to take me out before I do any more damage. My nemesis Mac might turn out to be my salvation, only he's got secrets of his own...and they may just kill us both.

Chapter One

Dear She:

My boyfriend is obsessed with video games. Like, that's all he ever wants to do. Even if I get him to take me on a date, we end up at Joe's Crab Shack, and the second we're done eating, he's dragging me into the back room arcade to make me play some stupid game with him. What can I do to get him to stop this B.S. and pay more attention to me?

Signed,
Sad and Lonely

Dear Sad and Lonely,

I'm going to skip the A and lob a Q your way: Why do you even want to be with a guy who's too dumb to recognize what he has? You might not want to hear it, but my advice? Bounce. There are some guys—even high school guys, if you look really hard—who are mature enough to realize there's more to life than video games. Join drama or chorus and maybe you'll find a guy who's interested in the arts. Like the intellectual type? Join the debate team or the academic squad. There are a ton of options out there just waiting for you. Don't sell yourself short or settle for less than you deserve.

    Forever yours,
    She

I clicked my mouse over the send icon with a satisfied sigh. Today's Q&A for my anonymous column, "That's What *She* Said," was officially in the bag and on its way to my loyal readers. Not bad for the back half of a forty-two-minute study hall on a Thursday.

I logged off the PC and then scooped up my messenger bag just as the bell rang. Next stop, chem lab. Not exactly my favorite subject, but at least my BFF, Libby, was in that class with me.

"Miss Raynard," a stern voice called.

Dread pooled in my gut as I pasted on a smile and turned to face Hortense Verbiglio, harpy of the computer science department. Mrs. Verbiglio was even less attractive—both inside and out—than her name suggested, and her stopping me could mean nothing good.

"Yes, Hort—erm, Mrs. Verbiglio." Pretty much the whole school privately referred to her as "Hortense," so sometimes it was hard to make the switch, but if she noticed my glitch, she didn't let on.

"What exactly did you accomplish today? I saw a whole lot of type-ity type-ity." She wiggled her stubby fingers like she was tapping a keyboard. "But I didn't see you print your work.

Do you mind telling me what you were doing all period? This is study hall not goof-off time."

"Oh, I know. It's just, I had a big report to do and didn't want to use up all your paper." Because I was a real sweetheart like that and all.

She crossed her beefy arms over her chest and stared me down for way longer than was comfortable. Finally, she tipped her head in a short nod. "Go ahead, then. Next time, though, I'll be expecting to see your work."

The tension in my shoulders released, and I shot her two cheerful thumbs up, then busted ass toward the door before she changed her mind and kept me there for more grilling. The school administration allowed us what felt like thirty-seven seconds to get from one class to another, and she'd just wasted twelve of mine. If I was late for chem, it was squarely on Hortense.

"Hey! Wait up."

Libby's musical voice had me skidding to a stop in the middle of the crowded hallway, which earned me a few dirty looks and someone's jam-packed book bag slamming into my shoulder blade. *Ouch.*

"Oh, good," Libby gushed breathlessly, her hazel eyes bright with relief. "You're late, too. Now I don't have to walk in alone. I was finishing up this test in psych. It was brutal."

She fell into step beside me, although her runner's strides were much longer, so I had to hurry to keep up. Yet another reason to despise being five-three. At five-eight, Libby liked to complain her height was a guy deterrent, but since she'd been asked to the Snowflake Swirl by four different people already and it was still technically autumn, I'd have to call bullshit on that theory. Either that, or the height issue was somehow offset by the fact that her legs went on for years and her bra could comfortably hold a grapefruit in each cup. Not that I cared. Being "blessed" with a solid set of oranges myself, I was of the opinion that boobs mostly just got in the way. Running in gym class was embarrassing as fuck, and forget about sleeping on my stomach. If they were any bigger, they'd be worthy of serious male attention and that was the last thing I needed.

I was done with guys.

Not in that fake, I-say-that-but-deep-down-I-really-want-a-boyfriend kind of way, but in, like, the seriously-I'd-rather-eat-maggoty-cheese kind of way. No relationships. Not for me. Not now and maybe not ever. Who I am…*what* I am, and what I'm capable of? Everyone's better off this way.

"I have to stop at my locker real quick." I veered to the right and cut through the crush of kids heading straight at me, like wildebeests to a watering hole. Libby followed and then stood by me as I fiddled with the lock.

"What's that?" She pointed to a white piece of paper sticking out half an inch from one of the slots in the olive metal door.

I tugged the padlock open and flicked the catch with my thumb. "Dunno." Maybe Bink had left me another note. Bink was my neighbor, bud, *and*—most days—my ride home. Last time I'd found a note in my locker, his cell phone had died and he needed to bail early. I seriously hoped this wasn't a repeat performance.

I mentally ran down the list of people I could bug for a ride and came up empty. Libby always had to stay after for some activity or another, and I only really had two other people I could call "friends" and neither lived near me. I wrinkled my nose in anticipation of the dirty-sneakers-meets-day-old-bologna smell of a bus filled with kids who'd had last-period gym and opted not to change clothes. With a sigh, I pulled open the door and the white rectangle floated to the floor.

Libby bent to grab it and read it out loud. "'Dear Sad and Lonely…'" She trailed off and went quiet for a few seconds until her peachy complexion went hot pink, and then she gasped. "Oh my God. Holy… Oh, Mags, you are so not going to like this."

I snatched the paper from her, trying to ward off the growing pit in my gut.

Dear Sad and Lonely,

Since I can almost guarantee She is about to give you some seriously shite advice like she does every week, let me be the voice of reason. Your boyfriend is just like most high school guys. Cut him some slack and, even better, why not offer to learn how to play some of the games he likes? He'd probably appreciate the effort and might even take you somewhere nice after. If that doesn't work, sit him down and let him know how you're feeling so he can tell you what's going on with him. Could be that constantly calling the things he likes stupid isn't the best way to get what you want in this situation, yeah? In any case, don't let the ramblings of some bitter emo chick who's probably never had a boyfriend ruin your relationship.

Hope it helps,
He

My skin prickled with alternating hot and cold flashes while my brain churned. The shock was too thick to let the anger in right away, but as stunned as I was, I knew exactly who was behind this. There was only one person in the whole school who would use the word "shite."

Mac Finnegan.

Opinionated, annoying, hot—did I mention annoying?—Mac Finnegan, who had barely given me the time of day since he'd come to Crestwood High. Mac Finnegan, who thought he was soooo cool with his Irish accent and his mocking smile. Mac Finnegan, who inexplicably made me want to lick him like an ice cream cone and then immediately rinse my mouth out with acid.

How had he discovered my secret? Only Bink and Libby knew I was the girl behind "That's What *She* Said," and I would have bet everything I owned that neither of them would have ratted me out.

Didn't matter though. One way or another, he knew.

Even worse, he'd chosen to taunt me with it. *Bitter emo chick who's probably never had a boyfriend*, indeed. I had a boyfriend once, and it hadn't ended well for either of us. I was in no rush to repeat the experience. Besides, what did this Irish asshat care?

Anger tightened my chest, and my vision went hazy. I could feel the power rising in me, clawing to get out, roaring to be heard. The hair on my arms stood on end as I tried to breathe through it, to let the fury dissipate and flow out of my pores in harmless pings of energy, but it was no use.

I pressed a hand to my locker and opened up the tiniest of escape valves, the spout of a teakettle, whistling off a stream of steam. The cheap metal instantly heated against my skin, the door buckling and warping on the spot just beneath my fingertips.

"Uh, Mags—" Libby whispered urgently, but a male voice cut her off.

"How's it going there, Libby? Maggie."

I turned around, still trying to catch my breath, and there he was, strolling by, a cocky grin splitting his sinfully beautiful face.

Mac Finnegan, who had decided that being the new kid wasn't bad enough, so he had to actively go out of his way to make enemies. Mac Finnegan, who wanted to turn my world upside down rather than minding his own business. Mac Finnegan, who didn't know the meaning of live and let live.

Mac Finnegan, who clearly had no idea who he was fucking with.

• • •

It was one fifty-three, and I stared at the clock, willing the hands to move faster. Dr. Pepper—I so wish I was kidding— droned on endlessly and everything seemed like it was moving in slo-mo as I seethed.

I'd get a tardy for cooking class if I went to track down Mac at his locker on the opposite wing before sixth period, but my head would literally explode all over these avocado walls if I didn't. So for the good of the school, I'd suck it up and take the detention if I was late.

Earlier when Mac had strolled past my locker, I'd tried to get my shit together and let him know exactly what I thought of his little note. To hit him with one of the dozens of cutting put-downs that would've been on the tip of my tongue had I been a different person. A regular person. The kind of person who used her brain to come up with kickass comebacks instead of letting anger get the better of her, making her think—and sometimes do—bad things.

Instead, I watched him walk by, impotent rage writhing under the surface of my skin like a nest of vipers.

Now that I'd had time to settle down some—I was still mad, but I had things under control—a gazillion witty comebacks waited in the wings, each one carefully crafted and designed to wipe that smug fucking smile right off his face.

Still, I needed to find out what the hell was going on with him. More importantly, I needed to figure out why he'd chosen *me* as the person he wanted to screw with most.

It seemed so random. He'd barely even acknowledged my existence at school since he'd enrolled in September, and now he was all in my business. I couldn't understand for the life of me what I'd done to deserve it. Did he really just hate my column so much he felt like he had to put me on blast like that?

My cheeks grew warm again, and I wondered who else, if anyone, had read his response. Was he passing them out everywhere, or was that a special edition just for me? While neither was ideal, option B was at least less humiliating. It was also the less likely one, but a girl could hope.

I looked up again and realized, while I'd been stressing, the clock had finally decided to cooperate and Dr. Pepper started wrapping it up. About time.

"So with that, I need you to read pages eighty-three through eighty-nine for homework and answer the questions at the end of the chapter for tomorrow." The bell cut him off, and per the status quo, we all stood, grabbed our books, and walked out with his nasally voice chasing us. "Make sure you restate the question in your answer, and — "

I didn't wait for the rest of his speech or for Libby, and went barreling down the hall.

"So what are you going to do?" she asked, rushing behind me to catch up. Funny how much faster my stubby legs could go when I was hella pissed off.

"I'm going to call him out, and then I'm going to tell him…" What? What *exactly* was I going to tell him? That my unauthorized and highly frowned-upon little school column was the only one allowed, and he'd better stop stepping on my turf? I pictured a bad dance-off à la *High School Musical* between us and smiled despite my fury. Mainly because, in my imagination, I'd saddled Mac with a pair of red leather pants and a faux-hawk, and he looked like a friggin' idiot.

"You know what? I'm just going to ask him flat out what he thinks he's trying to pull. I mean, we don't even know each other."

Guilt pricked me at the white lie. We knew each other *a little*.

He'd just moved in two streets over from me, and one night, when I'd gone out for a walk to clear my head, I'd seen him at the park on the corner playing with his dog. He was impossible to miss. Tall…so frigging tall, with shoulders wider than any guy on the Crestwood football team, even with their pads on. I'd tried so hard not to look when he squatted low to give his German shepherd a pat, but his button-fly jeans pulled tight over his muscular thighs and it was a wonder I didn't wind up drooling on his hand right next to Fido. So. Hot. I don't know if I whimpered or he just sensed my presence, but when he looked up it only got worse.

His face was beautiful. The kind of face with the power to make even a seriously badass girl start scribbling her first name next to his last name in the margins of all her notebooks. Straight, masculine nose, chiseled cheekbones, full but firm lips, and perfectly groomed light brown hair made for a pretty fine picture. Then he smiled and "pretty fine" became "holy-mother-of-God" and my stomach bottomed out.

Luck was with me, for once, and before I could make a total fool of myself, his unleashed shepherd came at me fast, barking like he meant serious, unpleasant business. An animal lover through and through, I stayed chill and waited, grateful for the reprieve and using that time to get my shit together before I became a stuttering idiot or worse. The dog stopped barking and sniffed my leg, eventually licking my hand while I patted him.

Mac had come running up, breathless and semi-apologetic. Ish. The blood was pounding in my ears, but I think I made some sense as I responded. Then again, who's to say? We talked for a minute but things got…weird.

If it had only happened that day, I could make sense of it. First sighting of a gorgeous guy around my age, maybe my insta-lust had made it awkward. But months had passed and things had never gotten less weird. We only had two classes together—Art II and Mythology—so it wasn't like we had to spend a whole lot of time together, but the time we did spend?

Weird.

Like I wanted him in a way that made no sense. Like I was drawn to him even though I knew almost nothing about him. And when he looked at me a little too hard, and his smile was always sort of mocking… I wanted to grab him tight and smack the shit out of him all at the same time. Yeah, weird. Enough that I wanted to turn away the second our paths crossed. But that was before. Those days were over.

If anyone should be uncomfortable now, it was him. Because I didn't care about his body or his stupid face anymore. I was about to get medieval on his ass.

Libby continued chattering from behind me. "At least if he does go public with his column, he didn't name you in his response. Maybe he'll keep it to himself."

I didn't get my hopes up because although she was right so far, there was still a very real chance that he'd blow my cover whenever it suited him.

"Maybe he just wants to make more friends and thinks this will make him popular or whatever," Libby said, not even bothering to hide her disgust at that theory.

Libby was like the patron saint of nerds, which was pretty odd if you were on the outside looking in. Blond, beautiful, funny, with a body from long-distance running that made most of the cheerleaders want to rush to the bathroom and hork up their chicken nuggets and tater tots after lunch. She was exactly the type of person you'd think would be all about her image and what people thought.

Not even close.

Libby was a theater geek, with a passion for woodwind instruments and Victorian literature. She loved clothes and dressing up but always seemed to miss the mark, with kooky stuff like berets and leg warmers making appearances, sometimes simultaneously.

Today she had on a pink puffy skirt with matching flats and her blond hair was secured in a bun at the top of her head with a pair of chopsticks. All in all, she looked like either the prettiest girl to ever escape a mental hospital or like she'd jacked a ballerina on the way to school and stolen her gear. And she didn't give a crap. She was entirely unconcerned about popularity, so the idea that Mac had stooped to some stealth attack on me to gain street cred had made her even more indignant on my behalf than she'd been before.

I rounded the corner to the east wing and was about to shoot down her theory about Mac, since in the few months he'd been at Crestwood, he'd amassed a shitload of groupies and a bunch of male imitators. He might not hang out with the jocks or be part of the way "in" crowd, but he was definitely on everyone's radar.

And now he was on mine. Literally. I zeroed in on his annoyingly broad shoulders covered in that dumb too-fitted tan jacket he always wore and cut a path toward him. Libby slowed and called after me. "I, uh, guess I'll see you in Mr. Weston's class. Be careful, Mags…"

Another thing about Libby: she always knew when I was going to make a scene and magically seemed to melt into the background. I didn't blame her, but I didn't respond either. I was too focused on my target.

"What the hell, Finnegan?" I spat when I was close enough for him to hear.

He turned around casually, like it was every day that an irate female came from behind and bitched him out in the hallway. Who knew? If he treated the girls at his old school the way he was treating me, that was probably the case. And even so, I still felt the odd little pull in my stomach.

Want.

I shoved it back and glared at him.

"Hey, Maggie." His gray eyes seemed to twinkle with a

challenge then flickered lower. Was he seriously checking me out right now? I scowled at him harder and his lips twitched a little before his face went blank and his gaze zeroed back in on mine. "What can I do for you?"

He said it like, "Fer ya," in that accent that both irritated me and always somehow made me want to repeat him out loud, which made me even madder.

"What do you think you're doing?" I bit out through gritted teeth.

"Just now?" His brows drew together. "I was thinking how they must have some shirts in the girls' section and wondering why you opted to get yours from the guys' department instead." He leaned back against his locker and shrugged. "Then I decided to be polite and keep my thoughts to myself."

My mouth dropped open, because WTF, and I barely resisted the urge to tug on my standard-issue vintage concert T-shirt that, aside from being a little big, looked just fine, thank you very much. "Do you have a specific problem with me, or are you just a pain in the ass in general?"

He tipped his head to the side like he was considering each word. "Hard question to answer, but I'm going to have to say no on both counts, although my mother might disagree on the latter."

"Don't play stupid. You know what I'm talking about. I got your little letter in my locker." I jammed a hand on my hip and tried not to let my voice go all shrill, like it did when I got really pissed. It was a short trip from that to the prepubescent boy cracking stage, and that always felt like it undermined my credibility.

I glanced around at the thinning crowd and hissed in a furious whisper, "The advice column thing is my deal. You starting your own is bad enough, but doing it just to argue with my points is crossing the line. And the name calling... What the hell?"

I tapped my booted foot in a furious beat on the scuffed black-and-white linoleum. I started to say more, but his brow was furrowed like he was deep in thought. Maybe that was all that needed saying. Maybe he hadn't realized what a dickwad he was being, and now that I'd pointed out the error of his ways, he'd stop and—

"Thing of it is, Maggie...your column is shite."

My brain booted down, and I stopped tapping, staring up at him in shock.

"What did you just say?"

He shrugged a ridiculously wide shoulder and shook his head, sending a lock of brown hair slipping onto his forehead, which he shoved away impatiently. "Come on. It's the ranting of an unhappy, boyfriendless teenage girl with no real understanding of relationships or guys at all. Not to mention the terrible, Dr. Phil advice you always give. That's not real life."

He shifted his pile of books to his other arm and slammed the door of his locker shut as I stood there, speechless, still trying to process what he was saying. But he wasn't done yet. "They'd be better off cracking open a fortune cookie and getting an answer there. I'm just trying to offset your damage."

My jaw was still swinging when the bell rang and he walked away.

Walked. Away. Seriously? If I was mad before, *this* time, the anger that tore through me was a living thing, with breath and pulse and depth and color.

Red.

When I called after him this time, my voice was the furthest thing from shrill, and it echoed down the now-empty hallway. "Don't move, Finnegan. Or else."

He slowed and then stopped, but he didn't turn to face me. Instead, he shifted to peer at me over his shoulder. "Or else what, Maggie?" The icy look in his eyes made me pause, but only for a second.

My nails dug deeply into the palms of my hands as a thousand ancient curses I didn't even realize I knew flew to my lips, unspoken.

That should have been a good thing, the unspoken part. Problem was, they didn't need to be spoken. All I had to do was…nothing. I didn't have to *do* anything. It was there. Ready. Waiting. I just had to take the cap off and let it flow. It would be a relief I only knew when I was sleeping. Even earlier, my little locker meltdown had only been the barest minimum leak. The finest of cracks in the eggshell, with a trickle of power allowed to ooze out.

If I really let it go—

"Get to class, Mr. Finnegan. Miss Raynard." Hortense's stern voice called from the open doors of her classroom.

Mac finally turned then to face me fully, and his gaze held mine for what seemed like an eternity but was probably only a second. What I saw there confused me enough that when Hortense repeated herself, I obeyed without argument. Disgust? Challenge? Hatred?

The haze clouding my vision dissipated as more questions flooded my already overloaded brain, but I dragged my ass down the hall to my next class, refusing to give in and look over my shoulder to see if *someone* was still watching me.

Who was Mac Finnegan, and why did it feel like he knew

me? Like, *knew* me knew me. The way Libby and my mom and my grandma knew me.

And why did it feel like he had so much loathing for me?

It might have made sense if he knew what I was. That I had this power living inside me that had been fighting its way out for the past six months. The thing that had indirectly almost killed a boy…

But he didn't know that. He couldn't. Still, the shame that came every time I thought of Eric filled me, and I fought the slick of nausea battering my belly.

By the time school ended, I'd talked myself in mental circles only to come to the realization that I was being paranoid. Mac was a jerk, but it was nothing more than that. Still, I was totally wrung out. I felt like I'd gone to the dentist for ten fillings, stopped by the doctor for a tetanus shot and some stitches, and then took a midterm all in the same day. When I pushed through the heavy metal doors to the outside world, the icy air that hit me was a relief.

"Hey."

I tensed until I turned to see Bink swaggering toward me. I couldn't take another run-in with Mac right now without imploding.

"Hey yourself. How was your day?" I asked, working up a grin. Bink wasn't what I'd call intuitive, but he had a sixth sense when it came to my moods, and I wasn't in any shape to answer questions or discuss a certain arrogant asshole. Not yet.

"Pretty good. Coach says if I ace my English paper, he can start me again next game." His face broke into a wide smile, and a group of girls walking by stared at him. I could hear their whispers when they passed, and the words "hot" and "dimples" were definitely in the mix.

It was hard to judge objectively after fifteen years of friendship, but I stole a glance up at him as we strolled side-by-side toward the parking lot. At six-one, one hundred and ninety pounds, he was a wall of muscle capped off by a mop of dirty blond hair and the chronic chin stubble that had some girls referring to him as Thor behind his back. He was one of those kids who had looked like a man since eighth grade but whose maturity level hadn't quite caught up with the rest of the package.

That aside, he was easy to look at. I probably should have been affected by it, but most of the time, I saw him as the same scrawny kid I used to catch salamanders and share PB&Js with during long summer days.

I was no fashion model, but the old Bink hadn't really cared what he looked—or smelled—like when we were kids, and he was pretty ripe most days. While I didn't miss that, there was one thing I did miss…

Being able to tell him everything. Because the fear of him knowing? The fear of him looking at me differently? It was more than I could stand. With all the changes going on in my life, he was one of the few constants, and I needed us to be exactly what we'd always been. Only we weren't.

I wished I could've blamed the recent change on our respective social standings at school. Before the "incident," I was pretty much invisible. Then, I became all too visible.

The past few months, since I'd started the column and some time had passed from the thing with Eric, I'd slipped back into a semi-comfortable state of anonymity. Sure, girls liked the column, but they didn't know I wrote it, and even if they did, I doubted I'd ever be really popular.

Despite having overheard my mom's friend say that my

black hair and green eyes made for some "striking coloring," anything notable about my looks stopped there. I had a decent figure, but it wasn't what I'd call standout. My nose wasn't small and it wasn't big. My cheekbones did their job as advertised and held my face up adequately, but they weren't going to cut glass or anything. My lips weren't Jessica Alba plump or Kate Middleton thin. I was pretty with a lowercase p. As for standing out in other ways, well…I just didn't.

I was a decent student, but I was nobody's valedictorian or any kind of laude. I didn't play a sport or have the urge to put on a short skirt and shake plastic tassels for anyone who did. In fact, aside from the whole semi-god thing, I was basically regular.

But Bink? Bink was not only gorgeous, he was fun to be around and also the starting quarterback of the football team, which all the girls seemed to like even more than my column. Through it all, though, he hadn't changed much.

When push came to shove, he'd not only have my back, he'd also keep a watch on the front, side, top, and bottom if I needed him. If anyone had changed, it was me.

I had secrets now that hurt too much to tell. I had done things…terrible things, and the thought of seeing the disappointment in his eyes if I said them out loud made me keep my piehole shut. And this was creating a thin but very real wall between us that I fucking despised but felt helpless to stop building. Maybe some quality time with him was exactly what the doctor ordered on a craptacular day like this one.

"Do you need help with your paper? I have some time tonight if you want."

He turned grateful baby blues on me and nodded. "That would be excellent, thanks."

We slowed as we reached his car, a red classic Firebird that looked way better than it ran. We'd had to get my mom to jump it that morning when it wouldn't start before school, and I crossed my fingers that we didn't run into the same problem again. It had already felt like the longest day in history.

"So what's your paper supposed to be about?"

"Jane Austen. I tried to read the books, but jeez, Mags. They're so boring." His brow wrinkled, and he looked pained. "How could anyone like that crap?"

I shrugged and tugged open the passenger door. "You're asking the wrong girl."

Although Bink and I were the same age, I was a better student and had taken a lot of the classes he was taking now the year before, so I'd already choked down my dose of Austen. My taste ran more toward Veronica Roth and Sarah Dessen, so it hadn't been fun times.

"But we don't have to like it to write a paper on it. We'll make it fun. No worries."

He slid into the driver's seat, and we both held our breath as he turned the key. It sputtered but then caught, and the engine roared. Maybe things actually were looking up.

"Sweet," he murmured under his breath and clicked on his seatbelt.

It wasn't until we'd pulled out of the lot that I managed to let go of some of the tension that had knitted my neck into knots since I'd found Mac's little note. I had a reprieve. Another sixteen hours or so before I had to go back there. Before I had to face *him* again.

It wasn't long enough, but I'd take it.

Determined to make the best of the afternoon, I turned to Bink. "I heard some gossip today. Talk to me. What's up with you and Ally?"

His cocky smile made his response unnecessary, but I let him crow about it anyway. "I asked her out at lunch and she said yeah. She's going to see family in Vermont this weekend, but next weekend we're going to the movies to see *House of Demons*. I figure I'll pull the old 'it's okay, I'll protect you' arm around the shoulder move and see if I get a chance to touch her boob."

He looked at me expectantly, and I gave him the patented deadpan eyes he'd set me up for, which made him laugh.

"Speaking of which, Libby wants to go out tomorrow and see the new *Spiderman* movie. You down?" He turned hopeful puppy dog eyes on me, and I nodded.

"You and Libby, eh? Sure I won't be cock blocking you?" I teased. Bink and Libby were always arguing, and I'd been teasing them for years it was pent up sexual tension. Neither of them had taken the bait yet, though Bink's face turned an interesting shade of pink all of a sudden.

"Yeah right. Libby?" He coughed. "Not likely. So you down or what?"

I stared at him hard, for the first time wondering if maybe there *was* something weird brewing between the two of them. I didn't know how I'd feel about that either. Probably not good.

"Sure," I said.

I *was* down. It would likely do wonders for my mood to get out and be around people who loved me. And who knew? Maybe today was just a fluke. Not an omen of a lot of crappy days to come, but only one crappy day. Maybe Mac would forget about whatever he'd been trying to pull and leave me alone altogether and tomorrow would be better.

Then again, maybe not.

Don't miss Kelley York's haunting and beautiful

MADE OF STARS

Available online and in stores now!

When eighteen-year-old Hunter Jackson and his half sister, Ashlin, return to their dad's for the first winter in years, they expect everything to be just like the warmer months they'd spent there as kids. And it is—at first. But Chance, the charismatic and adventurous boy who made their summers epic, is harboring deep secrets. Secrets that are quickly spiraling into something else entirely.

The reason they've never met Chance's parents or seen his home is becoming clearer. And what the siblings used to think of as Chance's quirks—the outrageous stories, his clinginess, his dangerous impulsiveness—are now warning signs that something is seriously off.

Then someone turns up with a bullet to the head, and all eyes shift to Chance's family. Hunter and Ashlin know Chance is innocent...they just have to prove it. But how can they protect the boy they both love when they can't trust a word Chance says?

HUNTER

When we first met Chance Harvey, he was playing with Barbies.

Not in the dressing-them-up sense. He had Malibu Barbie tied to the end of a fishing pole by her ankles and was reeling her in from the creek behind Dad's house. Even at eight years old, my half sister, Ashlin, and I both thought this was pretty bizarre.

Chance turned to stare at us with wide, round green eyes that didn't really fit his face. He was covered in grass and mud from crawling up and down the banks, camouflage paint smudged across his cheeks, and he stared at us like *we* were the weird ones.

"Who are you?" he demanded.

He was a runt, closer to Ash's size than mine, and I knew I could scare him off if he was there to cause trouble. My eyes narrowed. "That's my dad's house," I announced, pointing to the rooftop visible through the trees. "And this is *his* part of the creek. He's a cop, and you're gonna be in trouble if I tell him you're here."

In retrospect, I don't know why I felt the need to be

so mean. I was a kid, and I guess being tough seemed like the thing to do, especially in front of my sister. But Chance, frustratingly unbothered by my threat, turned his back to us. "Well, let me finish this and I'll go away."

I crossed my arms to wait for him to get lost, but didn't it figure that Ashlin, in her mouse-sized voice, piped up with, "What are you doing?"

Chance regarded her with a crooked smile over his shoulder, like he'd been waiting for one of us to ask that very question. "I'm doing a rescue operation. Duh."

Ash's eyes widened and she took a step closer. "You're rescuing Barbie?"

Chance stood up, straightened his back, and placed a hand on his hip. I remember thinking that with that one simple gesture, he looked more grown-up than we did. "Yeah! But see, there are so many down there, I don't know where to start. You should help."

My sister didn't even wait for my opinion. She darted past me in her summer dress and grass-stained sneakers and crouched by Chance's side while he gave instructions on how, exactly, we were supposed to go about this rescue mission. He spoke to Ash, but his eyes were always on me.

That was how it all started. Fishing Barbies out of the creek.

HUNTER

We've spent our summers with Dad since I was five. Every year, when school let out, Ash flew to Otter's Rest, Maine, from her mom's on the West Coast, and I was put on a bus or train because my mom's place is only across the state.

And, when we showed up, Chance would be waiting. "It's about time," he'd say, hands on his hips where he stood on our back porch in his bare feet with his messy hair and big glasses. I'm not even sure he *needed* those glasses, seeing as half the time he took them off and propped them on his head or lost them altogether, and we'd spend hours searching for them while Chance wandered in circles, hands outstretched, claiming he was too blind to help.

I couldn't tell you where Chance lived, what school he went to, or what his parents' names were. But I could tell you his favorite type of ice cream and exactly how he ate it (rocky road, picking out the nuts and marshmallows to eat last), how he could recite every lyric from every Queen song in existence, and that he had a soft spot for animals and sad movies that made him tear up.

In my opinion, I knew all the things about Chance that mattered most. Chance was strangeness and whimsy in human form. Chance was our friend unlike any other friend Ashlin and I have ever had.

Chance *was* our summer.

We didn't see or talk to him through winter, but when we arrived for summer vacation, the three of us came together like we'd never been apart. For seven years, all I looked forward to as I plodded through school and my monotonous life with Mom and her boyfriend was the day I could pack my things and see Chance.

This is the first I've been at Dad's for more than a few days since I was fifteen, and I know a lot can change in two years. I had to fight with Mom just to get here now: she wanted me at college, and I wanted to take a year off. To spend with Dad. To spend with Ashlin. To think about my future and what I want out of it. Maybe, just maybe, to see Chance again.

It's weird showing up while there's slush on the ground and the air is damp and cold. Dad's house nestled off the side of the road looks different surrounded by skeleton trees instead of green, green, green.

There is no Chance waiting for me on the porch.

Not that I expected there to be; how would he know we were coming? We were here every summer without fail until Dad took a bullet to the spine in the line of duty two years ago, and while he recovered, we were kept at our respective homes. Away from Dad, away from each other, and away from Chance, with no way of contacting him.

I have no clue where or how to find him. Don't know where he lives, don't have a phone number, don't know if he has any other friends in town… I called information once, but I didn't know his parents' names. Dad wasn't exactly in the physical state to be doing some detective work to find out, either.

Ashlin and I will have to put our heads together on how to find him when she shows up. Until then, I'll keep stepping outside, forgetting how cold it is even as the deck freezes my feet. I'll keep watching and waiting for the guy I haven't been able to get out of my head after all this time. That's the sort of person Chance is. He gets under your skin, and even when he's gone, you still feel him there like a dull ache. A warm memory you can never quite reclaim.

Ashlin arrives the next day. Dad and I pile into his old truck for the long drive to the airport. I haven't seen my half sister in six months—not since I flew out for her high school graduation. We only had the money for one of us to buy a ticket, and because I wanted to get the hell out of my house for a while, it was decided I'd be the one visiting her.

When I see her emerging from her gate, she still has the remains of a summer tan and a splash of freckles across her nose and cheeks. Once upon a time, she hated those freckles, until Chance told her they were cute and now she never tries to cover them with makeup. She goes to Dad first, careful in the way she hugs him. A rare smile pulls at his mouth as he puts an arm around her, the other not leaving his cane for support.

"My girl." He sighs. "I've missed you."

"Say that again after you've had us around for a few months." Ash pulls away and turns her attention to me.

"Hey, short stuff," I say with a grin.

Ash smiles a mile wide, throwing her arms around my neck. She smells like fruity body spray and shampoo and home. Being away from her and Dad all winter never felt right. *This* is how things were meant to be: me, my sister, and Dad.

All we're missing now is Chance.

Get tangled in our Entangled Teen titles

Allure by Lea Nolan

Emma Guthrie races to learn the hoodoo magic needed to break The Beaumont Curse before her marked boyfriend Cooper's sixteenth birthday. But deep in the South Carolina Lowcountry, dark, mysterious forces encroach, conspiring to separate Emma and Cooper forever. When Cooper starts to change, turning cold and indifferent, Emma discovers that both his heart and body are marked for possession by competing but equally powerful adversaries. A magical adventure where first loves, ancient curses, and magic collide.

Darker Days by Jus Accardo

Jessie Darker goes to high school during the day, but at night she helps with the family investigation business. Cheating husbands and stolen inheritances? They're your girls--but their specialty is a bit darker. Zombie in your garage? Pesky Poltergeist living in your pool? They'll have the problem solved in a magical minute. For a nominal fee, of course...

Origin by Jennifer L. Armentrout

Daemon will do anything to get Katy back. After the successful but disastrous raid on Mount Weather, he's facing the impossible. Katy is gone. Taken. Everything becomes about finding her. Taking out anyone who stands in his way? Done. Burning down the whole world to save her? Gladly. Exposing his alien race to the world? With pleasure. But the most dangerous foe has been there all along, and when the truths are exposed and the lies come crumbling down, which side will Daemon and Katy be standing on? And will they even be together?

Get tangled in our Entangled Teen titles

The Summer I Became a Nerd by Leah Rae Miller

On the outside, seventeen-year-old Madelyne Summers looks like your typical blond cheerleader. But inside, Maddie spends more time agonizing over what will happen in the next issue of her favorite comic book than planning pep rallies. When she slips up and the adorable guy behind the local comic shop's counter uncovers her secret, she's busted. The more she denies who she really is, the deeper her lies become...and the more she risks losing Logan forever.

Out of Play by Nyrae Dawn and Jolene Perry

Rock star drummer Bishop Riley doesn't have a drug problem. But after downing a few too many pills, Bishop will have to detox while under house arrest in Seldon, Alaska. Hockey player Penny Jones can't imagine a life outside of Seldon. Penny's not interested in dealing with Bishop's crappy attitude, and Bishop's too busy sneaking pills to care. Until he begins to see what he's been missing. If Bishop wants a chance with the fiery girl next door, he'll have to admit he has a problem and kick it.

Relic by Renee Collins

In Maggie's world, the bones of long-extinct magical creatures such as dragons and sirens are mined and traded for their residual magical elements, and harnessing these relics' powers allows the user to wield fire, turn invisible, or heal even the worst of injuries. Working in a local saloon, Maggie befriends the spirited showgirl Adelaide and falls for the roguish cowboy Landon. But when the mysterious fires reappear in their neighboring towns, Maggie must discover who is channeling relic magic for evil before it's too late.